D1568357

HONEY ON THE PAGE

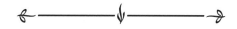

HONEY
ON THE
PAGE

A Treasury of Yiddish Children's Literature

Edited and translated by

MIRIAM UDEL

NEW YORK UNIVERSITY PRESS
New York

NEW YORK UNIVERSITY PRESS
New York
www.nyupress.org

References to Internet websites (URLs) were accurate at the time of writing.
Neither the author nor New York University Press is responsible for URLs
that may have expired or changed since the manuscript was prepared.

Library of Congress Cataloging-in-Publication Data
Names: Udel, Miriam, editor translator.
Title: Honey on the page : a treasury of Yiddish children's literature /
Miriam Udel [editor and translator].
Description: New York : New York University Press, 2020. |
Includes bibliographical references and index.
Identifiers: LCCN 2020016514 (print) | LCCN 2020016515 (ebook) |
ISBN 9781479874132 (cloth) | ISBN 9781479860364 (ebook) |
ISBN 9781479859139 (ebook)
Subjects: LCSH: Children's literature, Yiddish—Translations into English. |
Authors, Yiddish—Biography. | CYAC: Short stories. | Poetry.
Classification: LCC PZ5 .H7525 2020 (print) | LCC PZ5 (ebook) |
DDC 839/.10809282—dc23
LC record available at https://lccn.loc.gov/2020016514
LC ebook record available at https://lccn.loc.gov/2020016515

New York University Press books are printed on acid-free paper,
and their binding materials are chosen for strength and durability.
We strive to use environmentally responsible suppliers and materials
to the greatest extent possible in publishing our books.

Manufactured in the United States of America

10 9 8 7 6 5 4 3 2 1

Also available as an ebook

To Yitz, Kobi, and Manu

This book is for you, your children, and the generations to come.

זע, ווי גוט און ווי ליב איז דאָס איז דאָס זיצן פֿון ברידער באַנאַנד

How good and how pleasant it is that brothers dwell together.

—PSALM 133

CONTENTS

FOREWORD

Reviving Yiddish Children's Literature

Jack Zipes

Children's literature was never truly recognized as a field of study until 1953, when the International Board on Books for Young People (IBBY) was founded in Switzerland. Today, there are more than seventy national chapters in the world that sponsor meetings and research, and in many countries, the scholarly study of children's literature has been dignified by superb historical and critical works. Almost every aspect and topic of children's literature has been examined, investigated, and debated throughout the world. And yet there remain serious gaps to be filled in the histories and approaches to children's literature.

Yiddish children's literature is one of them, and now, thanks to Miriam Udel's comprehensive anthology *Honey on the Page*, we can finally gain a sense of how dynamic and fascinating Yiddish children's literature was not only in Europe but also in North and South America. A superb translator and scholar, Udel has divided her collection into eight categories so that readers can dip into Jewish history, culture, and education through fables, poetry, allegories, folklore, and fairy tales. Moreover, it is a book that can be read and shared by young and old. Of significant importance are the short historical biographies before each entry, restoring these words and images to their proper authors, ensuring they will not be forgotten. In fact, we can now include their works in general studies of different genres in the history of world children's literature.

What is extraordinary about Udel's collection are its international origins and an ethical storytelling that is closely tied to Judaism and socialism. Most of the writers were born in the Pale and moved about in central

Europe before emigrating to North and South America or the United Kingdom, that is, if they managed to avoid the Nazi concentration camps. They
wrote for a network of Yiddish publishing houses, magazines, and newspapers before, during, and after the Holocaust. Since they had no "home,"
so to speak, it is difficult to detect a nationalist tone or aspect in their writing. Their home was and is rooted in an ethical belief in social justice that
reverberates throughout the tales. In the wonderful ballad "Where Stories
Come From," Ida Maze (1893–1962), who wandered from a village near
Minsk at the beginning of the twentieth century to New York and then to
Montreal, wrote,

> Somewhere very far away,
> Where wagons will not go—
> There stands a little cottage
> As it's stood for years, just so.
>
> Sitting quiet and abandoned
> Doors and shutters bolted shut,
> Days and years pass; only wind blows
> Through the chimney of the hut.
>
> Everybody's known for years:
> Its people all have gone away
> Only wind blows in the chimney
> Not a soul has come to stay.

In the remaining stanzas in this ballad, Maze relates that stories emanated
from a cottage where a grandmother and grandfather tell stories to a
child, with the wind spreading the tales to children throughout the world.
Although the ballad is somewhat idealistic and optimistic, as many of the
stories in Udel's anthology are, it carries a strong and convincing belief that
stamps the entire anthology—the sun will always bring truth to light, no
matter how powerful predators may be. It is a faith in Enlightenment that
is reflected in almost every narrative, fiction and nonfiction, in *Honey on
the Page.*

One of my favorite tales that encapsulates this notion and more is Jacob
Reisfeder's touching narrative "A Boy and His Samovar" (1920). Born in
Warsaw in 1890 to a Hasidic family, Reisfeder began writing for various

magazines and newspapers as a young man. He left Warsaw for Argentina in 1923 and later returned to Warsaw, where he died in the ghetto in 1943. His story concerns a poor young boy who is given a samovar as a gift by his parents; when the ruler of his country runs out of metal and brass and cannot produce bullets for his soldiers' guns, he orders his people to deliver anything made out of metal or brass to his army. If they do not obey, they will be harshly punished. Since the samovar reminds the boy of his father, who was killed in one of the ruler's wars, he refuses to contribute his samovar. Eventually, the ruler's officers take the obstinate boy to the ruler to explain why he will not give up his samovar, and Reisfeder writes,

> The ruler already knew what the boy had come to ask of him, so he said to him with a smile, "Why do you need it so much, little boy, this samovar? I will order that you be given other toys in return, even nicer ones than the samovar."
>
> "I don't need *any* toys," the boy replied. "I can get along without playing. . . ."
>
> "But then why don't you want to give up the samovar?" the ruler asked, interested.
>
> At this point, the boy burst into sobs and whimpered, "Because I don't want my samovar to be made into bullets that will kill someone else's dear Papa as my dear Papa was killed. . . ."

After hearing this, the ruler is moved and enlightened. He realizes how disastrous war is and decides to end it and begin living in peace. Almost all the stories in Udel's book, whether fiction or nonfiction, carry this sentiment—the resolution of conflicts and problems such as war, injustice, and poverty must be attained not with force but through intelligent mediation and discussion. Remember here that the writers and collectors of the narratives in *Honey on the Page* experienced conflict most of their lives. They did not live lives filled with honey, yet they bravely wrote to make a contribution toward a better world.

Udel's work, I hope, will inspire other scholars of Yiddish children's literature to study, translate, and republish the tales of Jewish writers whose work has been neglected and forgotten. The stories in this book were not written or told just for Jewish children, nor are they religious tracts. Before the Holocaust, Yiddish-speaking people sought simply to live in peace, and their stories, so sensitively translated by Udel, have survived to foster understanding and empathy for children throughout the world.

TRANSLATOR'S NOTE ON AUTHORS' NAMES

The question of how to render a Yiddish author's name in English is not always a straightforward one. Some authors were closely—or even exclusively—associated with their pen names, particularly when writing for children. I have usually chosen to reflect how a given work was signed and then to include a legal name in parentheses in the notes. Because most of these authors migrated over the course of their lives, their names often changed with a new locale, sometimes conforming to the conventions of their new coterritorial languages. Rather than applying a single orthographic standard in rendering their names in English, I have tried to respect the historical contingencies under which these writers' careers unfolded.

To the Young Reader

When I started working on this book, I had three very important readers in mind, one of whom wasn't even born yet. They are my sons. They all like books, and right now, as two teenagers and a preschooler, each one likes different kinds of books than his brothers. I tried to put stories into this collection that would appeal to each of them and teach them about faraway places and times that were different from our own but also about ideas and experiences that are very familiar because they are already important to our family.

The stories and poems you'll read here were originally written in Yiddish, the language that the Jewish people spoke in eastern Europe for almost a thousand years and a language that they carried with them as a precious heritage when they left Europe for places like the United States, Canada, Mexico, Argentina, South Africa, Australia, and Israel. The number of Yiddish speakers today is relatively small, but people speak Yiddish on almost every continent!

A language isn't just a way of saying things: what you hope for, what you're afraid of, what you dream about, or what you ate for lunch. A language is also a way of carrying a culture with you. In fact, the things that you hope for, fear, dream about, and eat for lunch are all influenced by your culture. So when you read this book, which is full of stories and poems that I've translated into English, you are also catching a glimpse of the culture and civilization of kids who spoke Yiddish fifty, seventy-five, or a hundred years ago. Some of them lived in Poland or Lithuania, others lived in New York, and still others lived in Buenos Aires, Argentina, or Havana, Cuba.

What were their experiences like? Some of the kids who originally read these stories went to schools with Jewish teachers and students, where they studied all day in Yiddish. Others attended public schools during the morning and Yiddish after-schools every afternoon. Still others went to schools where boys and girls were taught very differently from one another and couldn't even really be friends with each other. Some of the children for whom these stories were written lived in places where it was difficult or dangerous to be Jewish. Their families lived their Jewish lives in many different ways: some observed Shabbat every week, others had a Passover Seder or special Hanukkah dinner and went to synagogue for major holidays, and still others didn't do much at all to mark the Jewish holidays but spoke and read Yiddish, the language of a large part of the Jewish people.

A lot of the events described in these stories could happen to any kid, almost anywhere: getting lost, going skating, having a birthday party, visiting grandparents, making a snowman (or snow *grandma*), or feeling nervous the night before the first day of school. And some of the events couldn't really happen anywhere *other* than a story: catching a ride on a lion's back, getting snatched by a giant, talking with a goat, or losing a calf in a farmer's long beard.

Who wrote these stories and poems? Some of the authors were teachers, who spent almost all their time with children and were used to thinking about the world from their students' point of view. Several of them devoted themselves to writing for children, and others wrote mostly for adults and only occasionally for kids. One of the special things about Jewish children's literature—in Yiddish and Hebrew—is that almost every writer, including the ones who wrote the best grown-up books, tried to write at least sometimes for children.

These stories and poems are very different from each other. You might like some of them better now and appreciate others as you grow older or even sometime after you become an adult. But I hope that just like the families that originally read these stories and carried Yiddish with them, you will carry these stories and poems with you and share them someday with the children in your life when you are grown up.

Introduction

When I started Hebrew school at age nine and received my *alef-bet* primer, Mrs. Wasserman instructed us to open the book to its first page, reading as we now would, from right to left. She then walked around the room majestically, tumbling a little cascade of chocolate candies onto the open booklet on each desk. She explained that the custom was to smear honey on the page, which students in the olden days would lick up to make the start of learning sweet; since honey was too messy, she was opting for chocolate. We pinched up those chocolates, and the adventure began. The books stayed spotless, and, after a little lick here and a rub there, our fingers passed for clean as well. It was all very civilized.

Now able to take the perspective of both the child eager for sweets and the adult responsible for cleanup, I think the chocolates were a logical choice. Yet I look back on that memory and suspect that ours was a different, more circumscribed sensation than new students enjoyed "in the olden days": the tongue lapping atavistically at the flat page, symbolically incorporating its letters together with the drippy sweetness of the honey. The chocolate stood in for the honey, just as the translations in this volume attempt to stand in for their originals. But as my teacher did so long ago, I hope to use the chocolate to evoke the honey: the painstakingly selected, translated, and annotated English to gesture at the wild, glorious, messy profusion of Yiddish children's literature.

Throughout the process of creating this book, I have been asked repeatedly whether it is meant for children or for adults. If for children, of exactly what ages? Perhaps because my parents always took such joy in the books they gave me, and I have tried to do the same with my children (even upon multiple consecutive readings), I continue to find myself flummoxed by the question. I could tell you all the reasons this is a book for children: the care with which I chose these works to educate, amuse, and inspire. I could dwell on the resources marshaled to create an inviting visual experience that outstrips that of the originals, which were often cheaply printed. Addressing adults, on the other hand, I could tell you how essential this corpus is to understanding Jewish history and culture in the twentieth century.

We would be getting warmer if I broke down the literary marketing barrier between adults and children altogether and told you that this was a "family" book, meant for multiple generations to enjoy together, both by reading aloud and by reading independently and then discussing the content. But it's not a book only for families, or only for scholars of Jewish civilization for that matter. It's a book for adults and children *in proximity to one another*. What I mean by that peculiar phrase is that as I have gone about the work of selection and translation, I've envisioned a child reading, with sympathetic and curious adults nearby. Such a child might receive this book as a Hanukkah gift from a doting Bubbie or Zeyde, Savta or Saba, Nana or Grampa, or pluck it off a library shelf at a public school where Jewish pupils are few and far between. At the same time and in equal measure, I have envisioned a sharply intelligent adult reader for whom the concerns, emotional intensity, and wisdom of childhood remain near at hand. Such adults might be parents or teachers trying initiate conversations about creating a more just world or seeking fresh takes on marking the Jewish holidays or grappling with threats and even violence against the Jewish people—or they might be students of children's literature or of the modern Jewish experience. Several of the most passionate readers so far have been contemporary children's authors, looking for inspiration in authentic Jewish storytelling of fifty and a hundred years ago as they create new cultural artifacts for today. Some of this book's readers might even belong to that special category of human between childhood and adulthood but open to transmissions on both frequencies: the adolescent.

In the Yiddish-speaking communities of New York, Europe, and Israel, children's stories are still being published in the *mameloshn*, but this book draws on a literary heritage that extended only through the first three-quarters of the twentieth century. As I shall explain shortly, this heritage arose in tandem with secularization and the progressive politics to which it gave rise; these political commitments, in turn, accelerated the processes of religious and social change. The corpus of children's literature that we are concerned with is quintessentially *in between*. Linguistically, it is written in Yiddish, a resplendently hybrid tongue drawing on several of the other languages that vied for its speakers' and readers' allegiance. Historically, most of these stories date back to an era in between a firmly implanted traditional religiosity and widespread assimilation. The very essence of this literature was to affirm what Jewishness meant in a newly secularizing world. That affirmative vision carved out a place for Jewish holidays, an awareness of tragic, hopeful, and resilient dimensions of Jewish history, an appreciation for Jewish folklore and the voice of the people, and a distinctive brand of insouciant humor. At the same time, it held space for stories that had little to no explicit Jewish content, in which characters were only incidentally Jewish or might not be Jewish at all.

A tension between the particular and the universal animated the entire seventy-five years of this literature's flourishing. How could authors—to say nothing of their readers—strike a sustainable balance between expressions of particular Jewish identity and gestures toward universal human belonging? Because this tension was so central, it often gave structure to early Yiddish anthologies, which tended to progress from the narrowly Jewish to the broadly humanistic. Correspondingly, I have adopted a similar organizing principle for this volume. There is an inevitable degree of overlap in my thematic categories, and the decision of where to place a given text frequently hinges on subjective questions of emphasis. I begin with the three *H*s: Jewish holidays, history, and heroes. However, these aren't straightforward tales of the piety of yore or collective mythmaking. Even the stories that seem to valorize traditional Jewish practices like Sabbath observance are nonetheless reflective of the socialist, antinomian spirit of their time. The section on "history and heroes" includes a mix of nonfiction and historical fiction that realistically portrays episodes from Jewish history through a modern lens.

Next come folktales and fairy tales, several of which bear a Jewish stamp but could be transposed readily to a non-Jewish cultural milieu. The same is true of the "wisdom literature" that features such Jewish comic staples as the Wise Men of Chelm and Lemekh the Fool (or Lemekh the Lummox). The chapter on allegories, parables, and fables includes many works set in the realm of (talking) animals, a mainstay of children's literature the world over. As the book moves to scenes of instruction, which involve both formal "school days" and casual learning "in life's classroom," the stories grow increasingly universal in scope and theme, while still marked by the trappings of the *kheyder* or *shul*—traditional and modern forms, respectively, of the Jewish classroom. The volume ends with a series of stories that emphasize family dynamics, perhaps the most universal theme of all, albeit with a decidedly Yiddish accent.

A literature for Yiddish-speaking children emerged and flourished during the first decades of the twentieth century, a politically tumultuous time for Jews living in eastern Europe and a moment of dizzying cultural and religious transformation for Jewry throughout the world. In broad terms, it was an era of large, multiethnic, and multiconfessional empires giving way to nation-states. Since 1772, Poland had been partitioned (and periodically redivided) among its neighbors. The largest of these was the Russian Empire, which, upon engulfing an area thickly populated with Jews in 1795, decided to manage the undesirable minority by restricting them to a vast but mostly undeveloped region known as the Pale of Settlement. For a great swath of eastern European Jewry, the long nineteenth century was a time of poverty, dramatic demographic growth, and relative insularity. Both populist and elite forms of religious piety flourished, even as cultural and intellectual tendencies took root that would eventually lead to widespread secularization. The term "pale" comes from the Latin for stake (think of the Spanish word *palo*, or "stick"), and it evokes an imaginary fence around the vast region. The borders of the Pale changed over the course of the nineteenth century, but by its demographic peak as recorded in the census of 1897, the area housed a Jewish population of over five million, the largest single concentration of Jews in the world at that time.

Even before the Bolshevik overthrow of the tsars in 1917 that formally ended Jewish confinement to the region, its Jewish inhabitants had already begun to dismantle some of the symbolic "fences" that had hemmed them in and marked them off from the larger society. The dawn of the twentieth century found many Russian Jews undergoing rapid processes of modernization and secularization and increasing their involvement with radical politics. Across eastern Europe, the years between world wars extended and intensified the nineteenth-century trends of urbanization and industrialization, whereby Jews and their Gentile neighbors alike flocked from small, diffuse towns and cities to large urban centers, where labor at artisanal crafts was supplanted in short order by factory-driven industries. Rapid but highly unequal economic growth fueled a radical labor movement, with Jews at its vanguard. Functioning in Lithuania, Poland, and Russia, the Bund established an address for Jewish labor activism and Yiddish cultural striving alike. Although it was transnational in nature, the Bund was not internationa*list* in philosophy. Its power was ultimately harnessed to the cause of Jewish cultural nationalism within the diasporic communities in which Jews were already living.

This commitment contrasted with both the Zionist aim of reconstituting Jewish life in the historical homeland of Palestine and the communist goal of uniting the world's workers without respect to national, ethnic, or religious divisions. Although only a small percentage of Jews were communists, the Jewish minority was nevertheless vastly overrepresented among the leadership of the revolutionary parties in Russia, the Bolsheviks, and even more so, the Mensheviks. Meanwhile, Poland regained independence with the conclusion of the First World War in 1918. Urbanized Jews living in metropolises like Warsaw and Lodz were able to secure unprecedented political representation in the Polish parliament through the Bund and other Jewish political parties, but their prominence also attracted all-too-familiar expressions of anti-Semitism.

The 1880s had ushered in a surge of Jewish emigration from eastern Europe, chiefly to the United States, that would not abate until this country promulgated the Immigration Act of 1924, which severely curtailed immigration from southern and eastern Europe, including the vast majority of Jews. Throughout the latter half of the 1920s and until World War II and its aftermath, some of the slack was taken up by Jewish immigration to Canada, Argentina, Mexico, Brazil, Uruguay, and Cuba. The destination for the largest number of interwar migrants was Mandatory Palestine, or as they usually wrote and spoke of it, the Land of Israel.

Whether in Vilna (as Vilnius, Lithuania, was known in Yiddish), Warsaw, or New York, at the turn of the twentieth century, Yiddish found itself subject to competitive pressure from other languages. The competition extended not only to the practically useful and prestigious national languages of the surrounding cultures (Polish, Russian, German, etc.) but also to Hebrew, with its classical tradition, which was undergoing its own concurrent revival as a spoken, written vernacular. Nevertheless, the hybrid tongue of the past thousand years, long disregarded as a mere *jargón*, remained the preeminent vehicle for Jewish political and cultural self-expression both in eastern Europe and wherever Ashkenazic Jews had already made new homes in the preceding decades. Yiddish was the lingua franca of Jewish political life, and it was not just the medium but even the organizing principle for a new kind of thoroughly secular yet avowedly Jewish educational endeavor that was inextricably linked to politics.

History does not transpire in a vacuum, and historical phenomena don't proceed by sequential stages neatly cordoned off from one another. Instead, there is a great tangle of simultaneities. With the Russian Revolution in 1917 and the independence of Poland in 1918, several of the hindrances to Jewish political activity fell away. Between the world wars, the political landscape in central and eastern Europe, as well as in New York, burgeoned with the socialist Bund, the Communist Party, the Zionist Po'ale Zion ("Workers for Zion," known in Yiddish as the Farband), and the traditionally religious Agudas Yisroel. The intensification of Jewish political engagement occurred in tandem with the spread of secularism, and Jewish secularist education in turn coincided with the adoption of new pedagogical theories and methods, known as the *kheyder metukan*, or reformed school, movement. Eventually, each political party established an affiliated network of schools, which took root in eastern European cities like Warsaw and Vilna, as well as in New York and Montreal. In North America, an aggregation of after-schools filled the afternoons and weekends of the public school student with *yidishkeyt*— knowledge of Jewish history, heroes, ethics, folklore, and music, all transmitted in the Yiddish language. The school systems, in turn, established their own publishing houses and recruited seasoned Yiddish and Hebrew writers to create suitable literary materials for their students.

Other factors combined to foster the growth of a children's corpus in Yiddish. The events of 1917 not only toppled the tsars from power but also swept away a host of restrictive censorship laws and other regulations curtailing Yiddish cultural activity. The first few years of the Soviet experiment were marked by radical cultural and linguistic freedom, conditions that persisted with respect to Yiddish until after the Second World War. In fact, the new Soviet state took an active enough interest in eradicating illiteracy to warrant generous support for children's literature in the diverse languages of its constituent ethnic populations. In the Soviet Union broadly speaking, children's literature was a high priority, viewed as an efficient medium of transmitting communist values and perspectives to a new generation. It didn't hurt the cause that Vladimir Lenin's wife, Nadezhda Krupskaya, was a veteran educator who used her prominence to promote librarianship and to foment the ongoing revolution through library science. If made widely accessible, children's stories, poems, and plays could help to refashion the citizenry organically and from within.

Communists were not the only ones who saw children and their reading materials as a shortcut to national reform. Socialist-affiliated schools flourished between the wars in Europe and the United States. Headquartered in Warsaw but eventually reaching one hundred locations, the Tsentrale Yidishe Shul-Organizatsye, or Central Yiddish School Organization (known as TSYSHO or CYCO), boasted over twenty-four thousand students by its peak in the late 1920s. Its leadership drew from both the Bund and Po'ale Zion to create a comprehensive system that served kindergarten through high school students, as well as running a teacher-training seminary and a network of evening schools for adult learners. Recreation as well as education was on the agenda, with party-affiliated summer camps and youth groups that promoted athletics, scouting, and comradeship in tandem. Just as the Soviets hoped to create a new kind of class-conscious citizen, so too the Jewish nationalists hoped to fashion a new kind of Jew: physically and mentally fit, culturally literate, ethically grounded, and manifestly courageous.

As progressives sought to use educational innovation as a means to cultural renaissance, they were nonetheless making lemonade out of some unmistakably bitter lemons. The Great War and the Russian Civil War had produced tens of thousands of orphaned, homeless, and deeply impoverished children, and the Jewish community's response to the crisis was to establish "children's homes" or orphanages that undertook the education of their charges. Here was a generation of children whose need for stories would not be met informally on the knee of a beloved grandparent (as imagined in Ida Maze's tender poem "Where Stories Come From"); the widespread institutionalization of Jewish childhood called for more formal educational and leisure reading materials as well.

It would be mistaken, though, to dwell *only* on the vulnerability of the interwar generation of children without also recognizing their latent power—soon to be actualized in adulthood—as possessors of immense cultural and political capital. The freedom that had enabled them to step out of the Pale, actually and symbolically, might lead either to Yiddish cultural renewal or to Jewish obsolescence, religious *and* cultural. Urbanization and secularization were mutually reinforcing: in large cities, association and religious affiliation became ever more voluntaristic in nature, and old forms of persuasion and social control fell away. Secularist leaders who remained passionately committed to their hybrid language and its culture could plainly see the specter of unchecked assimilation. Yiddish children's literature developed in an atmosphere of urgency, as an effort not only to bring about an affirmative vision but also to forestall a catastrophe of neglect. Cultural and educational leaders perceived keenly that the future of both Yiddish and *yidishkeyt* lay in the hands of the youth and that the grown-ups' task was to engender not only literacy and cultural competency but also ardent, abiding love.

The efforts of these leaders, as modern political and cultural exigencies asserted themselves, coincided with an unfolding transformation in the Western understanding of childhood itself. Corollary to the widely hailed "invention of childhood" was the setting aside of entrenched assumptions that children constituted blank slates or vessels to be filled with knowledge and virtue. The TSYSHO schools not only foregrounded content that they considered "modern," such as the sciences and literature of aesthetic and ethical (rather than narrowly religious) interest, but also adopted modern pedagogical methods, eschewing the corporal punishment that was widespread in the *kheyder* system.

Basic literacy had long been taught throughout the Western world, Jewish and Christian, using biblical texts that were minimally mediated by explanation or even illustration, but over the course of the nineteenth century, the idea that children required distinctive reading materials gained currency. Eastern European Jews had long enjoyed higher-than-average rates of literacy, but the key distinction the culture made was less between adult and juvenile readers than between male and female ones. An elite religio-legal discourse had long been the exclusive province of men, while more accessible narratives assumed an audience of women, "men who were like women" insofar as they lacked access to Hebrew and Aramaic, and implicitly, young children still in the orbit of female caregivers. Some works were religious and moralistic in nature, like the *Tsene Rene* (literally: "Go out and see"), known as the "women's bible," or tales of Hasidic wonder workers; others, like the romance-adventures of the *Bove Bukh* (the true etymological origin of the so-called *bubbie mayse,* or old wives' tale), were what we would now call essentially secular.

The bulk of reading material at the start of the twentieth century retained didactic aims, but crucially, the methods of moral instruction had shifted from inculcating fear of wrongdoing to teaching by modeling and positive example. Imprinted with the mark of Romanticism, the emerging literary output stressed innocence, imagination, whimsy, and idealism as the particular province of childhood. Aesthetic merit was a strong desideratum as well. Figuring out the best educational practices became a major preoccupation for Yiddish cultural leaders, and there was a proliferation, in Europe and New York, of pedagogical journals where a range of issues could be debated. Were progressive children better served, for example, by fanciful storytelling with imagined locales, talking animal characters, and supernatural episodes or by recognizable depictions of everyday life and realistic events? Was imagination itself a kind of bourgeois luxury or the universal inheritance of childhood? Did work aimed at children require a "happy" or redemptive ending? Generally, the more doctrinaire theorists tended to be in their leftist political commitment, the more they hewed to strict (and eventually *social*) realism. Fortunately for us, Yiddish literature found room for both whimsy and mimesis, and both tendencies enrich this volume.

The foregoing history has offered a bird's-eye view of the context in which Yiddish children's literature emerged. But what was this literature actually like? How did it grow from a sporadic trickle of texts in the first two decades of the twentieth century to a mighty stream in the interwar years? And how did it come to span the globe? The story of Yiddish kid-lit begins with stories that were not so much *for* children as *about* them. All three of the "classic" Yiddish authors, S. Y. Abramovitsh (fondly known by his most famous creation, Mendele the Book Peddler), Y. L. Peretz, and Sholem Aleichem, wrote memoirs describing—and burnishing in memory—their own boyhood days. Mordkhe Spector published a collection of holiday tales as early as 1888; but they were minimally illustrated, and many didn't address children.

Sholem Aleichem was renowned for holiday tales featuring youthful protagonists, often ridden with guilt over some religious infraction or other childish mischief. His great theme was the loss of innocence, which might come about through a character's own misdeeds or when a child observed the vagaries of the adult world. While he started by gradually reworking darker adult stories for younger audiences, he truly hit his stride only at the turn of the century with "Di fon" ("The Flag"), an initiation-cum-holiday tale similar to dozens of his others—but for its programmatic insistence on ending happily. During the last few years of his life, he worked on retrofitting some of his tales about children to conform to "the spirit of true children's stories," aiming for their publication in Warsaw. As a holdover of the nineteenth century, much Jewish literary consumption, both for adults and children, still took the form of newspapers and periodicals rather than free-standing books. The first children's periodical, *Grininke beymelekh*, or "Little green trees," began to appear in Vilna in 1914 and was named for a 1901 poem by the Jewish "national" poet Hayyim Nahman Bialik, renowned in both Yiddish and Hebrew letters. The poem, as well as the magazine's cover illustration, romanticizes Jewish children as markedly precocious and vulnerable.

Already in 1912, the increasingly prominent critic Samuel Charney had complained that works being marketed to Jewish youth lacked the requisite "joy and sunshine," which he proposed to redress by encouraging translation of world children's classics into Yiddish. A decade later, he would take matters into his own hands and begin a twenty-five-year tenure as the editor of the New York–based *Kinder zhurnal*, affiliated with the Shalom Aleichem schools. Sholem Aleichem himself died in 1916, just a year before the revolution that would do so much to transform Jewish life in eastern Europe and catalyze the development of a children's corpus in Yiddish. Coincidentally, 1917 was also the launch date of the first Yiddish children's periodical in New York, *Di yidishe kindervelt* (The Jewish children's world), affiliated with the Zionist Farband system of Yiddish after-schools. In Warsaw and Vilna, a smattering of free-standing story- and picture-books began to be published around the same time, as well as multiauthor anthologies. These are variegated and do not conform to any singular description. While some works were folkloric and stylized, others were mimetic and grounded in the everyday. It is easier to draw broad contrasts between the didactic but less overtly political works of the 1920s and the more polemical stories that became prominent in the Soviet Union and the United States alike by the mid-1930s.

Who wrote these works? The writers fall into two main categories. One was a dedicated cadre of children's authors, many of whom were also educators. They wrote primarily if not exclusively for juvenile audiences. Because of the emphasis that European Jews placed on education as the pathway to national formation, and because of the zeal of a small but determined band of American Jews to maintain a vibrant Yiddish secular culture, these communities allocated hefty resources to establishing an infrastructure of specialized presses, publishing houses, and periodicals for children. The second group of authors attests further to this setting of communal priorities: canonical writers for adults who at least dabbled—and often did much more—where juvenile readers were concerned. From Sholem Asch to Kadya Molodowsky to both Shteynbarg/Steinberg cousins (Eliezer and Judah, respectively), they form a veritable who's-who list of twentieth-century Yiddish letters. Of course, not all of the celebrated adult authors' output was suitable for inclusion here. Israel Rabon's novel *The Street* offers an enchanting portrait of interwar urban desolation but his work was—predictably—too darkly violent, even when writing about a family of mice. Just when the reader has come to adore Dovid Hofshteyn's gray and white kitty, it gets torn apart by a rapacious eagle. Leyb Kvitko's lovable (and beautifully illustrated) dog Bertshik is killed by an angry mob. Indeed, it would be illuminating to publish a second anthology of Yiddish "children's" literature with the title *Nisht far kinder* or *Not for Kids*.

Of course, to many Yiddish readers and writers, it must have seemed altogether futile after the 1930s to insulate Jewish children from violence. After all, the reality of the Holocaust, with its slaughter of roughly one million mostly Yiddish-speaking children, outstripped any literary horror that might have been imagined in the 1930s. And indeed, most authors who tackled the dreadful events did so with frank realism and an emphasis on the agency and heroism of children. The European apocalypse did not spell the end of Yiddish children's literature, as is amply attested in this anthology by works published in the 1950s through the 1970s. However, it shifted the aims of the corpus from linguistic propagation to a desperate bid for Jewish cultural consolidation and preservation. With wartime and postwar emigration to the Americas, new centers of Yiddish publishing emerged, including work for children. Storybooks published in Buenos Aires, Mexico City, and Havana placed a new emphasis on modulating Jewish religious holidays into a secular key. The families and school systems that consumed these works did not wish, for the most part, to return to the religious insularity of the shtetl. But neither did they wish their children to be ignorant of the themes and motifs associated with Sukkot, Lag Ba'Omer, and Shavuot, to say nothing of Passover and Yom Kippur. For most world Jewry, the postwar period marked the transformation of Yiddish from a spoken vernacular language to a nostalgically cherished postvernacular tongue.

Yiddish children's literature, deeply preoccupied as it is with the themes of identity, narrow escapes, fortuitous twists of fate, and the exercise of power, seems more relevant now than ever. Which political systems or sensibilities best promote human flourishing? How do you counter cruelty? Such were the questions that Jewish parents, educators, and artists unfurled before the children in their charge, and they remain as relevant to our moment as to theirs. Their answers, ideologically varied and raucous, tender and harsh, have come under threat of extinction. The urgency of bringing these texts back into the contemporary conversation impels this collection. These artifacts of the twentieth century speak eloquently into the twenty-first less because of their surface-level political commitments (after all, doctrinaire writing doesn't age very well) than because of something deeper. Collectively, these unquiet and disquieting stories and poems furnish an account of children reckoning with the world as it is, witnessing and comprehending its unfairness, and grappling with their own contribution toward its amendment. I think of the first-person narrator of Judah Steinberg's "Questions," who is astonished and disturbed to realize that an entire economic order, encompassing not only various people but multiple *species*, exists for his benefit and pleasure. I think of Sarah Liebert's heroes "Moe and Nicky," ethnically unmarked but ethically remarkable in their determination to water the horses in their charge on a hot day. Again and again, these stories illustrate the disruption posed by radical kindness—a powerful form of social intervention that children can enter into fully and even initiate on their own.

> As clear as Today,
> And as sure as Tomorrow,
> There will come a day
> Without want or worry
> Without troubles or fear,

Without enmity or rancor,
Oppression or hate—
A day full of friendship and brotherhood,
Peace and joy,
Happiness and contentment.
To *that* day,
My book is dedicated.

Written to accompany his 1952 story *The Last Prince*, Moyshe Strugatch must have invested this dedication poem with nearly equal measures of hope and weariness. He had been born in Slutsky, Byelorussia (Belarus), in 1892 and made his way as a student to a cosmopolitan Warsaw that was home to a thriving Yiddish cultural scene. He had immigrated to New York upon graduating in 1920 and pursued parallel—and complementary— careers as a teacher and writer, including regular contributions to the leftist periodicals aimed at the juvenile reader of Yiddish. *The Last Prince* was the first full book that he published after the Holocaust, and its preamble would have been all the more poignant for appearing not quite a decade after a vast swath of his book's natural readership had been annihilated. The poem concentrates in just a dozen lines the optimism and utopian spirit that infused the almost century-long project of writing for children in Yiddish. The poem concentrates in just a dozen lines the optimism and utopian spirit that infused the almost century-long project of writing for children in Yiddish. As we suffer a global pandemic that has darkened our world with the loss of life, health, and prosperity for so many, these stories and poems promise both candor and solace. We could do with an infusion of Strugatch's resilient optimism.

In order to compile this collection of nearly fifty pieces of prose and verse, I have combed through hundreds of anthologies and free-standing picture- and storybooks, as well as several years' worth of periodicals. I sought materials that would represent their times and places of origin, but principally, I looked for work that would feel relevant to today's young readers, their families, and their caregivers. After all, I became interested in this body of literature through a convergence of two pathways: my work as a Yiddish language teacher and my vocation as a mother. I hoped to find authentic Yiddish cultural products that my students could appreciate after just a couple of semesters of language study. At the same time, I felt enlivened at the prospect of handing these works to my own children. The stories and poems that you'll find here delighted me, taught me something new, reframed what I already knew, charmed me, and astonished me. Many of these selections feel fresh and surprisingly contemporary, while others show their age and distance from our own mores—and some manage to do both at once.

One foundational selection principle for me was to prioritize works originally composed in Yiddish. A robust ethos of translation into Yiddish thrived among eastern European Jewry, taking in not only the Bible but classics of world literature and contemporary novels and poetry well into the twentieth century and even into the twenty-first. Yiddish-speaking children could access the fairy tales of the Brothers Grimm and of Hans Christian Andersen before they could turn to stories written for them in their own native tongue. The translators, moreover, were often literary masters in their own right. No less a figure than the modernist genius Der Nister (Pinhas Kahanovitsh) took on Andersen, and the eventual Nobel laureate Isaac Bashevis Singer ushered Knut Hamsun's *Hunger* into the *mameloshn*. Had I opened this project to translated texts, it might easily have been twice as long. As it is, only one delightful narrative poem by the humorist Yoysef Tunkl (widely known as "Der Tunkeler," or "The Dark One"), "The Horse and the Monkeys," originates in a language other than Yiddish. Der Tunkeler adapted several works by the German cartoonist Wilhelm Busch, and I felt that his hewing to the constraints of rhyming verse rendered the Yiddish version a "second original."

Even as I allowed myself to exclude fine work based on its already-translated status, I also tried to include as many high-quality pieces as possible by women. Although the number of female authors increased over the course of the twentieth century, it never reached parity with men, a gap that cannot but be reflected in the table of contents. However, women penned some of the most memorable pieces collected here, ranging from Zina Rabinowitz's multigenerational saga of shifting Jewish identity, "The Story of a Stick," to Ida Maze's deceptively simple meditation on age and empathy, the poem "???." Nor should it be forgotten that women formed a key part of the behind-the-scenes infrastructure that brought Yiddish children's literature into the hands of eager readers. Not only were most librarians female, but women were (and remain) prominently represented in children's publishing. Samuel Charney was the towering literary critic who put his abilities at the service of Jewish children by editing the *Kinder zhurnal* in New York for twenty-five years, but it was his daughter, Elizabeth Shub, the masterful translator and children's book editor, who first invited Isaac Bashevis Singer to try his hand at writing for children. The sole Yiddish-language Nobel laureate went on to publish nineteen volumes of fiction and two works of nonfiction aimed at juvenile audiences. Shub's foresight summoned forth the rose- and gold-tinged texts that would survive in translation to represent a mostly lost civilization.

In addition to Bashevis Singer, there are classic Yiddish writers, including Sholem Aleichem and Y. L. Peretz, whose work for children—whether originally written as such or subsequently revised for young audiences—does not appear in this volume because it has already been capably translated elsewhere. Solomon Simon's charming collection of linked stories, *The Clever Tailor*, is being translated by his grandson, but his wry poke at Jewish literalism may be found in "A Deal's a Deal."

And now, a confession and perhaps a challenge: there is a set of stories and poems that I would have liked to include but to which I could not do justice as a translator. Yiddish boasts a subgenre of poems designed to teach the alphabet, brimming with puns and other wordplay. Despite a few attempts at some of this material, I didn't get much further than a title for "The Stinging B." Similarly, I struggled to render the poem "Nisele's Tear," one of just a handful of works that opt for symbolic rather than realistic strategies of representing the sorrowful events of the Holocaust. I included some rhyming verse, but given its demands on the translator, I had to be especially judicious in choosing just a few of these texts. Many plays for children have survived as well; however, their dialogue sounds rather wooden now, and I have omitted them.

I would like to acknowledge a few difficulties entailed in these particular translations. There was a historical lag between the urge to write for (and market to) children and the development of a separate, simpler register of speech in which to address young readers. A great deal of Yiddish children's literature is written in a lofty vocabulary that a contemporary ear might deem more suitable for adults. Of course, this can make Yiddish children's literature more rewarding reading for mature readers even as it might frustrate some children. I have attempted to strike a balance between simplifying some of the diction and remaining faithful to the tone of the original texts. I have also had to come up with creative solutions to the surfeit of reflexively (and sometimes gratuitously) masculine language. In rendering

Judah Steinberg's tale "Roses and Emeralds," I opt for the second person rather than defaulting to the third-person masculine.

In representing a robust, wide-ranging literary tradition truncated before its time, this book strives to be an honest one. Certain aspects of these texts protrude uncomfortably, refusing to be smoothed over or sanded down to conform to contemporary mores. The mutual suspicion between Jews and Gentiles evident in stories like "The Mute Princess" or "A Sabbath in the Forest" announces these texts' origins in a time different from our own. At least, we *hope* for certain things to be different. "To *that* day," Strugatch dedicates his book; just when *that* messianic, brightly beckoning day could be heralded in thoroughly secular terms, it threatened to recede from view altogether. But friendship and brotherhood (sisterhood too, now), peace and joy, happiness and contentment, continue to beckon just over the horizon. This book offers up a panorama of Jewish approaches to how we—and the children we hold near—might chase after them.

FURTHER READING

Abramowicz, Dina. "On the Beginnings of Yiddish Children's Literature." *Judaica Librarianship* 3, nos. 1–2 (1986–87): 68–70.

Allison, Alida. *Isaac Bashevis Singer: Children's Stories and Childhood Memoirs.* Woodbridge, CT: Twayne, 1996.

Balina, Marina. "Creativity through Restraint: The Beginnings of Soviet Children's Literature." In *Russian Children's Literature and Culture*, edited by Marina Balina and Larissa Rudova, 1–18. New York: Routledge, 2008.

Cunningham, Hugh. *The Invention of Childhood.* London: BBC Books, 2006.

Darr, Yael. *The Nation and the Child: Nation Building in Hebrew Children's Literature, 1930–1970.* Philadelphia: John Benjamins, 2018.

Fishman, David. *The Rise of Modern Yiddish Culture.* Pittsburgh: University of Pittsburgh Press, 2010.

Gennady Estraikh, Kerstin Hoge, and Mikhail Krutikov. *Children and Yiddish Literature: From Early Modernity to Post-modernity.* Oxford, UK: Legenda, 2015.

Gottesman, Itzik. *Defining the Yiddish Nation: The Jewish Folklorists of Poland.* Detroit: Wayne State University Press, 2003.

Kadar, Naomi Prawer. *Raising Secular Jews: Yiddish Schools and Their Periodicals for American Children, 1917–1950.* Waltham, MA: Brandeis University Press, 2017.

Kelly, Catriona. *Children's World: Growing Up in Russia, 1890–1991.* New Haven, CT: Yale University Press, 2007.

Mickenberg, Julia. *Learning from the Left: Children's Literature, the Cold War, and Radical Politics in the United States*. New York: Oxford University Press, 2005.

Moss, Kenneth B. *Jewish Renaissance in the Russian Revolution*. Cambridge, MA: Harvard University Press, 2009.

Noah Cotsen Library of Yiddish Children's Literature. Accessible on the website of the Yiddish Book Center. www.yiddishbookcenter.org.

Parush, Iris. *Reading Jewish Women: Marginality and Modernization in Nineteenth-Century Eastern European Jewish Society*. Waltham, MA: Brandeis University Press, 2004.

Peretz, I. L. *The Seven Good Years: And Other Stories of I. L. Peretz*. Translated by Esther Hautzig. New York: Jewish Publication Society, 2004.

Quint, Alyssa. "Yiddish Literature for the Masses? A Reconsideration of Who Read What in Jewish Eastern Europe." *AJS Review* 29, no. 1 (April 2005): 61–89.

Seidman, Naomi. *A Marriage Made in Heaven: The Sexual Politics of Hebrew and Yiddish*. Berkeley: University of California Press, 1997.

Shevrin, Aliza, ed. and trans. *Holiday Tales*. Mineola, NY: Dover, 2003.

———, ed. and trans. *A Treasury of Sholom Aleichem's Children's Stories*. Northvale, NJ: Jason Aronson, 1997.

Shmeruk, Chone. "Sholem Aleichem un di onheybn fun der yidisher literatur far kinder" [Sholem Aleichem and the beginnings of Yiddish children's literature]. *Di goldene keyt* 112 (1984): 39–53.

———. "Yiddish Adaptations of Children's Stories from World Literature." In *Art and Its Uses: The Visual Image and Modern Jewish Society*, edited by Ezra Mendelsohn, Studies in Contemporary Jewry: An Annual 6, 186–200. New York: Oxford University Press, 1990.

Stromberg, David. *In the Land of Happy Tears: Yiddish Tales for Modern Times*. New York: Penguin Random House, 2018.

Udel, Miriam. "The Second Soul of the People: Secular Sabbatism in Yiddish Children's Literature." *Jewish Social Studies* 21, no. 2 (Winter 2015): 78–104.

PART I

JEWISH HOLIDAYS

A Sabbath in the Forest
Yaakov Fichmann

YAAKOV FICHMANN
November 25, 1881–May 18, 1958

Born to a dairyman father in Belz, Bessarabia, Fichmann received a rudimentary Jewish elementary education but read widely on his own among Jewish Enlightenment writers. As a teenager, he left Belz and spent an itinerant period working at all kinds of odd jobs, including as a baker, a waiter, a coachman, a porter, and an attendant to a traveling organ grinder. Fichmann learned Russian and German and began writing poetry.

In 1901, he made his way to the Odessa of H. N. Bialik. From 1903 until his first collection of Hebrew poems was published in 1911, Fichmann moved between Odessa and Warsaw. In 1912, he emigrated to Palestine to accept a position editing a youth journal. On a return trip to Europe in 1914, he was stranded by World War I. Evading detection, he traveled from Berlin to Odessa, before moving on to Moscow. In 1919, he returned to Tel Aviv and took up editing.

Over the course of his lifetime, Fichmann spent long stretches in Warsaw and Tel Aviv, finally settling in the latter city. He wrote more in Hebrew than in Yiddish but composed poetry in both languages and greatly enriched the nascent children's literature of both as well. He is remembered as a cultural Zionist and as the father of the Hebrew lullaby. A literary prize was endowed in Israel in his memory, awarded to writing in Yiddish or Hebrew. He died in Tel Aviv.

"A Sabbath in the Forest" recasts folk motifs in a lyrical wonder tale celebrating the dignity of the common laborer and his Sabbath rest. Although the central character is religiously observant in the traditional mold, the story celebrates values that would appeal to more secular Jewish readers as well, including family togetherness (valued in the breach), special Sabbath food, and the right to a regular period of rest from the week's labor.

— ℘ —

I

Once upon a time, there lived a Jewish tailor in a small shtetl. He was known as Lipe the Tailor. He was a simple Jew who barely knew all the prayers, and he was very poor—it shouldn't happen to anyone. But he managed to earn a crust of bread for himself, his wife, Nechama, and their children, and he never—God forbid!—had to accept charity. From Sunday until Friday, all week long, he traveled well beyond the shtetl, going from village to village and doing jobs for the peasants. Sewing, patching, turning coats—Lipe wasn't picky. Just imagine what he suffered during the week! That's why, come Friday (thank God!), you could offer him the most profitable job, but Lipe the Tailor headed home no matter what. It could be thundering and lightning outside, but he had to make it back to his tidy little home to spend Shabbos, the Holy Sabbath, with his wife, Nechama, and their children—to recite the kiddush blessing over the wine and sing Sabbath songs at the table, as God had commanded. You see, the most important commandment for Lipe the Tailor was to keep the Holy Sabbath properly. He believed that it was thanks to his keeping Shabbos that the Eternal One provided his bread for the week. Lipe really made a point of observing the Sabbath, for truth be told, how better could such a simple Jew, a village tailor who hardly knew the prayers, serve God?

It had become Lipe the Tailor's habit over many years to rise at dawn on Fridays and finish up his work in the morning so that he could leave in plenty of time to be home for Shabbos. From the very moment he set out for home, he could feel all the cares of the week leave him, and his heart would fill with the joy of the holy day. This was especially true in the beautiful summer weather, when the fields were so green and fragrant that they seemed to sing and God himself took pleasure in the little world he had created. Nobody was happier then than Lipe! He didn't even notice the hardships of traveling or the burdens he carried but only thought about how quickly he could make it home and get ready for Shabbos. Even in fall and winter, when the roads were muddy and heavy clouds hung in the sky, the fields lay bare and gloomy, and the whole world waited silently like a mourner—even then Lipe didn't fall into sorrow. He had only to remind himself of home, where his wife, Nechama, had probably already put up the Sabbath stew, or *tsholent*, to cook, and bathed the children, where every corner sang with cleanliness and warmth, and his heart quickly turned joyful and his footsteps lightened. He already felt the pleasure of Shabbos and the joy of fulfilling God's commandment.

That's how Lipe did things year after year, and God's blessing rested on his humble home. He lived through the entire week, whatever it brought, just so that on Shabbos, the Good Angel would gaze upon him and beam with joy. Nothing had ever disturbed the holiness of the Sabbath day in the home of Lipe the Tailor.

II

Once in deepest winter, when the cold is strongest, Lipe rose as usual at dawn on a Friday and worked hard through the morning, his fingers flying. He wanted to be early because the winter days were short and the road difficult. He hardly noticed the great sheets of snow that had fallen throughout the night. The cold was so bitter that you wouldn't let a dog outside in such weather. Lipe was happy to have finished his work early, and he began to prepare for the journey home.

Meanwhile, a dangerous blizzard was stirring itself up outside, so windy and dark that you couldn't see a living thing. It tore the straw roofs off stables and blew such snowdrifts among the houses that it was impossible to open a door.

When one of the villagers came in from outside and saw Lipe standing with his pack on his back, ready to set out, he crossed himself fearfully and muttered, "How can anyone think of going out, when all the roads are blocked and ghosts are dragging about in the fields?" But did Lipe listen to a word of this? No, all he could think of was getting home for Shabbos! "Ghosts don't scare me," he said. "It's not my first time, and I have a great God who will bring me home safely." And in his heart, he trusted that his concern to always keep the Sabbath would stand him in good stead now, and this particular Shabbos wouldn't be ruined.

The villager saw that he could get nowhere with Lipe, so he let him go on his way; he thought to himself that the stubborn Jew would meet his end, because the wind and the frost were picking up force with every passing moment. Although he was a Gentile, he took great pity on Lipe. "How awful!" he told his wife. "Even if he's a Jew, our tailor is a God-fearing man. May the Lord have mercy on him!"

III

Meanwhile, Lipe made his way all alone through the desolate fields. He had his pack on his shoulders, and he groped along the road with a long stick so that he wouldn't fall into a snow-covered pit. But where *was* the road in fact? Snow covered bush and tree, mountain and valley, and the whole area was unrecognizable. Heaven and earth were one, and wherever Lipe's eye fell, he saw only white. If only there were some sign of a rock, a pole, a glimpse of forest or hill! What's more, icy snow blew right into his face, sticking him like needles so that he had to shut his eyes and couldn't see a single step of what lay ahead. But Lipe the Tailor didn't fall down, and he went on his way with great faith. At one point, he got stuck in a deep hole where he could have broken his back and hip, but instead he stood up unharmed and went on. He knew God was with him and would bring him safely home.

The farther he went, the harder the going became. His feet sank deeper and deeper into the snow heaps that blocked his path, and the wind lashed his face harder and harder. But Lipe mustered all his strength to go on until he reached a forest. He sat there for a while, his heart pounding. Just on the other side of the forest, Lipe imagined, must lie his town. But what if he'd figured it wrong and was lost? He would be doomed. Perhaps the dense forest stretched on for miles, full of wild animals and thieves—which are worse than animals. Others had fallen into their hands, and nobody knew what had become of their remains.

So Lipe entered the forest with terrible fear. He looked around constantly, searching for any sign of a roadway or footpath. Surely, he thought, he must be about to reach the far side of the forest. He trudged on and on, but still the forest stretched before him. The wind was calming down a bit, but the sky was growing steadily lower. Night was coming on. Lipe thought he might fall down, dead tired, in the snow and meet his end, but he wouldn't let himself and instead wandered even farther into the snow, even deeper into the woods.

Meanwhile, the forest was growing darker and more frightening. The frozen branches were all motionless, the tree trunks buried to their waists in snow. A sadness fell over everything. Lipe could hardly wander on his feet any longer. With the sun setting, he could see that it was time to welcome the Sabbath. Soon it would no longer be permissible to carry, so he threw off the pack from his shoulders and settled under a tree to recite the afternoon prayer. With a broken heart and streaming tears, he begged, "Dear, faithful God! Please do something so that my Sabbath won't be spoiled! I, Lipe the Tailor, surely don't need to tell *you* how!"

And suddenly he felt his heart lighten, as if he weren't in a dangerous place at all. Warmth flowed through all his limbs, and he truly believed that God, blessed be he, had heard his plea. He waited to see what would happen . . .

IV

After reciting the afternoon prayer, Lipe looked up and made out a little fire burning among the trees. It struck him as very strange: How could a fire suddenly appear when, as far as he knew, no one lived in the forest? He grasped that it was not a simple matter, so he left his pack under a tree and approached the beckoning flame. After just a few steps, he saw the fire right before him; and there loomed up before his eyes a marvelous palace made entirely of marble, and every window was aglow with Sabbath candles. *He turned and turned, but none was there; no living creature, not hide nor hair!*

Thinking it a dream, Lipe rubbed his eyes. But he saw that it was a real palace, the likes of which he had never before seen. It occurred to him that perhaps bandits or evil spirits lived here . . . but he saw the candles beckoning so kindly, as if inviting him, "Come in, Lipe the Tailor! We were kindled for your sake, so that your Shabbos wouldn't be spoiled . . ." Lipe gathered his courage, quietly opened the door of the palace, and went inside.

And there Lipe the Tailor saw things with his own eyes that he had never before even dreamed of. His eyes twinkled with the light burning in expensive crystal candelabra, and he smelled the aroma of delicacies that lay on long tables covered with pure-white cloths and saw rare wines in sparkling bottles. Yet . . . *He turned and turned, but none was there; no living creature, not hide nor hair!*

He came to a door and passed into a second chamber, where he saw tables of gleaming silver. Silver chairs surrounded them, and the pure-white table-cloths had the same rare delicacies and wines in sparkling bottles. But . . . *He turned and turned, but none was there; no living creature, not hide nor hair!*

He passed into a third chamber. There the tables were of pure gold, and golden chairs surrounded them; and the food smelled fragrant, and the wine sparkled. But . . . *He turned and turned, but none was there; no living creature, not hide nor hair!*

So he went from room to room, and the farther he went, the more rich and beautiful it all was—until he reached the sixth chamber, which was inlaid with diamonds and other precious stones such as captivate the eye. But here too . . . *He turned and turned, but none was there; no living creature, not hide nor hair!*

Lipe stood there, dazzled by all that his eyes had seen. "Master of the Universe!" he said to himself. "I am just Lipe the Tailor; how am I worthy of such a miracle?"

V

Suddenly he made out a soft song arising from somewhere, floating from afar and coming closer. And what a song—notes pure enough to break your heart, then a moment of silence, falling like soft dewdrops and pouring out like a lively stream amid the grassy steppe. The song arose from the depths and spread itself, like the wings of a mighty bird, over all the chambers of the palace, reaching higher and higher. Lipe didn't move a muscle but let the sweet song pour into every part of him. It lifted him up and carried him around as if he were light as a feather. He was amazed that the melody seemed so familiar. Couldn't he have sworn he'd heard it once in his own little synagogue? But never had he sensed its sweetness as he did now. He listened intently, and it flowed, like a pure golden sound, flooded with divine joy. The words were the first phrases of the Friday-night psalms: "*Lekhu neroneno lashem*. Come, let us sing to God . . .".

And as he stood frozen there, the door opened, and in came a gray-haired old man, garbed in white. He handed Lipe a prayer book and, winking, invited the tailor to follow him. Lipe followed the gray old man into a seventh chamber, where he saw a whole congregation of Elders, all dressed in white, their faces alight like burning suns, and they were all standing and singing a song of praise to the Sabbath Queen. Then Lipe realized that he was in the paradise of the lower realm, and the men before him were the purely devout and scholars of great renown; he stood as if stuck in place, too shy to meet their gaze. "Master of the Universe," he thought, "how did

I, Lipe the Tailor, come to be here?" He stood there like that until after the kiddush blessing that closed the prayer service. The Elders got up from their places, approached Lipe, and greeting their visitor with warm delight, wished him, "Good Shabbos, guest!"

Addressing him this way, the Elders invited Lipe to the table, where all sat down to eat. You can imagine what a feast it was, what Sabbath songs were sung at the table! They sat Lipe at their head; but he didn't forget who he was, and he was abashed to eat with such holy ones. The Elders encouraged him with their conversation, and everyone said to him, "Eat, Lipe, and may all be well with you! We haven't had such an honored guest in a long time!"

So he ate, and to his amazement, the food tasted familiar. He could have sworn that they were the same delicacies that his wife, Nechama, always prepared for Shabbos.

VI

From sundown on Friday to sundown on Saturday, Lipe the Tailor enjoyed the kind of Shabbos we should all wish on each other! He only regretted that it had been without his wife, Nechama, and his children, whose Sabbath had surely been marred by his absence. But just as soon as the sun set on Saturday and the conclusion of the Sabbath was marked with the *havdalah* ceremony, the entire palace disappeared, and Lipe saw that he was standing once again under the tree where he'd been the day before. His pack lay in its place, and his walking stick was stuck in the snow. He took a few steps, and oh! Where was the forest? *What* forest? He found himself standing in his town, not far from his own cottage.

Once home, Lipe kept quiet and didn't tell anyone where he had spent Shabbos. But from then on, whenever his wife, Nechama, would bring to the table her fragrant fish and tell him, as usual, "Time for the fish, Lipe—it has the taste of paradise!" Lipe the Tailor would smile to himself and reply, "Yes, yes, my Nechama! I've known for a long time that your Shabbos cooking has the *true* taste of paradise . . ."

And nobody else in their household knew quite what he meant by those words.

The Magic Lion

Yankev Pat

YANKEV (JACOB) PAT

July 19, 1890–April 25, 1966

Born to working-class parents in Bialystok, Pat was educated in Musar yeshivas, academies emphasizing ethical self-cultivation, in Slobodka and Slutsk. After breaking with religious observance, he worked as a weaver, was radicalized in the workers' movement, and served time in tsarist jails.

Starting in his twenties, Pat became a lifelong member of the Jewish labor Bund. He was a natural orator. He helped found institutions to care for and educate children, serving as secretary of the central Yiddish schools commission in Vilna. Pat lived in Warsaw from 1922 to 1938 and assumed leadership roles in the TSYSHO network of schools both in Vilna and in Warsaw. He wrote for socialist and communist periodicals, and he also wrote fiction and plays for children as well as contributing to journals on pedagogical theory.

Pat traveled widely to Israel, western Europe, and the United States, where he arrived in 1938 as part of a delegation of the Jewish workers' movement; when the war broke out, he remained in New York. Together with the other delegates, he formed the Jewish Labor Committee and served as its secretary general until 1963. Pat helped to rescue labor leaders from the Nazis and agitated for the founding of Israel, in addition to working for the Arbeter Ring (Workmen's Circle) throughout the war and postwar years. In 1945, Pat was among the first visitors to liberated Poland and the displaced-persons camps in Germany.

After a debut novel and children's stories published in Hebrew, Pat spent the rest of his career writing in Yiddish. He was a prolific author of short stories, children's tales and plays, articles, plays, novels, travelogues, polemics, criticism, essays, feuilletons, journalism, and textbooks. There was scarcely a Yiddish publication in the world to which he did not contribute. Of special note is his series of children's stories published between 1918 and 1921 in Bialystok and Warsaw. After the Holocaust, Pat penned a detailed account of his various family members' activities during the war, especially the heroic actions of his niece Haneke. In the 1950s, Pat worked to preserve Yiddish culture by compiling a compendium of profiles on prominent writers. The Yiddishist Emanuel Patt was his son. Yankev Pat died in New York.

"The Magic Lion" reworks a popular folktale, which has continued to generate subsequent adaptations in several languages, including English. Pat's version incorporates detailed information about Sabbath observance, including the fact that the kiddush blessing may be recited over bread in the absence of wine. His text is also richly lyrical in its portrayal of the natural world.

A long time ago, there lived a great rabbi who always kept the Sabbath faithfully and never forgot to act as it is written in the Torah and the Holy Books.

On Fridays, as Shabbos approached, the great rabbi would don his special clothes and beaver-fur hat, and with his white beard, he looked just like a real angel. Then he would say to his family, "Come, let us welcome the Sabbath Queen!"

His face would light up, and his eyes would shine with a pious glow just like that of the holy Shabbos candles that illuminated his household.

The great rabbi had never been on the road at the start of the Sabbath. He had always been at home, made the kiddush blessing in his own synagogue, and sung the *zemiros*, the Sabbath mealtime songs, at his own table, full of guests.

But once it happened that the rabbi had to go on a long journey for a matter of life and death, in order to save another Jew. The route he had to travel was a long and gloomy one, twelve days in a row through the wilderness. The road passed through dense forests and empty fields, where wild animals live and thieves lurk. No one had ever traveled there alone. Whoever needed to go that way would gather a caravan of armed travelers and go together. Skillful and well-armed guides led the way so that no ill might come to pass.

The rabbi did need to go by that route, so he bought a camel, loaded it with his necessities, waited for an armed caravan, and then set out with it.

He knew, of course, that a Sabbath would fall during his journey, and he didn't plan to violate it. So what did he do? The rabbi made an agreement with the eldest member of the caravan that he would be paid handsomely to forgo travel on that day and rest instead with the rabbi over Shabbos in a field along the way. The old man promised to do so because he really wanted the reward.

The caravan set out, and the great rabbi, riding on his camel, set out with them. The road was sandy and so hot that glowing sand burned the soles of their feet. Along the way were neither grasses nor trees—and no water. They started on a Monday, and by Thursday their water was gone. To quench their thirst, they milked all the animals they had brought along. The guides got angry and started shouting. They hurried the camels along, hoping to complete the journey faster.

Friday afternoon, the eve of the Sabbath, arrived. The daylight dwindled, and soon it was time to light candles—but no one wanted to stop and rest until after Shabbos. It was dangerous to stay there; they must hurry on.

What could the rabbi do? He asked his fellow travelers to stay with him so that he wouldn't have to violate the Sabbath by traveling. But none of them heeded his pleas, for they didn't want to risk their lives by remaining there. If the rabbi wouldn't come along, they would leave him there alone.

Different ideas about what to do battled within the rabbi. To go? Then he would violate the Sabbath, which he had never done in his life. Stay in the desert alone? Wild animals might tear him to pieces and devour him, or robbers might attack him.

But he took courage, dismounted from his camel, took off his pack, and said, "I'll stay here for Shabbos!"

So he split off from the caravan, and an extraordinary holiness shone forth from the great rabbi's face. Some laughed at him, and others pitied him, because here in the forest, his piety would surely be the death of him.

The rest of the group moved on together, screaming and cursing, but the rabbi was left alone in the wilderness. All alone. Stars lit up the sky, and shadows fell across the road. As it did every week and everywhere, Friday night arrived—and, with it, the Holy Sabbath.

The rabbi donned his festive clothing, and for him, it was Shabbos. He turned to face east and began to welcome the Sabbath with prayers and songs. He chanted, "*Lekho doydi.* Come, my beloved, let us greet the Sabbath bride. . . ."

As with every dusk, one side of the sky—the western side—glowed a wonderful red, and the sun set in a golden sea and withdrew itself into night, while on the eastern side of the sky, the darkness was heavy with lonesome shadows. From the east blew an evening wind that wafted the night clouds around the sky. The rabbi stood facing the dark east and recited the evening prayers alone in the wilderness.

He prayed out loud with his whole heart, and the louder he prayed, the calmer and safer he felt, secure in the knowledge that nothing bad would happen to him in the wilderness.

After he finished his prayers, he took out two loaves of challah from his pack and recited aloud the kiddush blessing over them. Then he recited *hamoytzi*, the blessing over bread, and tasted the challah and continued to take bites in between singing the traditional Friday-night *zemiros*.

He was so engrossed that he didn't notice his surroundings. He didn't see a lion approaching from the edge of the wilderness: a real, terrifying lion, the king of the jungle, taking long, quick lion steps right over to the rabbi. Only when he looked up did he make out in the darkness of the Sabbath night the flash of the lion's eyes, and by then, the beast was standing right in front of him. The rabbi was certain that he was about to give up his soul to the lion. It was hopeless; when one's appointed time came, one must die.

The rabbi looked at the lion and saw that the terrifying beast had lain down near him and was looking back at him mercifully, as if to say, "Don't be afraid."

So the rabbi's fear was dispelled a bit, and he stared and stared at the beast, before finally breaking off a piece of his challah and offering it to the lion. The lion took the piece of bread and ate it. When the great rabbi saw the king of beasts lie down, calmly eat the Shabbos challah, and do no harm, he also resumed eating his Sabbath "feast" and returned to singing the Friday-night *zemiros*, chanting, "*Kol mekadesh*. All who sanctify the seventh day. . . ."

After eating, the rabbi recited the grace after meals. It was already late at night, and the desert was quiet. The stars shone in the sky above, while down below, the lion's breaths dispersed through the air.

The rabbi placed his pack under his head and surrendered his soul to God—come what may. . . . He closed his eyes, recited the Shema prayer, and fell asleep. Likewise, the lion lay down his head and his regal mane and dozed off. The whole wilderness grew quiet, and both the rabbi and the lion fell fast asleep.

The night passed, and morning dawned gray in the wilderness.

The rabbi awoke while the lion still lay dozing calmly in his place without stirring. The sun began to rise—on a Shabbos morning in the desert wilderness. The rabbi started reciting the morning prayers. Just then, the lion woke up too and began to roar into the wilderness, roaring to the far corners of the fields and forests and upward to the heavens.

"That's his way of praying," thought the rabbi, and he wasn't afraid of the fearsome beast's roar.

When the rabbi had finished praying, he divided his meal in two: for himself and for the lion. Both ate together, and afterward, the lion got up and left. The rabbi thought he had left for good, but the lion was only taking a stroll around the edges of the desert, striking his paws against the distant, empty fields and bounding from one side to the other, then glancing back at the rabbi—who was sitting and studying Torah and reciting the weekly portion by heart.

So passed the entire day. The sun began to set; and soon the Holy Sabbath would be going on its way, and the rabbi would have to resume his journey alone on foot. For he must arrive at his destination in time to save the life he was trying to save.

Dusk fell. An evening breeze blew into the scorching desert, which glowed with heat. Dark shadows played about. The rabbi said the afternoon prayers and then ate, as is the custom, the third meal of the Sabbath. Following the grace after meals, evening arrived. The rabbi looked to see whether he could make out a star in the sky so that he could say the evening prayers. He waited until the sun had set completely and he could see the first stars. He knew that the Sabbath was over, and he had only to pray and recite the *Havdalah* blessing to conclude the holy day.

And because he was so happy to have made it through the entire night and day without violating the Sabbath or coming to any harm, he swayed and sang though his prayers, chanting them out loud and clapping his hands in joy.

He recited *Havdalah* the same way; and then the Sabbath was gone, and it was back to the work week.

Suddenly, the lion appeared before the rabbi and began to wag his tail like a loyal dog and to lick the rabbi; he sat down on the ground as if to say, "Climb up on me."

The rabbi understood the lion's meaning. He laid his pack on him together with his prayer shawl and then mounted the creature and took hold of his mane. The lion straightened up and began to carry him, running swiftly as an arrow, like a warhorse that scents battle. The lion sprinted nimbly over the desert, sending off his hot breath in every direction. The rabbi held on fast to the lion's regal mane without knowing where he was taking him. The king of beasts carried him all night long without resting and struck the ground so hard with his feet that all the other animals roared in fear throughout the night.

By daybreak, they had caught up to the caravan with the guides and the camels resting in the desert. The lion stayed silent as a stone. The rabbi dismounted unharmed. The lion roared loudly and triumphantly, and with his mane disheveled, his tail erect, and his eyes flashing, he ran swiftly back into the desert.

The lion disappeared from view, but his footfalls thundered across the wilderness.

The Mute Princess
Zina Rabinowitz

ZINA RABINOWITZ

1895–June 25, 1965

Born in Bender, Bessarabia, Rabinowitz attended elementary and middle school and later studied at university in Moscow. She spent 1913–14 living in Palestine, passed the years of World War I in Russia, and then returned to the Land of Israel. She moved to New York in 1921 and taught Hebrew, traveling frequently.

She began publishing in 1918, with stories and poems written in Hebrew. She went on to author poems, stories, novellas, and novels for children in Yiddish, as well as reportage for adults. Much of Rabinowitz's work appeared in both languages, and some was translated into Spanish. Her work is notable for its realism and frankness in addressing children. She was published very widely in Latin America, including in Buenos Aires and Mexico City. She settled in Israel in 1961 and died in Tel Aviv.

"The Mute Princess" is drawn from her collection of holiday tales, *Der liber yontef* (The precious holidays), as is "Señor Ferrara's First Yom Kippur" (which appears later in part 1). Both stories unfold in "exotic" settings that are not commonly represented in Yiddish literature.

— ℬ —

"I see that you too like our little princess!" said the matron of the new Jewish orphanage that I visited in Casablanca. "Everyone is amazed at her beauty."

"I've actually never seen such a beautiful child," I added. "But why do you call her 'princess'? Is that her name?"

"Let's sit down for a bit right over here in the shade, and I'll tell you about how she received the name," the matron of the orphanage suggested.

Following this advice, I sat down near her on a low bench, without ceasing to gaze from afar at the eight-year-old girl, who was playing by the swings with her friends.

"One morning, when we hadn't quite finished breakfast," the matron began to relate, "one of the older boys came running into the dining room and told me that someone was waiting for me on the playground.

"When I came out of the dining room, I spotted an Arab. He stood there bent over a sack that was lying on the ground.

"'Who gave you permission to come into the children's yard with your wares?' I asked the Arab angrily. 'Don't you know that all peddler's goods must go to the kitchen? Go there with your merchandise!'

"'This isn't the kind of merchandise you take to the "black market!"' the Arab answered, smiling and loosening his sack . . .

"I spotted a child's face in the sack. . . .

"'Get out of here!' I screamed at him. 'You're bringing me a dead child?'

"'She's not dead! She's alive, Madam, and breathing! She's one of yours, a Jew! I swear by Allah!'

"'How do you know that she's Jewish?' I asked, wanting to catch him in a lie.

"'How do I know? I know that the attic where her parents were hiding with her is now empty. Her parents died from the epidemic, and she ran to the well of the *mellah*, the Jewish Quarter, so people would see her there and take pity on her.'

"'But how do you know that her parents died in the epidemic?' I asked, still hoping to catch him out in a lie.

"'Do you think, Madam, that the epidemic kills only Arabs in the *mellah*?' answered the cunning Arab, turning to go. 'The epidemic doesn't spare anybody in our dirty *mellah*! She snatches whomever she comes across! She swallows up all the hungry, the thirsty, the filthy and the weak. She would have swallowed up this poor girl too, had I not taken her into my home and kept her there all night. . . .'

"'If it's true that you saved her life,' I said to the Arab, 'then how come you don't keep her? She's just famished! When she recovers, she'll pay you for her board. You'll put her down at the corner with a beggar's bowl, like all of your people do with orphans, and she'll beg for you with a crying voice and a little jingle, as others do.'

"'Not her!' the Arab shook his head. 'After all, she's mute!'

"'Mute?!'

"I bent down toward the child, who was still lying down with her eyes closed. When she felt my breath, she opened one eye, took a look at me and closed it again. . . .

"Doing as I did, the Arab also bent down toward the sack. . . .

"'She is mute!' the Arab said, and pointing to the child in the sack, 'I can't raise a mute child, so I want to sell her to you at a low price.'

"My heart trembled with pity. I paid the Arab a couple hundred francs and got rid of him.

"We quickly gave the poor child a bath and dressed her in a little white dress. She looked like a little angel, but she didn't speak a single word.

"Soon I called our doctor. 'Where did you find this princess?' he broke into a grin as he looked at her. 'Such a beautiful child! A true princess!'

"'In the meantime let's call her Princess,' the idea seized me. 'Until we can find out her real name.'

"'She's forgotten her name?' asked the doctor, listening to her breathing with his stethoscope.

"'She's mute, Doctor!'

"'She isn't mute! She hears every word. She turns her head in whichever direction she hears a sound. . . . The fact that she isn't speaking? It's a sign that she has been very badly frightened. . . . When she recovers, she'll find her tongue again! Be patient! Pay attention to her! She will speak!'

"But the beautiful princess didn't speak. She only smiled at the children, at me, but she didn't let a word out of her pretty little mouth.

"A day passed, a second day, a third—our princess smiled but kept silent. Was she really mute? Would she ever speak? Would we ever find out whether she's really a Jewish child, as the Arab assured me . . . ?

"It was already Thursday, the fifth day since she found herself in our splendid institution. She ate and drank like all the other children, she played like the other children, but she did it all by signs.

"Would she ever talk . . . ?

"My heart was full of pain and pity for the mute princess. And then it was Friday morning.

"On Fridays, we all prepare for Shabbos. Bathing, shampooing and combing hair, decorating all the rooms with flowers . . . In the dining room, we cover all the tables with snow-white tablecloths, and we put out vases with fresh flowers from our garden. Next to each place lies a little challah bread. . . . At the head of the table stands a candelabrum with five candles in honor of Shabbos. All the children are dressed up in white. They sit at the tables and wait for me to make the blessing over the candles, and when I finish, we all sing in unison, 'Good Shabbos' and '*Sholem aleykhem*. Welcome to the Sabbath angels.'

"But that Friday night, something happened that disturbed our usual program. . . . As soon as I had kindled the fifth Shabbos candle and covered my face with my hands, a hoarse cry broke the deep quiet of the dining room: 'Shabbos! Shabbos candles!'

"The princess was so surprised by the three words that had escaped from her mouth that she burst into loud tears, ran up to me, and hid her sweet face in the folds of my dress. . . .

"'She's talking!' Happy cries could be heard in the dining room.

"'She's no longer mute!'

"'Our princess recognized the Shabbos candles! . . .'

"There was such joy in our dining room that we forgot to make kiddush, to sing our Shabbos songs. We all held hands and started a happy dance around our princess. . . .

"And she kept marveling to herself and repeating, 'I can talk now . . . ! I'm not mute anymore! I can talk again! Good Shabbos! Good Shabbos!'"

Children of the Field

Levin Kipnis

LEVIN KIPNIS

August 17, 1894–June 20, 1990

Kipnis was born in Ushomir, in the Ukrainian region of Volhynia, to a family of twelve. He studied in *kheyder* and quickly showed artistic promise, painting and woodcarving. His parents helped to channel his artistry into calligraphy; he wrote out mezuzah scrolls to supplement the family's income. Reading the Hebrew children's magazine *Haperahim* (The flowers) led him to want to become a writer. His literary debut came in 1911, with a poem in the same publication.

In 1913, he went to Palestine to study art at the Bezalel Academy of Art and Design. During World War I, he resided in Jaffa, where be founded a children's publishing house. After the war, he was invited back to Jerusalem to write and edit materials for preschoolers and their teachers. He managed an orphanage in Safed in 1921 and left the following year to further study art and education in Berlin. In 1923, he returned to the Land of Israel to teach at the Levinsky Teachers' College in Tel Aviv.

Kipnis swiftly became a founding figure in modern Hebrew children's literature; he published over eight hundred stories and six hundred poems in Hebrew. He edited children's periodicals and textbooks, and his work was widely translated into Yiddish. He was also deeply involved with children's theater. For forty years, he wrote only in Hebrew. After the Holocaust, he began to write work in Yiddish that appeared in New York, Argentina, and Tel Aviv. He was active as a writer for eighty years: from 1910 until his death in Tel Aviv.

His story "Children of the Field" is part of a holiday collection conceived as a "gift" to the Yiddish-speaking children of the diaspora. It embroiders and secularizes a legend related very briefly in the Talmud (*bSotah* 11b). Emphasizing the idea of cultivation suggested by the garden of children, Kipnis's text manages to straddle the centuries between the biblical Exodus and the modern Haskalah and its aftermath. Reading beyond the story's plain meaning in connection with the Passover liberation tale, "Children of the Field" offers an allegory for the cultivation of new, post-Enlightenment Jews.

Who has ever seen or heard of such a thing: children sprouting out of the earth like grass in a field?

Of the kind sun sending her golden rays onto their little heads and the heaven's dew dripping its pearly drops upon them?

Of songbirds singing cheerful songs and butterflies fluttering by them all around and around?

Of a soft breeze caressing their hair and of angels covering them with their wings and rocking them with lullabies?

1. An Apple Field

A large, wide field extended not far from Goshen in the Land of Egypt. The field was overrun with tall, thick grasses and a lot of large, branching apple trees.

In the shade of the apple trees sat Jewish shepherds, trilling on flutes, and all around them grazed the sheep: reddish, spotted, and speckled—like flowers amid the grasses.

But there arose a new king in Egypt, a wicked one, and he forced the Jewish shepherds to abandon their sheep and toil with bricks and mortar. The wicked king issued an edict: "Every little boy that is born to the Jews must be cast into the river!"

The Jewish mothers didn't obey the villain; they hid their newborn boys, and each night when it grew completely dark, the mothers would zigzag their way to the apple field, where they lay down their tiny newborn boys by the roots of the trees and prayed:

> Apple tree, apple tree!
> The grief, it drives me wild.
> As you guard your apples,
> Please protect my child.

And when the dew fell and polished the grass with its pearly drops, the mothers cried:

> Pearly little blades of grass,
> The grief, it drives me wild!
> From burning heat and frigid cold,
> Please protect my child.

When the morning star appeared and the birds began to sing, the mothers lamented:

> Tuneful little songbirds,
> The grief, it drives me wild.
> Sing your happy little songs
> Lull to sleep my child.

2. In the Cradle Pits

The apple trees cared for the tiny little boys, the blades of grass kept them hidden, and bright-eyed angels with clear wings flew down from the heavens: an angel for each and every child. They stroked the children's little heads so that their hair grew very long, soft and silky, and covered their whole bodies. . . . They gave every child a pebble in each hand, one a milk-stone and the other a honey-stone. After that, they dug out pits near the roots of the apple tree and padded them with grass—as a mother makes a bed for her child; they laid the children in the pits—as a mother lays her child in the cradle; and they sang heartfelt songs—as a mother lulls her child to sleep.

They sang:

> Sleep, my child, sleep,
> Sleep in peace, itty-bitty ones
> Close your eyes, pretty little ones
>
> Sleep, my child, sleep
> There will come a day of days
> When the sun will brightly blaze
>
> Sleep, my child, sleep
> Your rescuer soon will come to you
> You'll rise, a generation new!

3. In the "Kindergarten," or the Garden of Children

The tiny little boys slept peacefully in their dark cradles, sucking milk from the milk-stones and honey from the honey-stones; they slept peacefully and dreamt of the bright day to come.

One lovely dawn, the sun came up large and dazzling, shining seven times more brightly than usual, and spread its rays over the apple field, warm, sweet rays—one for each and every child.

This made the earth split open, and little heads began to sprout forth like pretty flowers. In the blink of an eye, the entire field was full of little children, like a very large *kinder-gortn*, or garden of children.

The children raised their eyes to the sun and asked, "What happened, dear sun, to make you shine so brightly today?"

The sun replied, "Today is the first day of spring; you should know that during this spring month, the liberator will come and lead you out of Egypt."

The children asked, "Is this the day about which the angels sang, 'There will come a day of days'?"

"Soon! That day will come soon," replied the sun.

So things turned very happy: the children of the field, the flowers of the field, the birds of the field—every last one of them grew joyful.

4. The Day of Days

The anticipated day arrived.

The sun blazed like fire and said, "Pharaoh, the Egyptian king, has a hard and wicked heart, and he doesn't want to free the Jews; so I will withdraw my light from Egypt and leave it in the dark for three days and three nights.

And that's what the sun did: for three days, she sent all of her light only to the Jewish children in the apple field.

This is what the sun said:

"Dear, wonderful children! Long have you lain in dark little beds, and you haven't seen me shine in many days; wicked Pharaoh has robbed you of my light, but now I'm going to repay the debt to you by lighting up seven times brighter."

The children replied happily, "Dear, good, bright sun! In the darkness, we dreamt of your shining; we have missed it, and we love your light!"

So the sun illuminated the field: beams of sunlight flooded in, and the children bathed in light. They got up, found their footing, and began to grow bigger and taller—and just like that, they were already young men, tall and handsome as date palms, strong and brave—a large army of heroes standing at the ready and waiting for their liberator.

And the rescuer came.

It happened at midnight.

Moses the Liberator came and called, "Stand up, free children! You, who were never slaves to Pharaoh, you who never felt his heavy hand, you who never molded any bricks and mortar, stand up and lead the way for the entire people!"

"We're going! We're going!" they all cried out with one voice.

And with courage and pride, with loud singing, they strode to the gates of Egypt, and the entire people, the Children of Israel, marched after them with their heads held high!

What Izzy Knows about Lag Ba'Omer

Malka Szechet

MALKA (BIEGUN D') SZECHET
July 18,1907 (or 1908)—December 1991

Little record exists of the early life of the author, who was born in 1907 or 1908 in Poland to Tamar (née Sheinbein) and Yitzkhok Biegun. She married Mendel Szechet, a rabbi and kosher slaughterer. When kosher slaughter was banned in the region where they lived, they departed Poland, sailing from Liverpool to Havana in January 1936. She was pregnant with her first child during the journey, and she would later recount to him that there were two hurricanes during that winter voyage, "one on the outside and another on the inside." In Havana, Szechet published this story and a similar one, "What Khayiml Knows about Hanukkah." Although pictures of her and of a group of Cuban schoolchildren appear in these slight volumes, no publisher or date of publication is listed. She worked as a teacher throughout those years, both in the Zionist Colegio Yavneh and the Centro Israelita de la Habana.

With her three children, Máximo, Golda, and Jacobo, Szechet left for New York in 1954. Her family settled in Cincinnati, although she was widowed in December 1956 when her husband succumbed to lung cancer. Around this time, she was on faculty at the Chofetz Chaim Day School in Cincinnati. She remarried, to Rabbi Yochanan Spiegel. She taught in Hebrew and Yiddish religious schools for over thirty years but does not appear to have published further in the United States. She was living in Lakewood, New Jersey, at the time of her death and had thirteen grandchildren and three great-grandchildren.

"What Izzy Knows about Lag Ba'Omer" is a simple, didactic presentation of the details of the minor yet child-friendly spring holiday of Lag Ba'Omer, or the thirty-third day of the counting of the Omer: a period of seven weeks stretching from Passover to Shavuot whose days are counted individually according to rabbinic interpretation of a biblical verse.

— ℬ —

"Grandpa! Give me twenty-five groschen. The teacher said tomorrow is Lag Ba'Omer, and we're not going to do any work in school.

"We're going into the forest and shooting arrows, having a picnic, and telling the stories of Rabbi Akiba, Bar Kochba, and Shimon bar Yochai. Whoever tells the best story about Lag Ba'Omer will get two colored eggs. All the other boys will get one colored egg. This year, I have to contribute to the picnic because I'm old enough to study *chumash*, the Five Books of Moses. I get to go along to the forest!"

Breathlessly, Izzy appealed to his grandfather with these words. Grandpa was sitting at home, chanting over a large volume of Talmud, "Rabbi Eliezer said that Rabbi Hanina said . . ."

"Oh, you rascal! First off, you scared me," said Grandpa to Izzy, turning away from his Talmud.

"No, Grandpa! I didn't mean to scare you. I ran home, so I was out of breath. That's just how it came out," Izzy answered his grandfather.

"Okay! So if you're really an honest boy, and you didn't mean to frighten your grandpa, then sit down here next to me on this stool and tell me calmly what you want. You've said so much I don't know where to begin," said the grandfather to his grandson in a different tone.

"Give me twenty-five groschen, Grandpa. Tomorrow is Lag Ba'Omer," said Izzy to his grandfather more calmly.

"Tomorrow is Lag Ba'Omer, so I should give you twenty-five groschen. . . . Very well, very nice. . . . Now I understand. But I want to ask you, isn't that a little much? And do you think that I'm always obliged to give you money?" Grandpa interrupted Izzy.

"No, Grandpa: I'm not saying you have to give me any money. I'm just asking you to lend it to me, and Mama will surely repay you. Little Esther is sick, so we have to buy her medicine, and that's why Mama can't give me any money," Izzy replied to his grandfather, embarrassed.

"Oh! Well, if you're not demanding but rather asking, that's a different story. Please tell me what you know about Lag Ba'Omer, and I'll give you the twenty-five groschen right away," said Izzy's grandpa.

"Long ago, when the Jews lived in the Land of Israel, they used to bring the Omer to the Temple on the second night of Passover. In the olden days, the Omer was a measure of first grains that grew on their own land each year, and it was brought to thank God for his goodness to the Jews.

"And the Torah says that from the time when the Omer is brought, we have to count fifty days, seven full weeks. And then we celebrate the holiday of Shavuot, the Feast of Weeks. The fifty days that are counted from the second night of Passover are called *sefirah*. It comes from the Hebrew word *sefer*, which means "count." Originally, *sefirah* was a time of joy. Everyone rejoiced over the precious holiday of Passover, which commemorates the miraculous Exodus from Egypt. And also because they'd lived to see a time when the Omer was brought, all thanks to God, from the newly ripened crops of their own fields in the Land of Israel. They counted the days and waited to celebrate Shavuot, which commemorates the day when God gave the Torah to the Jews.

"But over time, the *sefirah* days were transformed into a time of sorrow. To this day, we don't hold weddings or other joyous occasions during the fifty days from Passover to Shavuot. Observant Jews don't get haircuts or don new clothing during those days.

"An exception is the day of Lag Ba'Omer, which means the thirty-third day of the Omer and falls on the eighteenth day of the Jewish month of Iyar. Even though it occurs during the *sefirah* period, the sadness of that time doesn't apply on this day. You can get a haircut, wear new clothing, and make weddings and other celebrations.

"This is all because when the Romans conquered the Land of Israel and burned the Temple, some of the Jews were left behind in their own land under Roman rule. The Romans collected enormous taxes from the Jews for Jupiter's Temple in Rome. They oppressed the Jews very badly. Then the heroic Bar Kochba arose with his strong army, and they were joined by the great and learned Rabbi Akiba with his twenty-four thousand disciples, and they led the fight against the Romans. Their struggle was successful. The Romans were almost entirely driven out. And Israel became a free nation under the leadership of the heroic Bar Kochba.

"But Israel wasn't destined to become free at that time. For just four years after Bar Kochba assumed the leadership of Israel, a stronger Roman army came and fought the heroic Jews. And after a year of war, the Jews were defeated. According to legend, a plague spread among Rabbi Akiba's students in the fifty days between Passover and Shavuot and killed many of them. That's why we mourn even to this day."

"Very good, my child! You tell it very nicely," said Izzy's grandfather in the middle of the story. "But I want you to explain to me how the word 'Lag' comes to mean 'thirty-three,' and why is *lamed, gimel ba'omer* different from all the other *sefirah* days?"

"That's very easy: it's because the letters of the Jewish alphabet, which are for reading and writing, can also be used as numbers for counting. Every letter corresponds to a number. And according to this alphabet numbering system, the number thirty-three corresponds to the letters *lamed-gimel*. The thirty-third day of *sefirah* is different from all the rest because on that day, none of Rabbi Akiba's students died. That's why that day is a holiday for children and a memorial to those times. It's like a Jewish Children's Day.

"When the Romans beat Bar Kochba's armies and crushed his uprising, they began to wreak even more havoc on the Land of Israel. They wanted to completely uproot and destroy the Jewish people. They enacted many decrees against Jewish practices. And anyone who did not obey their laws was punished severely. They gave an especially harsh penalty to anyone who decided to study Torah. They caught the great and learned Rabbi Akiba and used iron combs on him. They tore his body until he gave up the ghost.

"What they wanted was for the Jews to blend in with the Romans and other nations and to cease to exist as a people with our own beliefs and morals that we inherited from our ancestors.

"The Jewish children understood all of this very well back then. They would take daggers and arrows and pretend they were going into the forest to practice shooting. But really, they would go into a cave where one of Rabbi Akiba's students, Rabbi Shimon bar Yochai, was hiding, and they would study Torah with him.

"That's why Jewish children observe the holiday of Lag Ba'Omer—as a remembrance of those times and as a lesson about how Jewish children should take pride in their Jewishness in every era."

This is how Izzy, with great pride, told his grandfather the story of Lag Ba'Omer. Finally Grandpa took twenty-five groschen out of his purse and, with a joyful smile on his lips, handed it to his grandson, saying, "Great indeed is our Jewish life. And greater still are you, our children, who are carrying on that life!"

A Village Saint

Sholem Asch

SHOLEM ASCH
1880–July 10, 1957

The precise date of Sholem Asch's birth in Kutno is uncertain. His father was a scholarly, philanthropically inclined businessman, and his mother was from a learned family. It was his second marriage, and theirs was a blended family that included ten children. Asch's full brothers were adventuresome men of affairs who eventually made their way to the United States, while his half brothers dressed in gabardines and followed Hasidic practice.

Asch's parents hoped to raise him into a rabbi, and they hired tutors to oversee his elementary education. He began to read nonreligious books as a teenager, starting with maskilic works in Hebrew. With friends, he pieced together a knowledge of German by reading Mendelssohn's translations of the Psalms and then moved on to Schiller, Goethe, and Heine. Dogged by rumors of heresy and his parents' disapproval of his secular studies, he left home at seventeen for the nearby village of some relatives. He tutored the family's children and observed the lives of the Polish peasantry, a period he would later refer to as his "elementary school in life."

His "high school" came during the subsequent two years, when he found steady work writing letters, including love letters, for illiterate workers. During those years, he also read widely in the German and Russian literary traditions as well as the more nascent modern Yiddish and Hebrew canon. Asch began to write, initially in Hebrew, but he was deeply influenced by reading Y. L. Peretz's Yiddish fiction. During a visit, the "classic" writer encouraged the newcomer to write in Yiddish. At Peretz's home, Asch also met other emerging Yiddish literary talents. Peretz smoothed the path toward publication for Asch's first short story, "Moyshele." Peretz also secured Asch an exemption from compulsory military service.

The young author relocated to a bustling Warsaw and began in earnest what would become a prolific career writing fiction and plays. In Yiddish and in Hebrew translation, in periodicals and in books, he made a name for himself and earned the esteem of Jewish cultural leaders. In 1903, he married Mathilde (Madzhe) Shapiro, the daughter of a prosperous Hebrew teacher and poet.

His plays addressed important current events and trends, including the abortive 1905 revolution in Russia, Zionism, pogroms, and messianism. His work enjoyed translation not only into Hebrew but into German, Polish, and Russian as well. His 1906 play *God of Vengeance* was a sensation that saw its director and cast arrested for obscenity at a 1923 performance on Broadway; the controversial episode fueled the 2015 play *Indecent*.

In 1908, Asch made his first trip to Palestine as well as participating in the watershed conference on Yiddish language and culture held in Czernowitz, Romania. He subsequently took part in relief efforts for victims of World War I and traversed Europe on behalf of the American Jewish Committee. The year 1914 saw him leave Poland for New York, returning to Europe in the 1920s and '30s. He settled in New York in 1938. In 1929, Asch published the first volume of his landmark trilogy of Jewish life in Poland and Russia before World War I, *Before the Flood* (translated in 1933 as *Three Cities*). Later, in the 1930s and '40s, Asch stirred further controversy with novels about the figure of Christ and essays on philosophy and theology.

He continued to travel widely throughout his life in the United States, Europe, and Israel. He died in Bat Yam, near Tel Aviv.

The master critic Joseph Sherman wrote that Asch "clothed romantic idealism in a realistic style." The selections in this volume are drawn from the 1929 collection *Far yugnt* (For youth), published by Warsaw's prestigious Kultur-lige (Culture League). The short stories offer lyrical portrayals of traditional, pre-urban Jewish life in Poland. "A Village Saint" describes the spiritual life of a child who learns differently than his peers do, climaxing with the Hasidic motif of the unlettered Jew whose whistle penetrates the heavens where the *tsaddik*'s prayer alone cannot.

— ℘ —

In a dew-covered sea of green grass, he lay hidden, tending the lambs entrusted to him by his father. He was called "Yashek." Even he didn't know his proper Jewish name. After all, he'd never yet been called to the Torah.

Everyone knew that he was a peasant, a coarse fellow. His father, Isaac the Milkman, had given up on him entirely; he didn't even expect him to recite the Kaddish.* And it was only to fulfill his fatherly obligation that he had brought his son to a tutor in town.

The tutor had tried his very best. Hundreds and hundreds of times, he would repeat each word, but the boy looked on as if it was meant for someone else—"say long 'e' as in 'good week'!"

"Go try and deal with a mule-brain," the teacher would say, shaking his head, and the boy's mother would look at her son and sigh.

You couldn't get him so much as to pick up a prayer book. Pray? He, Yashek, should pray?! How could he approach God? It would be a disgrace before his Holy Name, were he to recite the Shema!

Nonetheless, Yashek understood God according to his faculties and felt him in his heart.

He saw God everywhere, wherever his eyes looked: he saw him right *there*, where the stream flowed quietly and murmured deep secrets to the quiet, calm, grassy bank; and over there, faraway, where the cloud pulled itself across the sky with a sad darkness—at those times, he sensed something, wanted something, longed for something. . . .

Whenever a large cloud passed by, a thunderclap sounded, lightning crackled . . . whenever rain poured down . . . or a heavy feeling enveloped the village, like the time they took out Old Maciek from under the threshing machine and the blood ran from his lopped-off foot . . . the village mourned . . . *then* he felt God! And God didn't live only in the heavens, and one didn't have to look up to the sky in order to see him; no, it seemed to him that God lived somewhere far, far away in a big city, like the master landowner to whom the village belonged. And over there, all the high overlords and bigwigs were nothing more than God's hired hands, just as Stach and Woytek were hired hands to their own village's nobleman.

But he, how could *he* approach God? Not even by being a shepherd of his. A shepherd of God's, he thought, must also be a distinguished "sir," a great nobleman! And who knew whether the master of their village was

* The memorial prayer recited upon the death of parents and other close relatives. The obligation to recite this prayer is so strong that it was considered a basic part of Jewish literacy even though the text is in ornate Aramaic.

even a coachman of God's horses? So then, were they really going to let Yashek through?

But occasionally when the sky, clear and bright, rested dreamily in a flowing blue veil; and the grass grew peacefully, with each blade rooted in the earth and gazing quietly into the sky; and across the way stood the old rampart, the green grandfather of the village; and beyond that, the road stretched on amid the grasses—a wagon rolled along, and somebody was going far, far away. . . . And up above, the sky also extended far and wide, sinking lower and lower until it lay at the door of the barn, watching. . . . At such times, it seemed to him, God had slipped out for a little while from the lords and nobles and had himself come into the field,* stretched out, and lay waiting. . . .

Then Yashek felt like giving thanks and praising everything all around him.

And occasionally he wanted to walk all the way until he reached the big city, where God dwelt and where his palace stood!

"I want to go and kiss God's hand," he thought.

Quickly, though, he sighed and wondered, "But would they let me?"

He might get to God's palace, but there would be "Swiss Guards" stationed there, tall ones with blue ribbons, yellow turned-down boots and red tailcoats, like those he saw on the lords who came to a ball at his village nobleman's—and they would chase him away. . . .

Then it occurred to him that he needn't go anywhere, that God was in the open field, and that actually the Swiss Guards kept watch over a palace empty of God.

"God is a faithful king,"† the rabbi taught the boy from the prayer book. He supposed that the declaration "God is a faithful king" was like a magic formula, the kind that when you said it, the Swiss Guards had to let you into God's palace.

But he had another kind of prayer for God, a prayer without words, a prayer that grew in his heart until he could feel it overflowing, and then the prayer escaped with a whistle!

---

* "The King is in the fields," drawing on Ecclesiastes 5:8, is a motif associated with the late-summer month of Elul, when one prepares spiritually for the accounting taken on Rosh Hashanah, the New Year. God is unusually accessible during this time, as Yashek perceives.
† This declaration immediately precedes the recitation of the Shema prayer.

When he felt like praying, he would place two fingers in his mouth, close his lips, and blow. And his prayer resounded through the whole forest!

And God understood him. God understood his prayer very well!

He only whistled when he felt like whistling to God, when he felt that he *needed* to whistle . . .

God, it seemed to him, lay somewhere far away over the empty, fragrant field and listened closely to how he whistled and took pleasure in his whistling and rejoiced in it.

Oh, he wasn't the only one whistling! Everyone, he knew, "whistled." When Sneezy the village dog would suddenly wag his tail, look up at the sky, and start barking—Yashek would say, Sneezy is praying. When Snowy the lamb walked home in the evening from the field, stuck out her tongue, and let out a long, plaintive bleat: maaaaa, he thought, Snowy is praying. The billy goat prayed in a different way: he would kick out in all directions, rear up on his hind legs, cock his head stiffly, and go, "burrrr!"

Each one prayed, even the frogs in the stream . . . one murmured to the other, "*kva, kva!*"

When Yashek turned thirteen years old, he still couldn't recite the Shema, and Rosh Hashanah was coming.

The rabbi worked with Yashek so that this Rosh Hashanah he could at least recite the Shema—and be taken along into town.

In honor of the holiday, they bought Yashek a new suit, a pair of boots and a new hat . . . now if he could just say the Shema!

The synagogue in town was crammed; small and big, everyone was dressed in white, draped in prayer shawls, everybody was standing and swaying in prayer, crying and calling louder and louder.

At the prayer lectern, where seven tall wax candles burned, the cantor stood with the choir . . . The sounds of drawn-out weeping could be heard, accompanied by half-torn, ragged voices:

"Who for life, and who for death . . ."

A broken wail suddenly tore forth from the women's balcony. Yashek had been standing still, dressed up in his suit, his fair hair poking out of his pushed-up cap. With a sudden motion, he pushed forward to the place of honor next to the cantor, and the prayer book that his father had given him so that it would at least look like he was praying slid from his hands; he stood there wide-eyed, gazing about.

A pair of impudent boys noticed Yashek, one winked at the other, they pointed at him and laughed quietly, and soon one came up to him and flicked his nose.

He didn't hear it, didn't feel it! He kept on gazing with wide-eyed devotion, his eye roving from the cantor to the crying congregation. He saw the white curtain covering the ark, with the large gold letters that spelled out, "Sanctified to God."

God must be here now—right there behind the curtain, he thought to himself.

From the women's balcony, his mother looked down and noticed her son standing and staring, the prayer book slipping from his hand—and she sighed and said to herself, "Peasant—a goy from birth."

His father threw him a glance from under his prayer shawl and sighed heavily, "Master of the Universe, Remember him too!"

Yashek stood there staring. Everyone cried, everyone prayed, everyone called out to God, and he suddenly felt the urge to do the same!

He also wanted to pray to God. He just wanted—not to cry, not to scream—but to thank and praise God. To give thanks, in front of everyone, absolutely everyone!

He picked up his prayer book, opened it to the Shema prayer, printed in bold letters, and began, "G-o-d i-s a f-a-i-t-h-f-u-l k-i-n-g."

But he couldn't put his heart into that kind of a prayer.

He didn't understand it. It was just like a magic spell to him, a dry formula. . . .

He wanted to thank and praise God honestly, faithfully from his heart—he was afraid in front of everyone, in front of so many people who prayed differently, but his urge grew stronger—and God was higher than all of them! He must!

So he brought his fingers to his mouth—

And a sharp whistle cut through the crying synagogue. . . .

The congregation was startled.

Who was that? *What* was that? Who was whistling in a holy place?

His father wanted to grab him by the shoulders, and the congregation wanted to beat him.

But suddenly the holy rabbi turned from the eastern wall and asked, "Where is the holy saint who managed to rend the evil decree? Who punctured the heavens and conducted our prayers up through the leaden clouds?"

But that saint was no longer there. . . .

He had slipped out of the synagogue, thrown his boots over his shoulder, and was already striding back to the village.

Señor Ferrara's First Yom Kippur

Zina Rabinowitz

ZINA RABINOWITZ

1895–June 25, 1965

For biographical information on Rabinowitz, see "The Mute Princess" in part 1. "Señor Ferrara's First Yom Kippur" is from Rabinowitz's collection of holiday tales, *Der liber yontef* (The precious holidays). Like "The Mute Princess," it unfolds in an "exotic" setting that is not commonly represented in Yiddish literature.

— ✄ —

After Mr. Auerbach had spent a couple of hours showing me around Port of Spain, he said to me, "Now that I've introduced you to all the Jews of our capital city here in Trinidad, I want to take you to see Señor Ferrara."

"Who is Señor Ferrara?"

Mr. Auerbach broke into a smile but did not answer.

I felt that he wanted to draw me in with his long silence, and I decided to wait. But my curiosity was growing, and so I repeated my question, "Who is Señor Ferrara? Why does he live so far outside the city?"

That's what I thought about in the car while watching the road that Auerbach was taking me on as it wound from one side of Port of Spain all the way down to the Caribbean seashore. . . .

Mr. Auerbach smiled once more, and after a long silence, he spoke again:

"His ancestors were from the small group of Jews who escaped the Spanish Inquisition at the beginning of the sixteenth century. . . . They wandered onto little ships that were allowed to sail anywhere, as long as it was away from the Inquisition. . . . After a long sea voyage, they spotted this island.

They settled here and began to trade and do business. . . . As it turned out, many of them married Christians, and over time, they also became Christians, Catholics. . . . Señor Ferrera was no exception. . . . He was a devout Catholic; he went to church and gave the most charity of anyone to the Catholic priests on the island. . . .

"When Hitler began his terrible atrocities, Jews from eastern Europe came to our town. They rented a large house and made it into a shul, where we could pray on Shabbos and holidays. Once, during the Kol Nidre service,* Señor Ferrara was passing by the shul when he caught the sound of the somber prayer melodies. He stopped and stood by the door for a long time. One of the congregants noticed the wealthy businessman and invited him inside. . . .

"Señor Ferrara waited in shul through the whole evening, until after Kol Nidre. The next morning, he came back to shul and sat there for several hours. After that Yom Kippur, he would steal into shul every Friday evening and sit there with his eyes closed until the end of services.

"'An evil spirit has gotten into Señor Ferrara!' The rumor spread among his children and grandchildren, friends and relatives. 'He doesn't want to go to church anymore! He no longer wants to serve our God!'

"'He's just old and doesn't have the strength to go to church,' his sons tried excuse him, when they saw how the town buzzed with the terrible rumor that was spreading about their father.

"The devout priests decided to visit Señor Ferrara at home and pray with him there.

"As soon as Señor Ferrara saw the cross with which the priests wanted to bless him and save his soul, an awful feeling overcame him. When he recovered, he pretended not to know what was going on, so that the priests would leave him alone and let him rest. . . .

"'Señor Ferrara is old and weak,' they said in the Catholic church, and they let him be. . . .

"From that time on, Señor Ferrara would wander about day and night all alone, talking to himself. Only when he stole into the Jewish synagogue of Port of Spain, could he sit calmly and gaze with his deep, longing eyes at the candles burning before the Holy Ark.

---

* The evening prayer ushering in Yom Kippur, the Day of Atonement, commonly regarded as the liturgical climax of the year.

"One fine day, all the bells in Port of Spain began to ring. A rumor spread through town that Señor Ferrara had died.

"All the Catholic priests donned their vestments to go and bury the good Catholic, Señor Ferrara. Nobody let slip even a single word about how old Ferrara hadn't been devout in the last months of his life. . . .

"They decorated the carriages, washed the horses, and bought the most expensive flowers, in order to beautify the way to the cemetery.

"But right when all the town's devout Catholics were already dressed in their finest and impatiently standing around Señor Ferrara's villa waiting for the Catholic funeral, the most distinguished local lawyer appeared, with a sealed paper in his hands. This was the will that Señor Ferrara had made a couple of weeks before his death.

"The will laid out all the details of how Senior Ferrara had divided his wealth among his children. At the end was this codicil:

"'Let nobody say that I was not in full possession of my senses when I wrote this will. My doctor is a witness that I am healthy and in command of all my faculties but not entirely robust in my beliefs. And since I'm not dying as a believing Catholic, I think that I have no right to occupy a plot in the Catholic cemetery. So I request of all my children that they should fulfill my final wish and take the casket with my remains out to sea, to the place where I hereby indicate. The great-great-great-grandson of the onetime Sephardic Jews who settled on the island when fleeing the Spanish Inquisition should be placed beneath the waves.'

"The priests would not help. Ferrara's children and grandchildren didn't help at all. According to English law, a will must be carried out just as it is written. . . .

"And here we come to the place where Señor Ferrara had his proper burial, as he instructed!" Mr. Auerbach smiled, stopping his car.

He took me up to the high cliffs, which cut deep into the sea and said, "From that last cliff, they threw down the casket with the Catholic who had apparently wanted to go back to being a Jew. Right into the sea . . . see the high waves? It's just as if they're still fighting over Señor Ferrara . . . !"

I regarded the high cliff. Tall, foamy, white waves crashed all around it— some on one side, and some on the other. Gazing at them, I imagined how in the depths of the sea, the waves were still fighting over the Catholic who hadn't quite managed to die as Jew.

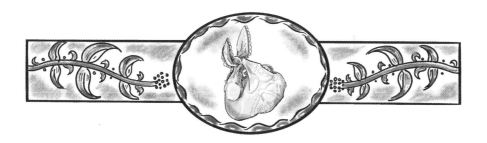

Kids

Mordkhe Spektor

MORDKHE SPEKTOR (MORDECAI SPECTOR)
May 5, 1858–March 15, 1925

Born in Uman, near Kiev, Ukraine, Spektor was the youngest child of his father's second wife. His father, Yankev, was a Talner Hasid who died when Spektor was two. His mother placed him in *kheyder*, but he spent a great deal of time outdoors. After his bar mitzvah, Spektor was sent to live with relatives; as a young teenager, he met important Enlightenment figures and cultural leaders. By the age of fourteen, he was increasingly devoted to Enlightenment thought, and his older brother sent him back home to his mother in Uman.

His mother died when he was nineteen, and Spektor moved to Odessa, a major Jewish cultural center. He worked in a paper factory and was proud to be earning his bread as a laborer. Following the pogroms of 1881, he moved to Medzhybizh, where he published some short pieces of journalism and worked at writing longer fiction. His *Novel without a Name* was published serially in *Yudishes folks-blat* (The Jewish people's paper), and he was invited to move to St. Petersburg to take up an editorial position at the paper. He published a great deal there and married Izabella Fridberg, whose father was a Yiddish writer and censor. He hoped to establish a newspaper of his own, but after failing to gain permission, he moved his family in 1887 to Warsaw—then a sleepy outpost on the Yiddish literary map.

Between 1888 and 1896, Spektor published five issues of an anthology, *Der hoyz-fraynd* (The house friend), as well as an almanac. His literary anthology found itself competing against Sholem Aleichem's *Yudishe folks-bibliotek* (Jewish people's library), but he nevertheless became friendly with the "classic" Yiddish writers Sholem Aleichem and Y. L. Peretz. In fact, he and Peretz were arrested together for attending an illegal meeting of labor revolutionaries in 1899, and they served a sentence at the Warsaw Citadel.

Over the next decade, Spektor continued to contribute to and edit various periodicals. In 1903, he edited the anthology *Hilf* (Help), directing the profits to benefit victims of the Kishinev pogrom. With the German army advancing on Warsaw in 1914, he and his second wife fled to Odessa. His health deteriorated there. In 1920, they left on a circuitous route through Europe that eventually took them to New York in autumn 1921. He published new novels and memoirs before he passed away in New York in 1925.

The story included here, "Kids," is a holiday tale that places the emphasis on children's own power to aid others and make the world a better place. The story subtly distinguishes between adults who regard children as a nuisance or with reflexive suspicion and those who treat them with affection and respect.

This story took place back when Notke was ten years old and his friend Leybitshke was twelve.

Notke and Leybitshke were friends, and like true friends, they walked together to school and back, went together to and from synagogue to pray; and even though each of them had his own little prayer book, they prayed together because of course it was more fun to pray from one prayer book. . . .

The entire town knew of the friendship between the two boys; even Shmerl, the water carrier, had noticed it.

All day long, Shmerl carried water on his old shoulders. He would bring home the groschen that he'd earned and then go back out to the synagogue, take a seat under the heating stove, and dry out his wet clothes, warm his old bones, and sometimes take a look at the Mishna* that lay open before him on the broken lectern that had been put into "early retirement" from the eastern wall.

But the old water carrier found many different uses for the "retired" lectern: sometimes, it actually served him as a lectern and at other times as a pillow for his head, and at still other times, he used it to fend off the rascals who often disturbed his study.

---

* Skeletal collection of rabbinic oral law, accessible even to those without an advanced Talmudic education.

II.

One Purim morning, when Notke and Leybitshke had just finished praying and were about to go home, Old Shmerl called them over out of the blue. The friends were very surprised, because all the rest of the year, Shmerl only spoke to them to call them "rascals." Nevertheless, they went over to him.

Shmerl stroked both of their cheeks, said nothing for a while, and looked at them with a very friendly expression. The children noticed a look of embarrassment on his wrinkled, old face. Suddenly, Shmerl began to speak in a quavering voice: "Children, I have something to ask of you. . . . You know that today is Purim. . . . Passover is coming soon. . . . And my grandchild doesn't have a pair of shoes. . . . She's been sitting at home for the past three months and can't even go outside. . . . I have nothing with which to buy shoes. . . . I don't even know whether we'll have a Purim feast at my house today. . . . I had pinned all my hopes on Purim. Go around town, children, both of you, and 'make' me a few groschen. . . . I swear I would go myself . . . but God knows I can't. . . . If only I could, I wouldn't be a water carrier in my old age. If I were capable of begging, I wouldn't be carrying heavy buckets of water on my old shoulders. . . ."

The friends were so embarrassed by Shmerl's words that they ran out of the synagogue without saying anything. But they stopped as soon as they reached the street.

"Why did you run away?" Leybitshke asked.

"Because you ran away—so I did too," Notke replied.

"Let's go back and give him a couple of groschen."

"That's silly. What can he do with four groschen?"

"So then let's go give him as much as we have. . . ."

They counted out their money: all in all, they had twelve groschen.

"It doesn't amount to much," Leybitshke said.

"It's practically nothing," Notke agreed, "because for my shoes, which are small, my mother paid maybe three rubles."

"Well, what should we do?"

"We'll go around and collect money together, like the teenage boys do on Purim."

"But can we? After all, they're big, and we're . . . I'd be embarrassed. . . ."

"Nah, what do we have to be ashamed of? I'll just ask my mother if she'll let me."

They both decided that right after breakfast, Leybitshke would come over to Notke's and they would let each other know what their mothers had said.

III.

Old Shmerl no longer had his children to care for. But God had punished him: his only daughter, who had gotten married long ago to a wagon driver and had children of her own, was suddenly widowed, and the children had become orphans.* The horse and wagon had been sold off quickly to pay debts, and once she'd gone through the few remaining guilders, the widow had needed to bring her children to live with her old father.

Reb Shmerl didn't drive his daughter and grandchildren out of his home; on the contrary, for their sake, he began to toil as he had in his youth— but with all his hard work, they barely managed to get a dry crust of bread. Nevertheless, Old Shmerl felt lucky because when he came home, his grandchildren would run up to meet him, hug him, stroke and kiss him, and affectionately call him "Zeydenyu," or "Grampy-gramps." Above all, he felt fortunate whenever, after his labors, he had a couple of groschen with which to buy his grandchildren a string of pretzels, because those pretzels brought the children great pleasure.

But the last time the grandfather had brought home pretzels, the eldest grandchild had kept her distance and didn't want to take any.

The grandfather said, "Why aren't you taking any pretzels, Leahtshke?"

"I don't want pretzels, Zeydenyu. I want you to buy me a pair of shoes! I want to go outside on the streets and see how people walk and ride around. I want to be able walk outside as they do. . . ."

"Right now, my child, I don't have any money. But, God willing, by Purim, may I live and be healthy, I'll buy you a pair of shoes," the grandfather had promised.

IV.

"Why not, my child?" Notke's mother said, when he asked her whether he could go around with Leybitshke to collect alms on behalf of a poor man.

* Losing one parent is considered orphanhood in Jewish culture.

"If you go around now for someone else's sake, God will help you so that you'll never need others to go around collecting for your sake."

Right after breakfast, Leybitshke came running over to Notke's to tell him the happy news that his mother had also said yes; and the proof was that he was already dressed in his Sabbath caftan and cap, and his mother herself had given him a donation of ten groschen.

Notke's mother dusted off her son's caftan, straightened his cap, smoothed his earlocks, gave him a colored kerchief to take along for carrying the donations, told them to walk slowly and with dignity, and advised them to go see Uncle Zalmen and Aunt Gitl and all the other wealthy notables and leading townspeople.

Notke's mother also made a donation of ten groschen, and the two friends headed out to the street.

Outside, everything said Purim: the sun was shining and melting the snow, as it ought to in the early-spring month of Adar. Water was dripping from the roofs. The white snow was stained yellow. Maids and servants were delivering *shalekhmones*, festive Purim food baskets.

"Where should we go first?" Notke asked.

"How should I know? Let's go to Reb Shloyme the Rich."

They began to argue over which one of them should enter first, until they decided that it would be simpler to go first to Notke's uncle.

But at his uncle's house they were received as guests, treated to Purim pastries, honey cake and layered fruit cake, and it simply never occurred to Notke's uncle that the children had come to collect charity. It was the same at his aunt's and at the home of her neighbor Gella, whom Notke also knew. They were too embarrassed to say what they had come for. And so, two full hours passed, and they hadn't yet "made" anything. . . .

Finally, they went to see Reb Shloyme the Rich. Gasping and sweaty, they made it inside.

Reb Shloyme the big shot was lounging about in a luxurious holiday robe. He knew Notke and Leybitshke as "rascals" because he had often seen them in synagogue, and as soon as he recognized them, he began, with a little laugh, to pull them by the ears.

"So, rascals, now you're going around collecting too? Surely so you can buy sweets?"

The children barely managed to pull their ears away from Reb Shloyme's rough fingers; they ran out of his house before taking a breath.

They themselves didn't know how they ended up in another well-to-do home. Trembling, they blurted out their errand.

"Ha, ha," the wealthy man's son-in-law burst into laughter. "Well, this is rich! Nice, new, freshly baked Jews—and they too want money! New "charity trustees," and they're already coming after alms? Ha, ha ...!"

Notke and Leybitshke felt so ashamed that they couldn't figure out how to open the door; they couldn't get out of there fast enough. The rich man's wife even shouted after them, "Come back! We'll give you something to buy apples with!"

But they were already far away.

So they visited a third notable.

"What do you want, rascals?" asked the rich man jovially.

The friends pointed to their colored kerchief, which one of them was holding in his hand.

"What? You're already up to wanting money? Ugh, brats! Bring me the switch, and I'll give them a spanking!" And he dragged them both over to a bench.

The rich man's wife and children, who had been laughing all the while, asked the rich man to let them go.

The two friends ran out to the street, barely alive.

V.

Out on the street, the friends started to cry; but they immediately felt ashamed, so for a couple of minutes they looked at each other in silence.

"Are you listening, Leybitshke, to what I'm going to say to you?"

"What?"

"I want to tell you that if we had money, we would buy a pair of shoes from Khaytshe the Cobbler, who's sitting over there in the market. Just look at how many pairs of shoes are lying around her."

They went up closer to Khaytshe's stall without taking their eyes off her.

"Why are you standing there, kids?" asked Khaytshe, who knew them well.

With her question, Khaytshe imbued them with new life. They went up even closer and told her the whole story of what had happened to them that day.

"You know what, kids? Buy a pair of shoes from me...."

"But we have no money."

"No matter, I know you, you'll settle up with me, you're honest kids. . . . You'll pay me back, right? You know I'm not a rich woman myself. . . ."

The friends swore on their lives to pay her back, though it might take a while because their mothers gave each of them only two groschen a day for breakfast at school.

"No," said Khaytshe. "You're not allowed to pay me back with those groschen. I'll give you a pair of good shoes for eight guilders, and you go around collecting a little more: however much you make, you'll bring me, and the rest you'll pay back gradually."

"But where else should we go? We've already been to almost all the rich people, and we don't want to keep going; we'd rather pay you back with our breakfast money."

"Then you've already gone through *all* the houses in town?"

"No."

"So, get a move on, kids. Skip the wealthy houses, and just go wherever you see a Jewish home; the home might look poor, but it doesn't matter: a Jewish household won't let anybody leave without a donation. . . . Have no fear," Khaytshe reassured them. "They won't make fun of you in those houses. Only the rich, who have it very good and want to make merry on Purim, poke fun; they think the whole world is their plaything. . . ."

Khaytshe chose a good pair of shoes, without knowing the size, naturally, wrapped them in paper, and gave them to the children.

The children walked away happy, with the shoes under one arm.

The young friends were convinced that Khaytshe had been right in advising them to skip the wealthy houses. They went to common householders. Wherever they went, they were received in friendly fashion and given a donation, as well as Purim pastries for themselves.

All day long, Notke and Leybitshke traipsed around, and it was only at night that they ran with great joy to Khaytshe and brought her eight guilders—and they had change left over. Then they ran to the old water carrier's.

VI.

Night had already begun to fall. The sun had set long ago, but in the windows of Jewish homes, it was light, as befits a great holiday. People everywhere were sitting happily at their Purim feasts. The tall, beautiful loaves of rich Purim egg challah, fish, and other delicacies shone from the tables. Children's pockets were full of Purim pastries, hamantaschen, little horses and birds made of sugar, and boxes of sweets wrapped up in gold paper. In their hands, they held layered fruit cake, honey cake, and saffron-spiced cake, with big raisins. The door almost never closed: one went in, and another came out with *shalekhmones*, gift baskets of food from relatives or good friends.

Everybody rejoiced on the holiday, and the kids rejoiced most of all.

But far away from town, near a hill, stood a low-lying hut. Here too lived a Jew: Reb Shmerl the old water carrier. Here too were children whose grandfather loved them no less than other parents loved their children. But what could be seen here on this merry evening . . . ? A penny candle flickered on the table, no Purim-worthy yellow egg challah, just one stale roll, which had been set aside for the purpose since Shabbos. . . . At the table sat Old Shmerl, the water carrier, feeling very sad. The dim candle didn't bother him, nor did the stale roll. He was already used to it. He too would have had a happy holiday in his low hut if only his beloved grandchildren had been happy. But how were they sitting at the table? One child sat sound asleep in his chair; another dozed. One child sighed, and the eldest grandchild, Leahtshke, was even more forlorn: she had lost all hope—no shoes . . . ! She wouldn't be going out for a walk so fast. . . . Maybe barefoot in summer, but summer was still a long way away. . . . Even in summer it wasn't so good to go without shoes, because feet could get pricked. . . .

Suddenly the door opened, and in ran Notke and Leybitshke. They immediately put a pair of new shoes down on the table, and from the colored kerchief, they shook out a paper basket with several coins left over from the donations and also several pieces of layered fruit cake and candy.

The two young friends, their cheeks aflame, were bashful but full of joy, and, hardly pausing to catch their breath, they blurted out to Old Shmerl, "This is the *shalekhmones*, the Purim 'gift basket' that Khaytshe the Cobbler and our mothers sent for your children." All the children jumped up as if awakening from a bad dream to a beautiful dawn and, with their big, innocent eyes, gazed at the table, at the boys, at their Zeyde, and each child took something from the table and ran to their grandfather with great joy, and each child called out, "Zeydenyu, Grampa! Just look, today is Purim . . . !"

"Just look, dear children, today really *is* Purim!" Leah came bounding over to Shmerl with the shoes on and hugged him hard.

With tears in his eyes, the grandfather kissed his grandchildren and then hugged Notke and Leybitshke, and tears from Shmerl's old eyes dripped onto their faces. . . .

Even though by now the penny candle was no longer giving much light, the old water carrier's home was suddenly as bright and cheerful as the houses where plenty of candles and lamps were burning.

The next day, on Shushan Purim, the children saw a girl walking down the street in brand-new shoes.

That was Leahtshke, Shmerl the water carrier's grandchild, and even though the shoes were too big for Leahtshke's little feet, she was quite pleased with them nevertheless, for they were her first pair of shoes.

PART II

JEWISH HISTORY AND HEROES

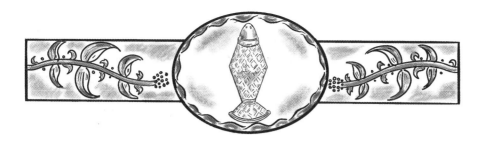

Gur Aryeh
Rokhl Shabad

ROKHL SHABAD
1898–1974

Regine-Rokhl Shabad's family lived in Vilna. Her father, Tzemach, was the "dean" of Vilna's Jewish medical community, and his wife, Stefanye-Shifre, descended from an aristocratic background. They married when she was nineteen or twenty and he was thirty-five. Rokhl's parents believed strongly in the value of agriculture, which had not traditionally been a Jewish pursuit. Rokhl was sent to do graduate work in botany in Frankfurt. The university was new, having been established in 1914. Its first class, of six hundred students, included one hundred women—an astronomically high proportion at the time.

Rokhl met the linguist Max Weinreich while they were both working as teachers; he would become the twentieth century's most preeminent scholar of Yiddish and found the YIVO Institute for Jewish Research, first in Vilna and then in New York (with an additional branch in Buenos Aires). They married in 1920. After she completed her PhD in 1925, the couple returned to Vilna; their son Uriel was born the following year.

Regine Weinreich, as she was then known, worked as an elementary-school art teacher for the rest of the family's years in Vilna. She cultivated warm relationships with her pupils and was referred to informally, with her first name, as "Lerern [Teacher] Regine." The Weinreichs were traveling with Uriel in Denmark when World War II broke out. Max and Uriel continued on to New York, while Regine returned to Vilna to collect their younger son, Gabriel. The family was reunited in New York soon thereafter.

Regine's aunt ran a dressmaking and secondhand couture resale business from her home, with a clientele of displaced Polish Jews with aristocratic tastes. Regine worked there as a fitter and seamstress. The Weinreichs lost Uriel, already an accomplished linguist, to cancer in 1967. Regine was widowed at seventy and diagnosed with abdominal cancer five years later. She died in New York and was buried in Ann Arbor, Michigan, where Gabriel had become a professor of physics.

The record of Regine Shabad Weinreich's writing career is sparse. "Gur Aryeh," published in Warsaw under the name "Rokhl Shabad" (spelled "Szabad" in Polish), is undated. A wonder tale resembling traditional stories of Hasidic masters and their spiritual exploits, the story has the trappings of a fairy tale, with its geographically vague setting and rabbi interacting with royalty.

In fact, the Gur Aryeh was an authentic historical figure of the sixteenth century, also known as the Maharal of Prague. "Gur Aryeh," or "lion's cub," is a metonym closely associated with his given name, Judah, and it is the title of his supercommentary on Rashi's Torah commentary. He is most widely remembered, through a nineteenth-century legend, as the creator of the clay Golem who defended the Jews of Prague from anti-Jewish violence. In light of the legend's prevalence, it seems significant that Shabad chose to embroider (or perhaps invent) a lesser-known episode that focused on the Gur Aryeh's spiritual acuity and faith that God would provide for his needs.

— ℬ —

Once upon a time in Prague, there was a great rabbi called the Gur Aryeh, or Lion's Whelp.

The Gur Aryeh possessed a sterling character and great wisdom, and people from all the surrounding villages, cities, and towns would come to him, seeking advice and an encouraging word.

His reputation eventually reached the king, who ordered that the Gur Aryeh be brought to the palace.

When he came before the king, it was clear that the rabbi was very wise, and the king came to prefer him to all his courtiers and to seek his advice always.

But the courtiers took a dislike to the rabbi, and they constantly looked for some kind of trick whereby they might drive the Jew away from the king's palace.

It was the courtiers' custom to make a feast for the king each month. The king would come and make merry with them for an entire night. Fires would burn in the palace like golden suns, and the sweet sound of violins would drift about the brightly lit palace windows.

But the Gur Aryeh was not rich, because he always distributed his money among the poor and oppressed. He had never made a feast for the king, and once he even declared, "Better to spend the money from the feasts on poor people."

One time the senior courtier said to the king, "Your Royal Highness! All your courtiers and all your lords always make a magnificent feast in Your Majesty's honor, and you spend a very enjoyable night with them, but the Jew who sits in your palace has never yet done so. He has never hosted a single feast in His Majesty's honor."

As soon as the king heard those words, he called for the rabbi and said, "Listen, my friend! My courtiers say that you don't like me. They always make me jolly feasts, but you have never done so. It seems that you really *don't* like me. . . ."

The rabbi replied, "Your Royal Highness! In a week's time, I will make a feast in Your Majesty's honor, and I will also invite your courtiers."

That same day, the king saw his senior courtier and told him what the Gur Aryeh had said, but he only burst out laughing and replied, "Don't believe him, Your Royal Highness. You should know that he is quite a pauper. He has empty pockets. How will he make a feast?"

The king shrugged and said, "Well, that Jew is a very honest man. He always does what he says he will."

A few days later, the courtiers quietly sent a man to see whether the rabbi was preparing for the feast. He returned immediately, splitting his sides with laughter. Tears ran from his eyes, and he whinnied with glee.

"Why are you laughing so hard?" Tell us already, what did you see there?" asked the courtiers in unison.

Even once his laugher had died down a bit, he could scarcely spit out the words, "The rabbi is sitting and studying, and his house is dead and empty . . . there's nary a hint of a feast."

The eyes of the senior courtier began to flash.

"Good, good," he said. "The little Jew will soon come to an unhappy end. The king will surely chase him from the palace."

A few more days passed. Again the courtiers sent a man to check. They still couldn't rest easy. Perhaps by now the rabbi had begun his preparations for the feast?

Well, the man left and returned—and laughed some more.

"Eh, I don't know! Nothing's been started. The rabbi is sitting and study-ing. He seems to have forgotten about the whole thing."

The courtiers clapped their hands and stroked their fine beards and said happily, "Good, good! Soon he'll meet his miserable end. The king will see presently that the little Jew has made a fool of him. . . ."

The day appointed for the feast was approaching. The night before, the courtiers were too impatient to sleep. They couldn't close their eyes. They were eager to see vengeance against the Jew who was so beloved of the king. As soon as the day dawned, they jumped out of bed, dressed quickly, and ran to take a look at what was happening with the feast.

Meanwhile, the time rushed by. Now it was just an hour until the feast was to begin—and the rabbi wasn't there yet; now it was half an hour—and it was quiet as a graveyard all around. No work, no preparations for the party.

"He's definitely not coming," they said quietly to one another, and their eyes burned with joy.

But at that very moment, the rabbi appeared, dressed in holiday clothing, and he invited the king and the courtiers to the feast.

The courtiers exchanged glances, but nobody uttered a word.

Soon they were seated in fine carriages, and together with the rabbi, they journeyed out of the city, with the king in the lead. They rode on and on, until suddenly they spotted a fine palace surrounded by a garden; and in the garden stood gigantic trees, and on the trees grew golden fruit.

The rabbi stopped the carriages and invited the king and all the guests into the palace.

As soon as they entered, slim, young waiters with white hand towels on their shoulders appeared through the tall, open doors. The courtiers looked at one another once again, their faces flushed now with anger and shame, but they remained silent, speaking not a word.

Suddenly, a tall door opened, and the guests caught sight of a large room with tall golden chairs and golden tables; on the tables was the very best of everything. The golden dishes on which the delicacies lay were radiant as fire. Among the dishes and utensils lay strands of pearls and individual diamonds and gems, and the walls were hung with a blue light, as if from the sky.

"How good and how beautiful it is here," the king thought, but he didn't say anything at all out loud.

"My honored guests!" the rabbi called out. "Seat yourselves at the table, eat, drink, and be merry."

So the king sat down at table, and all his courtiers sat around him. Behind each chair stood a waiter, anticipating each guest's smallest command.

The guests first enjoyed themselves and then ate. A light, fine wine that wouldn't cause drunkenness was poured from crystal bottles into tall, thin goblets. Each guest felt that he had never seen such a lavish and beautiful feast.

Nor was music lacking.

From time to time, the strains of an orchestra could be heard although not seen; joyful sounds drifted softly around the bright windows.

The king, who was accustomed to golden palaces and jewel-encrusted dishes, had never in his life seen so much luxury and splendor. A seeming trifle: he had never before seen such a beautiful saltshaker. Strewn with little gems, this saltshaker glowed with fiery greens and reds.

The feast lasted a long time, and finally they went out into the garden. The slender trees, dappled with sun, stood proud and silent, but the branches, laden with ripe fruit, bowed down to the guests and begged, "Enjoy my fruit. . . . Enjoy my fruit. . . ."

The fruits were easily plucked and lay on the tongue like sugar.

So the king tasted of the fruits, walked along the smooth, tree-lined paths, just as if they were paved with gold, and gazed about astonished. Everything there was new and fine, as things can only be in a dream. But he kept silent and said not a word.

The sun burned red behind the gigantic trees, and it grew late.

Happy and grateful, the king took one last look at the garden and readied himself to go home. Around him gathered all the courtiers, and with slow steps, they left the garden.

But one of the courtiers, the very most senior, could not move: as if he were bolted in place, he couldn't walk.

One of the courtiers asked him, "Why are you sitting there? Come with us!"

The senior courtier answered with a pained expression, "I can't get up. . . ."

The other one went over, bent down, and asked again, "Who's holding you here? Surely something not of woman born . . ."

But the senior courtier cried out in a muffled voice, "Help, I can't stand up! Help, what's happened to me?!"

The other one urged, "Just try again, maybe you'll be able to stand up. . . ."

He tried with all his might, but he couldn't. As if he were bound to the spot, his feet wouldn't budge, and his rage-filled eyes looked ready to pop right out from under his furrowed brow. He screamed and cursed the Jew together with his palace and his feast.

The second courtier ran and told the whole story to the king. The king, agog, went to see for himself what had happened to his senior courtier.

He reached the spot and saw the old man sitting as if riveted, with his eyes bugging out of their sockets. The king said to him, "Stand up and come with us. . . ."

But the senior courtier croaked, like a wounded animal, "I can't, I can't, Your Royal Highness!"

The king called over one of the other courtiers: "Go tell the rabbi. Maybe he can help."

So he ran to the rabbi, who was standing at the far edge of the garden, and told him what had happened to the senior courtier.

Upon hearing the news, the rabbi replied, "He probably took something from the feast table. He won't be able to rise from his place until he returns what he stole. . . ."

The lord ran back and passed on the rabbi's words. The senior courtier was searched, and they found the beautiful saltshaker in his pocket. They handed it over to the rabbi, and the senior courtier got up immediately from his place and slunk off by himself, because he was ashamed before the king and the other courtiers.

But the Gur Aryeh said to the king, "Your Royal Majesty, if the saltshaker finds favor in your eyes, you may take it with you for a month. But when the month is up, you must hand it back over to me."

So the king took the saltshaker and returned to his palace.

He slept well that night, and in the morning, he summoned his courtiers, saying, "Now I see that whereas the rabbi is a great man and very righteous, the senior courtier is wicked and false. From this day onward, I wish to see his face no more."

And so it was: the senior courtier never again appeared before his eyes.

Many years passed, and the king grew old; but he could never forget the palace with the garden. Quite often he thought, "How did the Gur Aryeh come by such a palace and such a garden? And how ever did he make such a feast? This is the sort of marvel that can't be grasped."

Once, the king was sitting with guests from a faraway kingdom, and they told him the following story: one day the king of a distant country wished to make a great ball for his high-ranking guests. When the day of the ball arrived, a miracle occurred: the palace with the delicacies, the serving dishes, and the waiters disappeared from before his very eyes. The lords arrived for the ball but all in vain—there were neither wines nor delicacies nor waiters. A dead place. Three days passed, and then the palace returned with its waiters and wines. Everything came back to its place, but one thing was missing: a precious and beautiful saltshaker. But do you know how it happened? A saintly rabbi was somehow mixed up in it. . . ."

Upon hearing these words, the king lost himself in thought. For three days, he did not speak, and on the fourth, he summoned the rabbi.

He wanted to question the rabbi about that marvelous palace with the garden that revealed itself so suddenly before his eyes, but he couldn't bring himself to ask. It seemed to him that he oughtn't speak of the matter, for it was the sort of grand mystery to which only a good and beautiful heart could receive an answer.

He said to the rabbi, "My whole life, I've been preparing myself to ask you about something, but I feel that I mustn't do it, because I am not good enough and because I have spilled blood in my wars. But there is one thing I would like to request of you: be my friend. . . ."

The rabbi lifted his two pure, kind eyes and replied, "I hear what you are saying."

The king added, "You are a righteous saint, a pure and godly man; you will be my best friend."

And so it was: until the king's very death, the Gur Aryeh was his best friend and his closest adviser.

Don Isaac Abravanel

Isaac Metzker

ISAAC METZKER

July 1901–October 6, 1984

Born in a Galician village to a family that owned its own fields, Metzker and his siblings were tutored at home during their elementary years. He began studying Polish and German at age six and then attended a Polish secondary school in Ukraine and then the Humboldt Gymnasium in Berlin. He reached New York in 1924 without a visa, working by day and studying in the evenings. He attended the Jewish Teachers' Seminary in New York, becoming a teacher in the Workmen's Circle schools in 1933.

Metzker began to publish in 1927, contributing stories, poems, and reportage to several periodicals for adults and children alike. In 1944, he became a regular contributor to *Forverts*. Between 1942 and 1952, he published three novels for adults, and his career writing for children spanned three decades. He wrote a great deal about the Jewish immigrant experience in America, and in 1971, he selected and annotated a book in English, *A Bintel Brief*, drawing on sixty years' worth of advice columns in *Forverts*. He also wrote lyrically about the Galician land to which his family had been connected for generations. He died in Bridgeport, Connecticut.

The life of Don Isaac Abravanel that appears here shows a teacher's concern with a child's understanding of the precarious political situation for Jews on the Iberian Peninsula leading up to the Inquisition and expulsions from Portugal and Spain. The story is notable both for its emotional acuity and for its celebration of America as the land that Columbus "discovered" and that would eventually offer a safe haven to many European Jews—who, centuries after the reign of the Catholic monarchs, found themselves in desperate need of refuge. The book is one of several, aimed at children and published during the Holocaust, that implicitly contextualized contemporaneous atrocities in terms of medieval and early-modern violence against European Jews.

— ℬ —

Judah Abravanel's House Is Blessed with a Son

One early morning in the year 1437, the news spread across the city of Lisbon that Judah Abravanel's house had been blessed with a son.

"May he grow up with good fortune in the care of his noble and generous parents! May God grant that he be as intelligent and learned as his father! Rich and poor, Jew and Gentile spoke affectionately about the newborn, as well as his house and his family going back generations.

Judah Abravanel was the finance minister of Portugal, and he was distinguished and well liked. He made his home in the beautiful city of Lisbon, where many Jews lived. The Jews regarded him as their leader and defender, who was always ready to take their part.

The new parents named their son Isaac and educated him with great devotion. They watched over him and gazed with delight into his clear, intelligent eyes.

Little Isaac began to talk early. And he spoke so cleverly and intelligibly that people couldn't help being amazed at his wisdom.

"Why are people so small and the sky above them so high up?"

"Why can't the sun shine at night too?" he asked his mother when he was two years old.

"Why don't all the people live in one big house?" he once turned to his father and wondered.

He always had another "Why?" and after the answer, he would sit for a while absorbed in thought like a grown-up. He wanted to learn everything, to know everything.

Judah Abravanel was a pious Jew, and he raised his gifted son in God's ways from an early age, teaching him to be kind and pious. Before Isaac was sent to school, his father had already taught him the Ten Commandments by heart. His father told him many stories from the Bible. Little Isaac loved the stories.

"Ah, I wish that the stories about Jews would never end," he once remarked dreamily to his father.

"Don't worry, my child!" his father comforted him. "The stories will never end. They've already lasted for thousands of years, and they will go on like that until the end of time."

Freedom of Faith

Judah Abravanel was known for his wisdom and knowledge. Learned people would come to visit—Jews, Christians, and Muslims—and they all felt at ease in his home. From the time Isaac was little, he liked to spend time among the guests. Religion was often spoken of, and Isaac was too young to understand the conversation. Many times he heard the words "freedom of faith."

"Papa, what does 'freedom of faith' mean?" he inquired several times, with great curiosity.

"When you get older, I'll explain it all to you," replied his father.

But soon enough, Isaac understood what the words meant. He was six years old then.

It was an evening in springtime. Isaac was sitting with his father in their beautiful garden, surrounded by many guests. Among the assembled were notables, prominent doctors and men of great learning. They were all sitting around a table under a mature, old tree. Fruit and wine had been served, and they were having a cozy, comfortable time together. The gold of the setting sun spread itself serenely over the garden's many-colored flowers. The air was fragrant with blooms, and the sky was high and clear, without a wisp of cloud.

Suddenly, a stranger appeared in the garden. His face was troubled, and his clothing was dusty and torn.

"Peace to you, stranger," Judah Abravanel greeted him in friendly fashion. Isaac, who was examining the stranger with large, childlike eyes, jumped up at his father's signal, and fetched a pitcher of water.

"Wash your hands, have a bite to eat, and take a rest from the road," Abravanel invited the guest to the table.

The foreign Jew washed his hands, piously recited a blessing, and drank of the fresh water.

"Tell us where you come from and what kind of news you bring," inquired one of those who were assembled.

"I come from Spain, and I bring sad tidings from the Jews there," the stranger began. "The Spanish priests won't allow the Jews to serve God freely. On Sabbaths and holidays, when Jews gather in the synagogues to pray, priests force their way in with crosses in their hands. They station themselves by the ark and scream loudly that the messiah came long ago, and they try to drive everyone to apostasy by force.

"The priests in my city, just as in many other cities throughout Spain, issued an order: to herd all the Jews into the middle of the market square, to force the rabbis to debate the priests on matters of faith; the rabbis were strenuously warned to choose their words carefully. They were cautioned several times that they would pay dearly for the slightest word they let slip against Christianity. At first they were frightened, but when the priests began to interpret the words of the Torah and the speech of the Prophets, our defenders forgot all about the warning. With enthusiasm and great erudition, they started to rebut the priests while everyone listened in silence.

"Suddenly a gang of men with swords drawn attacked us and started to chase us into the church, toward apostasy. Together with our rabbis, we resisted the murderers, and many Jews were killed on the spot. As if by a miracle, I saved myself from death and from the cross. I left my home and my property in the bloody hands of the robbers, who took away our freedom of faith, and I escaped to Portugal."

With this, the stranger concluded and slumped, exhausted, on a chair.

The whole time, Isaac gazed, enchanted, into the glowing black eyes of the Spanish Jew and very attentively heard him out. It was as if he had suddenly grown older. Now he understood clearly the meaning of the words "freedom of faith."

Not Everything Can Be Taken Away

The red sun set between the trees, and the day began to pass away.

After the stranger's speech, those sitting around the table were left sad and quiet.

Judah Abravanel went over to the stranger and touched his shoulder: "My house is open to you. Your fill of bread is ready for you on my table, and a bed is made for you too," he said cordially, and he sent him into the house in the company of a servant.

After that, the guests left one by one until only Judah Abravanel and his son were left in the garden.

"The priests want there to be no Jews left? All of them should convert together at once?" Isaac asked of his father in a sorrowful voice, like that of an adult.

"That's what they want," his father replied. "But this isn't the first time that someone has tried to alienate the Jews from their faith by force. They have always resisted and not capitulated."

"And did they take everything away from the stranger from Spain? He has no home left?"

"No, they didn't take everything away from him. They only robbed him of his worldly goods, but they couldn't take away his courage or his steadfast faith. They couldn't take those things away from my father and your grandfather, Samuel Abravanel, either, when he fled from there."

"My grandfather? Did he also have to flee from Spain?"

"Yes, my son. The same thing that happened to the stranger from Spain happened way back when to your grandfather."

Isaac moved over closer to his father, looked up at him with sad, intelligent eyes, and peppered him with questions. He wanted to know everything about his grandfather and his ancestors.

His father listened to all his questions and began to tell the story, as if to an adult.

"Over two thousand years ago, a cruel ruler of Babylonia destroyed the Jewish Land of Israel and drove the Jews into exile. At the end of their wandering, some of the exiles arrived all the way in Spain and settled in Seville, and among the first Jews in Seville was our ancestor, who descended from the line of King David.

"Was King David also our ancestor?" interrupted Isaac.

"Yes, a long chain of generations extends from you back to David," his father explained and went on with the story. "Many years later, the Romans destroyed the Land of Israel for a second time and dispersed the Jews all over the world. Tens of thousands of the homeless then came to Spain, where their brethren had already been living for a long time. The Jews built houses there, planted vineyards, worked in workshops, sailed on ships, and engaged in trade. They came to love that sunny land, and they enriched and beautified it.

"Once upon a time, the life of the Jews in Spain was so beautiful and so happy that Jews from all over the rest of the world couldn't stop talking about them. In other countries, such as Germany, Jews were persecuted terribly at that time. They invented false accusations against the Jews: that they practiced witchcraft, that they used Christian blood to make their Passover matzahs, that they poisoned wells—and thousands of them were killed. At that time, when Jews in other lands had to live locked up in dark ghettos and wear yellow patches on their clothing as a sign of shame, Jews in Spain were free citizens of the country. The rulers of Spain in those years were Muslim, and they made no distinction between Jews and non-Jews. Under their rule, Jews were court physicians, leaders, and educated people, who loyally served king and country. At that time, Spain produced many great Jewish poets and philosophers, whose names would remain known for several generations.

"But the Golden Age ended. Christian rulers had gone to war against the Muslims, and gradually, they had captured Spain. The country became Christian, and the priests, with honey and vinegar both, had started to trap Jews in the nets of the Catholic faith. They spread hate against the Jews who didn't want to become Christian and, as in other countries, took away many of their freedoms. This infuriated the proud Spanish Jews, and they began to fight courageously for their rights and freedom.

"Your grandfather Samuel Abravanel lived in the city of Seville, where our ancestors had once settled, over two thousand years ago. He was the finance minister of Spain, the representative of several Jewish communities, and the protector of the poor.

"This happened some fifty years ago. At that time there lived in Seville a fanatical priest by the name of Fernando Martín, who always incited the Christians in the churches against the Jews. With venomous words, he awakened in them hatred against their Jewish neighbors and instructed them to rob and murder Jews.

"Once, the congregation was so strongly stirred up by his talk that they all attacked the Jews of Seville like wild animals. They plundered Jewish homes and synagogues, mercilessly killed men, women, and children, and set fire to the city's Jewish quarter from all sides. The Jews defended themselves heroically at that time. Thousands of Jews perished in one day, and the entire Jewish community of Seville was destroyed. What few synagogues were not burned down the priests seized for use as churches, and the Jews who remained alive were sent off to apostasy. Among the unfortunates, who were forced then to accept the alien faith, was your grandfather Samuel Abravanel."

Fat tears appeared in Isaac's eyes.

"Did Grandfather remain a Christian, then?" he asked between sobs.

"Oh, no, my child! In their hearts, Jews remained Jews. In their homes, they carried on as before. They taught their children to keep all the commandments of the Torah. They told them again and again that they were going to church because they were being forced to.

Your grandfather didn't even want to go to church for the sake of appearances, and he no longer wanted to keep living among those who had caused him such shame and suffering. Robbed and humiliated, he left the country that he had loved so ardently and came over to Portugal. Here in this country, where Jews have freedom and rights just like everyone else, your grandfather renounced the faith that had been forced upon him and began everything anew. In short order, the king of Portugal appointed him as finance minister. His fortune was left in Spain, but he had brought with him his good name, his education, and his devotion to the faith of his parents. That, my son, is always worth more than gold and silver, because it can never be taken away from a person."

"It can never be taken away from a person," Isaac, lost in thought, repeated his father's last words.

The Torah Is Deeper than a Spring

Isaac grew up in wealth and comfort. His parents always sought to give him everything. But from early on, he was not drawn to any luxurious pleasures or noisy amusements. He was quiet and pensive, and he conducted himself differently than the other children of his social position did. Most children of parents as wealthy and distinguished as his liked to enjoy themselves at various sporting events. They loved to dress up and go out riding in fancy carriages and on fine horses. But Isaac loved just one thing—learning. With all the fire of his soul, he devoted himself to learning. This was his greatest pleasure and his greatest fun.

"The Torah is deeper than a spring," his mother nodded with satisfaction, when he told her, enthusiastically, what he had learned.

He studied the Bible with great affection. He wanted to understand each word clearly, and he wasn't embarrassed before his teachers to repeat questions over and over again. The book of all books became so dear to him that even at night, he didn't want to part from it, and he always slept with it under his pillow. More than once, he dreamed that the book lying under his head had opened of its own accord, and out of it stepped the people about whom he had been learning. He recognized them right away and spoke to them as to old friends.

Isaac's knowledge surpassed that of all his friends, but he never lorded it over them. He also never put on airs in front of them just because his father was so esteemed by the king. His friends all liked him, and they submitted more than once to learning from him. Even though he was the youngest among them, they all looked up to him as their leader.

He did often boast that King David was his ancestor; he wanted everyone to know it. As soon as someone so much as asked him his name, he always answered in one breath, "Isaac Abravanel of the Davidic line."

Already during his youth, he began adding his distinguished lineage to his signature on all his letters. Later, he would place this long name on all the books he wrote.

Since childhood, Isaac dreamed of being as courageous as his ancestor David. In his fantasy, he had more than once imagined that he himself was the heroic shepherd of Bethlehem who had gone fearlessly into battle for his people.

But neither the bow and arrow nor the sword was the weapon that Isaac chose in fighting for his brothers. The young Abravanel was entirely absorbed in learning. Rabbis and great scholars who were his teachers and friends spoke with admiration of his mastery and acuity.

In addition to Portuguese and Hebrew, the languages that he had learned as a child, he had also mastered Spanish, Arabic, Latin, and Greek, and he studied the history of various nations.

The Finance Minister

Years passed. Don Isaac Abravanel lived in the house he had inherited from his father. He was blessed with knowledge and wisdom, with wealth and honor. He was a great merchant, and he conducted his business affairs wisely; and as he and his erudition came to be known far beyond the borders of Portugal, Jews from other countries called upon him by letter as their teacher and leader.

Don Isaac Abravanel had become a regular in the royal court during his father's lifetime. Court doctors and ministers were his closest friends. The king of Portugal himself liked him very much and more than once listened attentively to his intelligent words.

When Judah Abravanel died, the king called for Isaac in short order, so that he might take his father's place.

"Isaac Abravanel," the king had turned to him, "I've known you since your youth, and I know that you are worthy to take the place of your fine and honest father. I would like for you to be not only my finance minister but also my closest adviser."

Isaac Abravanel was deeply moved by these words. His eyes grew moist when the king mentioned his late father. He could foresee clearly that in the royal service, he would not be able to fulfill his dream so quickly of writing a book about the Bible. Nevertheless, he soon reached a decision.

"My lord, my king," he bowed obeisance and answered, "I am ready to loyally serve the crown and the country that gave to my grandfather and many of my persecuted brothers the right to live in freedom and equality. I will pray to God to help me as he helped Joseph, when he placed himself before Pharaoh, so that I might not dishonor my father and grandfather."

Don Isaac Abravanel kept the sacred trust that the king had bestowed upon him, and he served him loyally. In wealthy palaces and poor huts alike, they spoke of his honesty and generosity, and his name was mentioned everywhere with respect and affection. With his own money, he helped many poor people, and with his wisdom, he stood up for Jews in the surrounding countries and saved them from various false accusations and harsh decrees.

Abravanel dedicated a great deal of money to freeing Jewish captives. During his travels, he spent a lot of time in the marketplaces, where human beings were sold like animals, and he would always redeem all the Jewish slaves and set them free. He was well-known in the slave markets, and as soon as they saw him coming, the cost of Jewish captives would climb; but Abravanel would see the Jews released at any price.

Don Isaac Abravanel always provided the tattered, starving captives with clothing, foodstuffs, and homes. He cared for them as he would his own children, and he supported them out of his own pocket for as it long as it took until they could earn their bread themselves.

Years passed. In the same house where Don Isaac Abravanel had been born and grown up, his four children were also born and grew up—three sons and one daughter. His dear and quiet wife, whom he had married when he was still quite young, had educated the children with motherly concern to follow in the footsteps of their father and their grandfathers.

Even though Abravanel was busy with the concerns of the king of Portugal, he nevertheless always found enough time for his children. He sought out the best teachers for them and also taught them himself.

He sent his elder two sons, Judah and Joseph, to study the science of healing the sick. His youngest son, Samuel, he taught Torah and business. When Samuel was free from his studies, Isaac took him along on his travels and also into the royal court.

"The king will soon need a new finance minister," he often joked with Samuel when he took him along to the court.

Sunrise, Sunset

The king of Portugal, Alphonse V, did not need a new finance minister, though. After a hard-fought war, which he had waged against Castille and lost, he died of heartache, and his younger son, Joan II, assumed rule of the country.

Abravanel had lost a devoted friend in the king, and he mourned deeply for him. He felt that he must remain in the royal court longer, close to the king's young son, whom he had known since since he was a child.

It wasn't long before the young king ordered Abravanel to rush to the court because he was needed urgently. Don Isaac Abravanel had just returned from a long trip when the young king's messenger came. And although Abravanel hadn't even rested properly from the journey, he immediately called for his horse to be saddled.

"You'll travel tomorrow. It's already almost nighttime. Take a rest first," his wife begged him.

"And it's getting cloudy over in that direction," his old servant added.

"First tell us about the trip," said his children, surrounding him.

But Abravanel, already dressed in his riding coat, answered them curtly, "The king is calling."

The members of his household understood his reply quite well. They had known from early on that nothing could hold him back from his work for the king. They took leave of him and accompanied him to the gate.

Don Isaac Abravanel rode through the streets of Lisbon, where everyone knew him and greeted him respectfully from their windows or their balconies. He loved his beautiful hometown, where he was born and raised, and when he was abroad, he missed it very much. Now he felt fortunate to be home once again and traveling once more by the familiar road to the king and palace. When he rode out of the city and set out on a narrow bridle path between vineyards, his thoughts were occupied with the new plans that he would carry out for the young king—plans for how to help the nation, which had been impoverished by the war.

"The sun rises and sets," from somewhere in the fields a song carried to him and startled him from his thoughts. Abravanel raised his eyes to the setting sun, which had begun to withdraw to the edge of the sky, and he sang cheerfully, "The sun rises and sets."

Suddenly, a rider appeared right before his eyes, barring the narrow path. The rider was entirely covered by a black mantle from which only two eyes were visible. He quickly pressed a letter into Abravanel's hand and swiftly disappeared. Abravanel opened the letter and began to read, "Don Isaac Abravanel, you are hereby informed that King Joan II has placed all of the blame for the lost war onto his closest advisers and friends of his father's. He's accusing them all of being traitors, and he is quietly killing them off. Death at the king's hand awaits you there as well."

Abravanel stood there stunned and stared at the unfamiliar handwriting as if it were a riddle. But soon he began to laugh at it. "No, it couldn't be." The king who had grown up before his very eyes knew him too well to accuse him of treason, he thought, spurring his horse.

He rode a little farther, and another rider overtook him. This time it was a household retainer of Abravanel's childhood friend Baron Fernando.

"Which way are you headed?" Abravanel greeted him.

"To you, Don Isaac Abravanel," the rider replied. "Don't appear before the king, because you won't come out of his bloody court alive. The sentence is already signed: that all your property be expropriated into the royal treasury and that you die the ignominious death of a traitor."

"But how is this possible?" Abravanel was stupefied. "I will make the trip to my loyal friend the baron and speak with him."

"Your friend, Baron Fernando, is dead. The king sent for him just as he has for you and swiftly ordered him killed," the baron's retainer reported with tears in his voice. "Don't lose a minute. Flee from Portugal and save your life," he said by way of good-bye to Abravanel and turned back onto the same road by which he'd come.

"Oh, God, do not forsake me!" Abravanel said out loud and rode off across the fields.

Later that night, Don Isaac Abravanel rested in a field, under a starry sky, his head lying on a stone. He knew that soldiers would be pursuing him on the roads with orders from the king to bring him in alive or dead. He could clearly imagine how frightened his family would be when the king's soldiers attacked his house and seized his possessions. But he accepted his fate calmly.

Abravanel closed his weary eyes and pictured the times when he was a very little boy sitting with his father in the garden. His father was telling him about his grandfathers and ancestors, how they were persecuted hatefully into sleeping in the open fields more than once.

When the morning star appeared, Abravanel picked himself up from his hard bed and, with renewed courage, set off for the border with Spain.

In Spain

Once Don Isaac Abravanel had set foot on Spanish soil, he wrote a letter to the king of Portugal. It was a matter of life and death to him to clear himself of the disgraceful accusation—himself *and* his friend the baron, who had been killed as an innocent man. In moving words, he demonstrated clearly how loyal and honest the baron and he had been to the country. Abravanel had a lot of faith in people. He hoped that the king would realize how unjustly he had treated him and that he would allow him to return home to his family, to his country, and to the Jews of Portugal, who were left "orphaned" without him there. He impatiently awaited a reply. But the letter did not move the young king. Instead of a reply, what came to Abravanel from Portugal was his family, dispossessed and humiliated.

Abravanel and his family settled in the city of Toledo.

With great honor, the Jews of Spain received the Jewish leader whose name had already been known to them for a long time. Educated people began to gather around him, many friends and admirers came to see him, and they all took pains so that he might forget that he was among strangers.

With great desire, Abravanel now resumed his life's work, a commentary on the Bible. He was absorbed in learning, and now, with his pen, he placed himself in the service of his people. In his writing, he encouraged Jews to hold fast to their faith.

The life of the Jews in Spain was sad when Abravanel arrived, and to them, his words were like a beacon for sailors on a stormy sea.

The servants of the Catholic Church were becoming more and more relentless against the Jews, who did not wish to convert. In the name of Christianity, new laws were always being promulgated against them. Jewish merchants weren't allowed in the marketplaces; Jewish government officials had their royal robes torn off in the middle of the street and were driven from their positions. False accusations were lodged against the greatest Jewish doctors, that they carried poison under their fingernails, and they were forbidden to treat Christian patients. The country swelled with robbers and murderers, who lay in wait for the Jews from all sides.

At that time, the priests would seize Jewish children by force and convert them. The number of new "Christians" grew, and the priests rejoiced.

But how disappointed and irritated they became when they found out that the thousands of new "Christians" led a double life: that although they went to church, they behaved in their homes like pious Jews.

"With glowing tongs, we will tear the old faith out of your hearts, accursed creatures that you are! We will punish you severely for your obstinacy," fumed the fanatical servants of the church, gnashing their teeth. They branded the New Christians with the nickname "Marranos,"* which means "cursed."

But the New Christians weren't ashamed of the nickname, nor were they alarmed by the warning. Just the opposite: the Jewish laws and customs became only more and more dear to them, and in their cellars and other hiding places, they upheld them as holy.

The priests realized that their efforts over many years were all for naught, and they would not rest until they came up with a new plan.

The rulers of Spain at that time were Ferdinand and Isabella. The royal couple was very devout *and* very fond of riches. Queen Isabella had received a church education. Her tutor had been the fanatical priest Torquemada.

---

* This pejorative term for crypto-Jews meant "swine."

For many years, she had worn a simple nun's habit. She had been taught from early on to conduct herself with simplicity. Once she became a queen, she liked to dress up in the most expensive clothing and wanted to have as much jewelry as possible. The well-to-do who visited the royal court would bring her the most precious pearls and diamonds.

A wealthy Marrano gifted her a rare necklace that was worth tens of thousands of ducats, but her passion for getting more and more did not subside.

The priests certainly knew of the rulers' love of money, and with royal assistance, they exacted a dispensation from the pope in Rome to institute an ecclesiastical court in Spain, an Inquisition to punish all Christians who were not sufficiently devout.

"The richest people in the country wear the cross and profane it. They must be severely punished, and their property must be taken away and placed in the royal treasury," they kept repeating to the royal couple—blinking piously all the while.

The large fortune of the Marranos tempted Ferdinand and Isabella, and they helped things along so that the holy court could be established as soon as possible.

With great fanfare, in the year 1481, the first fire of the Inquisition was kindled in Spain, to burn the heretics. Christian priests became like the idolatrous priests of old, who brought living human beings as sacrifices before their pagan gods.

The priests, together with fanatical Catholics, set about catching Marranos like hunters with bloodhounds. With a thousand eyes, they began to watch and spy on each one.

"Holy Father, yesterday I saw my master standing facing east before sunset, and it seems to me that his lips were moving."

"At my neighbors' house, no smoke came up through the chimney on Saturday. It can't be anything other than them observing the Jewish day of rest!"

Every tidbit about the New Christians was passed along swiftly to the priests. For the slightest little thing, the Marranos were dragged to the deep subterranean prisons of the Inquisition, whence few ever returned.

Over time, the queen's tutor, the holy Torquemada, became the Grand Inquisitor of the Ecclesiastical Court, and he devised the cruelest torments for the accused. His name cast fear even into Christians. The Marranos ran wherever their eyes led them. They hid in the mountains, in deep pits, and in thick forests. The wild animals of the forest frightened them less than the bloody nails of the Inquisitor did.

Wearing a black monk's cassock, with a large crucifix in one hand and a wax candle burning in the other, Torquemada spent whole nights walking around the deep, dark dungeons of the Inquisition and observing how the unfortunates were tormented. He enjoyed hearing the sighing of the tortured, and he liked to smell the blood that dripped from their bodies.

"We want to save your souls," he panted with savage glee, his eyes burning like those of a wolf holding its living victim between its teeth. "Kiss the cross!" he said to the bloodied wretches, who—hovering between life and death under the wheels of the torture rack and between the glowing irons—looked him right in the face, with contempt.

"Fifteen thousand Marranos have already been locked up in the prisons; three hundred heretics have already been burned alive," reports came into the royal court. And the royal couple, with religious fire in their eyes, counted the gold that had been robbed from the condemned.

Don Isaac Abravanel in the Royal Court

Don Isaac Abravanel could no longer sit calmly and write his books. The helpless and persecuted started coming to his door in ever-greater numbers.

"Protect us! They have invented the charge that we slaughtered a Christian child in order to use his blood for matzahs!" "Help us! We are Marranos. We want to teach our children Judaism and cannot, because the murderers are watching us from every side! Help us, protect us!" the unfortunates stretched out their hands to him, begging.

The fires of the Inquisition robbed Abravanel of his sleep.

Even at night, he watched long processions snake along the polished streets of the city. The condemned walked at their head. They were barefoot, but their footsteps were firm. Their faces were emaciated and pale, but their eyes shone with confidence. Their lips moved silently, and even though they were accompanied by the song of a church choir, it seemed to him that he heard the marvelous sound of the Psalmist's words, "And yea, though I walk through the valley of the shadow of death, I shall fear no evil, for you, God, are with me."

The condemned Marranos wore yellow sackcloth robes. On the robes were painted red crosses and weird devils, surrounded by flames. But those who escorted them, the priests, were dressed up in colorful clothes and black robes. They carried crosses, flags, and long, burning torches, and their faces shone with the joy of triumph. A large audience flowed from all sides and accompanied the procession with wild cries, all the way to the burning at the stake. From a platform, a priest spoke about the Christian religious principle of loving one's fellow man, and everybody listened attentively. For the last time, the priest turned to the condemned, so that at least before they died, they could save their souls by renouncing the Jewish faith. He waited for an answer, and the entire audience waited with him, tensely. But the Marranos didn't even hear him. Now they were singing out loud with great exaltation their last song to the God of Abraham, Isaac, and Jacob. A judge, dressed in royal apparel, read out the sentence, and the bright, red fire began to leap out from the burning stake. With song and with heads held high, the condemned walked into the fire, and the flames enveloped them. The fire flared up stronger, leaping higher and higher, and the words thundered out, "Shema Yisrael," "Hear, O Israel!"

"Into the fire with all the heretics! Let them burn!" resounded cries from all sides. But others in the audience crossed themselves and murmured quietly, "They're burning a blemish into our religion; forgive them, Lord in Heaven, for they know not what they do."

The fire consumed the courageous Marranos, but it seemed to Abravanel that swaddled in flames, they were striding away over the heads of the large audience. "Eternal are those who can die so for their faith," he thought at the time.

More than once, in the middle of the night, Don Isaac Abravanel rose from his bed and paced across his room like a caged lion. He wanted to help everyone, to protect everyone—but against the savage Torquemada, he was powerless. During the sleepless nights, he often thought with longing of that happier time when he had lived in Portugal and had a lot of power with the king there.

But a new light of hope arose for him. In the spring of 1484, Ferdinand and Isabella sent a messenger to him and invited him to enter the royal service.

Abravanel had just then begun writing a book about the persecution of Jews in various time periods, and even though it wasn't so easy for him to leave this work unfinished, he decided to go right away to the royal court.

"In every person some goodness is hidden. I must now go look for the good in the rulers of Spain. Perhaps through my service to the country I will awaken in them some mercy for the tormented. Perhaps I'll be able to have the decrees against our brethren repealed," he said to his family and friends, as he was about to leave. Abravanel's high forehead, his clear, intelligent eyes, his wide, dark-gray beard, his proud carriage, and his entire bearing called forth great esteem from the royal couple, and they appointed him as a nobleman.

"We have in our country often heard the name Abravanel mentioned with great praise," the king said to him amiably. "Our country is in need of educated and judicious statesmen," the monarch appealed to him.

This warm reception quickly made Abravanel at home. It was difficult for him to believe that this royal couple, who spoke to him, a Jew, in such a mild and friendly way, had signed all of the cruel death sentences of the Inquisition. First he thanked them for the hospitality that they had shown him in Spain and then informed them that he was ready to serve.

"I have returned to the land where the bones of many generations of my ancestors rest, and with my service to the crown, I shall strive to be worthy to call the country of Spain my home as well. I know that the long war that Spain fought against the Moors from Granada undermined the well-being of the country. But . . . ," and Abravanel immediately began to propose various plans.

The royal couple and all the courtiers were amazed as they listened closely to Abravanel's intelligent words and to his substantive plans. They were dazzled by his wisdom and astonished that although he was almost a total stranger to the country, he was so well acquainted with the state of the entire Spanish kingdom. Even the priests, who came to remind the rulers of the laws that forbade a Jew to take a government position, virtually lost their tongues and listened carefully.

A New Ray of Hope

The fires of the Inquisition spread across many cities, and their smoke turned the skies black. The Marranos had a great deal of property, which flowed into the royal coffers. But the bloody gold was unlucky for the rulers. It ran right through their fingers. The war that Spain had fought for years against the Moors of Granada swallowed up everything. The kingdom became poorer and poorer. Only when Abravanel became finance minister did the country begin to recover.

Abravanel's esteem in the royal court and with the Spanish people grew day by day.

At that time, when the savage Torquemada and his cronies were seeking, with various false accusations and with fire and sword, to abase the reputation of the Jews, a new ray of hope made the hearts of the tormented Spanish Jews and Marranos beat faster:

Don Isaac Abravanel became the right hand of the crown!

"The Prince of Israel will now be able to stick up for us, and he will release us from our suffering!"

"The noble leader will help quench the hellish fire that's burning our footsteps!"

"He'll bring us back the Golden Age of yore!"

This was also Abravanel's dream. He did everything to make the country rich and strong. He wanted Spain to blossom once again, so that peace and friendship could rule, as they once had, among all—Jew and Gentile.

Thanks to his loyalty to the nation, along with his honesty and wisdom, Abravanel quickly made many friends in the royal court and in the country at large. He became more and more able to stand up for the Jews and for all the persecuted. Quietly in his heart, he planned to prevail eventually upon the rulers of Spain and the pope in Rome to extinguish the flames of the Inquisition.

But Grand Inquisitor Torquemada, who was also the priest of the royal court, was always in his way. The fanatical priest's hatred of the Jews burned even hotter when he saw how the royal couple had bent the laws of the church and elevated a Jew to such prominence. His eyes blazed murderously when once, on royal orders, he'd had to release from his bloody hands a victim against whom he himself, or his loyal servants, had invented a false accusation. "It's the Jew Abravanel's decree and not the king's," he fumed, enraged.

Abravanel was a thorn in his side. All the courtiers in the royal palace and even the rulers kissed the hem of Torquemada's holy robes, but not Abravanel. While everyone piously bowed to the court priest, Abravanel sat by serenely and thought of Mordecai, a pious Jew of ancient times and the only man in the royal court of the Persian King Ahashueres who did not kneel and bow before the wicked Haman. The implacable Torquemada smoldered with rage when he saw the serenity of the Jewish finance minister. But Abravanel pierced the bitter enemy of the Jews with his steady gaze and said silently to him, "Your effort is in vain! Are you the first one, then, who has beset my people and my God? My lineage and my faith have outlasted them all."

The Jews of Spain began to breathe a little more freely. The Marranos too, who remained close to the Jews, became more courageous in their struggle, and they even dared to attack their tormentors.

One day, Torquemada was informed that one of his loyal inquisitors had been stabbed. The news inspired great fear in him, and he surrounded himself with hundreds of armed escorts. The tormentor of thousands had always been a fearful man, but now he started to be afraid of his own shadow. It began to seem to him that even bishops and priests were lying in wait for him. It so happened that his most trusted judges of the Inquisition were themselves Marranos, and he ordered that many of them be burned alive.

Abravanel's prominence and the daring of the Marranos wouldn't let Torquemada lie still in his bed. He sought to forget about the dungeons of the Inquisition and the blazing fires of the burnings at the stake. He had not only allowed people to be burned alive but also disinterred the skeletons of those who were long dead, whom he had accused of not being devout enough during their lifetimes.

In the dungeons among the tortured and at the fires, his heart had hardened, and he had developed new plans against the "heretics."

In the Name of the Father, the Son, and the Holy Gold

Over the course of a few years, the finance minister Don Isaac Abravanel had set the country on firmer footing and helped Spain to bring the protracted war against the Moors to a decisive victory. At the beginning of 1492, Granada fell, and the Spanish nation celebrated the conquest with great joy. Dressed in royal robes and accompanied by Torquemada and a whole procession of priest and courtiers, Ferdinand and Isabella entered the beautiful city of Granada with much fanfare. The royal couple were inspired by the victory and the riches that had fallen into their hands.

"Our Lord in Heaven is rewarding us for our piety," they said to Torquemada. In Granada, they confiscated the luxurious palace of the Moorish ruler, and the court priest came to sprinkle it with holy water.

"In the name of the Trinity," Torquemada murmured quietly, thinking that now would be the best time to suggest to the royal couple the plan that he had thought up long ago.

"We have vanquished and driven out the heretical Moor," he began. "But Spain is still not Christian. Hundreds of thousands of the Jews, who crucified Christ, live in the borders of our country under the protection of Christian rulers. It's not enough that they've been stubborn and haven't wanted to accept the sign of the cross, but they are detaching thousands of New Christians from the church. In the name of the Trinity, I swear to you that you should sign an order that the Jews must all as one deposit their gold and silver to the royal treasury and that they themselves must leave Spain!

"In the name of the Trinity . . . ," the rulers crossed themselves, ". . . and in the name of gold," they thought to themselves, and they began to prepare the order.

Abravanel's oldest son, Judah, who was the court doctor to the royal couple, found out about the terrible decree before it was published, and he immediately went to notify his father about it. But he found several Christian courtiers with his father, Abravanel's close friends, who had already come with the news.

"Torquemada has blinded our rulers, and they no longer see the great usefulness that the Jews bring to the country."

"This law not only will bring misfortune upon the Jews but will also ruin all of Spain," they said to the Jewish minister, and they offered him their help in having the decree repealed.

"It won't be our first exile," said Abravanel to his good friends and to his son the court doctor, a sad smile on his lips. He could imagine exactly how the court priest had stirred up the royal appetite for the property of the Spanish Jews and how he had bewitched the Catholic rulers with his pious saucer eyes and his devout words. Nevertheless, Abravanel took bravely to the task of preventing the law from being issued.

But Torquemada lost no time. Before Abravanel had even managed to see the royal couple, they had signed the law.

With a blast of trumpets one spring day in 1492, the edict was announced everywhere: "In the name of the king and queen, it is hereby ordered that all the Jews of Spain must either accept the Christian faith or leave the country within four months. Those who do not obey the edict will be punished with death."

The news fell suddenly as a thunderbolt on the heads of the Spanish Jews.
"We must leave the fatherland? Why?"

"Leave behind my home and my garden, that I inherited from my ancestors? But how is it possible?" they asked each other, stunned, and couldn't quite believe their ears, after hearing the new decree proclaimed.

"Our guide and our leader, who is so close to the crown, won't allow it," said many, seeking Abravanel's help to drive away the despair.

From every corner of the country, Jews now turned to Abravanel. Jewish leaders from several cities, fathers, mothers, and children besieged his house and trailed him down the streets.

"God is our light, and you are our support."

"Where to go? Show us the way! Save our children," the voices that reached him from all sides were full of tears and entreaty.

"The Watchman of Israel neither slumbers nor sleeps! So what can mortal men do to us if our faith is our fortress?" Abravanel comforted and encouraged the Jews from near and far, and with all his might, he awakened the conscience of his Christian friends against the law. Together with other Jewish leaders and rabbis, he collected a large fortune of hundreds of thousands of ducats. With this gold, he went to see the royal couple in the hope that he might succeed in rescuing his brethren from the terrible decree.

Far Away, a New World Dawns

Things hadn't been so lively around round the royal court in a long time. It hummed with the joy of the victory over the Moors, and the expanded borders of Christian Spain were spoken of with pride. The news was recounted again and again, that the king and queen had finally consented to send out the daring sea explorer Christopher Columbus on a distant voyage to discover new lands for Spain.

At that time, all kinds of stories began to spread about the dreamer and seeker of new worlds who had come from Portugal to Spain. People told with bated breath of how the wondrous man had already navigated many unknown waters and of how he knew where a great treasure lay hidden. Now he wanted to set about bringing the treasure to Spain. He wished to enrich the Spanish nation because although he was born in Italy, Spain had been the home of his ancestors, who had been Jews and had passed many years ago into the Christian faith. But to reach the place where the treasure lay would not be so easy. He'd have to sail for several months over great mountains of water and boiling seas. He'd have to elude the dangerous sea creatures that lie like mountains in the water, and he'd have to go to war against scorpions and great winged serpents.

"I've heard that he says the entire Earth is completely round, and pointy like a pear, and that it hangs on nothing and stands on nothing."

"It can't be. A pear is a bit lighter and smaller than the Earth, and yet it can't stay hanging in the air when it falls off the tree."

"If that were really true, then I wouldn't envy the people on the bottom part of the Earth's pear at all. After all, they'd find themselves walking around like on a ceiling, with their feet up top and their heads down below," young and old chatted, mused, and repeated to each other over and over again.

Columbus came several times to the royal court. He brought with him maps of unknown lands and territories, so that if he could just be furnished with ships, he might bring them back laden with gold. But the royal retinue and the rulers didn't take his fantastical stories seriously, and they always sent him away empty-handed.

Abravanel was one of the few who believed in Columbus's talk. He had read many travelogues by people who had wandered over the wide world. What's more, he also knew well the geography of the day. He was sure that entire parts of the world hadn't been discovered and that Spain could grow rich from them.

When the courageous explorer Columbus stood before the royal couple and all the courtiers and displayed his maps and told stories of the rich, unknown world, Abravanel strained to listen closely, as if he'd fallen into a sweet dream: somewhere far, far away, over seas and rivers, on untrodden earth, a new world would arise! People who'd been oppressed and driven out of their homeland, people persecuted on account of their faith, would be drawn to the new world and live there carefree and happy.

Together with several Marranos from the royal court, he kept trying to coax the royal couple to fund Columbus's voyage. They hoped that the riches from the new lands would satisfy the rulers fully and that they would repeal the cruel laws against Marranos and Jews. But the king and queen remained deaf to their words. Only when one of the Marranos laid out the money for the voyage did Columbus start preparing to set out in the name of the royal couple.

But more than anything else, there was talk in the royal court at that time of the law that would drive out all the Jews from Spain. People counted in advance the Jewish gold and silver that would remain in the country, and they tried to guess how many Jews would convert. Some were betting that only the eminent and wealthy would convert; then again, to others it appeared that almost all the Jews would seek protection under the wings of the church, as long as they didn't become homeless. There were also those who didn't talk but, mute and dejected, listened closely to the conversations. Those were the ones who were afflicted by the thought that it was a great sin to drive out people in the name of the Holy Church. But they trembled before Torquemada and the Inquisition and kept from saying a word.

His Request Could Move a Stone

By means of side corridors, Abravanel slipped almost unnoticed into the royal drawing room. The royal couple was favorably disposed, and they received their finance minister very cordially. They spoke nicely to him and hinted that the greater and richer Spain became, the higher he would climb and the more exalted his name would be in the royal court and throughout the entire country. They began to speak affectionately about his eldest son, Judah, of how well he knew the science of medicine, how intelligent and learned he was, and how deeply they felt his loyalty and friendship.

"But what does it amount to? After all, the royal edict is driving us away from serving you and from the country we love so dearly," Abravanel interrupted.

"The edict won't be allowed to touch you and your household," the king replied affably, as he glanced piously up at the crucifix hanging on the wall, right in front of Abravanel.

"Lord and Queen! I am just a branch of an old tree with wide, deep roots that grows in Spain and gives richly of its fruits to the country. Don't allow the tree to be chopped down!" Abravanel addressed the queen and also the king, trying to make them understand how useful the hundreds of thousands of Jews were to the country. He spoke at length, but the faces of the rulers just clouded over. They made no reply. Only when Abravanel offered them three hundred thousand gold ducats, as a ransom for the Jews, did their eyes begin to gleam.

Abravanel's heart was one large wound. Now more than ever before, he felt the sorrow and anguish of his desperate brothers and sisters, who were awaiting his help. Hot tears streamed from his large, bright eyes and rolled down onto his handsome beard, which had turned quite gray in recent days.

"These are the tears of thousands of little children who'll be left without homes, to wander in the rain and cold, in fields and forests. These are the tears of the elderly, who are drawn to their eternal rest near the bones of their ancestors."

His voice was soaked with tears. He was on bended knee, and with his proud bearing, he lowered himself down to the feet of the king and the queen.

"Worthy rulers of Spain!" he fell into pleading that could have moved a stone, "I beg you, be good to me and to my brethren! Reverse the edict and save hundreds of thousands of people from ruin! Spain is their home, and they have nowhere else to go. I will be your eternal slave. I will pledge to the crown all that I possess, if only you will show your mercy!"

"Stand up, good friend," said the queen, moved, to Abravanel as she wiped tears from her eyes. "You have a very kind heart."

"We'll think over the law again and see," replied the king, who was by then ready to negotiate the ransom money with Abravanel. Abravanel stood up from the floor with a new hope in his heart.

Suddenly, the door of the royal chamber opened, and Torquemada—enveloped like a devil all in black—flew in with a large crucifix in his hand.

"Judas Iscariot sold out Christ for thirty pieces of silver, and you rulers of Spain, the anointed of God, want to sell him out for three hundred thousand pieces of gold! Right here, you have Christ upon the cross, go ahead and sell him!"

His words dripped out of his mouth like venom from a snake. In a fury, he thrust the cross with the nailed-up Christ between the royals, scorched the queen with his burning eyes, and hurried from the palace.

With his glance and his few words, the wild Torquemada had once again won over the rulers as if they were both bewitched.

"The law remains the law!" the queen pronounced icily and crossed herself.

"The law must be carried out! But your place and your son Judah's place is with us in the court and in Spain. This country needs you, and you may not leave it," the king said to Abravanel.

"Our place is now among our outcast brethren. Their fate is also our fate," Abravanel countered, standing up straight, and with that, he left the royal couple.

The rulers of Spain brought everything to bear on detaining their finance minister and his son, the court doctor, in the country. But when they saw that both steadfastly refused, they tried to hold them by force.

Judah Abravanel had an only son, who was a year old. The royal couple knew that the child was the apple of his father's and grandfather's eyes. So it occurred to them to kidnap the child and hold him under arrest. On his account, the Abravanels would stay in the country too.

On a dark night, armed and disguised men forced their way into Judah's house. But when they reached the child's crib, they found it empty.

Good friends had informed the Abravanels of the dishonorable plan in time, and Judah had quietly sent the child, together with his wet nurse, to Portugal the day before. But the fanatical priests didn't sleep. Before the child could reach the nation of Portugal, pious soul snatchers were waiting for him. His nurse had just disembarked from the ship when several servants of the church attacked her and tore the child out of her hands. They immediately converted the little Abravanel and dragged him off somewhere to a Portuguese church, and the Abravanels never again saw their child, the apple of their eye.

The family mourned the child even more than if he had died, and they grieved over him for a long, long time.

In the Final Days

The spring in sunny Spain was clear and cheerful. The Spanish people were drunk with joy that all the property of the expelled Jews would remain in the country and that only Christians would be able to live in great and mighty Spain.

But for the Jews of Spain, that spring was a miserable one. Don Isaac Abravanel returned from the royal court with nothing, and the last hope for repealing the decree was extinguished. For many long weeks, the Jews walked around as if sunk in a bad dream and waiting for a miracle to save them. For many long weeks, the Spanish Jews couldn't and wouldn't understand that soon, very soon, they must leave their homeland.

Abravanel waited too, as if for a great miracle. At that time, he spent entire nights absorbed in the old holy books, and in them he found not only comfort for his distressed brethren but also the faith that the time of redemption must indeed be very near.

"The cup of our suffering has now become full. Human evil has already exhausted itself, and the injustice of the world is surely at its final limit. Messiah Son of David, our savior, can tarry no longer. His footsteps can be heard already! He will come to us draped in a cloak of our pain and sorrow, and the crown he wears on his head will be forged of our tears." With such words, Abravanel encouraged the Jews throughout the country and didn't allow them to despair.

With great sorrow and only in the final days, the Spanish Jews began preparing to leave. Fountains of tears poured from their eyes when they began to take leave of their beloved fatherland, where their ancestors had settled before Christianity had even existed in the world.

It was hard for them to leave forever their old synagogues and their beautiful houses and gardens that had passed through many generations as an inheritance from father to son. It was difficult for them to part from the hidden Jews, the Marranos, and it was hard for them to leave behind their good Christian neighbors, who, with tears in their eyes, cursed the fanatical priests together with the insane Torquemada, who had brought low their religion.

But hardest of all was for the Jews to part from their near and dear ones who rested in the cemeteries. Day and night, the graves were surrounded by young and old.

"Grandpa, stand up and look at what's become of your grandchildren! Look how we've become a laughingstock and a disgrace!"

"Mama, open your dark grave, and allow me into it with you, because I have nowhere to go! Mama, I'd rather die than leave you here alone!"

"Papa, we're being driven far from home, plundered, barefoot and naked!" Heartrending tears and cries carried from the cemeteries and reverberated far and wide. Jews pulled many headstones out from the earth and carried them along on their backs toward alien soil.

The Jews weren't permitted to take any gold or silver or any currency out of the country. Therefore, they sought to exchange their property for various kinds of merchandise that they could take with them. But the priests warned the Christians not to do any business at all with the Jews.

"It's a sin to buy anything from them now. They're going to have to leave everything behind anyway," they preached in the streets and in the churches.

Other Jews left their belongings in the hands of their trusted Christian friends and with the Marranos, who in recent days had risked their lives in order to help the Jews prepare for their departure. Still others had given away everything almost for free. They had traded a house for a horse and given away a garden for a coat or a bit of food. There were also those Jews who had hung strong locks on the doors of their houses, in the hope that they would soon be able to return home.

In the final days, when the Jews were deeply depressed, when the earth around them was wet from tears, the priests began to come at them from all sides.

"We can't stand to see your suffering. Our hearts are melting with pity. We want to protect you. We want to save your children from ruin!" they said sweetly and kindly, gesturing with their crosses in the air.

"We don't want your help!" the Jews drove them away derisively from themselves and their children and didn't even want to hear out their "merciful" words.

Like a heroic captain who finds himself in the middle of the ocean with a punctured ship, during those days Don Isaac Abravanel stood loyally by his unfortunate brethren. He gave the Jews additional courage so that they wouldn't be afraid to tread upon alien soil, and he awakened in them such friendliness and affection for one another that they shared among themselves their last bit of bread.

"Be strong, the day of redemption is near! With faith in our hearts, let us wander over the whole world like our ancestors of yore in the previous exiles and exalt the name of our people and of our faith!" His speeches and written words, like bubbling waters, delighted and revived their dejected spirits.

His friends from the royal court wanted to help him save himself and his property in time but he wouldn't even hear of it.

"No, my life and my property are worth no more to me than the lives and belongings of my hundreds of thousands of brethren. My ancestor two thousand years ago was among the first Jews to come to Spain, and I will be among the last to leave this country," he replied.

He divided his property generously among the poor, who were about to leave, and many wealthy Jews followed his example. Together with the representatives of many Spanish communities, he saw to it that the dispossessed would have something to wear and that their children would, at least during the first days of their wandering, be taken care of with bread and milk.

Without a Home

In one day, around three hundred thousand Spanish Jews were left without a home or a roof over their heads, for no other reason than that they had remained Jews. This was on the ninth of Av, the day when both Temples were destroyed. The expelled Jews recorded that sad day as the day of a third *khurbn*, or destruction, and a third exile. But with strength and courage and accompanied by music, they left their dear homeland behind.

Many priests followed the dispossessed and sought to persuade them to convert. But their efforts were in vain.

"Come back home! Misfortune and death await you among savage strangers. Come with us. Christ, our Savior, is calling you!"

"No, the Savior hasn't come yet. If he were here on Earth, then robbery and murder wouldn't rule the world!" the Jews countered bitterly.

"If we were to detach ourselves from our heritage and God's commandments, we would die a living death; but if we remain united with our beliefs and our people, we will live on even if we should die," the dispossessed wanderers comforted each other in the hour of need.

Along the way, sometimes good Christian women met the outcasts with water and milk for the children, who walked right in step with their fathers and mothers.

"Take some, dears. Refresh your little hearts!" they appealed, with tears in their eyes, to the little ones, whose lips were burning with heat and thirst.

"We won't take it. We want to remain Jews!" the weakened children said, pushing them away because they were afraid they would be made to kiss the cross in return.

At the nation's border, the expelled Jews divided themselves into groups and followed different paths.

The same day that Columbus set off to look for a New World, which would later become the home of the persecuted and banished, the homeless Jews of Spain set out to find a little bit of earth somewhere under the sun.

Packed onto ships, they wandered around for a long time over seas, floated from one coast to another, and begged at the gates of various countries, to have mercy on their children and let them in. Only seldom did a door open for some of the dispossessed.

In exchange for a steep head tax, some were allowed, just for a short time, to enter the neighboring countries, whence they were then driven yet farther. Many of the wanderers were saved in various ports by Jews the world over, who didn't stint on gold and silver and who provided the dispossessed with homes and with bread.

But thousands upon thousands of the unfortunate wanderers died on the way. They were attacked by pirates, wild men who robbed and murdered the helpless without pity. The captains of the very ships that were transporting them took everything from many of the wanderers and dragged them off to savage islands or sold them into slavery.

Gray haired and exhausted, Don Isaac Abravanel and his family, along with a group of Spanish Jews, arrived, after many months of wandering, in the city-state of Naples. Not only the country's Jews but also its king received the great Jewish leader and celebrated minister with respect and cordiality. He was invited into the royal court, and the ruler of Naples soon entrusted him with a high position in the government.

In short order, Abravanel once again had a home for his family, and with the power of the good king, who had shown a great deal of friendship to the Jews on his account, he was able once again to defend his unfortunate brethren.

But that bit of luck didn't last for long either. Before he could get properly accustomed to his new home, he had to take his walking stick in hand once again.

The French fought a war against his new king and captured the city of Naples. The king was expelled, and Abravanel, separated from his family, went with him into exile in Sicily. The French demolished his house in Naples, and his family left to seek protection in other cities.

In Sicily, the forlorn king died, and Abravanel had to flee from there. He left at first for the island of Corfu, and from Corfu, he wandered all the way to Monopoli.

Abravanel spent about eight years in Monopoli. All his time there, he didn't have to worry about a king or government finance. His only concern in Monopoli was to comfort and to cheer up the unfortunate Jews who were then wandering through various countries and always falling into different nets. There he took up his creative work anew, with fresh ardor, and he proceeded with his interpretation and explanation of the Bible. He wrote books there, through which he assured the Jews that the messiah would not tarry, that they ought to hope, wait, and believe.

Thousands and thousands warmed themselves with the hope that the messiah must soon come and thus saved themselves from despair and ruin.

From Monopoli, Isaac Abravanel went to Venice to spend his last years near his two eldest sons, who lived there.

He also met up there with his youngest son, who lived in Genoa. He wanted to be close to his children, who were a source of comfort and pride to him in his old age. He was proud of them because they hadn't dishonored his name. All three of them were learned, intelligent, and distinguished, and like him, they were bound to their people body and soul.

Abravanel was sixty-six years old when he came to Venice. But he was already old and weak. His wanderings and the suffering of the Jews had aged him terribly and broken his health. And yet in Venice he also served in the senate and conducted diplomatic negotiations for the government with other countries.

In Venice too his house quickly became a center for many learned people, and his life was full of work until his final moment.

On a winter's night in the year 1509, the light of his life began to be extinguished. His close friends and family were gathered around him. Apparently, in his last moments, Abravanel saw before him not only those who were standing at his bedside but also thousands and thousands of Jews from Portugal and Spain. He saw them on the stormy seas and on the roads to no-man's-land, and he told them in a soft, mild voice that their path of suffering was leading them toward a rising future, full of sunny clarity, with peace and joy that would never again depart.

After that, he smiled as serenely as a child and emitted his final breath.

The great Jewish leader and teacher had died, he who had refused riches and a high royal position, as long as he could remain true to his faith and his people. Jews from far and wide grieved over him for a long time.

His children and friends brought him to a Jewish burial in the cemetery in Padua, where many great Jewish scholars were laid to rest. But even his bones weren't fated to rest in peace. The Germans, in a war against Italy, disturbed the cemetery in Padua, and no sign remained of Abravanel's grave. His name, however, was never forgotten.

Only in the year 1904 did the Jews of Padua erect a large monument to the unforgettable Don Isaac Abravanel.

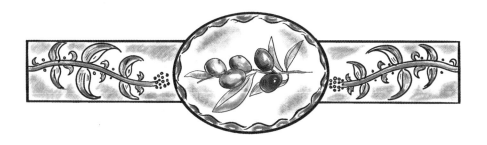

The Story of a Stick

Zina Rabinowitz

ZINA RABINOWITZ

1895–June 25, 1965

For biographical information on Rabinowitz, see "The Mute Princess" in part 1. This story offers a multigenerational saga of Jewish heritage, tracing an arc from Germany to Israel over the course of the modern period.

— ℬ —

Chapter 1

Many years ago, in the city of Frankfurt-am-Main, a wealthy businessman named Jacob Guttmann lived in the Jewish quarter, or "Judengasse."

Guttman was quite a pious Jew. He had a very kind heart and would always give a lot of charity.

The merchant's wife was also very pious, and she would distribute alms generously.

The Jews of the Judengasse loved and esteemed Reb Jacob and his wife because they always donated to the orphans' home, the yeshivas, the free community school, and the old folks' home.

Jacob Guttmann and his wife sent many donations to the study houses and the rabbis of their city. Everyone would bless the generous merchant and his wife.

Once, the charitable Frau Guttmann suddenly fell very ill. Her husband called one doctor and then another and then a third. Each doctor offered the patient a different remedy, each one called her illness by a different name, but none of them made her any better. . . .

Guttmann gave generously to each of the local charitable institutions. And in every one, people prayed for the sick woman's recovery.* Reb Jacob recited prayers on her behalf in his synagogue. He beseeched God day and night, before and after his formal prayers and in the midst of them.

Once, when Reb Jacob was praying for his wife between the afternoon and evening services, word went around the synagogue that an emissary from Jerusalem had come to Frankfurt to collect donations for the charities of the Holy City.

As soon as Jacob Guttmann heard this, he waited with great impatience to speak with the delegate. After the emissary had finished telling the worshipers all about Jerusalem and its charitable organizations, Reb Jacob beckoned him to step aside to a corner where nobody would be able to hear him and said, "Give me a list of all the institutions in Jerusalem; I would like to donate to each and every one of them."

When the emissary looked at Reb Jacob Guttmann with great surprise, like someone who hadn't quite caught his meaning, the merchant added, "I would like for every charity in Jerusalem to receive a contribution from me in the name of my wife, who is very ill. The doctors have not yet been able to find a way to make her well. . . ."

The delegate from Jerusalem wrote out a long list with the names of the charities of the Holy City, and Guttmann gave with a generous hand to all of them. But none of the Jews in synagogue was any the wiser, because Reb Jacob made all of his donations in secret—as was his custom.†

After the merchant had made large contributions to all the charities of Jerusalem, he quickly left the synagogue and went home to his sick wife. He asked after her health and told her quietly, "This evening an emissary from Jerusalem came to the Great Synagogue to collect donations from the Jews of Frankfurt for the benefit of the Holy City and her poor Jews. I gave to all the yeshivas and community schools, the orphans' home, and the old folks' home. I didn't leave out a single organization. . . ."

"You did very well, my husband, but . . ."

"But what, my dear?" the merchant wondered. He knew that his wife was always happy when he distributed charity. He bent down to his wife, in order to hear what she meant with her "but." Could it be that now she *wasn't* happy with his generous giving?

---

* Charity and prayer are two means of averting a bad outcome, according to traditional Jewish texts.
† Anonymous giving is the highest form of charity.

"But," his wife replied with a weak voice, "why shouldn't you go up to Jerusalem yourself . . . and make donations there yourself . . . with your own hands? Why shouldn't you yourself say a prayer at the Western Wall?"

"And what about you, my dear?" wondered Reb Jacob.

"Me?" said his wife. "I will wait for you and for your return."

Guttmann paced all around his wife's room in a state of great agitation, not knowing how to answer the patient. He thought to himself, "My wife is so sick. How can I leave her for such a long time?"

In those days, there weren't yet any airplanes, and the trains and ships moved very slowly. . . .

"I'm waiting for your answer, Jacob," demanded the sick woman.

Reb Jacob gazed at her with concern and answered with a quavering voice, "If you'll promise me that you won't be lonesome for all the days that I will be far from home and from you, then I will do as you wish. I will go up on a pilgrimage to Jerusalem and pray at the Western Wall. . . ."

"And you'll make more donations there, beyond what you gave the emissary," said the sick woman, gazing at her husband with eyes in which there flickered a new hope. "Start out as soon as you can, and may God bless you on your long journey—and may you succeed!"

Chapter 2

At that time, in the year 1868, there was just one good hotel in Jerusalem, where wealthy foreign guests could stay. The hotel was half empty when Reb Jacob Guttmann arrived, because not many guests came from abroad in wintertime.

In every corner of the city, they knew about the arrival of the great patron from Frankfurt-am-Main. Word spread quickly that the wealthy merchant from abroad was giving charity with a generous hand to all the institutions of Jerusalem and was refusing no one who came with a request.

Each day, alms seekers from every corner of the city came before the patron of Frankfurt: one requested money for a yeshiva and its students, who sat and studied day and night; a second, for the old age home, which suffered from pressing need; a third begged for money for the poor orphans and their establishment; a fourth, for the free community school; a fifth, for the study houses where Jews sat day and night, studying the Mishna and Talmud. . . .

Guttmann refused nobody. He gave generously to each and didn't let anyone leave his hotel room empty-handed. . . .

The rumors about the generous patron reached a scribe, who would sit entire days with his children writing out Torah scrolls.

So the scribe came by the hotel to ask that the patron buy a Torah scroll from him. When the scribe came into the hotel, he saw a clerk standing by the door of Guttmann's room, asking each visitor on behalf of which institution he was coming to solicit a donation.

The clever scribe thought, "If I tell the secretary the truth, he surely won't let me in to see the patron from Frankfurt-am-Main."

When the doorman asked him in whose name he was coming to make his request, the scribe said mysteriously, "That is a great secret, and I've promised that I would reveal it only to Reb Jacob Guttmann of Frankfurt-am-Main."

The clerk believed the scribe and opened the door for him to the patron's room.

When Reb Jacob Guttmann saw his guest, he bolted up from his chair, as was his custom, extended his hand, bade him "sholem aleichem" in greeting, offered him a chair, and picked up his record book in order to set down the names of the visitor and his organization. The patron took his pen in hand to record whatever the scribe might tell him, but the scribe kept silent and, in his great agitation, couldn't get out a single word. . . .

The patron noticed this and tried to set him at ease, saying, "Even if the organization for which you've come to collect charity is a very small one, don't be discouraged! I give to every institution in the Holy City, whether large or tiny. . . ."

"But I haven't come to ask for charity for any institution," the embarrassed scribe just managed to reply. "I am a scribe—I and my children. We write out Torah scrolls to sell to the pilgrims who come to Jerusalem from abroad. But now, in winter, there are no tourists and no pilgrims. . . . They come only for Passover, the Feast of Weeks, or the High Holy Days. It's still winter—a long time to wait until Passover. It's cold at our place, and we have to eat, and there's no money! So I've come to ask you whether you'd buy a Torah scroll from me."

"In our town of Frankfurt, there are many Torah scrolls in the synagogues," Reb Jacob replied. "But I'm always ready to purchase a Torah scroll from Jerusalem. Where is your Torah scroll?"

"I have several scrolls," the poor scribe said joyfully. "I didn't know which one to bring you because I'm not the only one who writes them. My boys write them too. Ask anyone who lives in Jerusalem, and they'll tell you, there are no better scribes than my children. Each one has his own handwriting. Each one writes the holy letters with his own artistry. I'll run home and bring back several Torah scrolls so that you can choose."

"Choose?" wondered the patron from Frankfurt in amazement.

"Yes, there are several to choose from, Reb Jacob Guttmann! Each one of my children has his talent, and so each Torah scroll is different...."

"If that's so," replied Reb Jacob Guttmann, "I'll come to your home and choose a Torah scroll there. And into the bargain, I'll see there with my own eyes how children write a Torah scroll. I have never before seen a child scribe."

The poor scribe left the patron's room as happy as could be. He did not walk home. He ran the whole way, while jumping for joy and humming all sorts of tunes and prayers under his breath. Even when he got home, he didn't stop singing. As soon as the scribe's children caught sight of their father, they were so amazed that they stopped writing because they had never before seen him in such a happy mood.

"Why are you looking at me like that?" asked the scribe, trying to pretend that he was cross with them. "What have you noticed about me? Have I grown horns, God forbid, since I left the house this morning?"

But the scribe couldn't pretend for long, because his joy was great, and he burst into loud laughter.

This frightened his children even more because they had never heard their poor father laugh. Seeing that he was scaring the children, the scribe stopped laughing and said to his incredulous family, "The Almighty has performed a miracle for us. He sent me a customer for a Torah scroll right in the middle of winter, when there are no pilgrims in Jerusalem. The Almighty inspired me with the idea to go to the great patron from Frankfurt and suggest to him that he buy a Torah scroll from me.... And he promised to buy one!" the scribe exclaimed with great joy. "He will come to our house himself to choose the Torah scroll.... So, gang, remember! When he comes, you should go on with your work, just as if he weren't here. Understood? Because it has nothing to do with you! Understood?"

Chapter 3

The scribe's children clearly understood what their father meant, and they didn't dwell on it. But the youngest was cleverer than his brothers. He thought over his father's orders and said to himself, "The rich merchant from Frankfurt donates to every single charity. He gives a gift to every single person who stretches out a hand to him. . . . Wouldn't it only be fair for him to give me a little gift too, a few coins?"

His thoughts raced on: "But it's beneath my dignity to stretch out my hand to the patron like the beggars who stand by the Western Wall. That I'll never do! I also won't ask for alms, like the blind who stand on street corners! That's out too. But if I could present the patron with some kind of souvenir of Jerusalem, then I would surely receive a couple of coins from him. But what can I give him as a gift, a souvenir of Jerusalem?"

Over the entire day, as he worked on writing out his Torah scroll, the youngest kept thinking about a souvenir for the patron. When he finished his work, the boy didn't go to play with his friends as he did on other evenings. He wanted to be alone with his thoughts about how to get a couple of coins from the patron—maybe he would have a brainstorm.

So the scribe's youngest son was standing among the olive trees that grew in his father's little courtyard musing, "If it were fall and the olives were ripe, then I could pick a bough of large olives and give them to the patron as a present. But is that what you give as a souvenir to someone who comes from abroad?" He laughed at his own idea. "A souvenir is something a person can take with him in his suitcase to the country he's traveling back to from Jerusalem. It's not a cup of olives."

Thinking along these lines, the boy broke off a small branch from a tree. Instinctively, he took out his pocket knife and began to strip the branch. He kept stripping it until a white stick lay in his hands.

"If I carved the word 'Jerusalem' into this very stick," the boy mused, "that would be a good souvenir for the patron, and surely he'd give me a coin or two when I present it to him."

But at that moment, he had another idea: "Why only the word 'Jerusalem'? Why not carve a whole verse into the stick? In that case, the patron will surely give me something for such a souvenir. . . ."

"But which verse? There are so many verses in the Torah. Which verse would suit him best?"

The scribe's son went over one verse after another from those he knew by heart.

But he couldn't think of one that fit the patron who had come to Jerusalem from Frankfurt-am-Main to give charity in the Holy City.

Suddenly the scribe's boy remembered the verse that he had just written that day in the Torah scroll, from the book of Leviticus. He went over it several times. "Yes, that verse fits him very well," he decided. "The patron has come into the Land and continually 'sowed' the seeds of giving. . . . Yes! *Here* was the right verse for him to carve into the stick: 'And when you come into the Land, you shall plant!'"

And the scribe's boy plunged his knife into the neck of the branch. He imagined that even the wood liked the verse that he had chosen. The branch lay still on his knees, while he carved one letter after another. . . . The letters turned out so beautifully that out of sheer joy, the boy gave the stick a kiss.

He read over the verse several times, and each time, he thought that no other verse was as well suited to the patron as the one he'd carved. Then he slipped the stick under his shirt, and when it got completely dark, he went back home.

Chapter 4

"Where to hide the stick until tomorrow? Until the patron would come to choose a Torah scroll?" wondered the scribe's youngest son all evening.

"Maybe I should hide the stick with the carved verse under my pillow? But what if my brother, who shares my bed, moves his hand in the middle of the night and feels the stick?"

"No, that's not a safe place for it," he decided. "So should I stay up all night?" he thought next. But he quickly realized behavior like that would surely arouse questions and suspicion from his parents—and then his secret, his stick, would be revealed, and his dream of receiving a couple of coins from the patron would come to nothing. . . .

"But then where *should* I hide it?" thought the boy, before his parents extinguished the candle in the house. Then suddenly, he got up from his place, ran out into the yard, and pushed the stick into a heap of old stuff that was lying in a far corner of the yard.

"Nobody will go out to the heap of old rags in the middle of the night," he thought, and with that, he went to bed.

But he didn't sleep through the night. Every so often another thought would awaken the boy. He imagined a voice taunting him, "Why did you leave your stick outside, in the heap of old stuff? Is that what you do with something that you want to give as a souvenir of Jerusalem?"

The boy, irritated by that voice, wanted to get up and go take a look and see whether anyone had noticed his stick, but his fear lest his parents hear him open the door kept him in bed. The long night finally passed. As soon as it was light, the boy stole outside, ran over to the heap of old rags, snatched his stick, and quickly slipped it under his clothing.

That entire morning, he wrote with the stick next to his body. He didn't want to eat or drink. Nothing else mattered to him, so great was his fear of somebody touching his back and feeling the stick. . . .

Finally he heard a knock at the door. The scribe winked at his children, so they would remain seated over their parchments, and he ran to open the door for the patron from Frankfurt. The scribe's children didn't raise their eyes from the parchment on which they were writing, and they pretended not to care a whit about the distinguished guest from abroad. The guest examined each one's work, chose one of the completed Torah scrolls, and left together with the scribe.

A moment later, the scribe returned with a brimming handful of money. When his wife and children saw the treasure, the joy in the house was so great that everyone surrounded him and started to dance and jump together.

The scribe's youngest had been waiting for that moment. He sensed that everyone was busy with the money that the patron had left their father, and he stole out of the house. On his thin legs, the scribe's youngest quickly caught up with the merchant from Frankfurt.

"Sir! Sir!" he barely managed to call out. "A gift . . . I have a souvenir of Jerusalem for you."

"From your father?" Reb Jacob wondered.

"From me . . . not from my father, just from me. For you . . . just for you . . . carved by hand, for you."

The patron looked over the stick, read over the verse, and asked, "Did you also choose the verse yourself? But why did you pick precisely this verse?"

"Because this verse is very fitting for you, sir!"

"Why do you think so?"

"Why? Because all over Jerusalem, they say you've come and 'sowed' much charity. A donation, my good sir, is like a planting. . . . Some benefit for Jerusalem will grow from it."

"It's true what they say: the children of Jerusalem are cleverer than all the rest," said the patron from Frankfurt," still looking over the stick and the carved letters of the verse.

Without taking his eyes off the beautiful letters, Reb Jacob stuck his hand into his pocket and took out two golden coins and handed them to the scribe's youngest.

"May God bless you, sir! Always!" the boy barely managed to pronounce before he ran off.

Reb Jacob Guttmann smiled to himself, looked over the stick and its fine letters once more, and placed it in the same valise as the Torah scroll that he had bought from the scribe.

During his entire journey back to Frankfurt, the merchant kept thinking about the stick and the verse that the boy had found fitting to carve for him.

The closer Reb Jacob got to home, the more he thought about the blessing the boy had bestowed upon him, when he had received the two golden coins.

"Perhaps the Almighty will heed the boy's blessing and send a remedy to my sick wife, who sent me to say prayers in Jerusalem and give charity in her name. . . ."

The thought of his sick wife wouldn't let him rest.

"Is she waiting for me, as she promised? Did her situation get a bit better at least than before I left home?"

With a trembling heart, Reb Jacob rang at the door of his house. . . . Dark and sad thoughts flitted through his mind, until the door was opened. . . . But how astonished he was when he came into the parlor! The room was full of guests. They were all dressed up and cheerful, but looking the most cheerful of all was a woman in a blue silk dress. The woman called to him with a sweet voice from far away, "Blessed is your return home, Jacob!"

Only then did Reb Jacob Guttmann realize that the beautiful, blooming woman was his own wife. He burst into endless tears of joy, but he didn't want to remind his wife that just a short while ago, she'd been so sick that the doctors hadn't had a clue how to cure her.

So Reb Jacob simply invited all the guests into the dining room to make a toast in honor of his safe return home from the long journey.

During the toast, he showed off the things he had purchased in the Holy City. At the end, he displayed the stick that the scribe's boy had carved for him.

When all the guests had taken a look at the finely carved letters, he said, as if talking to himself, "The boy picked out the verse for me himself . . . and blessed me . . . blessed me like an adult. . . . And it seems to me that the Almighty heeded his blessing," he concluded, looking at his now-healthy wife.

Reb Jacob's joy was so great that he asked his wife to make a large meal so that all the residents of the Judengasse, rich and poor, rabbis and learned Jews and their students, could be present for the festivities. And in order that she not suspect him of actually making a holiday because of her recovery, he added, "When a Jew travels across the great sea, he must recite the blessing *hagomel* * seven times. I of course have crossed over the sea twice, on the way to Jerusalem and back, so I want to thank God with a great feast day and lots of charity. . . ."

At the celebration, they spoke of Torah and of Jerusalem. When they looked over the stick that Reb Jacob displayed, all the guests praised the scribe's boy, who had chosen the verse so wisely and carved it into the olive branch with such talent. . . .

Chapter 5

For a long time thereafter, Frankfurt's Judengasse spoke of the feast day and of all the things that the generous Reb Jacob Guttmann had brought back from Jerusalem. For a very long time, all the poor people blessed him for the charity that he distributed at home before and after the feast day. Rich and poor alike wished the Guttmanns that they should have no misfortune ever again for the rest of their lives.

All these wishes were fulfilled, and for a while after Reb Jacob's return from Jerusalem, husband and wife lived happily.

But suddenly, a war broke out between Germany and France, and by that time, the Guttmanns had a grown son. Reb Jacob Guttmann was terribly unsettled by the worry that his one and only son would be called up by the German army. He was careful not to let his wife know about his dark

* A blessing of thanksgiving after surviving a dangerous incident or situation.

thoughts. When he went to synagogue, he would listen carefully, with a trembling heart, to what the city's Jews were saying about the war and about whether Jews would be conscripted into the army. Some were sure that the Germans wouldn't call young Jewish men into battle.

"It was only four years ago, in 1864,* that we received the rights of citizenship. So how can it be that the Germans are calling up our sons?" asked the Jews among themselves.

"Can the Germans really be trusting our boys to beat the French? Not long ago we were like slaves, prohibited from living in a decent house, prohibited from opening a large business, confined to a ghetto, where the Germans would lock the gates every night and not let us out on Sundays or Christian holidays. And now—they're already going to send our children to fight for them? No! No! It cannot be!"

But one fine day, all the Jews of Frankfurt received "invitations" to join the German army and to go defend Germany in her war with the French.

At first, Reb Jacob Guttman and his son didn't want to tell the boy's mother about the "invitation" for fear that she might fall ill again, God forbid.

The next day, Reb Jacob went to synagogue to ask the rabbi's advice about what to do with his son so that he wouldn't have to go into the army to fight for the Germans.

"My son is an only child, after all," said Reb Jacob, crying.

"We have other Jews in town who have only one son," was the rabbi's reply.

"But my wife, Rabbi," the merchant continued crying, "you must surely remember how sick she was just a short time ago! Only through a miracle did she recover. . . . And now, if she finds out that our only son is going into battle, she might, God forbid, get sick again. . . ."

"The Almighty cured her illness, and he will give her strength to bear all troubles, Reb Jacob. Have no fear! But your son has to go into the army to defend the Germans, right along with all the other Jewish children. . . . Now we're citizens of Germany, so we have to act like citizens, Reb Jacob. . . . We and our children have to pay for the rights of citizenship with all our might and with our money, if the government should require it of us. . . . Didn't we want to leave the ghetto and be equal citizens with all our rights? Then we must send our children into the army. Believe in God! He will take care of our children and bring them safely back home. . . . But there's one thing

---

* Guttmann's trip to Jerusalem took place in 1868, and there is no mention of a son until this point in the story. Near the end of chapter 6, it is clear that the son was already a young man in 1870.

you must do! Give him a prayer shawl and tefillin* to take along, and let him pray each day, whenever he has the chance. . . .

After Reb Jacob left the rabbi's house, the rabbi opened the door again and called after him, "And don't forget to send the stick along with your son! . . ."

"Which stick?" asked the merchant, amazed that the rabbi had remembered the stick he had shown all his guests after his journey to Jerusalem.

"The stick that you brought from Jerusalem, the Holy City," the rabbi said, adding, "the stick on which the scribe's boy carved the verse, 'When you come into the Land, you shall plant. . . .' That means giving alms and charity. . . ."

When Reb Jacob got home, he told his wife about how they were calling up their one-and-only to the army. He kept nothing from her. He also told her about how he had gone to ask the rabbi's advice and what the rabbi had told him.

Frau Guttmann listened quietly to all that her husband had to say. She didn't shed a single tear, and when she heard that the rabbi had instructed them to give their son the stick to take along with him to the army, the stick that her husband had brought from Jerusalem, she said, "I'm calm. I believe that the Almighty will bring back our son just as he brought back my health when we had no hope that I would ever recover. . . ."

On the eve of their son's departure for the army, she called for a large, festive meal to be prepared. The Guttmanns didn't invite any guests; just father, mother, and son spent time together at the holiday table. And when the time came for their son to leave home, Jacob Guttmann accompanied him to the bookshelf where the stick stood, took it down, and handed it to his son, saying, "This is what our rabbi instructed, my son! May you keep this stick with you throughout the entire war, until your safe return home! . . ."

Chapter 6

When Jacob Guttmann's son, Joseph, left his parents' house, his first thought was of how to get rid of the stick. . . .

"Should I throw the stick into one of the Jewish yards?" he thought as he walked to the barracks. "The Jews of the Judengasse will recognize the stick

---

* Also known as "phylacteries," these small leather boxes contain parchments with the Shema prayer and are strapped to the forehead and arm during morning prayers.

that my father brought from Jerusalem and take it back to my parents. . . . I don't want to bring my parents any more sorrow; they didn't cry at our parting, but surely they have enough pain in their hearts from my going to the army. I'd better wait a bit until I get to the barracks. I'll throw the stick away there, where nobody will find it. . . ."

But in the barracks, Joseph was surrounded by a lot of other soldiers, and he couldn't pull the stick out from under his clothing. So he waited until nighttime, for everyone to fall asleep.

When all the soldiers were sleeping, Joseph went out to the barracks yard intending to get rid of the stick.

But a watchman was seated by the door, and he asked Joseph to sign his name in a little book.

After Joseph had signed his name, he decided that it didn't make sense to throw away the stick in the yard, because when it was found, they would know that he was the one who'd thrown it out; besides, he didn't want the Christians to make fun of the Hebrew letters, which they would recognize on the stick. So he decided to wait until morning.

When the soldiers went to eat breakfast, he would leave the stick under his mattress, he thought.

But in the morning, it was announced that every soldier had to turn over his mattress before going out to the mess hall, because an officer would be coming to inspect their beds. . . .

With no other choice, Joseph slipped the stick under his clothing once again and went off to his first maneuvers.

Because of the stick that was tucked under his clothes, he had to march straight as an arrow, straighter than all the other soldiers.

"One and two, and one and two," cried the officer to his soldiers. "Follow the example of your comrade Joseph Guttmann. Look how straight he marches! You march that way too!"

Joseph found such favor with the officer, that the officer marched next to him throughout all the maneuvers, and when rest time came, the officer sat next to him and didn't leave the Jewish youth's side.

And so it was that Joseph couldn't get rid of the stick, neither by day nor by night. . . .

"I see that the stick won't leave me," he thought. "It seems that the rabbi's order that I keep it all the way until the war ends won't be in vain. . . ."

From that day on, Joseph kept the stick under his clothes, even though it bothered him not a little. He no longer thought about how to get rid of the stick. . . .

Once, during a big battle at night, Joseph's entire legion ran out of ammunition.

It fell to Joseph Guttmann to find a way to regional headquarters and notify them to provide bullets for the soldiers.

After Joseph had conducted his mission, he wanted to crawl back to his previous position, but in the meantime, the battle had ended. It was very dark because the shooting that had illuminated the area before had ceased.

Joseph crawled the whole time on all fours, but just at the moment when he thought he could stand up, he slipped and began to roll into a ravine.

After tumbling all the way down, he smashed into a rock that lay in a narrow stream between two tall mountains.

Only when he looked up at the sky did he understand what a deep chasm he had fallen into. His first thought was that he had to crawl out from the ravine. But both sides of the mountain were so slippery and muddy that as soon as he got a foothold, he tumbled back down. Joseph began to use his gun as a walking stick, but with just one walking stick, he couldn't use both feet, one after the other. Joseph Guttmann then remembered that he had on his person the stick with the carved verse that his father had sent along with him when he set off. Although the stick was not large or very strong, it could still be a second walking stick for him, and together with his gun, it could save him from slipping and rolling down again. And that's how, after crawling a long way, he was able to climb out of the abyss, where he would surely have died. . . .

When Joseph finally felt the firm ground under his feet, he brought the stick to his lips and mused with great joy, "You, stick, pulled me out of trouble. May you be blessed, you and every letter that's carved into you! Blessed be my parents, who made me take you with me. And blessed be the rabbi, who ordered my father to send the stick along with me on my way!" From that moment on, he didn't part from the stick for even a single minute, until the end of the war.

When the conflict was over and his legion came into Strasbourg in Alsace, Joseph immediately thought about finding the local rabbi, because his parents had told him that wherever he went, he should give charity through the rabbi. When Joseph received his first leave, he went to meet the rabbi and give alms through him to the needy Jews of Alsace.

"Your father is well-known to me," said the rabbi of Strasbourg, "even though until now we've never met. I have heard a lot about him and his charitable giving both in Frankfurt and other places where there are Jews."

From talking with the rabbi, it was evident that he knew of Joseph's mother's illness and how she had recovered suddenly, by a miracle.

Over the course of their conversation, Joseph pulled out the stick with the carved verse from under his clothes, saying, "My father would always mention with gratitude the Jerusalem boy who gave him this stick. He believes that the boy's parting blessings were fulfilled when my mother recovered. . . . And that's why he also believed that this stick would protect me from death and harm, if I kept it with me always until the end of the war."

Joseph told the rabbi of Alsace candidly about how at first he had wanted to get rid of the stick because it was no small nuisance to him.

"But it looks like this stick didn't want to leave me! And however much I tried to free myself of it, I couldn't do it," added Joseph Guttmann, seeing how the rabbi was examining every letter.

"A fine stick with finely carved letters," remarked the rabbi.

Joseph Guttmann took courage and told the rabbi about how he had tumbled down into the deep chasm in the darkness of night, after the great battle.

"You can believe me, Rabbi, if it weren't for this stick that served me as a second walking stick, I would never have managed to crawl out from the slippery, muddy ravine. . . . I have much to thank the stick for. . . ."

"Better yet, my son," the rabbi interrupted, "you should be grateful to the Almighty, who commanded the rabbi of Frankfurt to tell your father that he should send along the stick with you on your way. . . ."

"And because I came out safely from the deep abyss, Rabbi, I would like to make a donation through you for the needy of your town."

Joseph found such favor with the rabbi of Strasbourg that the rabbi invited him to come over whenever he could free himself of his military duties. He became a frequent guest at the rabbi's house. The rabbi would study a page of the Talmud with him, and after their study, Joseph would peruse the holy books in the rabbi's large library.

With his sterling character and his intellect, Joseph found favor not only with the rabbi but also with the rabbi's daughter, and when the country calmed down after the war, the two of them were married.

Rabbis and learned Jews from every corner of Europe came to the magnificent wedding, which was celebrated in Strasbourg-in-Alsace.

Eloquent speeches were given at the wedding, and all the guests blessed both the parents of the bride and groom and the young couple. It was wished upon them, by way of blessing, that their children might be as good Jews as their parents. . . .

The blessings were fulfilled. The son that was born to Joseph Guttmann and his wife had every advantage: he was smart, handsome, and a capable student.

At six, little Benjamin had already learned the Five Books of Moses. And when he turned eighteen, he was already versed in Jewish subjects, and at the same time, he was studying in a Parisian university.

His parents were very happy. And his grandparents were delighted with their talented grandson.

But their joy did not last long.

In 1914, war broke out once again between Germany and France. Before too long, the flames of war had ignited all of Europe and dragged all the young men to the front.

Benjamin Guttmann also had to go to war. But he hated shooting. His greatest pleasure was to sit over his books and study.

And so a great, dark cloud crept up on the Guttmanns soon after the war broke out.

The cloud of misery was even heavier and darker because Benjamin couldn't decide which side to join. . . .

Should he go defend the French—that would mean mean going to war against his own father, who came from Frankfurt, and against his grandfather, the distinguished merchant and benefactor, Reb Jacob Guttmann. . . .

But how could he go with the Germans, when his mother's homeland was France, the land where Jews had always had more rights and freedom than in Germany? . . .

Also, Benjamin had always loved his mother tongue, French, more than German. A great struggle took place in Benjamin's heart. The conflict robbed him of sleep and tranquility, and he stopped eating. Benjamin's parents grew sad, watching their son struggle with these feelings.

So Joseph Guttmann went to see the town's rabbi to ask his advice. The rabbi told the father that his son, Benjamin, must decide for himself which army to enlist in. . . .

Miserable, Joseph returned home from the rabbi's. When he opened the door of his house, his son welcomed him, with his mind made up. . . .

It wasn't long before Benjamin left his parents' home. But before he had to depart, his parents made him a holiday banquet, just as Joseph's parents had done for their son when he left for the army.

After the meal, Joseph took down from the bookshelf the stick carved with the verse, "When you come into the land, you shall plant." He hadn't given the stick back to his parents when he'd returned from the war.

"Do you recognize this stick, my son?" said Joseph Guttmann to his son, Benjamin. "When you were still a child, I used to tell you about how this stick had saved me from a slippery, muddy ravine in wartime, in the year 1870. Take this stick and keep it with you until the war's end, until you come safely home. . . ."

Chapter 7

When Benjamin Guttmann left home, holding the stick in his hands, he thought, "My father could carry around a stick in 1870, because in that war, people walked on foot or rode horses or mules. . . . But the War of 1914 is totally different. In this war, we'll be attacked by tanks. I must get rid of this stick because it will be a nuisance! I will get to Paris and leave the stick somewhere before I get to the barracks!"

Benjamin didn't want to leave the stick in the middle of the street, lest it fall into non-Jewish hands. So that's why as soon as he got to Paris, he went to the Great Synagogue.

He stayed there a little while, and when he got up to go, he left the stick lying in the same spot where he had placed it when he entered.

He left the synagogue feeling happy. He knew that all the custodians there were Jewish, and so he was sure that the stick with the verse carved on it would not fall into Gentile hands.

But before Benjamin Guttmann had managed to cross the street, one of the synagogue custodians chased him down, calling out, "You forgot your stick, sir! Nothing gets lost in our synagogue. I'm happy I caught up with you. . . . You would surely have been worried about this splendid stick until you recalled that you had forgotten it in the Great Synagogue. . . . It would be a shame to lose something so precious! . . .

"And why do you think that it's so precious?" Benjamin asked, taking the stick in his hands.

"You yourself know, sir, that only great artists can make such carvings in wood. . . . We don't even have such artists here in Paris."

Benjamin Guttmann slipped the stick back under his clothing and set off for the barracks. The whole way, he thought, "I take this as a sign that it's my duty to do what my father said: to hold onto the stick until the war's end."

Benjamin Guttmann got used to keeping the stick under his clothes so that nobody would notice it.

He would eat, sleep, and go to maneuvers—all with the stick. And when the time came for battle at the front, he didn't part from it.

Once Benjamin Guttmann got separated from his company of soldiers. Suddenly, he noticed that he was all by himself, surrounded by Germans. Seeing that one man alone couldn't cope with so many of the enemy, he tried to escape. The German soldiers chased him and shot after him from afar.

Running, Benjamin unbuttoned his coat so he could run faster. His stick, which had been under his coat at the time, fell out and tripped Benjamin so that he fell to the ground.

When they saw that "France" had fallen, the Germans thought that he had fallen from one of their bullets. So they stopped chasing him because one of them said to the others, laughing, "Who are we chasing after? Another dead dog? Another corpse?"

When the Germans went away, Benjamin began to crawl on all fours to the road back to his army. As he moved along, he thought, "The stick saved me from certain death. . . . It saved me from falling into the hands of the Germans. . . ."

How the stick saved Benjamin Guttmann from certain death a second time, he would not remember.

Benjamin recalled just one thing: he was lying on the ground in a forest, and the forest was burning from a great battle. The artillery fire was so close to him that he closed his eyes so as not to see it. How long he kept his eyes shut he couldn't remember. When he opened them, he saw that he was lying in a clean, white bed.

"Who brought me here?" Benjamin thought, looking around. "Is what I'm seeing here a dream?"

Benjamin closed his eyes again, the better to see the lovely dream. But then he made out a woman's soft voice, saying to him, "How long will you sleep, soldier? We want to give you some medicine, and you're sleeping . . . !"

Only then did Benjamin realize that the woman was a nurse and that he was in a hospital.

Who had brought him to the hospital? He wanted to ask, but his tongue wouldn't move.

"I'm wounded," thought Benjamin, "and that's why I can't speak! How long will I be unable to communicate? Maybe I'll never be able to speak again? Maybe I've become permanently mute . . . ?"

This thought upset Benjamin so much that he cried out loud. The nurse let him cry and shout for a long time, because she hoped that through his crying, he would recover his tongue and be able to speak.

The nurse had guessed right. After a long, helpless shout, he did recover his tongue and cry out, "My stick! Where is my stick?!"

Benjamin couldn't believe that his ears were hearing his own voice. That's why he kept shouting, "My stick! Give me back my stick!"

His shrieks summoned the head doctor: "What are you yelling about, you imbecile?! Don't you know that in a hospital, you're not allowed to yell?!"

But Benjamin Guttmann paid the doctor no mind. He kept screaming his demand, "My stick! Give me my stick!"

"And if I give you back your 'lucky charm,'" taunted the doctor, "then will you tell me what's carved on the stick?"

Benjamin sensed that the doctor was making fun of him. So he turned his back to him and wouldn't even answer.

"If you won't tell me the meaning of the engraved words," the doctor started again," then I will summon the rabbi. The chief rabbi of Warsaw will surely know what the letters mean. . . ."

Only then did Benjamin Guttmann realize that he had fallen captive to the Germans and that the doctor suspected that a secret code was engraved on his stick. . . .

He quickly turned back around to face the doctor and said, "My stick is engraved with the Hebrew words, 'When you come into the land, you shall plant'!"

"And that's exactly what I suspected," the doctor replied. "And what kind of trees do you intend to plant for espionage, ha?!"

"Sir! I am not a spy! And I don't come from a family of spies. I come from the distinguished Guttmann family. My father and my grandfather were great merchants! They could trace their lineage back several generations. . . ."

"But what did they engrave for you on the stick?" the doctor interrupted.

"They weren't the one who engraved the letters on the stick. . . . My grandfather Reb Jacob Guttmann brought this stick back from Jerusalem many years ago. A boy, who wrote out Torah scrolls, engraved a verse of the Torah on the stick, and he carved *this* verse because my grandfather always 'planted' donations wherever he went. And he told his son and grandson to do the same: to give charity wherever we find ourselves. . . . Believe me, that's the whole truth!"

The doctor believed that Benjamin was telling the truth, and he left him in peace. Just then, a man came into the hospital. On his uniform was a red cross.

The man with the red cross was soon questioning the doctor in German: "How is the 'French spy' that I brought in at night? Has he told you yet the meaning of the secret code that he carries engraved on his stick? If it weren't for that stick with the secret code, I would have let him rot where he lay, in the forest. . . ."

When Benjamin heard those words, he took his weak hand and pressed the stick to his wounded body and quietly murmured to it, as if to himself, "May you be blessed, stick. Blessed be each letter that the boy in Jerusalem once engraved upon you! Blessed be my parents, who sent this stick along with me! I'll never part from you, until we both return safely home after the war. . . ."

Chapter 8

As the doctor conversed more with Benjamin and found out that he was a student at a Parisian university, he grew quite friendly. After Benjamin's wounds healed, the doctor invited him to come visit his home.

At the doctor's house, Benjamin became acquainted with the doctor's daughter. She was very pretty. Benjamin liked her a great deal. But he wasn't pleased at how both father and daughter disliked the Jews, even though they themselves were Jewish. They would laugh at everything that had to do with Jews and the Yiddish language. That's why Benjamin hadn't told the daughter that he liked her.

When the war ended and all the prisoners of war were released, he was also freed and traveled home to his parents in Alsace.

He was gone for a while. Benjamin had almost forgotten the doctor and his daughter. But one fine day, he received a letter from them, from Warsaw. In the letter, they invited him to visit, this time not as a prisoner of war but as a free French citizen.

Benjamin felt that he was deceiving his parents when he told them that he was traveling to Warsaw to meet there with the doctor who had treated his wounds.

Regarding the doctor's daughter, he said nothing. Until one fine day, after spending a certain amount of time in Warsaw, he telegraphed his parents that he had gotten married to the doctor's daughter. . . .

Everything that had happened to him in Warsaw occurred so fast that he didn't have any time to notice that he wasn't really compatible with the father and the daughter. . . . He didn't even realize until it was too late that their good relationship with him was thanks to the fact that he had studied in a French university and knew European languages, not the fact that he was a good Jew and had a wealth of Jewish knowledge.

Before long, Benjamin sensed that a deep chasm lay between him and his young wife together with her father.

The first serious fight between them came about one day when he returned home from his office to eat lunch.

Coming into the corridor, he spotted his stick with the carved verse in the garbage that the maid was about to throw out.

Benjamin pulled his stick out of the garbage, wiped it as one polishes a holy object, and carried it into the room where his wife was waiting for him by the set table.

"Who ordered the maid to throw out my stick with the garbage?" he asked quietly, concealing his anger inside himself.

"Who? I did! I'm the lady of the house here!"

"That's true that you are the lady of the *house* here. But you're not allowed to throw away things that are precious to me! I've told you many times already that my life was saved twice thanks to that very stick."

"I don't want to hear that nonsense anymore," his wife swiftly interrupted. "I'm simply embarrassed on your behalf, that you, a learned man, make an idol of that stick. . . ."

"I don't make an idol of the stick at all!" he cut in angrily. "But I will never forget that this stick came from Jerusalem, from the Holy City, that it was passed down from my grandfather to my father and from my father to me . . . and, I hope, that it will be passed down also to my son. . . ."

"Certainly not!" replied his wife angrily.

Benjamin didn't listen to another word. He wrapped the stick in paper, carried it up to the attic, and hid it, so that nobody would find it and throw it away.

The second fight between Benjamin and his wife took place when their first child was born. They fought over his name.

Benjamin wished to name his newborn son after his grandfather, Jacob. But his wife didn't want the child to be called by the Jewish "Jacob" under any circumstances.

Benjamin's wife prevailed. The boy was given the name Stefan, in Polish. When he got bigger, people started to call him by the nickname Stefek.

Stefek grew up as a Polish child, hearing Polish songs and stories. When he was six years old, he was enrolled at one of the schools where children from the Polish aristocracy and merchant class were the only students.

Benjamin requested of his wife that they invite a Jewish tutor into their home several times a week to teach the child Yiddish. But his wife and her father laughed at him.

"Our Stefek has no time to learn a language that's written from right to left. . . . What would he get out of Yiddish?" Benjamin's wife asked sarcastically. "Stefek doesn't need to know any of the 'Holy Tongue'! Stefek needs to learn European languages: English, French, German, but not these foolish things that are more suitable for old Jews and country bumpkins. Stefek lives in Warsaw, among Poles, so he should grow up as a Pole. Our neighbors ought not suspect that he is a Jew. . . ."

Benjamin Guttmann knew that their conversation was pointless, and he stopped fighting with those who hated Jews and Jewishness.

But his heart hurt a great deal. Often, very often, he would stay up the whole night unable to close his eyes out of resentment and pain. He would awaken from his first sound sleep because he imagined that he heard a voice from somewhere saying, "Benjamin Guttmann! Have you forgotten that you are the grandson of Reb Jacob Guttmann from Frankfurt-am-Main? Have you forgotten that you are also a grandchild of the rabbi of Strasbourg, the distinguished rabbi from Alsace? Your parents taught you to be a Jew. Why aren't you teaching your son any Jewishness? He'll soon be bar mitzvah age, and he still doesn't even know the Jewish alphabet. . . ."

After such nights, Benjamin Guttmann would wake up rattled and miserable. He would look for a chance to speak with his wife and her father, the old doctor, to explain to them that his life made no sense if his son was to grow up as a Polish boy. But they never wanted to hear him out. So then Benjamin left home quite early for his office, in order to forget himself there in his work. . . .

Several days before Stefek's bar mitzvah, the Nazi army entered Poland. Guttmann's wife and her father, the "Polish" doctor, didn't believe that Hitler would capture Warsaw so quickly.

They had prepared a large celebration for Stefek's thirteenth birthday, as if times were peaceful and normal, just as if no danger lay in wait for the city and its Jews. . . .

Benjamin knew in advance that his wife would invite only Poles to the party, or such Jews as hated Judaism, just like her and her father. He already knew by heart all the wisecracks that would be made by the Polish children, Stefek's friends, all the stories that would be told, and all the songs that would be sung at his son's "bar mitzvah."

The words "bar mitzvah" drilled noisily into his brain when he recalled his own bar mitzvah. His parents' house was full of rabbis and teachers and their pupils, who understood the finer points of Jewish learning as well as he did. They not only ate and drank at the celebration but also tested all the children, asking more questions of the bar mitzvah boy than of anyone else. The guests from young to old listened to the bar mitzvah's speech with great interest. Not only had the bar mitzvah boy been well versed in Jewish matters, but he also spoke European languages. . . .

And what did Stefek know as his bar mitzvah approached?

No! He wanted no part of such a bar mitzvah! He would not be party to such a celebration!

And so Benjamin left his house very early on the day of his son's bar mitzvah, in order not to be at home while they were preparing for the festivities.

But the thought that this was the day of his son's bar mitzvah gave him no peace, even as he sat in his office. He couldn't even manage to forget himself in his work on that day. . . .

Around four o'clock, he left his office and wandered the streets of Warsaw. Strolling aimlessly in the vicinity of his office, he noticed that the gates of the Great Synagogue were open. This really surprised him because it was a weekday.

Curious why the synagogue was so wide open in the middle of the week, he went inside. That's when he saw that a great many Jews had gathered there, women and children.

Benjamin sat down in the synagogue in order to see and hear what was going on and to find out why the synagogue was full of people.

A young man ascended the platform, and in a fine Yiddish, addressed the assembled, saying, "Jews, save your children! Don't delay, as the Jews of Germany did, who didn't want to pay us any attention. If they had listened in time to what we are saying, their children would now be in England or in the Land of Israel, where they would be cared for with devotion and affection. But they didn't want to listen to us, and that's why their children are together with them in the various camps. . . . But you, Jewish parents, don't you hear how close the Nazis are getting? Entrust your children to us, and we will take them out of Poland, because we still have a little time, a few hours and no more! Hurry! The last group is getting out of here tomorrow night. . . ."

With a pained heart, Benjamin Guttmann left the synagogue. He wandered the streets of Warsaw for a long time. Walking around, he thought of his son continually.

When he finally got home, he didn't ring the doorbell but instead entered quietly, so that nobody would notice him. He got into bed deliberately and pretended to be ill.

He lay in bed like that until all the guests had left. Only then did he go down to the dining room, where only his wife and her father were left, in order to discuss with them what he had heard in the Great Synagogue.

"You're celebrating holidays like in the good old days," he began, "and in town, they're waiting for Hitler's invasion! You know of course what he'll do with us Jews when he arrives. Even if you don't want to escape from here, if your lives aren't dear to you, let us at least rescue our child, our Stefek!"

"And how can you rescue our Stefek?" the old doctor laughed at him. "Maybe with your long-ago magic stick that was carved with ridiculous words in your 'Holy Tongue' . . . ?"

"Stefek is a blond boy," Guttmann's wife said. "He looks like a true Pole! And Hitler won't do any harm to the Poles. . . ."

"And I'm telling you that our 'good neighbors,' the Poles, in whom you believe so deeply, will turn you in at the first opportunity. They'll turn you and our child over to the authorities! Let's rescue him from here!"

Benjamin sensed that he spoke in vain to his wife and to his father-in-law. He dismissed them and got back into bed. But the entire night, he kept thinking, "Until the day of my son's bar mitzvah, you've done with him what you've wanted. But from now on, I will do with my son what I feel is necessary. . . ."

The next day, Benjamin Guttmann left the house very early, after a long and sleepless night. All that day, he couldn't sit still in his office. Once again he wandered the streets of Warsaw; thoughts of how to save his only son troubled his mind continually.

This time too, while strolling through the streets, he went inside the Great Synagogue. Again, it was full of people. Benjamin looked around and approached the youth who had spoken the day before from the platform to the assembled crowd in a fine Yiddish. "Sir," be began with a weak voice.

"I'm not a 'sir,'" replied the youth. "My name is simply Erik. Call me Erik!"

"I want to rescue my son, Erik!"

"And where is your son? Did you bring him here with you?"

"No, how can I bring him here when my wife and her father won't allow him to be taken away from here? They still believe that Hitler won't do them any harm."

Erik looked at Guttmann with great compassion.

"So should I 'kidnap' your son for you and bring him here by force?" he asked, shaking his head. "And how old is your son, sir?"

"My name is Guttmann. My son became a bar mitzvah just yesterday. He's thirteen, Erik."

"I understand very well, Herr Guttmann, that you want to save your son. But can one seize a boy of thirteen by force and take him from home, if he himself doesn't want to go?"

"No, he won't come on his own. His mother won't let him go . . . ," said Benjamin quietly, as if to himself.

Just then, other Jewish parents surrounded Erik and pulled him aside, in order to pass along details about their children, whom they were entrusting to him.

Once Guttmann was alone, he couldn't stop ruminating on Erik's words: "Kidnap, seize him by force, and bring him here. . . ." But how? And perhaps Stefek would listen after all to what he was going to tell him about the great Hitler danger, which was creeping up on all the Jews and on him too? No! No! Stefek had been poisoned by his grandfather, the doctor, who took himself for a true "Pole." Stefek's mother also believed that his blond hair and his light-blue eyes would save him and that they would be able to fool Hitler's race specialists. . . . No! He mustn't rely on them; Stefek must be brought here by force, by might!

Benjamin paced around the synagogue for a little while longer. Then he went into one of the large drugstores and said to the druggist, "I haven't slept in several nights, and I'm so tired that I can't do anything. Give me sleeping pills so that tonight I can fall asleep at least for a few hours. . . ."

"If you haven't slept in several nights, then I'll give you really strong pills, Herr Guttmann. I guarantee you that tonight you'll finally sleep. . . ."

The druggist gave Guttmann a little box of pills.*

Chapter 10

When Guttmann came home with the sleeping pills in his pocket, he didn't ring the doorbell. He let himself into the house with his own key. He wanted to see what kind of a mood his family was in. Perhaps the rumors about Hitler's approach had already reached his wife and father-in-law? But Guttmann didn't notice the slightest change in the mood of his household. From the kitchen wafted the delicious, tantalizing smells of good cooking. The table in the dining room was set for dinner as always, with a sparkling white tablecloth. The fine crystal and silver shimmered with hundreds of colors. Chandeliers burned in every corner of the large house. On a soft chair in the living room lay the Polish newspaper, waiting for the old doctor. On the divan lay a fashion magazine, with all kinds of new clothing styles on display. . . .

---

* Chapter 9 was not marked. The translation follows the chapters as numbered in the original.

"They hath eyes, but they see not what's going on around them," thought Benjamin Guttmann, looking over his comfortable home.

"Are you home from the office already?" his wife asked, coming into the living room. "What are they saying in town?"

"Everything's the same!" he strained to answer her in a calm voice.

"No news. Things are calm in town," added the doctor, who had also come into the dining room at that moment. "I've told you, Benjamin, that Warsaw isn't some small town that can be captured in an hour or two. It's going to cost the Germans plenty of blood before they'll succeed in taking Warsaw."

"But why talk now about war?" Guttmann feigned a smile, "when such delicious smells are coming from the kitchen? Let's go eat instead."

"I'm also hungry as a wolf," said Stefek, as he came in.

"But I don't want to go to dinner today without a cocktail," Guttmann said merrily.

"You're the 'Chief Cupbearer,' Papa. So go mix a cocktail for yourself."

"Today I want all of us to drink a toast together. I couldn't make it to your birthday, Stefek, because I felt very bad that day. So now I want to mix a cocktail for everyone. . . . And I won't forget even our servants. . . . I'm sure you forgot all about them at Stefek's festivities."

"You're right, Papa, we forgot all about them."

"So call everyone in now. Don't leave out even the doorman. . . . Everyone deserves a toast in honor of your belated birthday, Stefek!"

And Guttmann went into a small room where he always mixed cocktails. But this time, he made sure to mix the cocktails together with the sleeping pills. . . .

"And now let's all drink a toast, a *lechaim*! he cried happily, passing each one a large glass of the mixed drink. "But before we drink to Stefek's thirteenth birthday, I'd like to say a few words about the guest of honor. . . . Remember, Stefek, that you should always, wherever you are, think about those who are drinking this toast with you and your parents above all. . . ."

"You're not making sense, Papa!" Stefek interrupted. "What do you mean, 'remember' all of a sudden? Am I going away? That's how people talk when one of them is getting ready to hit the road, Papa!"

"You're right, Stefek, I'm not doing this very well! Next time, I'll prepare better in advance. For now, though, I'll end my speech with the wish that this *lechaim*—"to life"—bring you long years and a healthy life, Stefek!"

After everyone had drunk the toast and drained their glasses, the family sat down to dinner.

They ate with great appetite, all except Benjamin. He pretended to eat, but each bite stuck in his throat because he was worried: "Would the plan work? Would the cocktails have the proper effect?"

The doctor was the first to get drunk from the cocktail. As soon as he finished eating, he excused himself, saying that he had worked very hard in the hospital the whole day.

After the doctor, Stefek was next to leave the table. Without saying goodbye, he went running upstairs, where all the bedrooms were.

"What's your hurry, Stefek? Surely you're not as tired as your grandfather?" Benjamin tried to delay his son.

"I'm drunk from your cocktail, Papa! Let me go to sleep!"

"I won't let you go until you give your Mama a kiss."

"What's this about a kiss all of a sudden, Papa? I'm grown up! I don't kiss Mama anymore before I go to bed. . . ."

"Grown up?!" Guttmann forced a laugh, "Really: I won't let you go to bed until you give your Mama a kiss. . . ."

The thought niggled in his mind, "Maybe it's the last time he'll ever see his mother . . . ?"

"I'm also drunk from your cocktail," declared Frau Guttmann. She took the fashion magazine with her and went up to her bedroom. A few minutes later, everyone was sound asleep. Even the doorman was sleeping soundly next to his sentry box, sitting on a chair.

After looking around, Guttmann went up to the attic and brought down the stick that his grandfather had brought from Jerusalem. He took the stick out of its wrapping paper and wiped off the dust of a long time. After that, he went into Stefek's room, sat down by the boy's desk, and wrote a note. He placed the note into a coat pocket and slipped the coat onto the sleeping boy. After he had buttoned and belted the coat, he tucked the stick with the carved letters into the belt.

In Stefek's sound, drunken slumber, he looked like a little boy. His father took a good look at him and his delicate, childish face, hoisted him onto his shoulder, and with his "living package" descended from the second story to the street.

Chapter 11

The Great Synagogue was packed when Guttmann brought in his sleeping son. Erik ran over to him, in order to help lay down the "sleeping package" comfortably on a bench.

"I see, Herr Guttmann, that you pulled off your 'kidnapping,'" he smiled at the father. "Snatching a child doesn't always work. . . ."

"I needed it to work, Erik! We have to save him from the great danger that's hanging over all of us. . . ."

Guttmann turned his face away, so Erik wouldn't see the tears in his eyes.

Erik noticed everything, but he pretended to be absorbed in his record book, where he was recording the names and the histories of the children being entrusted to him.

"So, Herr Guttmann, now is the time to write down your son's history. We need to know everything so that we can find each other after the war. . . ."

"If that's the case, Erik, then write down that my son's Jewish name is Jacob and that I named him after my grandfather, of blessed memory, Reb Jacob Guttmann of Frankfurt-am-Main."

"Reb Jacob Guttmann was your grandfather, Herr Guttmann?!" cried Erik with great surprise, and again he offered the father his hand to shake.

"So that means that Stefek is a great-grandson of that distinguished Jew, whose name entered into the history of German Jewry? You may be sure that I will take care of Stefek, just as if he were my own child!"

"As long as you're writing, Erik, write also that my father, of blessed memory, Reb Joseph Guttmann, was also a learned Jew and a generous benefactor who walked in the footsteps of his father, Reb Jacob Guttmann, in this regard. . . . And if it interests you, I myself have also looked into the finer points of the law, even once I was a university student in Paris. . . . But I must tell you the truth: alas, my son doesn't even know the Hebrew alphabet. . . . His mother and grandfather wanted him to grow up as a true Pole. . . ."

Erik wrote down all of this in his record book. As he finished writing, there was starting to be a lot of movement in the synagogue. Men, women, and children began to push toward the doors.

Erik wanted to help Guttmann carry his sleeping son to one of the wagons, but Guttmann wouldn't allow it. This time he wanted to feel the "sweet burden" by himself, with all his limbs. . . .

He carried his son out and lay him down in a wagon. He remained standing in the middle of the street, until that wagon moved and until all the wagons and pedestrians had passed by.

And when the street in front of the synagogue was empty, he stood there still, murmuring to himself, "As long as my son is saved . . . nobody need worry about me. . . ."

Chapter 12

It was a clear and sunny autumn day at the beginning of September when Stefek was startled awake from his heavy slumber.

When he opened his eyes, he saw that he lay in a wagon, among small children. It seemed to him that what he was seeing must be a dream. . . . Stefek looked at the blue sky and waited for the dream to disappear. . . . But the dream didn't go away. He was really lying in a moving wagon. The horses were alive. Stefek patted himself . . . no! He wasn't sleeping. That meant that he wasn't seeing it all in a dream but in reality. And if it was for real, then how had he come to be among all these tramps who were walking alongside or sitting and lying in the wagons? No, something was not right! Not normal! It could be nothing else: he must have been kidnapped. If that was the so, he had to save himself from his "kidnappers"! What a piece of good fortune that they hadn't tied him up but just laid him down in the wagon. . . .

Stefek jerked himself forcefully from his place, hoisted himself up, and tried to jump down from the wagon.

Suddenly, two friendly hands stretched out toward him, ready to help him down.

But once he was standing on the ground, the two hands held him fast and a friendly voice asked him, "Where to, Stefek?"

"Home!" replied Stefek, tearing himself out of Erik's hands. "Home, to my father! To my mother! Who dared to kidnap me?!"

"Calm down, Stefek! Reach into your pocket, and you'll find a note, and then you'll understand everything. . . ."

Stefek did as Erik told him. He found the note, which was written in his father's hand. He read over the note:

"Stefek, our son, we're parting from you for a while. The fire of war has caught all of Warsaw. If with God's help we see each other again, I will tell you all about why we chose this path for you. We are going on a different road, but we are sure that the road down which we have sent you is best. In the belt of your coat, you'll find a stick with carved letters. You've never learned those letters. A long time will go by before you will learn to understand what is engraved on the stick. But remember one thing: guard the stick until the war ends, and when the land calms down, do all that is engraved there. . . ."

Several times, Stefek read over the note that his father had written in his own hand, in Polish. But he didn't understand a single word. The note was a great riddle to him. But when Erik asked him, "Do you understand, Stefek?" the proud boy replied, "Understood!"

Only then did he take out the stick that was stuck into the belt of his coat and examine it closely. The riddle grew even greater. He wanted to know very badly what was engraved on the stick and who was the young man holding him by the hand. He wanted to know why his parents had taken a different road and sent him on this road with this young man. And who were the tramps walking on ahead and behind him? Where were they taking him? And why had his father slipped this stick into his belt?

But most of all, he wanted to know what the carved letters on the stick meant. . . . Should he ask the young man who was leading him by the hand? No, Stefek was a proud boy, and it was beneath his dignity to ask. . . .

The wagons stopped, and those who were walking alongside sat down to rest a little from the hard road.

Erik took a candy out of his pocket and offered it to Stefek, but he pushed away the young man's hand. Then Erik went up to one of the wagons and brought back bread and sausage and offered it to Stefek.

"Why didn't you tell me that you were hungry?" he said to the boy with a friendly smile.

Stefek accepted what Erik offered him. As he chewed the bread, they smiled at each other like good friends. Smiling at Erik, Stefek couldn't help being struck by the thought that maybe he should read Erik the note that his father had written in Polish and placed in his coat pocket.

Stefek glanced at the note once more, and when he read through it again, he asked Erik, "Is there really a war going on, like my father wrote in the note?"

His question was interrupted by an airplane's ear-splitting roar.

All those who were on foot ran to take cover among the trees of the forest. After them ran those who'd managed to scramble down from the wagons. Holding Erik's hand, Stefek also ran into the forest and hid among the trees.

"The roar overhead must mean war," thought the boy.

When the noise had passed, Erik said to the boy, "You asked me whether there's a war going on. I didn't get to answer you. . . ."

"It's no longer necessary," said Stefek, pointing to the planes flying by.

"Meanwhile, that's just an introduction to the war, Stefek. But have no fear! I will always protect you."

"I don't even know your name," the boy smiled at him.

"Then I haven't told you yet that my name is Erik?"

These friendly words made Stefek feel so at home with Erik that he once again took out his stick from the belt of his coat and, showing him the carved letters, asked, "Can you read these letters, Erik?"

"What kind of a question is that? Am I not a Jew?"

For the first time in Stefek's life, he felt ashamed that he couldn't read the letters that a Jew was supposed to know how to read. He slipped the stick back into the same place where it had lain until then, and he didn't ask Erik any more about what the carved letters meant.

"Anyway," he comforted himself, "my father wrote in the note that I should do what's carved on the stick *after* the war ends . . . but the war is just getting started! The airplanes are still roaring overhead. . . ."

Several days passed, but Stefek couldn't manage to overcome his pride and ask Erik what the verse carved on the stick was telling him to do. Each time his curiosity surged, he would calm himself down and say, "There's still a war going on. So what's the hurry . . . ?"

But one fine day, he didn't hear the roar of a plane from earliest dawn until after midday.

So Stefek thought, "It could be that the war has ended as suddenly as it started. . . ." And he decided that today, right away, he would ask Erik what the carved verse meant.

But as soon as he tried to open his mouth and ask, he heard a sudden, loud roar overhead, and right from out of the sky leaped three big, iron birds with their wings outspread.

Before the refugees on foot could manage to run away into the forest and the wagons could stop to give the passengers a chance to climb down, it began to rain bombs and bullets.

Stefek saw Erik lying down on the ground, and he thought that was the thing to do so as not to be hit by the bullets. So he too lay down on the ground, near his old friend.

"Go farther on, don't lag behind them . . . ," Erik murmured with his last strength.

"I won't go on without you!" shouted Stefek. "Come with me! Stand up!"

Seeing that his friend wasn't getting up, he fell down and cried into his face, begging, "Come with me, come! I'll . . ."

"But don't you see . . . ?" Erik whispered weakly, closing his eyes. "Go, with your stick, go!"

Seeing that Stefek wouldn't move from the spot, his friends picked him up by force and sat him back down in one of the wagons.

The boy buried his head in a heap of rags that was crammed into the wagon, and he cried for a long time, calling out again and again, "Erik . . . ! Erik . . . !"

Chapter 13

Days and nights passed. Sometimes Stefek rode, and sometimes he walked because he had to give up his seat to those who were tired from walking. How many days and nights had passed he didn't know. He had grown very weak, hungry, and thirsty. Erik's friends divided the portions of food and water fairly, but the portions were very small because the food that their associates had been able to bring from other cities and towns had disappeared along the way, just like those who had transported it. . . .

Once, when the airplanes were roaring overhead and and everyone was running into the forest, Stefek was so weak from hunger that he couldn't make it back from the forest with the others. . . .

He lay on the grass and quietly called to his friend, "Erik . . . Erik . . ."

He didn't know how long he lay there on the ground calling "Erik." Suddenly he felt someone slap his head. With great effort, he opened his eyes and saw that whoever was hitting him held his stick in his hands.

"Hey, that's my stick. Give it back to me!" he screamed, but he couldn't hear his voice. And before he could manage to shout in a louder voice, the young man who was holding his stick hoisted him onto his shoulder and carried him off somewhere.

When Stefek finally opened his eyes, he saw that he was lying on a large table. Around him stood several men, examining him.

Suddenly he noticed that he was naked. A pungent smell of medicine entered his nostrils. The smell reminded him of his grandfather, the doctor, who used to come home from the hospital, after an operation. . . .

"Grandpa?" he thought. "And where is my father? And where is my mother? And where is my note that Papa left for me in my coat pocket? And where is my stick, which was in the belt of my coat?"

"My stick!" Stefek suddenly burst out. "Give me back my stick!"

Stefek was soon given back his stick and dressed in a long nightshirt, and a spoonful of medicine was poured down his throat by force. . . .

Stefek couldn't remember how long he'd been at that hospital. When he had relearned how to eat and drink like a human being, he was transferred to an orphanage.

In the orphanage, Stefek always ate off in a corner by himself, and he never played with anyone else. He didn't want to leave his stick for even a minute, lest it get lost. . . .

The teachers instructed the children not to touch Stefek's stick. But even so, Stefek couldn't be convinced to leave his stick and go play with the other children. . . .

Once, a young man who was one of the children's caregivers noticed Stefek sitting alone in a corner while the other children played. He asked, "Why don't you go play with the children? Are you afraid to leave your stick for a little while? Who will take it? Who else even wants your stick . . . ?"

The youth looked so much like Erik. And just because of that, Stefek didn't turn away, as he usually did with other children at the orphanage. He even allowed the youth to take the stick in his hands and to examine it closely. . . .

"A beautiful stick," said the young man, as Stefek kept looking at him and seeing Erik in him, "very nicely carved. But do you know, Stefek, what these carved letters mean?"

"No," answered the boy, embarrassed.

"The carving means, 'When you come into the Land, you shall plant.' . . ."

"I don't understand. . . ."

"You won't understand, Stefek, until you come into the Land."

"Into which land?"

"Into the Land of Israel, Stefek!"

"Are you sure that my father meant the Land of Israel?"

And Stefek thought, "Perhaps my parents actually traveled to the Land of Israel by another road? And that's why Papa wrote me that I should do what's carved into the stick when I get there. . . ."

Chapter 14

After a long journey on buses, trains, and a ship, Stefek arrived in the Land of Israel.

He had been rescued from the war, along with a group of children, and brought to a large village for refugee children.

The director of the village took Stefek and the others on a walk to show them the gardens that the children themselves had planted, the chicken coop, the calves, the donkey, and the sprinklers with which the children watered the orchard and the gardens.

Stefek liked the village very much, so he decided to remain there. But he kept the stick near him as before: he ate with the stick, studied in the classroom with the stick, worked with the stick, washed with the stick. . . .

The director of the children's village and the teachers told the children not to touch the stick . . . and not to bother Stefek. . . .

"A day will come when he'll leave behind the stick on his own," they promised. . . .

Months passed. Stefek became one of the best students in the children's village. He worked hard and studied hard. He would ride a donkey, take care of the horses so that they ate well, feed the hens—whatever needed to be done.

Once, during a hike, the teacher said to a group of boys including Stefek, "Guys, let's see who'll be first to climb that hill—but without holding onto anything. . . ."

At first, Stefek was in the lead, but his stick made trouble for him. . . . It looked to the boys like he was holding onto the stick. He lost the race, and that annoyed him a great deal. He thought he had lost because of his stick, and he figured, "In the note my father sent with me on my way, it said that

I should keep the stick with me until the end of the war. . . . Maybe by now the war has ended?"

"Guys!" Stefek called to his friends when he got back to the village, "just tell me, guys, is the war still on? I mean, has the war ended yet?"

"You don't know?" his friends laughed.

"If the war is still going on," he thought, "I'll wait a bit! I won't leave my stick behind in the middle of the war. . . . I'll do what it says in my father's note . . . !"

Chapter 15

Once, when Stefek was eating with his friends in the cultural center of the children's village, a voice blared from the radio: "Hurrah! Hooray! The war has ended! Peace has arrived! Peace!"

All the children in the village rejoiced. Stefek stood by the radio for a long time, thinking, "Now that the war has ended, maybe my parents will come by that other road they were going on. . . . I want to show them that I've kept the stick, exactly as it was written in Papa's note! But until they get here, I'll keep it in my closet, so that it won't bother me when I'm playing with the other boys . . . !"

When Stefek went to store his stick in the closet, he saw the old shoes and clothes that he and his friends wore to work. . . .

"No, that's not a nice enough place for my stick," he decided. "Now I have to look for the right spot for it! But where to find a good place?"

Unable to find a fitting spot for it on his own, Stefek decided to go to the director and ask his advice on where to keep the stick that was so precious to him.

Every time he thought about it, he put it off until the next day. So passed many tomorrows, and Stefek still hadn't gone to the director.

But one day, the director of the children's village sent for Stefek to come to his office.

"Stefek, do you remember Erik?" asked the director once the boy sat across from him.

Stefek looked down, so that the director wouldn't notice his tears. "Now that the war has ended, many papers have come to us from Warsaw. . . . And among them we found Erik's record book, where he wrote down a lot of things. And that's how we found out about your distinguished lineage, Stefek . . . !"

"I've said for a long time, of course, that my grandfather was one of the best doctors in Warsaw. . . ."

"A doctor isn't a distinguished lineage. Anyone who studies medicine can become a doctor! But your distinguished lineage is actually from your father's side, because your father was a grandson of Reb Jacob Guttmann, a merchant, who was not only a notable scholar but also a renowned philanthropist and supporter of all kinds of Jewish institutions. He became part of the history of the Jews of Frankfurt-am-Main. . . . Here, take the book and read for yourself who your great-grandfather was. . . . Your grandfather was also renowned for his love of Jews and Judaism and for the Land of Israel. . . . Your great-grandfather Reb Jacob Guttmann visited the Land of Israel back in the year 1868, when a journey here was no simple matter. He gave quite a bit of charity to the institutions of Jerusalem. And your stick, the one you always carry with you, also traces its lineage to your great-grandfather. He brought it from Jerusalem. From him, it passed as an inheritance to your grandfather, from your grandfather to your father, and from your father to you. . . ."

"Four generations!" Stefek exclaimed.

"Yes, four generations. . . . Now I understand why the stick is so dear to you and why you don't want to part with it."

"But I *will* have to part with the stick," Stefek interrupted the director.

"Why, Stefek?"

"Because in my father's note, it says that I should keep it only until the end of the war . . . and of course now the war has ended. . . ."

"What are you thinking of doing with your stick, Stefek?"

"I'd like to bury it in a pretty place. . . ."

"Have you found such a place yet, Stefek?"

"In our children's village, the soil is the most beautiful place . . . and besides, the carving on the stick says, 'When you come into the land, you shall plant. . . .' My father wrote to me in his note that I should do what's engraved on the stick. . . . So I'd actually like to plant it, if . . .'

"No 'ifs,' Stefek! If you want to put it into the ground, then all the land of the children's village is yours. . . . Just tell me when you want to plant it and where exactly. . . ."

"I think, Teacher, that the most appropriate time for it would be Tu Bishevat, the fifteenth of Shevat, the day when we plant in honor of the New Year of the Trees. What do you think?"

I think that's a very smart idea, Stefek. We're going to leave it for Tu Bishevat. . . ."

Stefek stood there awhile in front of the director without answering.

"What's the matter, Stefek?"

"About my name, Teacher . . . My name! It doesn't fit in the children's village. I want to change it now to something different. . . ."

"I've also found an answer to your very question in the record book. It says there that your father gave you your Jewish name after your renowned great grandfather Reb Jacob Guttmann. . . ."

"So then my name isn't Stefek but Jacob, Ya'akov!" cried the boy with great joy as he ran out of the director's office.

Stefek ran straight over to his friends, who were waiting for him in the shade of a tree in the courtyard of the children's village.

"Guys!!" he shouted. "Stefek is no longer! From today on, only Ya'akov! You hear me? My name is Ya'akov Guttmann, understood?"

Chapter 16

Many guests arrived on that Tu Bishevat at the children's village to witness the festive planting of saplings in honor of the New Year of the Trees.

With great fanfare, they walked to the small field outside the village.

The village orchestra played all kinds of tunes. The marchers sang along, each holding a sapling in one hand and a miniature flag in the other. But Stefek—Ya'akov Guttmann—held in his second hand a stick, on which an entire verse from the Torah was carved in Hebrew letters. When the marchers heard the beat of the drums, each one stopped at a predetermined spot, where holes for planting had been dug in advance.

The drummers gave another drumroll.

Before all the guests and marchers, a small boy stepped out from the first row, lifted his stick up high for all to see, and called out with a trembling voice, "I, Ya'akov Guttmann, the son of Benjamin Guttmann, the grandson of Joseph Guttmann, and the great-grandson of Reb Jacob Guttmann of Frankfurt-am-Main, am now fulfilling the instruction of my father to do what is engraved upon this stick: I am planting it together with a new sapling in honor of the New Year of the Trees."

Once again, the drummers burst into more drumming. Stefek bent down to the ground and placed a small branch into one hole and his stick into the other—but not all the way in. When he covered the hole with the dug-up earth, the tip of the stick could be seen near the top of the branch, with its last six letters of the carved verse spelling out, "and you shall plant. . . ."

After Stefek, all the children of the village planted new plantings in honor of the holiday.

With great fanfare, they walked from the newly planted field back to the village. They sang, the orchestra played, and when they reached the village school, where tables of food and drink awaited the guests and the children, the children locked arms with each other and began to dance a spirited hora.*

After that came speeches. They ate and drank their fill, danced and sang some more, and opened bottles of liquor.

But one boy ate little on that festive day.

Stefek—that is, Ya'akov Guttmann—was very agitated. It was hard for him to part with his stick, after keeping it with him for so long. . . . And so when he noticed that his friends were busy opening bottles for themselves and for the guests, he stole out quietly from the yard and ran back to the newly planted field. . . .

For a long, long time, Stefek—Ya'akov Guttmann—stood by his stick, stroking the six letters with his hand, shedding a tear, wiping a tear, kissing the letters, and whispering, "Four generations. . . ."

* Popular Jewish circle dance.

PART III

FOLKTALES, FAIRY TALES, WONDER TALES

Where Stories Come From
Ida Maze

IDA MAZE (MASSEY)
July 9, 1893–June 12, 1962

Ida Zhukovski was born in a village south of Minsk in what is now part of Belarus to Simon, an innkeeper, and his wife, Musha. The family was related to the "grandfather" of modern Yiddish literature, Mendele the Book Peddler. Ida had only about a year of formal schooling, although she listened to her brothers reciting their lessons and began a lifelong habit of acquiring her own education. In 1905, her family emigrated to New York and settled permanently the following year in Montreal, Canada. In 1912, she married Alexander Maze (Massey), a traveling salesman. The couple had three sons. She began to write poetry in her teens but published her first volume, *A mame* (A mother) in 1926, following the death of her eldest son, Bernard, at age ten.

Maze produced four books of poetry and an autobiographical novel, in addition to numerous poems and essays published in periodicals in the the United States, Canada, Poland, Argentina, Mexico, and Israel. She also coedited a literary quarterly from 1935 to 1937.

Maze served many authors as a mentor, helping them to achieve publication, and also as something of a patron who provided lodging and food in her own family's home when needed. During and after World War II, she aided in fund-raising and refugee resettlement. Her son Irving Massey, in his highly personal study *Identity and Community*, describes her activities as "the equivalent of a full-time job as social worker, placement officer, psychiatric counselor, and fund raiser, not to mention copy editor and literary agent." Maze died in 1962 in Montreal.

With an emphasis on rhythm and regular rhyme, Maze's poems can appear deceptively simple. "Where Stories Come From" offers a rich ars poetica for

Jewish storytelling, originating with generations past, located in the imagined preurban space of the isolated cottage and filtered through the natural world.

(*Ballad*)
Somewhere very far away,
Where wagons will not go—
There stands a little cottage
As it's stood for years, just so.

Sitting quiet and abandoned
Doors and shutters bolted shut,
Days and years pass; only wind blows
Through the chimney of the hut.

Everybody's known for years:
Its people all have gone away
Only wind blows in the chimney
Not a soul has come to stay.

One night when all are sleeping,
And the wind is sleeping too—
Lights come on inside the cottage
And smoke wafts up the flue.

Door and shutter are unbolted.
In a corner, by a light,
Sits a grandpa learning Torah;
A child listens with delight
To Grandpa's tales of wonder-beams,
Absorbs them through her dreams.

Hard by the hearth, a spinning wheel;
From silken thread, so thin and soft,
Grandma spins her lovely stories
And, with the smoke, sends them aloft.

The smoke takes up the grandma's stories,
Repeats them to a wind beguiled—
On its wings the wind will spread them,
Giving some to every child.

The Magnate of Jerusalem

Sholem Asch

SHOLEM ASCH

1880–July 10, 1957

For biographical information on Asch, see "A Village Saint" in part 1. "The Magnate of Jerusalem," with its plot of fortunes lost and gained, explores the link between generosity and prosperity. With its dreamy imagining of another's consciousness, the story calls to mind the short, experimental fictions of Jorge Luís Borges.

— ℬ —

Long ago, in the holy city of Jerusalem, lived a Jew who was both very wealthy and very charitable. People all over knew of his pious virtue. From Safed and Tiberias, from Damascus and Hebron, and wherever else our Jewish brethren had settled, the poor and needy would drag themselves to the wealthy man seeking help. And he would open his hand wide and give of his wealth to all who were in need. He did so because he thought of himself as God's messenger: he was simply doling out what God had entrusted to him for the poor and needy. Moreover, since the rich man was also very wise and devout, all those who were heartsick or suffering from bad thoughts or whose minds wouldn't let them rest—as happens to people who have sinned—they would all come to him to ask for advice both in matters concerning the soul and the body, such as money troubles, and in other such similar worries. The magnate would listen to each of them with great affection and loyalty, and to one he would offer sound advice with his sharp intellect, while he would heal another with a kind word from his generous heart.

It had always been the magnate's habit, before each day was done, to sit alone in his beautiful rabbinical chamber and to devote some time to making a spiritual accounting for himself of that entire day's deeds. For the good ones, he praised God, and for the bad ones, he felt regret and repented; his good deeds he swiftly forgot, but his bad ones he inscribed with a sharp quill in a book that lay open before him for hours at a time, so that he would see them and never again repeat them.

One evening, he was sitting in his rabbinical chamber, as was his custom, rendering judgment and account for the whole day's deeds. All around the room were expensive bookcases full to the brim with valuable holy books and rare manuscripts, selected from around the world, wherever sages and scholars happened to be dispersed—for the magnate had his emissaries in every far-flung place. As soon as a great scholar or sage was found somewhere faraway, in Egypt or Turkey, where the Muslims were settled, and that scholar or sage wrote up some novel idea in the realm of Torah or philosophy, it was immediately copied and the manuscript sent to the magnate in Jerusalem. The books were covered by curtains decorated with exotic fruits that were elegantly woven with gold and silver threads, the very rarest fruits that grow. The fruits were woven in the far reaches of India, and they were ordered specially by the rich man, so that there should be no images of animals or birds,* for those were forbidden.

On the table before the rich man stood an ornate spice box hammered from a single piece of silver, in the shape of a rare fruit that grew in the farthest reaches of the Land of Kattim. And into that fruit were carved pictures of others: lemons, citrons, hanging bunches of grapes, and pomegranates— but not a single picture of a person or an animal, as this was strictly forbidden by Jewish law. Each fruit was drawn in the same tint and hue as when it grows on the tree. As is well-known, the Kattites were great experts at imitating the colors and the light of nature. For example, the hanging bunches of grapes appeared so fresh and red, beaded with droplets of wine that flowed from the precious stones called rubies, which we no longer know the secret of melting—but the Kattites had kept a record, and they knew how. Thus was each fruit painted in its own color, so that they might remind the rich man of God's Creation and he would always remember God's works. The fruit-shaped spice box was filled with the most precious spices, which

---

* This is a strict interpretation of the biblical injunction against graven images, meant to convey the man's piety.

the Indians had exported from their faraway lands. He himself wore silken garments that gladdened his heart whenever he donned them, for they had a bright silver sparkle and a happy song woven into them.

The magnate was very pleased with himself and with the Master of the Universe, his Creator. He'd had a day full of good deeds and charity, with study and prayer, and he'd had nothing to record in his book of sins. He thanked God in his heart that he'd been chosen as his emissary and that he was the giver and not the recipient of charity. But on this day, the rich man was even more cheerful than usual, for he had performed a great mitzvah, a commandment, that can seldom be fulfilled. His accountant, who had just returned from a trip with the caravans that carried spices from India to Turkey, had informed him that while in Izmir, he had performed on the rich man's behalf the commandment to redeem the captive by releasing Jews from the Turks, who had brought them as captives from the Slavic lands. The magnate was overjoyed with the mitzvah, and he heard that his caravans had arrived safely at the seashore and their cargo had been loaded onto ships. His wife, who was both very beautiful and very virtuous, waited behind the door with their two children so that they could pay their respects before going to bed.

In the midst of all this, the door opened, and in came a poor man, wretched and lonely. The foul odor that preceded him overpowered the good smell of the spices, and the rich man felt weak because he was fastidious and couldn't stand bad smells. But the poor man didn't stop at the door; he entered and walked right up to the magnate, his hand outstretched in a hearty greeting. And the hand was full of grime and other ugly things that aren't nice to talk about and especially not to write about in detail. His whole body was wrapped in filthy clothing, from which bits of his naked flesh poked out, soiled with dirt, and locks of hair were matted onto his face and crept forth from his head. His was not the face of a human being but rather that of an ugly animal, God help us, with swollen lips, broken teeth, and bulging eyes. The closer he came, the stronger was the stench that he gave off, like the stink of a carcass or a rotting corpse, God help us, and the magnate couldn't stand it any longer, because as everyone knows, a fastidious man can take anything but a bad odor. So the rich man pulled back from the poor one, turned aside, and called for his attendant to lead the poor man out of the rabbinical chamber and into the kitchen, where he could get washed up, dressed in other clothes, and fed—all according to the custom of his house with anybody poor.

The magnate quickly entered his ritual bath, to immerse and change his clothes, and he called for his rabbinical chamber to be aired out with all sorts of fine herbs and spices to dispel the stench that the poor man had left behind. Then he sat down to wait in his luxurious bedroom, which was hung with silk and silver tapestries and was illuminated by a precious oil lamp with seven branches, which hung over his bed. The rich man couldn't sleep all night, and deep in his heart, he took up his complaints with the Master of the Universe, who had created such outcasts and wretches. He thought about the course of human life and how, if it had been up to him, he would have created only beautiful and clean people and not allowed such wretched outcasts into the world.

A bit of time passed, and the magnate heard that the ships carrying his spices overseas from Izmir to Venice had been overtaken by pirates and captured. Naturally, the rich man thought that perhaps it was a coincidence—just an accident. And he thanked God for the bad as well as for the good.

A bit more time elapsed, and he heard that the caravans carrying his merchandise from Egypt had been blocked by a desert sandstorm. He realized then that it was no coincidence; so he began to examine his deeds and opened up the book where he had inscribed his sins, but he didn't see anything in the record of his life to suggest that he deserved such punishment. He thought about it, though, and realized that if the Master of the Universe no longer wanted him to serve as the treasurer of his wealth, then that was his right. Thank God all he was losing was money.

But soon his body was affected: he was plagued with terrible afflictions that caused him great misery and made him feel disgusting, because he was fastidious. So once again he examined his deeds, looked over his actions and found nothing, and concluded that God was only taking out his anger on his body but would preserve his soul untouched. For this, God was to be praised.

But then his little daughter, to whose soul his own was bound and whom he loved more than ten sons, was suddenly taken from him. He was seized by a great terror before God's judgment, to which he was being called, with no idea of how he had sinned. So he began to probe and investigate himself, but he couldn't arrive at the reason for God's punishment. He didn't know any path forward, and the pain of his uncertainty grew even greater than the pain of his troubles themselves.

One night, when he was lying down and thinking over why bad things happen to good people and why good things happen to bad people, it occurred to him that he should go out and wander the world, and perhaps God would take pity on him and let him know his reasons. This thought was actually from God, who, in his mercy, could no longer bear the man's suffering.

So the magnate sold off his valuables and gave the money to his wife and children so that they would be able to continue living as they were used to: giving charity and hosting guests. As for himself, he took off his expensive woven clothing and donned sackcloth, according to the custom of the poor, and set out to wander the world.

He traveled with a band of beggars he met on the road. By day, he wandered with the poor people, eating what kind people donated, and at night, he slept over in poorhouses. He never spent more than one night in a single place. All day he'd make do with dry food, which kind people had given. On Friday nights, he stopped in a city where there was a Jewish community, went into the study house, and placed himself by the door with the other poor people, until a Jew who wanted to perform a mitzvah took pity and brought home a guest for Shabbos. Wherever he went, he heard stories about himself—the great magnate of Jerusalem. The mothers blessed their children that they should be so virtuous, rich, and wealthy as the magnate of Jerusalem. He heard them telling wonder tales about him, of his outrageous wealth, his wisdom, and his virtue. The poor people with whom he wandered mocked and shamed him for his fastidiousness. The fact was that he wasn't used to the hardships of the roads they traveled or to their manner of eating, sleeping, and speaking coarsely, and they scoffed at him, "What are you, the magnate of Jerusalem?" And they gave him a mocking nickname, in keeping with their habit, "the magnate of Jerusalem."

And that's what he came to be called.

Wandering around from one place to another, his body became very filthy, and in the way of beggars who go around in torn rags in order to awaken more sympathy, he didn't attend to his clothing either. Over time, parts of his body poked out through the torn rags and grew quite dirty, just like the body of the poor man who had come to call on him. The dirt also made him start to smell very foul. But he was no longer sensitive to the smell because now it came from his own body and not from a stranger's.

Very gradually, his name faded out, as is the way of the world; one soon forgets what was—and he was forgotten. No longer did anyone speak of the Jerusalem magnate and giver of charity, but instead they spoke of the new rich man who had arisen in Damascus. They told stories of his eminence and wealth, as they once had about the magnate of Jerusalem. Jews from all over were drawn to seek counsel from the magnate of Damascus.

He went to Damascus as well. He'd heard that the man in Damascus was very wise and very generous, and he wanted to seek his advice; perhaps he could explain the reason why God had taken away his wealth and given it to another, to the magnate of Damascus. So he traveled from one city to another until he came to Damascus.

His hair was matted with dust and sand. His body gave off a stench, like the body of a corpse, God help us, and his face was swollen and full of dirt—just like the face of the poor man who had come to him when he'd been the magnate of Jerusalem. But he didn't notice any of it, because it was his own body and not a stranger's.

When he arrived at the home of the Damascus magnate, he found him sitting in silken garments, as he himself had done long ago in his large rabbinical chamber. And the room sparkled and glowed, like the moon and stars, because of the gemstones that shone from the curtains and the crowns that were hanging across the large cupboards, and there was the pleasant scent of precious spices and all kinds of fragrant herbs, which the spice boxes gave off from every corner of the room. He thought that he had come back into his wealth, which he had just now lost—so he walked with an outstretched hand to greet the magnate of Damascus, his peer.

But the rich man of Damascus turned away and called to his attendant, "Take this poor man into the kitchen. The room is full of a foul odor."

At this, the magnate of Jerusalem suddenly recalled something, and at last he understood. Seized by a great joy, he proclaimed, "God and his judgment are correct!"

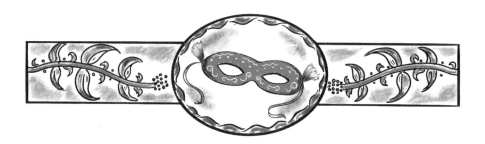

The King and the Rabbi
Solomon Bastomski

SOLOMON BASTOMSKI
July 1891–March 5, 1941

Born into the family of a poor locksmith, Bastomski was orphaned at an early age. He studied in both a traditional Jewish elementary school and a Russian public school for Jewish youth. After graduating from the Vilna Pedagogical Institute in 1912, he gained teaching experience in Russian Jewish schools until he was ready to open a school where Yiddish was the language of instruction. Bastomski's career teaching at and administering that school exemplified how Yiddish children's literature grew out of the needs of the Yiddish school system.

It is difficult to overstate his role in developing literary and educational materials for Yiddish-speaking children or the extent to which the needs of his charges would shape his career. He created a publishing house devoted to disseminating textbooks (in several subjects, including mathematics), school readers, games, folklore, popular science, travelogues, biographies, and literature. He authored several of the titles. Bastomski also founded and edited two children's periodicals and contributed to pedagogical journals. He was politically committed to strengthening Jewish life and Yiddish culture in the diaspora, supporting a group that advocated for a continued Jewish presence in Europe rather than emigration to Palestine.

In seeking authentically Jewish sources to enrich the lives of schoolchildren from secular-leaning families, Bastomski gave pride of place to folklore and folk materials. He worked as a *zamler*, or collector, of folk songs, legends, and proverbs. "The King and the Rabbi" reflects these tendencies, wedding some of the features of the European fairy tale (the royal setting, the significance of coincident birthdays) with the stuff of Jewish holidays (a wicked adviser plotting against the Jews as in the Purim tale), values (Torah study over the trappings of wealth), and history (the blood libel).

Bastomski's partner in his creative endeavors was his wife, Malka Khaymson, born in 1888 in the nearby town of Eyshishok. Bastomski died in March 1941, just before the Nazis occupied Vilna. Khaymson died in Vilna's Jewish ghetto shortly thereafter.

— ℬ —

Once upon a time, in a faraway land, lived a king. An old man came to him in a dream and said, "Your Royal Highness, something terrible is going to befall you, and the only one who can save you is a man who was born in the same year, in the same month, and on the same day as you."

As soon as the king awoke, he gave an order to search in all the cities and towns of his kingdom for a man who was born in the same year, in the same month, and on the same day as he.

They searched in every corner of the kingdom but couldn't find such a man.

Suddenly, word was brought to the king that somewhere in a far-flung town lived a Jew who was born in the same year, in the same month, and on the same day as the king—and even at the very same hour.

He was a famous tzaddik, a rabbi known for his wisdom and kindness.

The king was overjoyed at the good news, and he suddenly felt the urge to lay eyes on the man who could save him from the grave danger.

He mounted a horse and set out for the Jew's town. He traveled alone in disguise, without an entourage.

Arriving in town, he began to ask after the man by name, to find out where he lived.

He was shown to a little hut at the edge of town. He entered and saw how poverty blew like a wind into all the corners.

He asked of the woman who was there, "Where is your husband?"

She replied, "He's sitting and studying Torah in the study house."

So the king went to the study house, and as soon as he'd crossed the threshold, an old man approached him and recited the blessing over seeing royalty, "Blessed is he who has apportioned some of his glory to human beings."

The king wondered how the old man had recognized him.

The tzaddik said, "That shouldn't surprise you at all, and what's more, I know why you came."

He invited the king back to his home.

Stepping inside, the tzaddik told his wife that they had an esteemed guest and that they should honor him by setting out the best food and drink they could, whatever it was.

His wife replied that, in fact, there was simply nothing to offer him.

So he sent her out to a store and asked her to borrow a hand mirror there.

She brought back the mirror, and the tzaddik turned to the king, saying, "Your Royal Highness, gaze into this mirror, and you'll see something."

The king gazed into the mirror and saw in it the entire world.

"What do you see?" the tzaddik asked.

"I see the whole world," replied the king.

"Now think just of your kingdom," said the tzaddik.

The king gazed into the mirror again.

"Now what do you see?"

"I see my kingdom," said the king.

"Now think just of the capital city," said the tzaddik, and he asked, "What do you see now?"

"I see my palace."

"Now just think of your chambers in the palace. What do you see?"

"I see the prime minister sitting in my chambers on my own chair," replied the king, "and next to him sits my wife the queen."

"Listen to what they're saying," urged the tzaddik. The king bent his ear to the mirror and listened, and he heard them plotting to bring down the old king and seat the prime minister upon his throne.

The tzaddik looked at the king's face and saw that it had turned deathly pale. The tzaddik asked, "Your Highness, what is the punishment for plotting against the life of the king?"

"A rebel against the king is liable for the death penalty," replied the king.

The tzaddik instructed the king to gaze into the mirror once more.

Just then he saw in the glass the prime minister's dead body.

Then the tzaddik took the mirror, hurled it down to the ground, and shattered it into pieces.

"Now you know what's going on in the palace," said the tzaddik to the king. "Go home, make a ball there, and don't sit down at table until I arrive. And I'll ask of you one thing more: don't sign any piece of paper until that time either."

The king was beside himself with wonder.

"I see," said the king to the tzaddik, "that you are a great and holy man. Help me to understand one thing: why are you so poor? After all, you were born under the same stars as I was."

The tzaddik smiled and answered, "You, Your Royal Highness, are rich in belongings, and I am rich in my Torah. . . ."

The king parted from the tzaddik and set out for home.

Now let's see, what was going on in the capital while the king was away?

When the queen saw the prime minister struck dead, she was very frightened. She decided to cover up the whole matter.

She had a loyal servant whom she summoned and swore to secrecy. She ordered him to carry the dead body down to the cellar and to bury it there among the casks of wine.

By the next morning, people had begun to notice that the prime minister was missing from the king's court. They searched for him—nothing. They started to ask around and to investigate—but no one knew anything.

Since the Passover holiday was approaching, the courtiers reasoned that the Jews had probably killed him.* So the representatives of the Jewish community were brought into the court and told that they must produce the guilty party; if not, all the Jews would be exterminated. . . .

The Jews swore that they knew nothing about the matter. No one believed their oath, and the court pronounced all the Jews guilty of murder and handed down the following sentence: all the Jews must gather together in one place, they must all shut their eyes and form a line, and every third one would be killed. Their belongings would be taken out and divided in this manner: half to the royal treasury and the other half to the widow and heirs of the minister. Those Jews who survived must pull down their clothes and

---

* This sort of lie, or "blood libel," to the effect that the Jews used Christian blood as an ingredient for the Passover matzah, served as a pretext to attack Jews and Jewish communities. Matzah can only be made of flour and water.

strip naked, and several of them must shave half their beards and one side-lock and be chased out of town mercilessly by mounted soldiers.

This was all written down as a royal edict, and they waited only for the king to sign it.

When the king returned from his journey, the members of his entourage came to him and recounted the story of how the Jews had killed the prime minister and been sentenced to death.

And they held out the document for him to sign.

The king said, "We should set this aside for several days," for he wanted to celebrate first with a ball in honor of his birthday.

On the appointed day, the richest men and leading citizens of the whole land gathered in the palace, and a ball was arranged with splendor beyond compare.

They danced and leaped, played and sang, and they ate and drank the finest and best. Only one person felt like an outsider at the celebration. That was the king himself. He wandered around the halls preoccupied, without tasting a morsel.

Everyone wondered, "What could *this* be about?"

Everyone supposed that he felt that way because of the sudden death of his minister, who had served the king so long and so loyally.

When the ball was in full swing, an old Jew with a gray beard, dressed in rags, with a sack on his back, appeared suddenly at the door. No one had noticed how or whence he'd come.

There was a commotion: "How did a dirty Jew get in here, to the king's ball?"

But soon everyone was stunned, for the king himself went over to the poor Jew, led him to the table, and seated him right near his own place. Everyone watched and wondered what was going on.

The king was instantly transformed. Gone was his sorrow, and a radiant smile shone on his face.

The choicest delicacies were brought to him at table, and only now did the celebration properly begin.

The old man didn't so much as glance at the delicacies.

After the meal, the document was brought to the king for his signature. He set the paper aside and ordered his servants to bring him the best wine in his cellars.

They brought him a cask of the finest wine. The king passed the first cup to the old man. The tzaddik sniffed at it and said, "It smacks of a carcass."

The king held it to his lips and said, "Yes, indeed, it smells like a carcass."

Everyone tried it—when the king says it, there's no doubt he's right.

It remained only to check the cellar and see where the wine cask had been stored.

So they went down to the cellar but found nothing—just cask after cask.

The king commanded them to search underneath the casks.

They looked and saw fresh earth.

After digging a bit, they found the corpse of the minister. . . .

They came out and told the king. A loud clamor, a wild din, arose among the assembled.

The king wanted to turn to the tzaddik for advice. But he wasn't there; he'd disappeared.

It remains only to add that the king never did sign the death warrant, and the Jews observed a joyful and happy Passover.

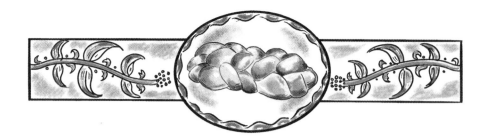

The Baker and the Beggar

Kadya Molodowsky

KADYA MOLODOWSKY
May 10, 1894–March 23, 1975

Kadya Molodowsky was a poet, an educator, and the author of many works for children in both poetry and prose. She was born into a traditional family that saw to her religious education but also schooled her in "modern" subjects such as Jewish history and Modern Hebrew grammar. She earned a teaching certificate and continued her education in Hebrew-language acquisition at a specialized institute in Warsaw. She was displaced from the city by World War I and began teaching refugee children in various settings. After the war, she settled down with her husband in Warsaw, where she taught in the secular school system and began to publish her poetry in Yiddish journals. She also worked as an editor at literary journals during this period. In 1935, Molodowsky emigrated to New York, where her husband joined her in 1938. She spent the rest of her life in the States, except for a two-year stint (1950–52) in Tel Aviv, and she published several volumes of poetry.

  "The Baker and the Beggar," along with "Zelig the Rhymester" (in part 4) and "A Story of a Schoolboy and a Goat" (in part 6), appeared in a section called "Schoolboys" of her 1970 collection of stories and poems for children, *Martsepanes* (Marzipans). These stories, set in the vanished European shtetl, incorporate many folkloric elements and reflect a child's-eye view whereby biblical figures are close at hand and keenly interested in the inner lives of children.

— ❦ —

Once upon a time, there was a baker with his own shop, who made bread, rolls, pretzels, bagels, and challah for Shabbos.

His wife would tie up her hair in a scarf and knead the dough, and the children would twist the bagels into circles.

The whole town delighted in their pretzels and bagels. Even the birds would swoop down from the sky in order to catch the crumbs, and their tail feathers twitched with pleasure.

Every Friday, poor Jews would come to the bakery to beg food for Shabbos. That was the custom of the time, the time of our grandparents. The baker would give them a roll, a bagel, a pretzel, whatever he could spare. And no one left empty-handed.

One of the poor Jews had very special eyes, so radiant that they sent forth beams of light. The baker liked him best of all, and each Friday, he would give the man an entire challah for Shabbos.

So it went week after week, Friday after Friday, over many years. The baker became so accustomed to the man's visits that he would look forward to them. He would hand the beggar the challah personally and say, "Eat in good health, and may all be well with you."

The man never thanked him; he just smiled with his bright eyes and replied, "May you live long, and may God repay you."

One Friday that happened to also be the eve of a holiday, the bakery was crowded with customers, who pushed and crushed against each other. This one wanted a challah with poppy seeds; that one, a loaf of white bread ("but make sure it's sweet!"). . . . The baker, his wife, and their children were so busy that by day's end, they could hardly stand.

Along came the bright-eyed man. He saw the great rush, so he didn't want to bother the baker just then. He stood there for a while and then left without saying so much as a word.

After that Friday, the beggar stopped coming. A week passed and then two and three. The baker thought of him many times and asked the other poor people about him—but eventually he forgot about the man. Who keeps thinking about a poor man? Perhaps God had helped him, and he no longer needed to beg.

The bakery prospered. The baker had built a fine house with a large oven. His wife had sewn herself a new woolen jacket, and their children now wore shoes without holes and flannel jackets. They had bought drinking glasses and spoons by the half dozen, and they thanked God for providing these little luxuries.

But no one's good luck lasts forever. One Friday, a fire broke out in the bakery. It burnt up the sacks of flour, the shelves, and the whole house; everything the baker possessed disappeared with the smoke.

The baker stood there slumped with worry, staring at the cinders of the burnt walls. And near him stood his wife and the children like lonely sheep. The baker thought, "God in Heaven, why have you brought such a punishment upon us? Why must I endure such a bitter blow? Shabbos is coming, and we're left without a roof over our heads."

The neighbors came and echoed the baker's sadness: "Really, why should this have happened to the baker? He's such an honest man!"

While the baker was standing there worried and despondent, not knowing what to do—*just then*, along came the poor man who had not come to the bakery in a long time.

The baker was dumbfounded. Of all times to return, the poor man had to come now to see him in the midst of this great misfortune? He ran up to the man and said with a broken spirit, "You see, sir, what has happened to me! Everything burnt, lock, stock, and barrel! Now I don't even have challah for Shabbos for myself."

With eyes beaming, the man said, "I didn't come to ask you for challah. God has changed my luck and freed me from poverty. Now I have what I need and can repay the debts of what I have borrowed from generous people."

From his pocket, the man took out a bundled kerchief and handed it to the baker, who was astonished. "Here," said the man, "you have the repayment for all the challahs you gave me week after week, from Friday to Friday, over many, many years. I have added it all up and thought of everything, and my calculations are right. You may be certain I've made no error."

It was enough for a house and an oven and a bakery and even for a woolen jacket for the baker's wife and for flannel jackets for the children. The baker was absolutely amazed: the price of every challah was recorded: each and every loaf, from week to week, Friday to Friday, year to year—and not a crumb was missing.

A Boy and His Samovar

Jacob Reisfeder

JACOB REISFEDER
September 18, 1890–January 1943 (Warsaw Ghetto)

Reisfeder was born in Warsaw to a Hasidic family and received a traditional education in *kheyder* and yeshivas. He began to publish as a young man. He left for Argentina in 1923 but subsequently returned to Warsaw.

His first publications were slices of life and feuilletons in Warsaw's daily press, and he worked as a staff writer for *Haynt* (Today) from 1911 to 1915. Later, he wrote sketches, longer fiction, poetry, and stories and plays for children. His work was published in Warsaw, New York, Riga, and Argentina. A three-act play that he wrote toured Poland. He died in the Warsaw Ghetto, and little record of his life and prolific work has been preserved.

"A Boy and His Samovar" dramatizes the ethical fantasy of a child exposing the illogic of (adult) warfare and persuading the powers that be to choose peace. The king's edict threatens to symbolically reverse biblical Isaiah's promise that swords will be beat into plowshares, but the innocent boy is able to prevent such a sad eventuality.

— ℬ —

Once upon a time, there was a ruler who waged wars of conquest with all the other nations for so long that he eventually began to run out of guns for his soldiers, and there was no longer any brass or lead left in his country to make bullets. The ruler was scared, because now all the other nations were ganging up and making a push to conquer *his* land. He didn't feel like surrendering.

So he issued an order to his people that within three days, everybody must turn over all of the lead, copper, and brass vessels that could be found in their homes. And out of fear, everyone brought their metal vessels to the collection points.

Among the poor folk, there lived a quiet, graceful boy with blond hair and clever, blue eyes of rare beauty. He was a very curious boy who wanted to know everything in the world and would gaze at everything for a long time and wonder, Where does this stream lead? Where are the little clouds floating to up above? How do birds build their nests? How do the flowers in the field grow, and how do people make the bread that I eat each day? He also liked to keep very quiet and listen closely to adult conversations, which nobody could stand. But worst of all were his strange questions: Why did some children go around in tatters and bare feet in the cold, while others were nicely dressed in overcoats and fancy pants? Who would get all the pretty dolls, hobby horses, and books that filled the shops—and that the poor children were dying for but would never receive? Why were there poor and rich in the world at all? Wouldn't it be better if everyone were equal? And his questions went on and on. . . .

The boy had a beautiful little brass samovar that was cleverly designed and decorated with red silk ribbons and colorful cut paper, which his parents had given him as a present for his fifth birthday. That had been two years ago; now he was seven. But the samovar still shone like new. It sat by the window on a special little table and sparkled in the sun like gold, so often did the boy polish and clean it. Of all his nice things, it was the very best toy he had.

He loved to pretend that his friends were coming over—ooh, here they were now!—and the little samovar was boiling. Once it was steaming, he would pour out the tea from his own samovar into his own little teacups and would drink it, beaming with pleasure: ah, that must really be what it feels like to be grown up. . . .

The boy gazed at his reflection in his samovar and guarded it like the apple of his eye. . . .

In those days, when they were collecting all the copper and brass from every household, the boy quietly and sadly listened in on the adult conversations about how the metal vessels would be used. After that, he went around silently, with tears in his little eyes and a grieving heart. . . .

He was thinking about his dear Papa, who'd been killed in the war somewhere. He had left, kissing him just like that, and never come back.

"Why?" wondered the sad little boy. "Whom had he ever hurt?" He was really such a good Papa. . . .

The next morning, as his mother was gathering all the metal vessels in the house to carry away, she cast a glance at his samovar and felt a surge of pity for her child. She knew quite well how precious the little samovar was to him, how unhappy she would make him by taking it away. But she couldn't leave it behind, because if it was found in her possession later on, she would be punished harshly. The ruler was mean, and his guards hadn't a glimmer of mercy in their hearts.

She reached out to take the samovar. But the little boy threw himself down on it with a clatter, gripped it tightly in both hands, and began to scream, as if with something more than his own little voice, "No! No! No! I won't let anyone take my samovar! I won't allow it!"

He stamped his feet and pitched a fit.

The mother took pity on her only child and let go of his samovar.

"But hide it really well so that they won't find it," she begged.

So the boy hid his precious samovar in a good, safe place. But from time to time, he would take it out when he was seized by a strong urge to play with it.

Once, the city guards were going from house to house, looking for any remaining metal vessels that hadn't been properly turned in.

They came into the boy's house unexpectedly and caught him playing right by the window with his little brass samovar.

"Hey, you scamp!" they shouted at him. "You're actually playing with brass?! You can play with plain paper, and your samovar can be used for more important things. . . . Quick, give it here!"

But with extraordinary strength, the boy grabbed hold of the samovar and begged the furious guards, "Have mercy, please don't take my samovar."

"You can play with something else!" screamed the policemen.

"I don't need to play with anything at all," cried the boy. "But I won't give up this samovar. And what's more, I know what you want it for . . . !"

The boy sobbed so pitifully that the policemen were moved.

"But it's no use, little boy," they said, stroking his head. "We can't help you at all. The ruler has ordered everyone in the land to turn over all of their copper and brass."

"So take me to the ruler," the boy blurted out. "I will ask him not to order me to give up my samovar."

The policemen smiled at that, and out of curiosity, they led him to their superior and told him about the boy's request. He laughed heartily and sent him on to someone even higher up, and so on, until the boy came before the ruler.

The ruler already knew what the boy had come to ask of him, so he said to him with a smile, "Why do you need it so much, little boy, this samovar? I will order that you be given other toys in return, even nicer ones than the samovar."

"I don't need *any* toys," the boy replied. "I can get along without playing. . . ."

"But then why don't you want to give up the samovar?" the ruler asked, interested.

At this point, the boy burst into sobs and whimpered, "Because I don't want my samovar to be made into bullets that will kill someone else's dear Papa as my dear Papa was killed. . . ."

And the boy wept even more bitterly.

The ruler trembled at the boy's words and bowed his head in thought. Then he took the child onto his lap and gave him an affectionate kiss. "You precious, clever boy! No, nobody's going to take away your samovar. . . ."

The ending was a very happy one: because of that boy's words, which had touched the ruler so deeply, he issued an edict before the day was out returning the metal vessels that had been taken from everyone. They would no longer be needed, because the ruler had finally realized that too much blood had already been spilled, and the war could finally come to an end . . .

Roses and Emeralds
Judah Steinberg

JUDAH STEINBERG
1863–March 10, 1908

The older cousin of poet Eliezer Shteynbarg, Judah was born in Lipkany, Bessarabia, to a devoutly Hasidic family. He was drawn to Jewish Enlightenment thought and taught himself mathematics, German, and science. His father pressured him to marry at seventeen in the hope that he would settle down into traditional religious thought and practice. The young couple lived with the bride's family in a village near the Romanian town of Shtepaneshty, a Hasidic center. Steinberg appreciated Hasidism in its rural guise and at the same time made friends with a local proponent of Enlightenment who offered him literature but did not seek to draw him away from Hasidic practice.

He returned to Lipkany to work as a teacher after about three years, but in 1889, the tension with his father led him to move to a nearby town. His first writing, a Hebrew style manual, grew out of his work in the classroom. His first anthology, *In Town and Forest*, established his literary talent and gained the notice of writers in Warsaw and Odessa. He moved to the shtetl of Liova in 1897 and continued teaching, but he also began to publish what would amount to hundreds of fables, stories, legends, Hasidic tales, and children's stories. In 1905, he left teaching in order to write full-time as the Odessa correspondent for the New York–based Yiddish paper *Di vorheyt* (Reality). In 1908, he was diagnosed with neck cancer, which proved fatal. After his death, Yankev Fichmann compiled his writing into four volumes.

Steinberg's work seamlessly fused neo-Hasidic and socialist values. "Roses and Emeralds" is a well-crafted folktale decrying selfishness.

— ℬ —

Once upon a time, there was a worldwide famine. Everyone went hungry, for there was nothing to eat. Hungriest of all were the residents of a small village that was very famous in those days. Only two people in that village didn't know hunger.

One of them was Korach the Miser. He didn't know hunger, but neither did he know satiety, because he was so stingy that he begrudged himself bread and meat—which are very expensive in times of famine. Every day, he sold off part of his own meal for cash. He didn't go hungry, though, because his warehouses were full of grain.

The second was Isaac the Blacksmith, who had saved up a little of his earnings from better times. When the famine began and he could no longer find work, he sat back and ate from his reserves. He also took pity on the poor and shared his few mouthfuls with them.

But this didn't last long, and the little bit of money he'd saved grew smaller and smaller until it was all gone. Hunger slipped into Isaac's house, and from time to time, his little boy, Hillel, went to bed without dinner.

Once Hillel was standing in the doorway, holding in his hand a small piece of bread that his mother had given him for lunch, telling him to leave some over for his dinner, because there was no more bread in the house. The boy stood there, chewing and considering the little piece of bread in his hand. He looked at it and wondered: Should he eat any more, or should he stop eating and leave the rest for dinner? As he stood there thinking, an old, lame pauper passed by, leaning on a cane, with a sack on his shoulder. The poor man came over to him, fixed a pair of sad eyes on him, and begged for a bit of bread.

The boy took pity on the hungry pauper and handed over his last crust.

The old beggar regarded the good boy with gratitude and asked him quietly, "You like roses, Sonny?"

"Sure," the boy replied cheerfully. "I love roses."

So the old man took a little bottle of pure, clear liquid out of his sack and gave it to the boy, saying, "When you sprinkle this liquid on wild grasses and thorns, they will turn into roses." With that, the beggar left.

Meanwhile, Korach's son, Nevel, a boy of fourteen, was standing on the street corner eating candy, which he had bought with money he'd stolen from his father. He saw what Hillel had done and what the beggar had given him. He was terribly jealous of Hillel. So he ran after the beggar, caught him, and said, "Here, Grandpa, take this candy and give me a better present than the one you gave the blacksmith's son, because I'm giving you candy, which is better than a crust of bread."

When the old man heard this, he smiled, took out of his sack a little bottle of dark liquid, and passed it to the boy, saying, "When you pour this liquid on dry grasses and thorns, they will turn into emeralds."

An emerald is a kind of precious gem that looks like a person's eye, and inside is a glistening point, like a teardrop. Here's the amazing thing about emeralds: as soon as you catch a glimpse of one, you want to keep on looking and looking at it. The eye and the soul cannot be satisfied even after an entire day of staring. But the longer you look, the sadder and more dejected you become. It reminds you of your own sorrows and the joys of others, and it makes you jealous. It reminds you of all the ways your friends have it better than you do and makes you resent them. And people who see emeralds can never again live without jealousy and hatred.

Nevel ran home as fast as he could, afraid to look back lest the beggar think twice and take back the magical little bottle he had given him.

When he got home, he began to calculate how many emeralds he could get out of the little bottle of magic liquid, how much money he could accumulate from selling them to the wealthy, and how many groschen he could gather from the poor, for letting them look at his beautiful emeralds. He reckoned and tallied up the great fortune that he would collect, until he had to stop because he could count no higher.

"If only enough thorns would grow," he thought happily, "then I could rake in the gold like sand."

Hillel was also pleased with the gift that the beggar had given him.

"Oh, how many thorns grow upon the earth!" thought Hillel. "They tear the flesh of anyone who touches them, and they serve no purpose. Everybody hates and avoids them, and now I can turn the wretched thorns into lovely, fragrant roses. Then, everyone will love them, and they will love everyone . . . especially me—'cause after all, *I'll* be the one who turned them into roses!"

So it was that both boys left their village and set out into the world to sprinkle their potions. Hillel passed through many desert wastelands, and wherever he went, he sprinkled his liquid and turned thorns into roses. In the morning and at dusk, the roses would spread their fine fragrance and fill the air with it, and the wasteland would turn into a Garden of Eden. The wild animals of the forest didn't dare trample on the beautiful roses, nor did the dark clouds dare to pour out their storms there; the hail clouds saw the roses and ran away, ashamed. Only the sunbeams and light breezes swirled about them and played with them.

Songbirds came and got to know the lovely roses, and with their song, they swore to them eternal love.

People also began to go and enjoy the beauty of the roses and their wonderful fragrance. And the roses possessed a magical power: just as soon as people saw them and breathed in a little of their fragrance, their hearts would be filled with joy and love beyond measure. Lifelong enemies would forget their hatred and embrace each other fondly.

Now people came to settle in the former desert.

Only the old folks could still remember that the place was once a barren and empty wasteland, where only wild animals lived. The children heard their grandfathers' stories and couldn't believe them. "Is it possible?" they would ask themselves, "that this Garden of Eden should have once been no more than a wilderness?"

And Nevel, Korach's son, had also left his home and village and come to a place where he bought a piece of land and seeded it with all kinds of thorns. When they were fully grown, he sprinkled them with the liquid from his bottle, and large, beautiful emeralds blossomed. When people saw the emeralds, they marveled at their sparkle and their similarity to human eyes. A lot of them really couldn't believe that they were *not* human eyes.

"Can't you see?" many insisted. "Don't you recognize that these are eyes, real eyes, unfortunate and lost?"

All who saw the emeralds turned sad and bitter. They were reminded of their own sorrows and of their friends' joy, and people couldn't look each other in the eye out of jealousy and hatred.

The old folks would often gather at dusk and talk about things that had and had not happened, what should and should not have been, and they spoke also of Nevel and his gemstones. One old man said, "True, the emeralds are wonderful. But I've noticed that ever since Nevel came to us, every day there's been less joy and love and more jealousy and hatred. The Devil is dancing among us, brothers!"

Everyone seconded the old man's words and agreed that Nevel was hated by everyone, not only because he was taking a lot of money from those who came to see the emeralds but also because he was a horrible person unworthy of affection.

One boy, an orphan without father or mother, told how he had long wanted to tear out the magical emeralds by their roots, because when he walked by them, it seemed to him that his dead parents were crying and wailing for him. But when he tried to touch them, he was singed as if with burning coals, and he felt as if he had heavy chains on his legs.

But Nevel didn't care about any of this. On the contrary, he took pleasure in seeing how his fortune grew day by day—while nobody else could touch it. And when all the town's residents banded together to drive him out, he went to another town and started his business over again. So it was that he traveled around from town to town to town and everywhere displayed the tear-like emeralds and received in exchange money and hatred.

Hillel also traveled around from desert to desert, and wherever he found thorns, he turned them into roses. Once Hillel came to a place where Nevel had planted his thorns, and he saw human eyes growing over an entire field. And the eyes looked at him beseechingly, with tears. So he took pity on them and doused them with his water, so that they soon closed their tearful eyes and were turned into roses with a wonderful fragrance.

People smelled that wonderful fragrance and went out to the field. A spirit of goodness and love overcame them, so that they hugged and kissed one another and began to dance from sheer happiness. And with joy and astonishment, they asked each other, "What has happened to us?"

When Nevel heard that people were dancing and enjoying themselves on his field, he went out to demand the fee for looking at his emeralds, and then he saw that no trace of them remained. Beautiful roses covered the entire field. So Nevel grew enraged and wanted to punish the people; but the spirit of the roses took hold of him too, and he began to dance with everyone else. With his feet, he danced and jumped, and with his mouth, he cursed the people and the roses both. He laughed and cried, danced and cursed, until his gall bladder burst and he fell down dead.

So the people buried him in his field, and on his grave there sprouted a thornbush on which emeralds grew. But they couldn't make people sad anymore, because the roses all around spread their good fragrance and gladdened the people's hearts.

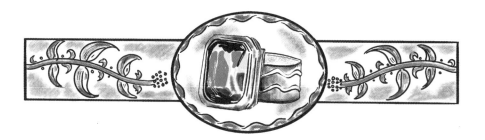

The Red Giant

David Ignatov

DAVID IGNATOV
October 14, 1885–February 26, 1954

Born into a Hasidic family in Ukraine, Ignatov attended religious schools before becoming a university candidate and a revolutionary in Russia. He was arrested for these activities in 1903 and in 1906 emigrated to the United States, where he worked at factory jobs in Chicago, St. Louis, and New York. He worked as a union organizer and began to write both in Russian and in Yiddish. Although his start as a writer was rocky, he contributed to several anthologies and was eventually recognized as part of the group of immigrant poets and writers known as "Di yunge" (The young ones).

This youthful creative circle, at the vanguard of American Yiddish culture, cared more about setting a mood and depicting internal emotional states in their work than writing about politics and outward-looking events. In 1921, Ignatov published a series of works for children that bore out the artistic vision of "Di yunge," including "The Red Giant." The story is a lyrical adventure tale folded into a nostalgically remembered Jewish setting in which children recite the Shema prayer every night before sleep. Romantic and highly imaginative, its events unfold in a dramatic, stormy emotional landscape.

Ignatov contributed to a lively literary scene of collections, small magazines, and annuals, both as writer and publisher, including the influential *Shriftn* (Writings). These publications helped to establish and develop Yiddish literature in America. He was also active in cultural and immigrant aid organizations, including the World Jewish Cultural Congress and the Hebrew Immigrant Aid Society. He took ill in 1950 and upon his death was buried in a place of honor in the Workmen's Circle cemetery in New York.

— ✿ —

Somewhere out there was a shtetl, a town, where many Jewish papas and mamas were born. The land over there wasn't covered with stone and asphalt; the earth there was free, bare and open. The houses were small, separate, and pretty. And the fathers and mothers there had gardens, orchards, geese, and chickens—and they had little children. The geese swam around in long rows on the town's beautiful river, and the cattle and goats grazed in the town's large forest. The river ran through the middle of town, and the forest lay below that. Almost every evening, the sky above the forest would turn red and gold, and all across the vast, distant forest, things would happen.

As the setting sun touches the edge of the forest, you can begin to paint yourself a picture with words:

Deep in the forest stood a large castle with a golden tower, and in the golden tower lived a red giant. His hair was curly and red as fire. Tall and big, the giant went out hunting with his lucky ring—whereby he could attain anything his heart desired. By means of the ring's magic, he had captured a princess, whom he was holding prisoner in the castle. Each day when the giant went out hunting, he would bar the princess in his golden tower and guard her jealously, locking her up behind seven locks. Only in the evening, when the sky turned fiery red and gold, would the giant return to the castle, take out the princess, and, through the ring's magic, have the two of them lifted up and seated out at the edge of the sky, where they would begin to feast upon their dinner.

But this time, the evening did not come on gradually, calmly, and quietly as usual. Rather, it happened suddenly: all at once, flames appeared in the sky over the forest and a haze began to rise from the town's gardens, its river, and the ground itself—it rose and fell and rose again, like someone who's had too much to drink, like someone caught totally by surprise.

The abrupt dusk also caught the red giant in the forest suddenly and unexpectedly. The giant was running late with his hunting that day, and he realized all of a sudden that the forest was on fire!

So he broke into a run toward his castle—to the beautiful princess. He ran between the flames, flinging the burning trees with his hands, hurling them right and left, breaking a path through the burning forest. But all at once, the giant realized that he had lost his magic ring and that he had lost his way. . . . He wouldn't be able to find the path again. . . . So he stood there terrified, and in his rage, he grabbed a flaming hundred-year-old oak, tore the ancient tree from the ground by its roots, and started to roll it over the rest of the burning trees. Those trees began to fall, crash, crackle, and burst into flames.

The giant stood there exhausted, and as the oak fell from his hands, he looked around, stunned. . . . He wanted to start running again—but where to? Where could he go? . . . His eyes burned big and red and wild, and he grabbed his curly red hair with his large hands. He let out a wild cry, "Vaaaaaaaa-h!" Then he jerked and fell down unsteadily between the burning trees.

The town's children, who were staring at the red sky, saw the giant's downfall, and meanwhile, his large castle at the very edge of the forest had also caught on fire.

The children watched fearfully as the golden tower where the beautiful princess was imprisoned broke off from the castle and began to teeter above the flames, as over a red sea. . . .

The beautiful princess ran up to one of the crystal windows and, trembling, looked down at the children of the town; her kind eyes fluttered as if to ask, "What will be, children? What will be? . . ."

Late in the evening, when the fires had long gone out of the red sky, when the children had already eaten dinner, when the mothers had bathed them and the fathers had recited the Shema prayer with them, just after the children had finally fallen asleep, they saw in their dreams the beautiful princess, freed, floating on a boat on the town's river, and with her kind smile, she thanked the children and told them that she was floating home now to her father, the king, and to her mother, the queen.

PART IV

WISE FOOLS

The Jews of Chelm and the Great Stone
B. Alkvit

B. ALKVIT (ELIEZER BLUM)
December 7, 1896–February 11, 1963

In Jewish folklore, the Polish town of Chelm, in the district of Lublin, came to be associated with perversely comical foolishness—although this storytelling tradition has nothing to do with the actual denizens of the town, whose Jewish community dates back at least to the fourteenth century. "The Jews of Chelm and the Great Stone," which appeared in *Kinder zhurnal* in 1925, is the rare Chelm story written by an author actually born in the town, Eliezer Blum.

Blum attended *kheyder* and was orphaned by age twelve. He made his way to Lublin, Warsaw, Vienna, and finally, in 1914, to the United States, where he worked as a tailor. A master of short forms, he published poems, stories, and essays in a variety of Yiddish periodicals for adults as well as in the children's magazine *Kinder zhurnal*. He allied himself with the Introspectivists, publishing his first poems and later serving on the editorial board of their flagship publication, *Inzikh*. He remained in New York until his death.

This story follows the typical plot of a Chelm tale, wherein the denizens of this mythic town of fools go about solving a problem in a ridiculous way that merely augments or displaces it. This plot inserts a witness to their folly. Shelishtsh (Polish: Siedliszcze), whence the guest hails, is a neighboring town to the west of Chelm, perhaps a bit of realistic local geography included by a native of the area.

— ✸ —

Once upon a time, the Jews of Chelm wanted to build a new shul. The old synagogue had grown too small for the Chelmers, who had been fruitful and multiplied so well that their numbers grew with every passing day and week. Being good and pious folk as God had commanded, they all wanted to pray in the large synagogue and nowhere else. The old shul was so crowded that on holidays, or even a regular Sabbath, they stood elbow to elbow. So it was left to them to build a newer, bigger shul.

The Jews of Chelm decided to build their shul only with large stones. Because the church spires all stood at the crest of the town's hill, the Chelmers decided that their shul, to mark the difference, should be built in the valley. All the good and pious folk took to the chore, and even the children helped to carry the large stones from the hilltop down to the valley.

It was hard, sweaty work. But the Jews of Chelm put up with it because each and every one of them knew that the town was carrying out a holy task.

One day, as it turned out, the Chelmers came upon a very, very large rock—a boulder—lying right on the peak of a high hill. They realized that this boulder could become the foundation stone of the entire shul, so they set out to carry it from the hilltop to the valley.

But it's easy to say "they set out to carry it" when you're standing far away and watching a whole community of Jews melt into sweat while carrying such a large, heavy stone—which hung over their heads like Mount Sinai did back when God gave the Jews the Holy Torah.* Two men had to run ahead and shout, "Careful, careful, hold it, hold it! Watch out!" If they hadn't, the huge stone might have broken loose and fallen from the hill toward the valley and with it, God forbid, dragged along the whole community.

No, no. The Jews carried the stone step by careful step downhill. Uh-oh, watch out! Looks like they're about to fall! But no, they never did. The idea that the stone would be the foundation of their new shul made their steps firm. And after a long, hard day of carrying and dragging, they finally brought the stone into the valley.

Having carried the stone step by step, the Jews of Chelm glanced at God's world and realized that it was time to recite the afternoon prayers. Looking around, they noticed a goat, which shone red in the setting sun; and near the goat stood a Jew with a small goatee of his own, and he was laughing.

---

* According to the well-known midrash (rabbinic interpretation of the Bible) appearing on *bShabbat* 88a, God hastened the Israelites' acceptance of the Torah at Mount Sinai by suspending the mountain above the people's heads while they considered the covenant being offered.

At first glance, they couldn't tell the man was a Jew. Between his goatish little beard and the way he bent over with laughter, he looked more like a goat standing up on its front legs and laughing a human laugh. The Chelm Jews knew right away that this must surely be a Jew from Shelishtsh.

But nevertheless they asked him, "Where are you from?"

"Where am I from? From Shelishtsh," he answered, chortling with laughter.

"And why are you laughing so hard?"

"Why shouldn't I laugh? All the Jews here are, beg pardon, such great fools that if you traveled the whole world over, you wouldn't find the like anywhere but Chelm. Is it necessary to carry down a stone from the hilltop— and such a huge boulder at that—on your *backs*? You just start rolling it down, and it's a done deal! Even a child can understand how easy it is to roll a stone down a hill."

The Jews of Chelm saw the logic in what he was saying, and they applied themselves to the task right away: all through that night, the Chelmers dragged and pushed the boulder back up the hill. Not one Jew remained in his house, and not one went home to bed. You can imagine for yourself how hard it was. Many of them fell down and fainted under the heavy burden, but just as the day began to dawn, the boulder lay once more in the same spot on the hilltop where they had found it the previous morning.

At last they could roll the stone down gently, very gently, from the hilltop. It reached the bottom once again. They took another look: there was the goat, and near the goat, a man—and both were laughing. The Chelm Jews immediately recognized the Jew from the day before. Nevertheless, they asked, "Where are you from, and why are you laughing?"

But he didn't answer them at all. He just hopped up onto the back of his goat, and rode away from Chelm, howling with laughter all the while.

Lemekh Goes Ice Skating
Leon Elbe

LEON ELBE (LEON BASSEIN)
September 25, 1879–August 30, 1928

Bassein's father, Bezalel, was known for his rich bass voice and served as an assistant cantor at the Great Synagogue in their hometown of Minsk. The boy distinguished himself scholastically and earned scholarships to offset the family's meager earnings. Lacking funds to continue his education in secular subjects, he handed out notes at a public park explaining his educational goals and in that way found free tutoring. He eventually became a tutor himself and came under the influence of revolutionary politics.

As a young man, Bassein was active with Poale Zion and helped to found the Minsk Labor Zionists. He was conscripted into the Russian army but managed to emigrate to the United States in 1904 before serving out the final year of his term. Arriving in New York penniless, with command of neither English nor a trade, he took various unskilled jobs and observed how shabbily management treated the workers.

Bassein wrote for a variety of leftist periodicals, both for adults and for children, and taught in Yiddish schools. He compiled *Di yidishe shprakh* (The Yiddish language), the first Yiddish chrestomathy, or anthology for scholastic use, published in America. While battling tuberculosis, he relocated for several years to the Catskills. He was principally affiliated with the Sholem Aleichem network of schools, and he became a frequent contributor to its associated periodical, the *Kinder zhurnal*. Indeed he penned the linked adventure tales of *Yingele ringele* (Little boy, little ring) for its pages and read the drafts gleefully to his own children.

He wrote under a number of pseudonyms, including Leon Elbe, Leybe der royter (Leon the red), Ben ha-bat (Daughter's son), and A Lamed Bat-nik (a play on his initials and the phrase denoting the thirty-six righteous souls in whose merit the world's existence is said to depend at any given time). His tuberculosis began to worsen until he collapsed in April 1928 on the brink of a rest-and-relaxation trip to Atlantic City. He declined rapidly and passed away at age forty-nine.

The modest adventures of Lemekh the Lummox (his name has become synonymous with "fool") animate several stories. They display a comical inverted logic reminiscent of the Chelm stories. Lemekh is a "wise fool": that is, he is certainly foolish, but he has such a kind soul that he cannot recognize the sarcasm that others direct at him. In that purity of spirit, there lies a sort of wisdom.

— ℬ —

Lemekh took the brand-new ice skates that his mother had bought him and went out to skate.

He walked along and wondered what he should do if he fell once he started skating. He thought it over for a while but couldn't come up with anything.

He passed a house and saw a man standing and sprinkling ash from a basket onto the sidewalk.

Lemekh called out to the man, "Why are you doing that? You're getting the sidewalk dirty, and the owner will yell at you!"

The man smiled and said to Lemekh, "You're a fool, boy! First of all, the owner will not yell at me because I myself am the owner. And second, I'm not getting the sidewalk dirty. Surely you see that the sidewalk is slippery, and people can fall when they walk on it; I'm sprinkling ash so they *don't* fall."

Lemekh said, "Wow, I've never heard of that, but it's such a good idea. I'm going skating right now, and I think that's what I should do so I don't fall on the ice. I'd like to take a little bit of your ash now to sprinkle on the rink."

The man smiled and said to Lemekh, "I see, boy, that you're very wise. What's your name?"

Lemekh answered, "Lemekh!" which actually means "fool."

The man smiled again and said, "A fine name, Lemekh. Wear it in good health. It suits you very well!"

"Thank you," Lemekh replied, remembering that Mama had taught him that when someone told him, "Wear it in good health," he needed to say, "Thank you."

"You're a nice person," Lemekh continued. "Nobody likes my name, but you said that it's a fine name. And since you're so nice, now maybe you'll give me the bit of ash I've asked for?"

"Here you go, Lemekh. Take the rest! I don't need any more," said the man as he handed over the whole basket of ash.

"Thank you!" said Lemekh. "You're a *very* nice person!" And he took the basket and went off to skate.

On the way, he ran into another boy, who asked, "Where are you going, Lemekh? Skating?"

"Yes!" said Lemekh.

The boy questioned him further, "And why are you bringing along a basket?"

Lemekh replied, "A basket of ash to sprinkle on the rink, so I won't fall."

The other boy laughed and waved, "Carry that basket, Lemekh! Carry it in good health!"

"Thank you!" Lemekh answered—and walked on.

He arrived at the rink and began to sprinkle the ash. The man in charge of the rink and the other skaters began to yell at him, "Hey, boy! What are you doing?"

"I'm sprinkling ash," Lemekh replied, "so that I won't fall, because I want to skate; I've never skated before, and I'm scared of falling."

They all burst out laughing.

Lemekh said, "Why are you all laughing? I saw how a man sprinkled ash on a slippery sidewalk so that nobody would fall."

Everyone just laughed harder and asked Lemekh what his name was. He told them. They laughed even harder, and one boy did a little dance on his skates and chanted,

> Lemekh is a fool
> A nail is a tool
> Flour is thick
> Ice is slick
> Slippery ice?
> Then sprinkle rice!

"Well, Lemekh!" said the man in charge. "Take your basket of ash and go home."

"What about skating?" asked Lemekh.

"When you stop being such a *lemekh*, a fool, you'll come back here to skate."

So Lemekh left, thinking about how to stop being such a *lemekh*.

A Snow Grandma

Benjamin Gutyanski

BENJAMIN GUTYANSKI

1903–1956

Born in the village of Glubochok, Podolia, Gutyanski attended high school in Bershad before going on to earn degrees in education and mathematics. He wrote sharp satires, fables, plays, textbooks, and children's literature as well as translating both contemporary works from the Russian and classics like *Don Quixote* into Yiddish.

He was decorated for his military service in World War II, and he served with the pen as well, by satirizing the Nazis. He was exiled to a forced labor camp in 1950, and while he was rehabilitated in 1956, he never regained his health and died shortly after his release.

"A Snow Grandma" displays Gutyanski's typical cleverness and charm. The poem was originally published in his 1940 collection of poems *Far kinder* (For children) and then reprinted in a 1986 Soviet anthology that collected children's portraits of their mothers and poetry intended for young readers.

— ℬ —

Look! A grandma made of snow
Two black eyes she has, just so
Her mouth's a hole
Filled up with coal
She has a crooked, little nose
But where her ears are, heaven knows!
It gives the grandma quite a fright

(And truth be told, the grandma's right)
It brings her—poor thing!—close to tears
Where to find a pair of ears?

Zelig the Rhymester

Kadya Molodowsky

KADYA MOLODOWSKY
May 10, 1894–March 23, 1975

For biographical information on Molodowsky, see "The Baker and the Beggar" in part 3. Along with "The Baker and the Beggar" and "A Story of a Schoolboy and a Goat" (in part 6), "Zelig the Rhymester" appeared in a section called "Schoolboys" of Molodowsky's 1970 collection of stories and poems for children, *Martsepanes* (Marzipans).

— ℬ —

All the boys liked Zelig because he told good stories and knew how to rhyme. He had a rhyme ready for every word. A goat—stood next to a moat; a *dreidel*—lay under the cradle; a bear—danced on a dare; a cat—wore a hat; and so on and so forth.

But most of all, the boys liked it when Zelig told stories.

One day after their lessons, Zelig told the boys a story about Elijah the Prophet. They sat around Zelig in a circle, and he explained:

"On a clear summer evening, when you can see each star shining, Elijah the Prophet goes out for a tour. He wants to check on whether kids are going to bed nicely and concentrating properly when they say the Shema prayer. He's pulled across the sky by fiery horses harnessed to a carriage with four wheels made of stars, and a pillar of light follows the carriage. His ride lasts just one instant; but in that instant, he sees the whole world, from one end to the other, and he hears how every kid says the Shema. When his carriage shows up in the sky, the stars start to fall: ten stars at a time, five at a time, and then lone stars. Whoever looks up right at that moment and sees the stars falling can make any wish at all. You just have to say what you wish for. If you want a ship, you'll get a ship; if you want a gold ring, that's what you'll get."

The boys all wanted to catch that moment when Elijah journeyed forth in the sky so that each of them could make a wish.

"Look out for falling stars," Zelig urged. "They have to fall in an open field where there are no roofs or trees and where nothing blocks the sky."

Every night, the boys waited for clear skies so that they could go into a field and look out for Elijah the Prophet's carriage with the four star-wheels. One evening, they couldn't go because it was cloudy; another was rainy; on a third night, not all the stars were shining; and a fourth night was so windy that dust blew into their eyes. Not until a week later did the sky clear, with all the stars shining and none missing. The boys went out to the field.

The crickets chirped, but the boys paid them no attention; the frogs croaked, but the boys didn't echo their croaks; two late crows flew by and cried, "Good night, good night," but the boys ignored them. They didn't want to take their eyes off the sky and miss making their wishes exactly when Elijah the Prophet appeared. Meanwhile, a rabbit ran across the field. Zelig couldn't keep himself from shouting a rhyme after it: "Short-nose bunny, your nose is runny. Your ears are long and very funny!" The boys lost their focus and glanced down at the rabbit.

Just at that moment, the sky lightened, and stars began to fall. The boys forgot to call out their wishes. But little Shayele remembered to call out, "You should come back in a year!"

The boys were angry at Zelig for distracting them with the bunny. Little Shayele consoled them, saying, "I told him to come back next year, so I'm sure he will."

The boys agreed that the next year, they wouldn't look away for anything, even a bunny rabbit; they would call out their wishes as soon as Elijah the Prophet showed up in his carriage with the four star-wheels harnessed to fiery steeds, and then they would have all that they could wish for.

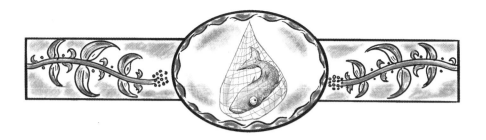

From The Three Braggarts
David Rodin

DOVID RODIN (ELYE LEVIN)
b. July 31, 1893

Elye (Eliyahu) Levin was born to his parents, Shmuel and Shayna, in Brahin, Byelorussia (Belarus), and emigrated to the United States in 1911. He attended *kheyder* as a child and was also taught Russian. In America, he furthered his education in various kinds of institutions: evening school, a Jewish teachers' seminary, and finally at the University of Pennsylvania, where he studied pedagogy and psychology. He pursued music as well, mastering the organ and then the piano and eventually directing a choir in Rochester, New York.

His first publication came in 1916 in the satirical newspaper *Der groyser kundes* (The great prankster), but the vast majority of his writing thereafter was aimed at children. He adopted the pseudonym David Rodin.

He spent some time teaching in Toronto and Nova Scotia. During World War I, he joined the Jewish Legion, a military formation organized through the British army to fight the Ottomans in Palestine.

After the war, he taught in two of the Yiddish secular educational networks, the Sholem Aleichem and the Workmen's Circle schools. He was also deeply involved in community theater in Russian and Yiddish. He lived in Memphis from 1924 to 1927 and founded a drama society there.

In 1955, he emigrated to Israel, where he continued to publish prodigiously throughout the 1970s. His work was always attuned to the power of children's imaginations. *The Three Braggarts* offers a rollicking cycle of one-upping tall tales, shared among three friends.

— ∝ —

Meet Moshe, Chaim, and Getsl—three little boys, all the same age, who live on the same street, go to the same school, and have the same interests.

All three are big dreamers and even bigger braggarts. All three like to go around the streets and parks and down to the river; they observe everything, think it over, ponder it some more afterward, and then fantasize and brag about everything.

Moshe, Chaim, and Getsl can solve the hardest problem—with the snap of a finger. For them, it's no difficulty. For them, *every* obstacle gets pushed aside. If Moshe can't solve it, then Chaim does; if Chaim can't, then Getsl will.

For Moshe, Chaim, and Getsl, there's no such thing as "too far" or "too high." For Moshe, Chaim, and Getsl, the farthest distance and the tallest height is as easy to reach as it is for me to tell you these stories.

So, listen. . . .

Their Uncles

How Moshe's Uncle Uproots Trees with His Bare Hands

Moshe, Chaim, and Getsl met up and started bragging to each other.

Today they were bragging about their uncles.

Moshe said, "My uncle has such big lips! He can pull his cheeks all the way out to here! And he can spread his lungs so far apart that his chest rises up to here! And when he blows out, it makes such a big, strong wind that it can tear out a tree by the roots!"

How Chaim's Uncle Blows over an Elephant

"Meh," said Chaim. "It's no big deal to uproot a tree! Now *my* uncle once walked a long, long way, until he came to the edge of a big, deep forest. He started through the forest, thinking nothing of it. Suddenly, he saw a large, wild elephant approaching him. But my uncle didn't get scared; he just kept going on his way.

"Then the elephant came right up to my uncle and swung its big head back and forth, this way and that; and his long trunk waved up and down, up and down. But my uncle still wasn't scared. The elephant opened its large mouth to swallow up my uncle. So my uncle gathered his strength and blew so hard that the elephant was sent flying for three miles, banged into a tree, and was killed.

"And then my uncle continued on his way."

How Getsl's Uncle Blew the Ground Out from Under His Own Feet

"Blah, blah, blah, is that all?" replied Getsl.

"What's so amazing about killing an elephant or pulling up a tree by its roots? Now, my uncle was once walking a *very* long way, so he kept going and going, and going and going some more, and he still couldn't see anything. He ended up walking until he got to a very large rock. It was so big—how can I put it?—like a giant mountain that reaches from one end of the world to the other. And it was as high as that little white cloud over there.

"So what was my uncle supposed to do? He needed to keep going. Without giving it a thought, he puffed out his cheeks, and with his big lips, he blew on the ground so hard that it started flying out from under his feet; and he started to float like a bird higher and higher toward the sky, until he flew right up to the very top of the rock.

"So what do you suppose he did then? Nothing. He just slid down the other side of the stone mountain and continued on his way."

Farmers' Beards

His Beard Sleeps in a Separate Bed

Moshe, Chaim, and Getsl spent the summer months in the mountains—each on a different farm.

When they returned to the city, they met up and started telling each other about the amazing things they'd seen on the farm, and they started to boast to each other.

Today they were bragging about the farmers' beards. Moshe said, "The farmer I was staying with had such a big beard! Whenever he needed to go somewhere, he would throw his beard over his shoulder, and it would hang down his back like a big, wide cape. When he had to lie down to sleep, he would spread out his beard on another big bed near his bed, and that's how they would both sleep: him in one bed and his beard in the other.

"Once there was a very cold night on the farm. And on that night, I happened to be sleeping together with the farmer's boys. They liked to hear my stories, so they invited me in; and I told them stories until we all fell asleep. In the middle of the night, we felt a draft so cold that we were practically frozen. And there was nothing to cover ourselves with—because the farmer had given out all of his comforters to the guests who were staying with him. So what were we supposed to do? We sat in bed, shivering with cold and thinking, 'Where can we find a comforter?' Thinking along these lines, we spotted the farmer's beard. So we jumped right up, dragged our beds over to the farmer's bed, and covered ourselves—all of us—with the farmer's beard. It was as warm as an oven for us, and we slept almost until noon.

"Once the farmer said to me, 'Are you going to take a dip?'

"I replied, 'Sure I am.'

"As I got to the river, I saw that the farmer was braiding his beard. I asked, 'Why are you doing that?'

"He answered, 'If I tell you, you won't believe me anyway, so it's better if you wait and see.'

"In the meantime, I went into the river and took my dip, and when I got out, the farmer was already in the water and swimming the crawl all the way across the river and up and down its length. Whoa, did he swim—like a fish!

"After a while, the farmer got out of the river. I took a look—and what was this? His beard looked like a big, stuffed sack, and its sides were trembling like the sides of a pregnant cow. So I asked, 'What is this? Is your beard pregnant with a calf?'

"The farmer burst into laughter, bent over, and said, 'Look inside. You'll see what kind of calves are in there.' So I looked inside his beard, and just guess what I saw there? A beard full of big, fresh, wriggling fish that were leaping over one another like calves! He had woven his beard into a net, and while he swam, he'd caught a beard full of fish.

"When we got back home, the farmer shook out the catch from his beard, and there were enough fish to bake, fry, and broil."

A Beard Where Children Play Hide-and-Seek

"Now I have a wonder," replied Chaim. "Catching fish with a beard? That's no miracle at all! There are birds that catch fish with their feathers.

"Well, the farmer I stayed with had such a big beard that it looked like a haystack. Once, when I played hide-and-seek with his children, they all hid under his beard. I looked around all day and couldn't find them. At dusk, when the farmer got up to go milk the cows, I saw that the children were sitting under his beard as chicks sit under the wings of a hen.

"Once the farmer said to me, 'Chaim, would you like to go and see how the hay gets taken down from the field?'

"I said, 'Sure.'

"So he harnessed two horses to a big wagon, and we rode to the hayfield.

"Once we got to the hayfield, the farmer spread himself out on the freshly mown grass and fell asleep. I frolicked about in the field and looked on as his ten workers with long pitchforks loaded the hay into the big wagon.

"By dusk, the wagon was piled as high as a mountain. They threw each other rope, tied up the hay, and woke up the farmer, and we all followed the wagon home.

"When we got there, the workers began to unload the wagon and carry the hay into the barn to the cows, but suddenly the farmer cried, 'Hey, guys, where did you drag my beard off to?'

"They looked around and saw that the wagon was loaded not with hay but rather with the farmer's beard.

"Don't even ask what happened next there! People laughed, and the farmer's wife shrieked, 'Some workers I have—I don't even know what to say! Just let people get a load of this! Ten adult men go out into the field to load a wagon with hay, they work a whole long summer's day through, and what do you think they manage to accomplish? Loading the farmer's beard onto the wagon! I ask you people, how am I supposed to stand it?'

"But that's still not the end of the story. Listen to the rest:

"Since they hadn't brought any hay home, the cows had nothing to eat. So what should the farmer do? He couldn't leave the cows hungry for a whole night—hungry cows don't give good milk—so he stood among the cows the entire night and let them chew on his beard.

"You're thinking, of course, that you'd be able to notice some difference in his beard after so many cows had grazed on it for an entire night? Nonsense! And if another dozen cows had come to graze on it, would it be noticeable then?

"When I took a look at his beard in the morning, it still looked like a haystack."

A Beard in Which a Calf Got Lost

"Well, so what?" replied Getsl. "What kind of a trick is it to load a beard onto a hay wagon and bring it home? Or to let a couple dozen cows chew all night on your beard?

"Now the farmer that *I* stayed with had a beard so big that it looked like a corn field. Once, when he was lying in his field and sleeping, the reapers came to cut down the corn, but they cut off the edge of his beard because they thought it was part of the field.

"It just so happened that his red cow gave birth to a black-and-white calf. One day when the calf was bigger, the farmer took her out to the field to pasture.

"When they reached the field, he took his red kerchief and tied it around her neck so that he would recognize her—since there were other calves like his grazing there—and he lay himself down to sleep. To the calf, all grasses were the same; so first she ate the grass around the farmer, and then she crept into the farmer's beard and got tangled up.

"The farmer woke up—and there was no calf. So he searched the entire field—but no calf. He thought, 'Wolves probably ate up the calf.'

"He went home but never stopped thinking of the calf. He saw her always before his eyes with black and white spots and with a red kerchief tied around her neck.

"Two or three years passed, and the farmer felt his beard grow heavier with each passing day—it was actually pulling him down to the ground. So he decided to go and cut off his beard.

"He went to the barber. The barber stretched him out on the chair and started to soap up his beard. While working up the lather, the barber heard a 'mooo!' coming from the beard. Immediately after that came a 'mehhhh!' The barber was scared to death. Before he could even recover, he saw a black-and-white cow with a red kerchief tied around its neck jump out from the beard. And following the cow, out jumped a red calf.

"When the farmer saw that, he jumped up from the barber's chair, embraced the cow's neck, and shouted joyfully,

> Look children, people hear!
> A miracle has happened here!
> My little calf's become a cow!
> And turned into a mama now!"

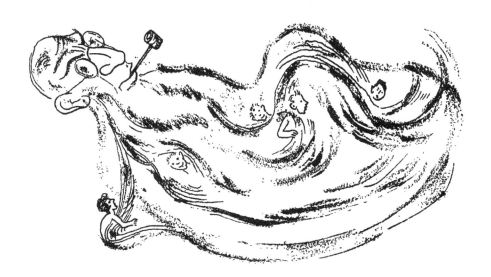

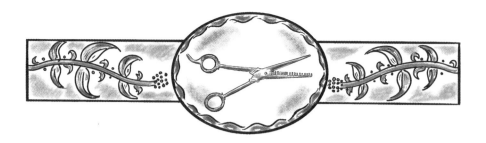

A Deal's a Deal

Solomon Simon

SOLOMON SIMON

July 4, 1895–November 8, 1970

Born Shloyme Shimonovitsh in the town of Kalinkovitsh near Minsk in Byelo-russia (Belarus), Simon was the fourth of eight children born to a father who was a cobbler and a mother who helped support the impoverished family by baking. A case of rickets left him unable to walk until he was nearly six, and this disability contributed to his developing a rich inner life. He was educated in traditional fashion at *kheyder* and then selected to attend a yeshiva in Kremenchug, at some distance from his home. His education continued at other Polish yeshivas until it was interrupted by conscription into the tsar's army.

He escaped by fleeing to America, arriving in New York in 1913 without knowing any English, and set about studying in the evenings, while working at various trades including the garment industry, laundering, housepainting, and driving a wagon. He Anglicized his name to "Simon." He served in the US Army beginning in 1918 and then taught Hebrew in New York and New Jersey. He studied dentistry at New York University, graduating in 1924, but he practiced only as much as he needed to in order to support his wife and three children, preferring to devote his time to writing and Yiddish educational and cultural activities.

Deeply involved with the Sholem Aleichem Folk Institute, he helped to found and lead one of its schools and its summer camp, Boiberik. Simon also devoted himself to various communal extracurricular activities, including a leading role in the Jewish Ethical Society in New York and a society for Bible study in Brooklyn. He began to write for children in Hebrew in 1912 and then published his first Yiddish story in 1915. He went on to publish in several periodicals for adults and children, assuming the assistant editorship of the *Kinder-zhurnal* from 1948 to

1951. His journalism, fiction, and criticism appeared in prestigious journals based in New York, Warsaw, Buenos Aires, Paris, and Montreal.

Simon was committed to secularist Yiddish culture and especially to the preservation of folktales and legends. Two volumes of his Chelm stories were translated into English, along with his storybook *Shmerl Nar* (translated as *The Wandering Beggar*). Later in life, he devoted his efforts to writing for adults, and he spent his final years working on an English-language series about the Hebrew Bible. He died in Miami Beach.

He often wrote in a comic vein, as with "A Deal's a Deal," which shares the stubbornly perverse logic of the Chelm tales.

It was a cold, rainy autumn night in Chelm. The wind had torn open door and shutters. In the middle of the night, Avrohom heard the door banging. So he woke up his wife, Mirtl, and said to her, "Wifey dear, did you lock the door?"

Mirtl replied, "Hubby dear, I thought that *you* had locked it."

"I didn't," said Avrohom. "Go and lock it."

"*You* go and lock it," said Mirtl.

Said Avrohom, "No, I'm not going downstairs in this cold, and surely you know that when I say 'no,' it's 'no.'"

Said Mirtl, "The whole world knows that when a man is a rabbi, his wife is a called a *rebbetzin*; when a man is Mr. Shoemaker, then his wife is Mrs. Shoemaker. You're Mr. Stubborn, my husband, so that makes me Mrs. Stubborn. I too am staying in bed and not moving a muscle."

Said Avrohom, "What you say makes sense. You know what? Let's make a deal with each other that whichever one of us is the first to speak will lock the door."

Said Mirtl, "Deal."

So they lay there in silence. The wind blew, and the open door banged and banged until the house shuddered; but both of them kept quiet, and neither moved a muscle.

The rain poured, the wind blew, inside the house it was wet and cold enough to drive away wolves, but Avrohom and Mirtl didn't budge.

Just before dawn, husband and wife heard footsteps and human voices.

Thieves were talking. One thief said, "Just look at that open door! Let's go inside and see what we can lift."

Said the second thief, "Don't talk so loud! Maybe the owners are home, but they're sleeping!"

"Don't be ridiculous!" answered the first one. "You hear how the door's banging? That would wake the dead. Chances are nobody's home. Come on."

Husband and wife heard the thieves come into the house and start to empty out all the rooms. But husband and wife didn't move a muscle.

The thieves did their work and packed up everything they could get their hands on. Husband and wife knew their home would be left naked and bare, but they didn't let out a peep.

The thieves gathered everything together and took off. They left the door open, as they'd found it.

Night passed, and morning came. Husband and wife got up and looked around. The house was empty. The thieves didn't leave even so much as a saucepan to cook up a bit of porridge for breakfast. Husband and wife exchanged glances but remained silent.

Mirtl went out to a neighbor's to borrow something for breakfast. But as for closing the door? That Mrs. Stubborn didn't do. She got to the neighbor's and lingered there for a long while chatting, as women will.

Meanwhile, a barber was passing by the house with the open door. In those days, barbers would go from door to door asking who wanted a haircut and clipping the hair of both children and adults right at home.

The barber saw Avrohom sitting silently on a chair in the middle of the house, lost in thought. So he said, "Perhaps you'd like a trim, Reb Avrohom?"

Avrohom kept quiet and didn't answer. Well, when you don't say "no," that obviously means "yes." So the barber laid out his towel, his scissors, his bowl, his soap, and his razor and went about the job. He snipped and snipped, and then he asked, "Enough, Reb Avrohom?"

Avrohom was silent. So the barber went on clipping. Avrohom began to look like a shorn sheep. The barber asked, "Enough?"

Avrohom was silent. So the barber thought, "What kind of a hard case is this? Well, so be it; there's only one thing to do!"

So he took the soap, lathered up Avrohom's head, and shaved it. Having done so, the barber said, "Such a long beard doesn't go with such a bare pate. Trim it a bit?"

Avrohom was silent: Mr. Stubborn through and through. The barber started in on his beard, cutting and cutting, and Avrohom was silent. The barber spared no effort in shaving off Avrohom's beautiful beard. Avrohom kept silent through it all.

The barber gathered his towel, his scissors, his bowl, and his soap and said to Avrohom, "Well, Reb Avrohom, I've trimmed and shaved you, so pay me."

Avrohom seethed and boiled inside. Who had asked the barber to cut and shave his hair? And what's more, he wanted to be paid for his lovely work! Some nice new look he'd gotten! A Jew without a beard and sidelocks— how could he show himself in public?"

Thus reasoned Reb Avrohom, but he kept silent. He surely wouldn't be the first to speak. The barber complained, "I'm a Jew, a poor man. I've worked. Now pay me!"

The barber talked and talked, but Avrohom said nothing. Eventually the barber got angry and said, "Is that how it is? You're stubborn? You don't want to answer? I'll teach you a lesson!"

And the barber didn't hold back: he went out into the street, picked up large handfuls of mud, and began to smear it all over Avrohom's shaved head and face, and then he left the house without even shutting the door.

No sooner did the barber leave than Mirtl, Avrohom's wife, came in. She took one look at Avrohom and clapped her hands together, saying, "Woe is me! Alas and alack! What did they do to you? You look just like a demon!"

Avrohom got up from his chair and said very calmly, "You were the first to speak. So please go and close the door!"

Mirtl went and closed the door. After all, a deal's a deal!

PART V

ALLEGORIES, PARABLES, AND FABLES

The Wind That Got Angry
Moyshe Kulbak

MOYSHE KULBAK
March 20, 1896–October 29, 1937

Born in Smorgon, a town near Vilna, to a timber merchant father and a mother descended from farmers, Kulbak received an education that combined modern and traditional elements. After years in both a "reformed" *kheyder* and a Russian Jewish public school, he attended several yeshivas.

During World War I, he lived in Kovno, teaching at the school for Jewish orphans. At the same time, he began to write poetry in Hebrew but switched to writing in Yiddish. In 1918, he and his parents settled in Minsk, where he helped to educate Jewish teachers and contributed articles and poems to Bundist publications in Vilna and Moscow. Soon after, he moved to Vilna to teach.

During a stint in Berlin that began in 1920, he encountered European modernism and was especially influenced by expressionism, though his German was not good enough for him to be admitted to the university there. Returning to Vilna in 1923, he worked as a teacher of Yiddish literature while continuing to write poetry and fiction. He enjoyed a great deal of popularity on the city's cultural scene. In 1927, he chaired the Vilna Yiddish PEN Club. In 1928, he relocated to Minsk, where he published *Zelmenyaner* (1929), the masterful comic novel about Soviet-Jewish life for which he is best known. He also published poetry and wrote plays during what turned out to be the final decade of his life. Kulbak was arrested in September 1937 and executed the following month. His family was misinformed about the circumstances of his death. Though he was officially rehabilitated in 1956, the details of his execution were not known until 1990, and his burial place remains unknown.

Kulbak wrote little for children, but "The Wind That Got Angry" shares several of the thematic and stylistic elements that predominate in his romantic poetry, including a preoccupation with alienated outsiders and a view of nature as vibrantly alive. This story works so beautifully for children (and their caregivers) because it sympathetically channels the emotional experience of a tantrum for a figure with limited resources for self-expression and an aptitude for being misunderstood.

— ℬ —

A gift to the children of the Dinezon Orphanage in Vilna.

A tired, old wind dragged himself across snowy fields. He had already traveled through many towns and villages, creeping round over all the roofs, running his long, cold fingers along the windowpanes, and blowing into the chimneys, without finding anywhere to rest.

There had been a sudden thaw in town, which could have spelled his end. As it was, the wind had barely managed to crawl out from the chimney where he'd been lying down and singing. He only just escaped with his life to the desolate fields.

The snow glittered pure white out there, the sky was blue, and the wind traipsed around exhausted, looking for a place to rest. In the distance, where sky met field, he made out an oak tree and thought, "Under that oak, I can lie down to rest." He managed to drag himself to the spot, and, drained of all strength, he fell down under the oak.

So the wind lay there. His tired eyes were closing, and he was just about to fall asleep. Suddenly he heard the oak grumble, "What kind of a wise guy plunks himself down here? Ow! Something is stabbing my roots with cold!"

The wind said to him, "Don't be angry, dear Mr. Oak! I'm a wandering, old wind. This year, I wanted to spend the winter in town, but a thaw came and took my breath away so suddenly that I just barely managed to escape to the fields."

The oak replied, a little more softly now, "Dear Mr. Wind! Right now, I'm not feeling very well. In wintertime, I'm left naked, without any leaves on my branches, and if I don't take care with my roots in the ground, who knows whether I'll come back to life in the springtime? It would be better, my dear, if you would go on a bit farther. There's a rock down there by the road, and you can sit down there and rest."

So the old wind picked himself up and headed for the rock.

He walked on and on and finally saw it at the side of the road: a big, silent rock. The wind sat down, tucked the edge of one sleeve into the other, and got ready to nap. The rock felt someone sitting on its back and snorted, "Who's there?"

The wind answered, "I am."

The rock asked, "And who are *you*?"

The wind replied, "I'm just an old, wandering wind. This year, I wanted to spend the winter in town; but suddenly, a thaw came along and took my breath away, so I escaped to the fields. I had hoped to lie down and rest under the oak; but he said that I was pressing too hard on his roots, and they're as precious to him as life itself. . . ."

"Roots, shmoots!" the rock interrupted. "Look, when you want to sit down on someone, you have to ask permission; you can't hurl yourself onto them just like that. See, I'm cold and dry inside too, fit to crack wide open—and this guy here plops himself right down on me?! What will this old tramp do next?!"

The rock disliked anybody who could walk or move, but the wind didn't know that.

What *could* he do? He went on. . . . Meanwhile, night was falling, and the sun was setting. It lit up the western sky like a big fire. It turned the white snow pink, and snowy crystals—white, pink, and blue—sparkled over all the fields.

The wind followed the road for another hour, until he had hardly any strength left. He made out a large inn with a big, red porch. His eyes lit up with hope, but he was afraid to actually sit down without permission. He thought to himself, "I'll ask the innkeeper if I may rest on the porch." He went and knocked on the door and called, "Mr. Owner!"

No one answered, so he began to beg plaintively, "Mr. Owner!"

There was no answer this time either. The innkeeper was asleep, lying on top of the oven to keep warm. You see, all the peasants came to buy at the market in town on Mondays, but it was a Tuesday. The innkeeper figured no travelers would come along on a Tuesday, so he decided to spend the time sleeping on top of the oven, where it was warm.

The wind slowly opened the door and stuck his head inside to take a look.

Meanwhile, when a cold wind started to blow under his collar, the innkeeper jumped down from the oven and shouted, "Ay, don't hurt me, you sharp wind! The door's blown open!"

The wind just managed to snatch his head out of the doorway before it slammed shut, and he took off running, breathless; and behind him he could hear the innkeeper shouting and cursing.

The wind started to feel angry at the entire world. Nobody would let him rest, and he felt terrible. He stood up, like a strongman, in the middle of a field, rolled up his sleeves, girded his loins, and began to blow with all his might. The snow flew off the ground and, like silver flour, began to fall anew. . . .

The wind blew at everything, as hard as he could. Then he began to whistle, to blow and whistle, whistle and blow, until he had whipped up a whirling, whistling, screaming blizzard. And the snow began to whirl and throw itself about like white handkerchiefs flying in a gale. The wind began to cry. He cried like a child, without stopping. Then he began to howl like a dog, and with all the howling, hard-driving snow and screaming, it grew darker than the white snow had ever seen it. The snow scattered through the darkness, from the sky down to the ground and from the ground up to the sky. And the wind began to wail like a cat and to cry, as cats wail and cry on a dark night. It was a great blizzard. The wind had covered all the roads with snow. The traveling coachmen had to stop their horses. No one could see which way to go. They scrambled down from their laden wagons, slapped themselves under the armpits to keep warm and exclaimed,

"What a storm wind!"

"What a whirlwind!"

"I've never seen such a blizzard!"

Mountains of snow were heaped up all around the villages and towns. Dogs stood by their dens with outstretched necks and howled. The shutters had been closed everywhere, the doors shut tightly, but the wind knocked against the doorposts; he wedged himself into the chimneys and cried for the whole world to hear. People lay in their beds but couldn't fall asleep, and even the bigwigs didn't know what to do.

In a tiny hut somewhere at the edge of town lived a poor woman with two children. The wind had covered their entire hut with snow. The children clung to their mother; they were very frightened. She had stroked their heads and tucked them in, but the wind knocked so hard against the windows that they couldn't sleep.

"Mama, go ask the wind not to knock so hard on the windows!"

Standing behind the wall, the good wind could hear what the children told their mother, and it choked him up. But he was still angry at the world.

"Mama, go ask the wind not to cry so loudly in the chimney."

This just made the wind cry more. It pained him that he had to spend his entire life outdoors, like a dog, and that small children were afraid of him.

"Mama, go ask the wind to stop being angry."

The mother quickly put on her shawl and opened the door—onto darkness. She stood in the doorway and spoke into the night, "Wind, wind, stop being angry!"

The wind didn't listen to her. He was still mad, and he shoved a big heap of snow into the mother's face. She wiped the snow off and spoke to him a second time, saying, "Wind, good Mr. Wind, think about what you're doing!"

The wind still wouldn't listen to her, but neither did he cast any more snow into her face.

So she turned to the wind again, this time with tears in her eyes, and said, "Wind, dear wind, do it for the sake of the little children!"

The wind quieted down right away. The snow gradually stopped falling. From behind the row of houses, a muffled cry could still be heard, but it grew quieter and quieter, until it finally stopped.

The wind was no longer angry.

In the morning, all the children pulled their hats down over their ears, put on thick gloves, and began to shovel and clear away the snow that had piled up in front of all the doors.

The Horse and the Monkeys

Der Tunkeler

DER TUNKELER (YOYSEF TUNKL)
1881–August 9, 1949

"Der Tunkeler," or "The Dark One," was the pen name of Yoysef Tunkel, born in Bobruisk, Byelorussia (Belarus), to an itinerant teacher. He was a talented painter and visual artist, studying drawing at the Vilna school of design before moving to Odessa and working as an artist and caricaturist. Poor eyesight interrupted his blossoming art career, so he turned his comic sensibility to writing instead. He wrote for several Yiddish newspapers and departed for the United States in 1906. In 1908, he founded the humorous illustrated weekly *Der kibitzer* (The joker), and in 1909, he founded a similar outlet, *Der groyser kundes* (The great prankster). He returned to Europe in 1910, working in Warsaw's Yiddish press. He went back to his hometown during World War I before going on to Kiev and Odessa.

Between the wars, he wrote a great deal for the stage and was altogether prolific. During late summer 1939, he was touring in western Europe when he got stuck in Belgium. He stayed ahead of the invading Nazis by escaping to France, but he was eventually arrested by Vichy police and sent to a camp, from which he escaped with great difficulty. In 1941, he made his way back to the United States, where his health worsened rapidly. He nevertheless managed to chronicle his European experience of the war in a 1943 memoir. He died in New York.

"The Horse and the Monkeys" is the only work in this volume that was not originally composed in Yiddish. Tunkl made a series of adaptations, some of them quite free, from the verse of the German cartoonist and fabulist Wilhelm Busch. The two shared a comic sensibility, although Tunkl often "Judaized" the content and even revised some of the illustrations that accompanied Busch's work.* This story-in-verse about a horse plagued by mischievous monkeys displays their shared command of a light, humorous tale that can also sustain a more adult, serious reading.

— ॐ —

In a meadow undisturbed
Grazed a horse quite unperturbed
But not far off, need I say more?
There roamed a pack of monkeys four

They thought they'd try and take a ride
Upon the horse's back and sides
Soon the foursome all, of course,
Was sitting up astride the horse

* See Marc Miller, "The Judaization of Wilhelm Busch," *Monatshefte* 99, no. 1 (Spring 2007): 52–62.

Clinging to his mane and tail
They gave a shriek, a scream, a wail.
Thought Mr. Horse, while keeping mum,
"Of this, I fear, no good can come!"

He jerked, he jumped, he spun around
And tried to shake them to the ground
But each devilish, little monkey guest
Held and held and held on fast

The horsie liked this not at all
He reared up, hoping they would fall
But that old gang, they held on tight
To mane and neck as if for spite

Eek! I fear they're killing him!
Scraping, scratching up his skin
Biting, tearing strips of flesh
Laughing, joking acting fresh

From sorrow, pain and misery
The poor dear falls down to his knees
The monkeys turn things upsy-daisy
And nearly drive a good horse crazy

Well, he must take a different tack:
He lets himself down on his back
And rolls around; the gang goes flying
Yowling, screaming like they're dying

But: soon as Mr. Horse stands up
The monkeys four are back on top
Tearing again at his horsey hide
They'll ruin him yet and woe betide!

But now a new plan makes him quiver
Giddyap! And to the river!
How those monkeys four did totter
When he dove into the water.

Back in the field, the horsie savors
All the pasture's tasty flavors,
While poor little monkeys, sick and wet:
Look back on a caper they won't soon forget.

A Nanny Goat with Seven Kids

Leyb Kvitko

LEYB KVITKO

1890–August 12, 1952

Born around 1890 in Holoskovo near Odessa and orphaned in childhood, Kvitko was raised by his grandmother. He was apprenticed to a quilter at age ten. He lived briefly in Nikolaev, Odessa, and Kherson and then moved to Uman in 1915. Despite—or perhaps because of—a working-class childhood, he harbored literary aspirations. He sent his poetry to the leading critic of the day, Shmuel Niger (Charney), who rejected it. However, the writer Dovid Bergelson was more enthusiastic and not only helped to circulate Kvitko's poetry in Kiev but also arranged to help fill in gaps in the young poet's education. In 1917, Kvitko arrived in Kiev wearing homespun garb and was embraced as a folk talent. He published four collections of children's poetry between 1917 and 1920, as well as modernist and folk poetry.

In the early 1920s, Kvitko spent time living in Germany, where he joined the Communist Party. In 1925, fearing that the German police would arrest him for his political activities, he fled back to Soviet Russia, where he was offered the editorship of a journal in Kharkov. His tenure there was rocky, thanks to internecine squabbling among Soviet Jewish literati; in 1929, he was removed from the masthead after publishing a satirical poem about a powerful Moscow editor. Kvitko was sent to work in a tractor factory for a couple of years. He was re-admitted into official favor only after being championed by the leading Russian children's writer, Kornei Chukovskii, whose support helped to ensure that as the Russified *Lev* Kvitko, his works in Russian and Ukrainian translation would enjoy print runs in the millions.

In 1934, Kvitko served as delegate to the First Congress of Soviet Writers, and in 1939, he was honored with the Order of the Red Banner of Labor. Despite these tokens of acclaim, Kvitko, along with other members of the Jewish Anti-Fascist Committee, was killed at Stalin's behest on August 12, 1952—the Night of the Murdered Poets.

Kvitko wrote for children in various modes, ranging from the allegorical and stylized ("A Nanny Goat with Seven Kids" adapts a tale of the Brothers Grimm) to the hyperrealistic. A feature common to all his work, though, was the absence or incompetence of children's parents and an implicit insistence that the state, and especially "Papa" Stalin, was the true and necessary parent of each Soviet child. In the Grimms' telling, the capable mother is the heroine of "A Nanny Goat with Seven Kids." But for Kvitko, it is the lame but thoughtful child who both masterminds his siblings' rescue and consoles their distraught mother.

Once upon a time, in a clearing in the wood, lived a billy and a nanny goat with all that was good.

Their home was happy, its own little heaven, and as for kids, they had seven.

Six of their kiddies were healthy, athletic—but the seventh one was truly pathetic.

His ribs poked out like needles, and what's more, he limped on one foot.

But where he *could* be, he was the best: more clever and cheerful than all the rest.

One day the billy goat up and died, and the nanny with all the kids had to abide.

She worried and fretted in her sorrow: how about today—and what of tomorrow?

What on earth is to be done? The children must have food—and there's none!

I must go into the forest and forage for food, but how can I leave the kids home alone?

But I must!

So she taught the kids, and repeated it twice, not to climb the walls or be naughty—in short, to be nice.

And the most important thing: while she was gone, to lock the door well and to open for none.

The goat went out to the forest and spent all day collecting food. She brought it home, and sang out by the door, where she stood:

> Kiddie-dearies, soft as silk
> The sun is setting
> You'll be getting
> Pitchers of milk, pitchers of milk

The kids recognized her voice and let her in.

The next day, the nanny goat went out to the forest again. Before leaving, she warned her kids once more to keep the door locked and not to open up for anyone. But a bear had overheard her singing by the door, and he too began to sing with his rough voice:

> Kiddie-dearies, soft as silk
> The sun is setting
> You'll be getting
> Pitchers of milk, pitchers of milk
> Open the door; Mama's home!

The little kids thought it was their mother, so they ran to open the door. But the lame kid stopped them, saying, "Fools, can't you hear that it's not Mama's voice? Our mother has a delicate, little voice, and this one is so gruff! It's the bear fooling us; he wants to eat us up." The kids listened to their lame brother and didn't open up.

Another day, when the mother was out again, the bear came back and sang with a thin, little voice:

> Kiddie-dearies, soft as silk
> The sun is setting
> You'll be getting
> Pitchers of milk, pitchers of milk
> Open the door; Mama's home!

The kids rejoiced, thinking it was their mother, and ran to open the door. And the lame kid cried out to them, "What are you doing, little fools? The bear is fooling us. Mama just left; she couldn't be back so quickly." The bear sang his ditty again. But the six kids didn't feel like listening to the cripple anymore, so they opened the door.

The lame kid saw that it was bad, so he hid himself behind the oven. The bear came in and snatched six of the kids, but he couldn't reach the seventh. "Just you wait," said the bear. "I'll be back for you after I hide these six."

The bear took away the kids and carried them to his lair. The lame kid came out from under the oven, followed the bear to his lair, noted where it was located, and ran home as quickly as he could. Meanwhile, the nanny goat had come home from the forest, seen that the door was open and the cottage was empty, and realized what must have happened. She burst into tears. Along came the lame kid came and said, "Don't cry, Mama. There's no time to cry now; the bear will be back soon. Better that we should dig a trap for him."

So the nanny goat began digging up the earth with her hooves, while the kid swept it this way and that and smoothed it out, so that the bear wouldn't notice anything unusual. They covered the trap with branches, spread dry leaves over it, and hid themselves behind the trees.

Along came the bear and tumbled right into the trap.

The kid knew where the bear's lair was, and he led his mother right to it. By the time the bear crawled out from the trap, the nanny goat had already rescued all her kids. And once again they were happy, and the kids grew bigger. Everything turned out well for them—and for us, may it be even better!

Stories from Genesis

How the Birds Learned Bible Stories

Eliezer Shteynbarg

ELIEZER SHTEYNBARG
May 18, 1880–March 28, 1932

Born in Lipkany, Bessarabia, Shteynbarg attended *kheyder* and learned to read German and Russian literature independently. His cousin was the writer and educator Judah Steinberg (represented in this volume in parts 3 and 7), and Eliezer followed in his older cousin's footsteps into a career as a teacher and educational administrator. He ran a secular school with Hebrew as the language of instruction. In 1919, he moved to Czernowitz, a Romanian city at the forefront of a Yiddish cultural renaissance. He also directed a Yiddish children's theater between 1920 and 1928.

He spent 1928 to 1930 leading a Sholem Aleichem school in Rio de Janeiro, Brazil, and then returned to Czernowitz with his wife, Rivke. As an educator, Shteynbarg wrote Purim plays for his students to perform and primers that displayed a progressive educational approach to teaching basic literacy. In his spare time, he wrote the 150 tightly crafted verse fables (*Mesholim*) for which he is best remembered; most of them were published only posthumously.

"Stories from Genesis" typifies Shteynbarg's fanciful use of Jewish folk culture. The text offers a retelling of some of the key stories in Genesis through an avian lens, delighting in homophonic wordplay and whimsical conceptual juxtapositions. The teacher is a rabbi (*rov*, a Yiddish word from the Hebrew) who is also a raven (also *rov* in Yiddish, but from the German). The pupils are asked to regard the "bleter" all around them: a word meaning both "leaves" and "pages." The open-air school room offers a portrait of a progressive educational setting that includes features like recess and gentle discipline when the students grow unruly.

Chapter 1

In which it is told why the crow caws, "kra, kra"; who studies Torah with the birds; what kind of books the birds study; what kind of letters those books are written with; and the meaning of this chicken scratch is further explained.

Kra, kra, kra!

"Who makes that sound?"

"The crow."

"And why does the crow scream, 'kra, kra'? Don't you know, child? Well, I'll tell you. In birdspeak, 'Kra, kra' sounds like 'kro, kro,' which is Hebrew for 'read, read.'"

"And why does the crow scream, 'read, read'?"

"Because the crow is the teacher of the birds, and the teacher shouts, 'Kro, kro! Read, bird, read!'"

"And is that why the crow is also called raven [*rov*], because *rov*-the-raven sounds the same as the Yiddish word *rov*-the-teacher?"

"Yes, yes!"

"So do the birdies have books?"

"Of course, and what books! Each and every tree is a book. . . . A book with leaves . . ."

"With green leaves?"

"Absolutely!"

"So do the leaves have letters on them?"

"Of course, and I'll tell you how you can see for yourself! Take a leaf, child, a green leaf from a tree and take a good look: you'll see little lines and scratches, fine little scratches."

"Really, really?!"

"Absolutely! The strokes aren't as straight, and the scratches aren't as smooth as the lines and curves that you sometimes scribble with your pen. No, but they are real letters! True letters. Once upon a time, human beings also wrote letters like that. 'Chicken scratch,' they used to call those letters."

"So then were they able to read the writing on the green leaves back then?"

"No, child! The writing on the green leaves is a totally different kind of 'chicken scratch.' They say that those who are as good and pious as little birdies are visited at night in their dreams by a tiny angel who's just the size of a sparrow. The little angel is called a 'cherub,' and that's who teaches you to read the writing on the green leaves."

"Really?"

"That's what folks say. And whoever can read the writing on the green leaves will know a lot of secrets and stories, secrets that only the birdies know."

"Only the birdies?"

"Only birdies! And maybe also little tiny children, who still drink mother's milk and laugh at the notion of sleep. . . ."

"And humans who can read the bird writing find that when they go to write—using our letters, of course—it comes out the same as when we birds write: short strokes, scratches, lines, and dots. . . ."

"I've seen those kinds of poems in books."

"And in an old holy book, I've read a story like that."

"I want to hear it!"

"And since you want to hear it, I will tell it. . . ."

Chapter 2

In which it is told how the birds came to school; what their teacher taught them about the old bird Sandy, who counts the stars; and about an old-timer who heard a nice story; and how the little birds blessed the new moon.

Once the rabbi, the teacher of the birdies, let out a cry: *Kra, kra!* The birdies quickly gathered around him and sat on the branches of an acacia tree, where the rabbi said to his little pupils, "Now, my little birdies, we're going to start studying Bible stories!"

"Bible! Bible! Bible!" the birdies cried and beat their wings with joy.

"I'll tell you how the world was created, and you'll be delighted."

"Tweet, tweet, tweet, sweet!" all the birds twittered at once.

The teacher gave three pecks at the branch, sniffed the sweet acacia fragrance, and slowly relaxed into his tale:

"My grandpa, of blessed memory, told *me* that he heard from his great-grandfather what an old-timer had once told *him*.

"The old-timer was in the forest once, near the Hidekel River mentioned in Genesis, over where the phoenix-bird Sandy* sat on a tall cedar tree and

---

* *Hol* is referenced in Job 29:18 and translated variously as "phoenix" and "sand."

counted the stars. Once he had counted all the stars, he would know how old he was. . . ."

"Sandy? Sandy? Why was he called Sandy?"

"Well, I'll tell you: This was a kind of bird that lived forever, growing and growing until he grew backward and became a little chick again, small as a grain of sand, and a fire rose up from his nest and burned him to ashes. Just one little egg was all that remained of him. Out of the egg would peck a new Sandy, and so it went on and on without ever ending.

"Fi, fi, fi!" the birdies cried. "Sooo, what story did Sandy tell?"

The teacher gave another three pecks on the branch, sniffed three times at the acacia fragrance, and said, "Did you know that the moon and Sandy Bird are sister and brother? The moon also lives forever, and she also keeps waxing until she begins to wane; and then she grows smaller and smaller, until a fire rises up from her nest and burns her to ashes. Out goes the moon! But no! An egg remains. She pecks her way out of the egg, and there's a new moon, a young one, a brand-new moon! The birdies bless the new moon, jump and dance before her,* and they sing:

> Tweetle dee, tweetle dee
> New moon, come to me.
> Cheep! Cheep! Cheep! Peep! Peep! Peep!
> I have in mind a tune so deep
> Tu, tu, tu, toowhit, toowhoo
> I will sing the tune for you!

All the birdies sang along.

"And that one gets burned up too," sang the teacher.

"And again, peck, peck, peck!" a dancing birdie sings. "Another new moon pecks her way out!"

"Whee! Whee! Tee heehee! How many new moons the world must have blessed by now!" sang a birdie.

"New, new, but still the same old moon," said the teacher. "She burns up over and over again."

"Shriek, shriek, shriek!" chirped all the birdies happily.

---

* This description mimics the Blessing of the New Moon, which incorporates rising on tiptoe as a way of symbolically dancing toward the celestial body.

The teacher reflected a little and went on: "Sandy is a silent one, a big silent one, because he's old as the forest and he's seen and heard everything and he knows everything, and those who know everything keep quiet.

"When the birds bless a new month, it makes Sandy happy. Then all the birdies from the forest gather together around Sandy, and by the glow of the new moon, they tell nice stories. Once—and the old-timer was *there*—he told a story like this. . . .

"Cheep! Cheep! Creeeeep! Stop fooling around!" Suddenly the birds got angry at one another and started jostling each other for a closer seat.

"Don't be angry, little brother, I want to hear too. . . ."

"Meh! Meh! Feh!" cried the others, "Why are you interrupting?"

"Don't fight, birdies," says the teacher softly. "Straighten up and come closer! That's it. Good, good. Now listen!"

Chapter 3

In which it is told of human beings who set out on a ship across the great ocean, of a woodchopper's stroke; and of how the birdies laughed when they really should have cried and how come the teacher shouted at them.

"Once upon a time, some people set sail on a ship across the sea. Suddenly they spotted a bird with its head in the air, its feet in the ocean, and water only up to its ankles. So they wanted to jump off the ship and go for a swim. After all, because of the bird, they thought it couldn't be that deep—only up to their ankles. Suddenly they heard a heavenly voice:

"'Watch out! Seven years ago, a woodchopper chopped wood here. His axe is still down under these waters. It's been falling and falling, and to this day, its still hasn't reached the bottom yet.'"

"Deep, deep, deep!" the birdies gaped in wonder. "So deep?!"

"So deep!" said the teacher.

"So very deep and yet only up to the bird's ankles?" wondered one birdie.

"Don't be surprised," answered the teacher. "That bird is Bar Yokhni!* Bar Yokhni, praised is he and praised is his name! Bar Yokhni, who measures the deepest depths with his ankles.

"And he's the one who warned the people to watch out?"

---

* Literally, "Son of the Nest," Bar Yokhni is a bird mentioned several times in the Talmud in connection with its gigantic size.

"Yes, he was!" said the teacher. "He tried to warn them but they didn't listen. . . .

"Ooooooo," trilled all the birdies at once. "Bar Yokhni is gooooood."

And one little bird, a lively and happy one, danced on one foot and sang:

Yokh Yokh Yokhni
Sweet and good!
Guard my dad, bless my mom
Understood?

"Ooooooo" all the birdies sang in unison.

"Yes," said the teacher. "Bar Yokhni is good, and he was good to the people, but

"What good is a sweet wheat crop—when there's no one to harvest it?

"What good is clever advice—when there's no one to praise it?

"Bar Yokhni is good, and he tried to do well by the people, but they didn't listen. . . ."

"Didn't listen? Why?"

"Because they were great swimmers. And whoever is a swimmer is boastful, like a duck."

"The swimmers bragged:

"'We'll do it,' they said. 'We'll descend to the deepest depths, fetch the axe, and use it to measure Bar Yokhni! We'll be world famous!'

"So saying, they jumped into the ocean. Soon a big storm wind came, from all the corners of the earth, the dark eagles converged, and they spread their wings, as large as the night, across the sky.

"And the blind eyes of the dark eagles were opened, and they flashed with excitement. And waves like mountains tossed up to the sky, and the eagles carried the ship on their backs—forty days and forty nights.

"And then Bar Yokhni—praised be he—gently flapped his wings and blew a soft wind that stilled the waters, and the ship was spit out on Mount Ararat.

"All the swimmers were drowned, except one who remained on the ship and could thus tell of Bar Yokhni's wonder.

"People wrote down the story of the drowning in the holy books. They call it The Flood, or Inundation."

"What? What?" asked the birdies.

"In-un-day-shun!" said the teacher. "It's hard for you; you won't be able to repeat it."

"Daysh," tried one.

"Hee, hee," laughed a second.

"Sh! Sh! You rascal," shouted the teacher. He gave the student a light peck on the head and added, "People drown, and it's funny to him. He's laughing."

The birdies turned sad.

The teacher went on:

"And Sandy told another story that night. . . ."

"We want to hear it! We want to hear it!" the birdies all encouraged him.

And the teacher told it as follows:

Chapter 4

In which it is told of a high tower, a black cat, and how a wise word came from a clever snake.

"Once upon a time, the people built a high tower that went all the way up to the sky! They wanted to reach up to Bar Yokhni.* They wanted to pull off bright feathers from his wings and sell them for money!"

"Money? Money?" asked the birdies. "What is money?"

"Who knows? It's a secret! Humans have a habit of hiding their money. . . ."

"But a canary, who spent an entire year in a cage living among people before he escaped, told me that he himself saw something black moving around in the house, a black thing with green eyes and sharp claws!

"At night, when they put out the fire and the entire household went to sleep, just then, in the dark, the green eyes of the black thing would light up—what a fright! They could burn up the whole world! Death would spread to every corner! . . . I thought, If this isn't some wild cat, then it certainly must be money . . . yes, yes, money. . . . I have proof. . . ."

"What kind of proof?" the birdies were eager to know.

"Once I spoke with a snake, who had lived for seven years in India with a fakir. She had learned much wisdom from him. The fakir would take her mouth into his own and, mouth to mouth, would reveal deep secrets to her.

"The snake told me this:

* According to *bBekhorot* 57b, "Once, the egg of a *bar yokhni* fell and flooded sixteen cities and destroyed three hundred cedar trees."

"'You'll see something that by daylight is dark and by dark night is bright, and you should know that you are seeing:

"'Either a glow worm, or rotten wood, or fools' wisdom, or money....'"

"Deep, deep, deep!" chattered the birdies—"that's so deeeep!"

"Definitely!" says the teacher. "When you grow older, you'll begin to understand it properly."

"Anyway why do people need the black thing with the eyes that burn in the darkness?" the birdies wanted to know.

"That, dear birdies, the people have not told us, but I surely do know that people love these black things very much. For money, sometimes a person will even give up his life!"

"Even his life?!"

"Yes! The canary, who had lived among them for an entire year, told me that everyone in the household, from children to adults, loved the black thing. Little ones would play and dance with it, and it slept on the same bed with the man of the house. The woman of the house would cuddle it close to her heart, even though it would scratch all over...."

"That's crazy!" pronounced one birdie.

"And they say that people are smart!" added a second.

"Ehh," said the teacher, "smarter than a duck, that's for sure.... But I shouldn't mix up two things; I'll tell you about the duck later on.... Where were we?"

"At the tower."

"So the people built a high tower. They built and built until it almost reached the sky, and suddenly—cr, cr, cr-ack!

"Bar Yokhni threw down the very smallest egg from his nest, and that brought down the whole tower.

"When the tower fell, many, many cities were destroyed under its weight—so many cities, as many as the number of birdies that can sit on a tree branch, with all their little wings and eyes, their little feet and claws."

"Fi, fi, fi!" the birdies cried.

"So do you understand now who Bar Yokhni is?" asked the teacher. "Now, my birdies, stretch your wings and get a little air, and when you come back, I'll tell you how Bar Yokhni created the world."

"Chirp, chirp, chirrrrrp!" the birds flew off with a song.

The birdies flew and frolicked over the open fields for about half an hour. In the blue air, they made circles and played hide-and-go-seek and duck,

duck, goose. And they came back lively and happy and out of breath to the teacher on the tree.

They sat quietly and obediently as the teacher began to speak again:

Chapter 5

In which the teacher poses to the birdies a difficult question and then answers it himself; the origins of the black eagles that wander around crying are explained; and the reason why there is thunder and lightning is given.

The teacher began with a question:

"Children! Where does a bird come from?"

"From an egg!"

"And where does the egg come from?"

"From a bird!"

"And the bird?"

"From an egg!"

"An egg comes from a bird, a bird from an egg," said the teacher. "But what came before that? At the very beginning? First of all came the egg! And where did the egg come from? The egg came from the dark mountains. . . .

"Once upon a time, long ago, before the very first egg, there were dark mountains—dark, slumbering mountains and nothing else! And beyond the dark mountains, Bar Yokhni hovered, like an eagle guarding its nest, anxious about its hatchlings. So Bar Yokhni—praised be he—circled over those hills, watchfully.

"All of a sudden, a bright flash struck the mountain peaks!

"A flame kindled in Bar Yokhni's eyes, and that fire lit up the peaks of the slumbering mountains.

"The mountains were startled out of their sleep.

"Bar Yokhni spoke to them, saying:

"'Let all the dark mountains gather in one place, and let one great egg come forth from them!'

"And so it was: all the dark mountains gathered in one place, and one egg came forth from them: the first egg!

"Bar Yokhni, praised be his name, cracked the egg with his beak, and inside was an egg white, a large yolk with a blood spot, and many, many smaller yolks.

"From the top half of the white, he created the sky; from the bottom half, the sea; from the great yolk, the golden sun; from the little yolklets, the moon and stars; from the hard shell, the earth and all that is in it; and from the blood spot, human beings.

"Then Bar Yokhni looked at it and realized, 'One dark mountain didn't come with the others!'

"When Bar Yokhni had commanded, 'Let all the dark mountains gather together,' that one hadn't heard. He had fallen asleep.

"Bar Yokhni got angry at him and said, 'Dark mountain! Because you alone stood still when all your brothers united to make a great Creation, you shall be a restless wanderer! You shall ramble around from place to place and never find any rest!'

"Just then, Bar Yokhni beat his wings hard, and great winds picked up and caught the mountain and tore it to pieces. And from those dark pieces came eagles: dark eagles that wander eternally!

"The dark eagles cried before Bar Yokhni and said, 'Our sin is too great to bear! We didn't participate in the Great Creation, so we were left distressed and benighted. We'll never find any rest; we'll be crying forever!'

"Bar Yokhni took pity on them and said, 'Well, then let your tears fall upon the earth and refresh it, and new creations will spring forth from your bosom.'

"And so it was. When the dark eagles cried out of great remorse and longing for Creation, their tears fell on the earth, the earth swallowed their tears, and new creations grew forth from their bosom: crops, trees, grasses, roses, flowers!

"The earth blessed the eagles.

"The eagles answered with one voice: 'Amen!'"

"Is that what thunder is?" asked the birdies.

"Yes," said the teacher. "That's thunder."

"And so what's lightning?" asked the birdies.

"Lightning is the first light that flashed in Bar Yokhni's eyes at the very Beginning, the flash that lit up the mountain peaks when Bar Yokhni—praised be he—had just thought of creating the world."

"How did that bright light come to the dark eagles?"

"Bar Yokhni, in his great mercy, gave the lightning to the dark eagles so that the world wouldn't be afraid of them. . . . When the dark eagles finally showed up and spread out their wings, as wide as the night, their blind eyes welled up, and they gushed tears, rivers of tears, over the whole world because they had slept through the moment of Creation. Then suddenly the light of Creation flashed forth from their eyes—a sign that from that darkness and from those tears, creation and blessing would come, . . . new life would sprout forth. . . ."

"And Cuckoo here is afraid of the lightning!" said one birdie, pointing one wing at his friend.

"Cuckoo! Cu—lookoo! Just look at him, that wise guy!" said the cuckoo, embarrassed. "Well, you're just as scared of thunder as I am, aren't you?"

"I . . . I . . . I . . . will never be scared of thunder again. . . ."

"And now I'll never be scared of thunder *or* lightning," promised the cuckoo.

"None of us! No one!" shrieked the birdies happily. "None of us will be afraid. Let there be thunder and lightning! Let new life come! Let there sprout new life! Tweet! Tweet! Tweet!"

The birdies swarmed about, with their beaks in the little green "book," and applauded with their wings and sang:

> Up, up, up, in the tree so green
> Up, up, on thin little branches
> Up, up, at the very treetop
> A star on a lightning bolt dances
> Let us sing: tweet, tweet, tweet
> Tweet, tweet, tweet!

And the teacher dismissed the birdies until the next morning.

The Birds Go on Strike

Lit-Man

LIT-MAN (SIMKHE GELTMAN/FREYLEKH)
1898–July 26, 1946

Born in Mezritsh, Poland, Simkhe Geltman emigrated in 1924 to Buenos Aires. There he became part of the editorial board of the newspaper *Di prese* (The press) and an educational leader. He wrote for adults under the name Freylekh and for children under the pseudonym Lit-Man (Literatur(e) + Man). He was a successful playwright in Argentina, and between 1927 and 1947 he authored several books, which saw publication in Buenos Aires and Warsaw.

His writing for children managed whimsically and imaginatively to reflect the realities of their lives. "The Birds Go on Strike" imagines birdsong as the critical "labor" that avian citizens perform so that the world can run smoothly. Their dismay at the captivity of some of their number, which leads them to strike, demonstrates an enviable fraternal solidarity. The story took up themes of both labor activism and environmental awareness before the latter became a widespread concern.

— ℬ —

A bird sat for three days and three nights shut up in a cage and then escaped. He flew for a kilometer and took a break and then flew two and three more—until he reached his sisters and brothers in the forest, where he raised a cry, "Friends! Birds!"

The birds were flying around playfully in the forest, singing and jumping; when they heard the voice of their newly freed fellow, they all rallied to greet him, but the bird wouldn't let them speak.

"Birds!" he said. "Do you see the city over there?"

The birds turned their little heads around, startled, and said, "Yes, we see it. . . ."

"Do you know how many thousands of our brothers and sisters are sitting in cages over there?"

The birds hung their heads sadly:

"We know."

"My poor child is there," said a mother, crying.

"My little sister," sighed a brother.

"My father . . ."

"My mother . . ."

All of a sudden the forest grew quiet and cheerless, and all the birds and animals fell silent. Only the rustling of the trees could be heard as they shook their heads sadly.

The bird looked at his colleagues and cried out, "Birds! We must not allow this anymore!"

"What should we do?" asked the rest of the birds.

"Tomorrow not one bird will chirp!"

The next day, the city woke up later than usual, and all the children were late to school.

"What happened?" everyone asked.

"Every day, the chirping of the birds wakes me up, and today, there was no birdsong," one boy said.

"Even the bird that lives in a little cage at my house stayed quiet; I didn't hear the slightest peep out of him."

"Could the birds have flown away to other lands right in the middle of spring?"

The day was gray and sad. When the children went outside, they noticed that a dark pall covered everything; all the trees and flowers stood there silently, their heads bowed.

"What's going on?" a boy asked.

"Yesterday the trees were so fresh and green, just starting to blossom, but today they look as old and yellow as in midautumn. . . ."

"Trees, trees, what happened?" a girl asked.

A tall tree gave a shudder, saying, "We don't know. The birds didn't come today, and we're sad and withering. . . ."

"When we don't hear them sing, we can't bloom and grow," said a second tree.

"They bring us the spring, the joy, the sunshine. . . ."

On the second day, the city was even grayer and sadder, and the sun only showed itself at midday, glanced at the city and its streets, and quickly tucked her head back down between the white pillows.

"You see," someone said, "when the birds aren't here, the sun is lonesome."

"Today the sun slept through the entire day."

"Of course! The birds wake up the day, the sun, the trees. . . ."

The children spent six cheerless days in the city: days without sun, without joy, without spring, and without games. And on the seventh day, they went out to the forest to talk things over with the birds.

"What do you want?" they asked.

"First of all," the birds said, "we want you to let our brothers and sisters out of your cages."

"Fine. What else?"

"No more catching birds by luring us with seeds or grains. . . ."

"Done."

"You can't mess with our nests anymore."

"Agreed."

The next day, thousands of birds were set free and went outside joyfully, and hundreds of thousands of cages were burned publicly—accompanied by singing.

The day after that, the sun shone warmer than ever before, and the trees and flowers bloomed and turned green. And when the birds burst into song, many great musicians lay down their instruments and said, "We've never heard birds sing like *that* before!"

The Bat

Meyer Ziml Tkatch

MEYER ZIML TKATCH
December 1894–1986

Born in the village of Priborsk, near Kiev, to a schoolteacher and his wife, Tkatch studied in *kheyder* before following his father into teaching. He came to the United States in 1913 and worked as a painter; the following year he began to publish poetry in Russian. Shortly thereafter, he switched to Yiddish, writing fables for a long list of publications in New York, Chicago, Philadelphia, Warsaw, Tel Aviv, Paris, Mexico City, and Buenos Aires. He began to publish books of poetry as well, beginning in 1927 and continuing into the 1970s. Tkatch translated the poetry of Sergei Yesenin and Robert Frost into Yiddish. A Yiddish literary prize was named for him.

Tkatch wrote masterful fables, often using the final lines to sharpen his moral. "The Bat" exemplifies the twist whereby a question of zoological taxonomy becomes a critique of human failure to live up to the potential of our species.

— ℬ —

Once upon a time there came
A bat to a zoologist to complain:
"Oh, Learned Sir, it's enough to make me cry!
I have wings, and I can fly,
But as if in jest, you have me classed
With the caste—
Not avian, as you might accordingly determine,
But rather like a mouse: among the vermin."

"Have you really come now, Bat,
 To raise this fruitless hue and cry?"
 And speaking thus, the Scholar did
 To Ms. Bat an explanation broach:
 "It's true enough that like a bird you fly,
 But verily you live more like a roach."
. . . .
 So, too, the human lives just like a pest,
 Though he may with wings of thought be blessed.

PART VI

SCHOOL DAYS

The Alphabet Gets Angry
Moyshe Shifris

MOYSHE SHIFRIS
April 5, 1897–February 13, 1977

Born in Kisnitse, Podolia, Shifris was educated in Belz, where his father was a ritual slaughterer. He was orphaned as a young child and continued studying in yeshivas until age fifteen. He came to America in 1914. In 1918, he enlisted with the Jewish Legion of the British Army to fight the Ottomans in Palestine, and he returned to New York in 1919. He worked as a hat maker and then a teacher, first in the relatively apolitical Sholem Aleichem schools and then, as of 1927, in the communist-aligned Ordn-shuln. He joined the Proletpen organization of leftist Yiddish writers.

After publishing his first poems in the Brooklyn weekly *Progress* in 1917, Shifris went on to contribute to a wide variety of periodicals, including a regular column for the *Vegetarishe velt* (Vegetarian world) as well as a host of more mainstream publications. He wrote poetry, stories, stories, and plays for adults and children as well as children's songs. He also penned literary criticism and translated books from English, including John Louis Spivak's lightly fictionalized novel condemning the harsh conditions, brutality, and racism that prevailed in Georgia's convict camps. He died in New Jersey.

His 1950 collection of children's stories, *Foygl kanarik un andere mayses* (The canary bird and other stories) focuses on the experiences of children in Yiddish schools. "The Alphabet Gets Angry" tells the more universal story of a schoolboy panicking on the eve of the first day of school about how much he has forgotten (and, in this case, failed to review!) during the summer break.

— ℬ —

Mikey's mother tucked him in and said, "Close your eyes, Mikheleh, and go to sleep. Tomorrow you have to go to school. Good night, son, sleep well and sweet dreams."

She kissed his forehead, turned out the light, and quietly closed the door behind her.

Mikey lay there in the dark with his eyes open and thought about the summer that was ending. What a good time he'd had in the mountains! There he was, rocking in a boat on the river and then taking a stroll in the forest with his friends. His eyes were beginning to close, and very soon he would be asleep.

All of a sudden, from a corner of Mikey's room, a classroom floated up before his eyes. The desks and chalkboard danced in a circle. Children with booklets in their hands swayed at the desks. The teacher stood in the middle, leading a choir, and all the children were singing,

> Enough already, sleepyhead,
> School is starting, out of bed
> Go on, Mikey, grab your book
> Come to school and take a look.

And that's when Mikey remembered that he hadn't looked inside a Yiddish book all summer long. The teacher had given him a book to read so he wouldn't forget what he'd learned and could go on to a higher class, but Mikey had never found any time for it. Who knew whether he could still read a single word of Yiddish?

Mikey turned on the light. He got out of bed quietly and picked up the book, which his mother had already gotten ready for him to take with him to school in the morning. He got back into bed and opened it to see whether he could still read any Yiddish.

He wanted to start reading, but it didn't work. The letters jumped off the pages and spun and whirled in circles before him. He closed his eyes. He rubbed them and opened them again, but the letters weren't on the pages; they were chasing each other around like fireflies in the dark. They danced up and down, back and forth, and Mikey didn't know which was which.

A *shin* (ש) planted itself, and next to it, a *vov* (ו) and a *tes* (ט) and a *hey* (ה). They stood straight as soldiers. And then, close together, came a *beys* (ב) and a final *nun* (ן), a *pey* (פ), a *yud* (י), a *kuf* (ק), a *hey* (ה), an *aleph* (א), a *lamed* (ל), and a final *tsadi* (ץ).

Mikey looked at them in amazement, but he couldn't begin to know what they wanted.

The *shin* (ש), with its three little heads, jumped forward and danced right up to his nose, and each little head gave him a flick—three heads and three flicks—and angrily spelled out the phrase they'd made, "*shoyte ben pikholts*, you complete idiot, why are you so surprised that you can't catch us or that you don't know which end is up, you bearish oaf who likes to loaf?! What did you think? An entire summer, you didn't so much as look at us, and suddenly you want to be our best friend?"

Here the *kuf* (ק) danced up onto Mikey and with its pointy stick started to jab him in the side, saying, "Not even once did you crack open the book, so that we could get a bit of fresh air."

The *daled* (ד) started to jump before Mikey's eyes and spin his head left and right, saying, "Why, you such-and-such, you've been living it up in the mountains, and we've—"

The thin final *nun* (ן) could no longer hold back his fury, so he jumped—with his point—right onto Mikey's stomach, and nodding his tiny head up and down, with his eyes glued to the heavens, hit him hard with these words:

> You ran in grasses free of cares
> And chased all day the mountain hares
> Breaking twigs with country bums
> Munching apples, biting plums,
> Sailing, swimming all day long
> But not *one* Yiddish letter
> While you were gone!
> And now, look who the cat's dragged in
> He's back, so we should let him in?
> And after all these summer harms
> Welcome him with open arms?

And the *aleph* (א) with both of its little heads, blew up in anger, flashing and blinking its eyes as if to make the point, and taunted Mikey, while dancing up and down,

> And to think he finds it a surprise
> When we letters spin before his eyes?

The *lamed* (ל) began to stride back and forth across Mikey's forehead, and with his long giraffe neck, swayed like a wagging finger before Mikey's nose and said,

> What you don't put in
> You can't get out.
> And if you don't look in a book
> You'll never know what it's about.

Mikey lay there stunned, not knowing what to do. He began to make excuses, saying, "How could I look inside the book and savor a Yiddish word, if I didn't even take the book along with me?"

Now the *beys* (ב) got angry* and, losing his temper, jumped right up onto Mikey and seized his ear with both hands, saying, "Why didn't you take along the book, you brilliant boy? Huh? What, during the summer it's forbidden to look inside a Yiddish book? Maybe you don't like nice stories, eh?"

"Of course I like nice stories," Mikey nodded. "I actually took along several English books with nice stories, so I could read on rainy days."

"Very nice—as far as *you're* concerned," railed the *beys*. "But why only English? Are there not enough stories in Yiddish?"

"When the teacher told stories in school, did you like hearing them?"

"I *really* enjoyed the teacher's stories," declared Mikey.

The final *nun* said,

> Is that how it is?!
> And when you're alone
> Are you too little-kid-ish
> To pick up a story
> And read it in Yiddish?
> Are you too lazy
> Or would it bore ye
> To read aloud
> A Yiddish story?

And now the *giml* (ג) clicked together the heels of its boots, saying,

> What a silly goose
> With his tongue so loose.

---

* The word used here for "angry" is *beyz*, a homonym with the name of the letter in Yiddish.

I'm afraid there's no sense
In forgiving his offense.
There's none to supplicate:
It's better if we separate.
There was a book without a Mikey
The whole entire summer,
So now there's a Mikey without
Yiddish books—ha, bummer!

And all the letters from *aleph* (א) to *sav* (ת) discussed it and decided on how things should go: they would have nothing more to do with Mikey. He would be a stranger to them.

With that, the book lifted itself up into the air and started to fly away, with all the letters trailing behind.

Mikey felt a tingling in his nose as if he had suddenly gulped down a spoonful of horseradish (as he had in fact done last year at the first Passover seder), the tears rushed into his eyes, and he began to beg,

Now I really see that you are right,
I've committed quite a wrong.
The book has lots of lovely stories
And also poems and also songs.
I beg you not to leave me then;
I promise not to goof again.

When the letters saw the tears in Mikey's eyes, they grew sad and returned to the book, and the book flew back into Mikey's hand, and . . .

Suddenly Mikey felt a hand on his shoulder, and he caught the strains of his mother's voice, "Mikheleh, Mikheleh, it's time to get up and go to school."

Mikey jumped out of bed, rubbed his eyes, looked around joyfully, and quickly ran to wash up and get dressed. Grabbing the book, he pressed it affectionately to his chest and went running off to school.

His mother shouted after him, "Mikheleh, you forgot to eat!"

"I'll eat later," he replied, running.

And like an arrow shot from a bow, Mikey flew off to school.

The Teacher
Mashe Shtuker-Payuk

MASHE SHTUKER-PAYUK
October 5, 1914–May 28, 1988

Born in a town in the Grodno district of Poland, Shtuker began her education in a Tarbut school in her town. Her family emigrated to Argentina in 1925 and farmed on the Montefiore settlement, one of several Jewish utopian agricultural settlements throughout North and South America. There she studied at a local colony school where her father, Binyomen Shtuker, was a teacher. She attended the Jewish teachers' seminary in Buenos Aires in the 1930s and became a kindergarten teacher. She was known in Spanish as Martha Stuker de Paiuk.

Her first poem, identified only as the work of "a girl from camp," was published at age sixteen. But her adult literary debut came in 1933 with a series of poems in a Buenos Aires newspaper. After that, her work appeared in several periodicals in Buenos Aires, Montevideo, Mexico City, and New York. She published several books, and her work for children was widely anthologized and translated into Hebrew and Spanish. In 1974, she moved to Israel. She is buried in Holon, Israel. Her epitaph reads, "It's good to be young and to sing your own song, aloud and free."

Shtuker-Payuk's poetry is written with a light touch and a child's-eye view of the world. "The Teacher" portrays a mischievous but wise child who recognizes in the new teacher a kindred spirit.

— ❧ —

Tomorrow a new teacher comes
Woohoo! It makes me very glad
I've worked so hard on all my tricks
And little ways of being bad

Before he gets to know the class
Each and every single one
I'll have my mischief at the ready
All my games and all my fun

But I'd rejoiced in vain it seems:
Before I could see my plans through,
He fixed me with just one good look
He knew just what I'd hoped to do

How did he guess before he saw
The slightest little thing at all?
Heh heh, the teacher must have been
Just like me when he was small.

A Story of a Schoolboy and a Goat

Kadya Molodowsky

KADYA MOLODOWSKY
May 10, 1894–March 23, 1975

For biographical information on Molodowsky, see "The Baker and the Beggar" in part 3. Along with "The Baker and the Beggar" and "Zelig the Rhymester" (in part 4), "A Story of a Schoolboy and a Goat" appeared in a section called "Schoolboys" of Molodowsky's 1970 collection of stories and poems for children, *Martsepanes* (Marzipans).

— ℬ —

Dovid was the best student in his class. He always knew the weekly Torah portion by heart. Once, when they were studying about Noah and the Flood, the students came into the classroom and saw a goat. Dovid ran out after the goat and pulled its tail. When he came back inside and took his seat, he found that he'd forgotten everything he'd learned, just as if all the words had flown out of his head. The rabbi got annoyed with him and asked, "Where did your memory go?"

The other boys were happy to see the teacher angry at Dovid and sang under their breath, "Now you're feeling quite forlorn. You lost your mind on a goat's sharp horn."

Dovid felt ashamed, and he cried all the way home from school. It was raining, and that made him even sadder. Suddenly, he saw Noah's ark floating toward him from out of the rain. Noah stuck out his head and asked, "Little boy, why are you crying?"

Dovid told him about how he'd seen a goat, pulled its tail, and then forgotten the Torah portion. The rabbi got mad at him and the other boys had made fun of him and chanted, "Now you're feeling quite forlorn. You lost your mind on a goat's sharp horn."

"And *that's* why I'm crying," he concluded.

Noah, concerned, said, "You should be careful of the goat, little boy. She will get the better of you—unless you can get hold of the little silver ring that she keeps hidden in one hoof. With that ring, you'll receive all that you could ever want. Remember what I'm telling you."

Noah patted Dovid's shoulder, and the ark floated away in the rain. Dovid went over the Torah portion that he'd learned, reciting it word by word from memory until he got home.

On his way to school the next day, Dovid saw the goat again. He ran after her, climbed up on her back, and while he was riding along, whispered into her ear, "Goat, goat, give me your silver ring that you keep hidden in one hoof."

As soon as she heard that, the goat gave a sudden jolt, Dovid wobbled off her back, and the creature ran away. But when he jumped up, the goat dropped the silver ring. Dovid snatched it, put it in his pocket, and went to school.

That day, Dovid knew the Torah portion better than ever before. All he had to do was touch the silver ring in his pocket, and he saw the words and their meanings right before his eyes. The rabbi was pleased, and he praised Dovid.

Thinking it over, Dovid asked himself, "Why do I have to study?" After all, he just had to pick up the silver ring, and he would know everything he needed to by heart. He no longer felt like listening to what the rabbi taught or how the children replied.

When the rabbi called on him to recite the portion, he dug his hand into his pocket to take out the silver ring—but poof! it was gone.

Dovid became very confused. He didn't remember how to recite or explain even a single word. The rabbi got very angry and screamed at Dovid. The other boys whooped and chanted, "Now you're feeling quite forlorn. You lost your mind on a goat's sharp horn."

Dovid was so distraught that he couldn't speak at all. That afternoon, he wept on his way home. To make matters worse, it was raining out, and this made him even sadder. Then he saw Noah's ark floating toward him through the rain. Noah stuck his head out the window and asked, "Why are you crying, little boy?"

Dovid told him all about the disaster that had befallen him. He had lost the silver ring and couldn't find it.

Noah shook his head and replied, "You have forgotten. I told you that with the ring, you could have everything that you could ever want. But you didn't actually *want* to learn. You didn't want to listen to what the rabbi was teaching, and you didn't want to listen to what the other children were saying—so the ring rolled away from you."

Dovid had nothing to say to that, so he kept quiet.

Noah patted Dovid on the shoulder, and the ark floated off in the rain. Dovid stood stock still while fat tears fell from his eyes.

When he was finally ready to go home, he saw something shining before him. He bent down, and the silver ring began to roll slowly but surely toward his feet. With great joy, Dovid snatched up the ring and put it in his pocket. He swore that from then on, he would treat the ring so well that it would never again want to roll away.

Although Dovid never saw the goat again, he saw Noah and his ark often—but only in his dreams.

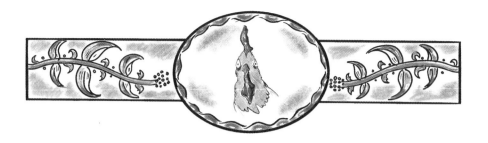

The Chickens Who
Wanted to Learn Yiddish

Moyshe Shifris

MOYSHE SHIFRIS

April 5, 1897–February 13, 1977

For biographical information on Shifris, see "The Alphabet Gets Angry" earlier in part 6. "The Chickens Who Wanted to Learn Yiddish" takes readers into the poultry-farming communities that Yiddish-speaking Jews established in Vineland, Toms River, Farmingdale, and Lakewood, New Jersey, in the 1920s through the 1950s.

— ℬ —

On the sandy beaches of New Jersey, only about two hours outside of New York City, lies the town of Toms River, surrounded by slender pine trees.

In and around the town live many Jewish farmers. Chicken farmers they're called, because they all raise chickens there.

Last winter, the Jewish farmers got together and decided to bring down a teacher and open a Yiddish school. It isn't right—the Jewish farmers reasoned—for Jewish children not to be able to speak a word of Yiddish, read a Yiddish book, or know any Jewish history.

No sooner said than done.

They set up school desks and a big chalkboard in the community center, and it became a Jewish school.

Every afternoon, children from the neighboring farms came to study Yiddish.

The children took a liking to the teacher and the school. They learned to recite Yiddish poems and sing Yiddish songs, and they listened very avidly to the teacher's every word when he taught them about Jewish history.

The fathers and mothers, grandfathers and grandmothers beamed with pride that their children and grandchildren wrote such beautiful compositions and recounted what they had learned in Yiddish school each day.

Once, on a lovely, mild day at the beginning of spring, when the children were absorbed in their learning and the class was so quiet that you could hear the summer arriving, there suddenly rang out an extended, tuneful "Cock-a-doodle-doo!"

All the children and the teacher lifted their heads and looked around amazed, wide-eyed, as if to ask, "What just happened here?"

And in the midst of this sudden quiet, everyone caught sight at once of a rooster's little head with a red comb peeking out from Pinchas's jacket pocket, and they made out the sound of a "cock-a-doo."

The rooster's crowing didn't end there. For nine-year-old Pinchas, who had turned redder than the creature's bright comb, was trying to stuff the bird's head back under his jacket, which was puffed up in front as if he had a hump there.

Suddenly the rooster jerked itself out from under the jacket with all its might and jumped right onto the teacher's desk. It spread its wings, pricked up its comb, and with all its youthful strength burst out crowing with a long, musical cock-a-doodle-dooooooooo—as if it thought it could wake up all the farmers in Toms River, from the midst of their work.

All the children burst into laughter. Pinchas sat there forlorn and didn't know what to do with himself—whether he should run after the rooster or just run home.

The teacher fixed his brown eyes on Pinchas and asked calmly, "What is this, Pinchas?"

Pinchas, blushing and playing with a pair of brown feathers that had been left in his hands, murmured quietly, "The chickens want to learn Yiddish."

"What?" the teacher trained his wide eyes on Pinchas.

The children burst out laughing again, and word passed along from the first row of desks to the last: "The chickens want to learn Yiddish."

"Enough laughing," the teacher said with a serious expression, although his brown eyes, surrounded by little wrinkles, were smiling.

The children stopped laughing, but they smiled in the light of the spring sun, which came pouring in through the window.

The teacher sat down and calmly said to Pinchas, "Tell us, Pinchas, about the chickens who want to learn Yiddish."

And with his serious expression, he showed the children that they should keep a straight face and hear out what Pinchas had to say.

Pinchas fixed his black eyes on the teacher. "Yes, Teacher, the chickens really do want to learn Yiddish. That's what they've decided. They told me so themselves."

"In English or in Yiddish?" cried out one pupil, exploding into laughter.

The teacher gave him a sharp look and soothed Pinchas, "Tell us, Pinchas, we want to hear."

So Pinchas began to tell the story: "Every day, when my sister Sarah and I came home from public school, we would eat quickly and go out to the yard to play. We would play behind the house where the chicken coops are. All winter, we kept the chickens in their coops, but when it got warm outside, Papa let out the chickens on the field, where they would go around pecking with their beaks, grubbing for food.

"Sarah and I would play with the chickens. Some of the chickens loved us so much that wherever we went, they would follow.

"It got so that the chickens would wait for us to come home from school and play with them.

"But since the Yiddish school was opened, we can't play with them anymore because we need to come here.

"So the sad chickens hung around the field, and some of them no longer even felt like laying eggs. They missed us.

"One day, a Saturday, when Sarah and I went out to the chickens, we saw that something had happened to them. They were going around clucking and getting mad for some reason. So I said to Sarah, 'What happened with the chickens? Why are they so sad and angry? Come on, let's take a look.'

"When we came closer, I heard all the chickens speaking at once, and one was trying to scream over the next; and this very cock, who just crowed here, flew up on one of the little hutches that we have in our field, the ones that have no walls or floor, just a roof, where the chickens hide from the burning sun during the worst heat, and he let out a crow and started to say, 'Hush! Be quiet! Why are you clucking like hens? Speak one at a time.'

"So one after another, hen and rooster, they stepped up to speak, and here's what they said: a while ago, we—that is, Sarah and I—their best friends, had left them, and instead of coming every morning to play with them, we had completely disappeared, to be neither heard nor seen—we were no longer friends but total strangers. . . .

"When all the hens and roosters had said their piece and it was quiet again, this very rooster here, who just crowed a moment ago, said, 'Well, if you're done already, then I'll take the floor. Let it be quiet. You all appointed me to find out where Pinchas and Sarah were disappearing to every afternoon. So I followed them and have found out everything that you want to know.'

"'Let's hear, let's hear!' all the chickens started to cluck.

"'When you stop clucking, you'll hear,' said the rooster. 'Pinchas and Sarah go to a Yiddish school to learn Yiddish, and that's why they don't come to play with us.'

"'Yiddish, Yiddish?' all the chickens clucked.

"'Yes, Yiddish!' the rooster screamed. 'They are Jewish children,* so they need to know Yiddish. Isn't that right?'

"'Certainly, certainly,' nodded all the chickens.

"'So there's no reason to be mad at them,' crowed the rooster, 'and no reason to scold them.'

"All the chickens grew quiet. But then suddenly the cockerel pushed forward, pricked up his red comb, and crowed, 'And what are we, huh? Do we or do we not live with a Jewish farmer? We were born here, we grew up here, and we live here, right? So we are Jewish chickens, are we not?'

"'Jewish, certainly!' clucked all the chickens in unison.

"'And if that's so, then why shouldn't we learn some Yiddish, huh? I'm right, am I not?'

"'Right, right, certainly right!' they all clucked in unison.

"'But how can we learn Yiddish?' asked the rooster on the roof of the hutch. 'Who will teach us?'

---

* The word "Yiddish" means "Jewish," as well as referring to the name of a language.

" 'It's very simple,' crowed the cockerel. 'You'll go with Pinchas to the school every day, and whatever you learn there, you'll teach us.' "

"And what came of this fowl assembly?" asked the teacher with a serious expression.

Pinchas answered, fixing his black eyes on the teacher, "It was decided that this cock right here," Pinchas pointed to the rooster on the teacher's desk, "would come to school with me to learn Yiddish, and then later he'll teach it to the chickens."

The teacher listened to the whole story with smiling eyes. And the sun itself smiled through the window.

PART VII

IN LIFE'S CLASSROOM

Questions

Judah Steinberg

JUDAH STEINBERG

1863–March 10, 1908

For biographical information on Steinberg, see "Roses and Emeralds" in part 3. "Questions" is a far more realistic and explicitly political treatment of a similar theme as in "Roses and Emeralds."

— ℬ —

Little Joseph, a rich boy, had a friend named Bezalel, a carpenter's son.

Once, Bezalel brought Joseph over to his house. Noticing that the large rooms were empty, Joseph asked his friend, "Bezalel, where is your furniture?"

"We have no furniture."

Joseph looked around and asked another question: "Where's the bed you sleep in?" Bezalel replied, "We don't have beds. We all sleep on the ground."

Joseph looked down at the ground and was astonished. "Why isn't there any floor in this room?"

"There's no floor in the other rooms of our house either."

"And where's the cabinet where you keep your books?"

"I keep my books in a bag; we don't have a cabinet."

As Joseph was going home, he ran into the servant in the courtyard, where she was laundering clothes.

Joseph turned to her and asked, "Tell me, Sarah, who makes furniture?"

Sarah answered, "Carpenters make furniture."

"Then why on earth is our house full of furniture, while Hanan the carpenter's house has none at all?"

"Do you have to ask about Hanan the carpenter?" the servant replied. "Ask about *me*. I wash and prepare clean clothes for all of you, and I myself go about dressed in dirty rags."

The boy left her and then ran into the geese in the courtyard, as they went about honking, "Goh, goh, goh!"

He turned to the geese and said, "Oh, babbling, white geese! I have two questions to ask you. Maybe you can tell me: Why is there no furniture at Hanan the carpenter's house? And why does the servant who washes our clothes go around herself in torn rags?"

The geese lifted their beaks skyward and said, "Ga, ga, ga! Why do you have to ask about Hanan and the servant? Ask about *us*! We give feathers, so why do you sleep at night on pillows stuffed with soft down while we lie on the naked ground?"

He left the geese and ran into the cow, as she stood there lowing, "Mrooo, mrooo."

He turned to her and said, "Mrs. Moo, Mrs. Moo. I have three questions to ask you, and maybe you can answer them. Why does Hanan the carpenter make furniture, while his son sleeps on the damp earth? Why does the servant Sarah, who launders our clothing, go about dressed in rags? And why do the geese, who give feathers to the whole world, themselves sleep naked on the ground?"

The cow fixed her eyes on him and said, "Do you have to ask about Hanan the carpenter, the servant, and the babbling geese? You had better ask about *me*! I give all of you milk, while my own little calf, my child for whose sake I make the milk from the marrow of my bones, stands locked all day in a dark stall. I 'moo' to him, and he 'mehs' back at me, and by the time I give you a full pail of milk, I have nothing left for my child to suckle!"

The boy took leave of her and ran into a donkey, who had been loaded with the hide of a dead animal. The donkey stood there braying.

"Hey, you loudmouth!" the boy turned to him. "I have four questions to ask you. Maybe you can give me answers. Why does Hanan the carpenter, who makes furniture for everyone, have no beds in his house? Why does Sarah the servant clothe all of us, while she herself goes about in rags? Why do I lie on soft pillows full of down feathers while the geese lie on the naked earth? And why does the cow nourish all of us with her milk while her own calf goes hungry?"

The donkey pricked up his ears and said, "Leave me to my troubles! I'm a mourner right now. My wife, the jenny, caught a cold and died, and I must carry her hide to the tanner to be made into leather; the cobbler will use that leather to make shoes for you. And the road is bad, and I'm barefoot; so how can *I* answer your questions?"

The boy left the donkey alone and ran into a sheep. He said to the sheep, "Lambie, lambie! I want to ask you five questions. If you don't answer them for me, I'll tell everyone that you're a fool. Why does Hanan the carpenter have no furniture? Why does Sarah the washerwoman dress in dirty clothes? Why do the geese, who give their feathers for pillows, lie on the naked earth? Why is the calf shut up in a stall while we drink his mother's milk? Why do the donkeys go barefoot and catch cold and die, while our boots and shoes are made from their hides?"

This is how the sheep replied to him: "Please leave me alone! I'm very cold. Don't you see that I've just been sheared? They took away my wool to make you a suit, and now while I'm standing here naked and shivering with cold, you come to pester me with your questions?!"

So the boy left the sheep and went to his mother and said, "Mama, I want to ask you six questions, and surely, you'll be able to answer them. After all, a mother is the smartest thing in the world."

"Ask, my child," his mother replied.

So he asked, "Who makes furniture?"

"The carpenter."

"Then why on earth doesn't Hanan the carpenter have any furniture in his house?"

"Okay, so that's one question. What else would you like to ask?"

"Who does our laundry?"

"Sarah, the servant."

"So why does she go around in torn, dirty clothing?"

"Why do we lie on white pillows while the geese lie on the ground?"

"Why do we drink the cow's milk while her calf stands there all day shut up in a stall?

"Why do the donkeys go barefoot and catch cold, while our shoes are made from their hides?

"And why does the sheep go around naked while my suit is made from his wool?"

His mother heard out his questions, heaved a sigh, and said nothing.

The boy saw that his mother wasn't going to answer his questions, so he heaved a sigh too and went out. Then he took out a little book from his pocket and wrote down his questions.

"When I grow up, I myself will find the answers to these questions!"

And with that, the boy consoled himself and really took the matter into his heart and mind.

Boots and the Bath Squad

Leyb Kvitko

LEYB KVITKO
1890–August 12, 1952

For biographical information on Kvitko, see "A Nanny Goat with Seven Kids" in part 5. In "Boots and the Bath Squad," the parents are simply not home; the "bathmen," agents of the Soviet state, provide the necessary care and sanitation for a child whose gluttony and dirtiness are regarded as a potential vector of disease.

— ℬ —

I can't tell you for certain
Whether or not the story's true,
Whether it happened exactly so.
But however it's told,
It's a cheerful tale—

This much I know,
So I'll tell it as I do:

Off somewhere in a shtetl far-flung,
Lived a boy: one of those guys
With shining eyes
And cheeks for weeks
And such a tongue!

To him, a book might as well be a brick;
Just keep the sweet crepes coming quick,
And pancakes and dumplings
For his tummy's grumblings:
Plate after plate—
And then, a smidgen more he ate.

Before the boy could even swallow
He'd wink and check what more might follow:
"Hey, is there anything left in the pot?"
He'd overturn it on the spot.

And hey, when you're gorging and noshing,
Who so much as thinks of washing?
And hey, when there's strudel and fruit cake for grazing,
Who so much as thinks of bathing?

No soap for him! No water to squirt!
He was completely encrusted in dirt.

The thing was bound to come to pass:
The door, it opened up, alas,
Without so much as a knock.
And who should come in,
In a flaxen smock,
So tall and thin?
The Bathman.
And then another and yet another:
Neither smaller than the other.

Thus spake the Bathman
No more, no less:

"Why, that's him, yes!"
And he pointed out the lad.
Soon as his words reached the boy's ears,
One of his eyes filled up with tears
And the dumpling he was eating?
Well, it knew not what to do;
That dumpling got stuck in his throat midchew. . . .

The Bathman
Sang out shrill as trumpet's metal:
"A cold is going 'round the shtetl
What a punk!
What a craw!
Such filthy funk!
His dirty maw!
Grab that Boots, that grubby schlub!
Drag him over to the tub!
Turn on the taps!
No time to cosset,
Hurry, get him to that faucet!"

The two men,
Neither of whom
Could be said to be small,
Reared up like bears
And lunged at the wall,
Thinking the boy would just—

I really don't know
What they thought he would do!
Boots snorted and hid
And continued to chew. . . .

Meanwhile, the two men who
(As I think you'll recall)

Could neither of them be said to be small
Began to comb the young man's locks
And to pull off his shoes and socks.

What socks?! Now this is quite a feat:
His socks were caked onto his feet!
And what a stench!
Enough to make them sneeze and blench,
First, the men who (as you'll recall)
Could neither of them be said to be small—

And soon enough, the Bathman too
Sneeze after sneeze, "Atchoo, atchoo!
Throw him in the tub—atch—
With his socks on—oo!
Atch—" through gaping mouth, "Atch—! Atch—!
Oo! Go ahead, turn on the taps!"

Around and over the lad, in a rush,
The faucet's stream began to gush
And warm him with its steam.
He started to give himself a scrub:
Like cymbals crashing
He set to roaring and to splashing.
Legs a'thrashing,
He gave his locks a rub.

Yes, he scrubbed his locks
Then suddenly—quiet,
And there they floated:
Two withered socks!

When they took him from the bath
He beamed with pride, began to laugh
Didn't recognize himself
Sitting on a chair so grand
He reached to shake the Bathman's hand.

"Hey, thanks!"
Then, facing the men who (as you'll recall)
Could neither of them be said to be small,
And taking his time lazy and sweet,
He chirped,
  "*Now*
      I could go
        For a bite
          To eat!"

The Girl in the Mailbox

Lit-Man

LIT-MAN (SIMKHE GELTMAN/FREYLEKH)
1898–July 26, 1946

For biographical information on Lit-Man, see "The Birds Go on Strike" in part 5. "The Girl in the Mailbox" playfully explores how technologies like international mail were making the world smaller and increasing mobility.

— ❧ —

A father went with his little girl to mail a letter at the mailbox. But he made a mistake and instead of throwing the letter into the box, he pitched in his daughter.

Before too long, along came a mailman none too clever, and he took the letters and the little girl out of the box and carried them to the post office.

Another fellow was at the post office. He looked over all the letters and found the girl among them.

"What are you doing here, huh?" he asked.

"My dad threw me into the mailbox."

"Wow! And where is the address?"

"He didn't write one down."

"And where are your postage stamps?"

"I don't know."

The man thought and thought. "We need to send you back, but I don't know where to."

One of the letters heard this and said, "Oh, don't send the little girl back. I have three cents of extra postage. I'll give them to the girl."

"That's too little."

"I also have one extra cent," cried out a second letter.

"And I have two. . . ."

Long story short, they scraped together enough postage to take the little girl along on the ship.

The girl had a cheerful journey. Each letter had a different story to tell: some were sad and others were happy, some told of good children and others, of bad ones.

When the ship arrived in Europe, a man showed up and asked each letter, "Letter, letter, tell me whether you know where you're traveling to and where you're going?"

The letters replied, "I'm going to Lithuania. . . . I'm going to Poland. . . . I'm off to Pitimite. . . . Me—to Reb Joel."

When he got to the little girl, she didn't know what to say, and the man sent her back to Argentina. She was taken to the city square, where they asked, "Who wants to buy a little girl? A little girl from the mail? Cheap and inexpensive, she costs just a groschen."

Soon the girl's father came running and said, "How much does the girl cost? A groschen? Here, take ten and give her back to me!"

???

Ida Maze

IDA MAZE (MASSEY)
July 9, 1893–June 12, 1962

For biographical information on Maze, see "Where Stories Come From" in part 3. Many of Maze's poems are miniatures containing worlds, including the lyric "???." In under thirty words, the poet evokes the question of empathy in the relationship between an older and a younger child.

— ℬ —

If you were me
And I were you,
I'd be in
Your shoes.

I would be eight,
And four's what *you'd* be;
So then would you
Play with me?

Moe and Nicky

Sarah L. Liebert

SARAH L. LIEBERT (SORE-LEYE LIBERT)
ca. 1891–January 28, 1955

Born in Kutno, Poland, either in 1891 or the following year, Liebert emigrated to America in her youth. She studied education at Hunter College and received a master's degree from Columbia University, becoming the first female teacher in New York's Yiddish schools. She was active in the new Sholem Aleichem Folk Institute and its schools and involved in teacher training. She also helped Jewish farmers living outside New York City to organize Yiddish schools for their children.

Her writing appeared in children's periodicals and newspapers for adults; she took a particular interest in highlighting the work of women authors throughout the world. She published a variety of books for children, including contemporary, realistic stories, biblical and Talmudic tales, and a textbook. She worked in New York's Welfare Department during her later years and died in that city.

Mirele's experiences on her family's farm outside Boston lie at the center of several of Liebert's tales. She portrays a loving Jewish family trying to balance maintaining their cultural identity and family cohesion with the desire to acculturate among their non-Jewish neighbors. "Moe and Nicky" offers a rare glimpse of a Yiddish-language story with only the subtlest Jewish ethnic markers or none at all. Based on their names, Moe and his boss, Jack, might be Jewish. Nicky's boss, Tony, who has named his horse Garibaldi, is almost certainly Italian American. Together, the heroes of the story's title uphold a value that is highly important in traditional Jewish culture, albeit one with universal reach: care for animals.

— ❧ —

1.

Around three in the afternoon, when the sun was burning its hottest, Jack the fruit peddler pulled onto Eleventh Street, between Eighth and Ninth Avenues, with his horse Max, and a wagon full of fruit.

"Giddyap!" Jack just barely managed to spit out as he pulled up to a garage.

Catching sight of Tony the vegetable peddler, his horse Garibaldi, and his wagonload of vegetables, Jack called out, "Hello, hello, Tony! Have you already sold your potatoes, onions, carrots, and cabbages?"

Tony wiped the sweat from his forehead with a red handkerchief, patted his thin Garibaldi, and replied, "Hello, hello, Jack! Sold who, sold what now? You could melt today from the heat. And you? Ha, ha, ha—I see there's no need to ask how it's going: your wagon's still full of fruit."

With his last words, Tony turned serious. He went over to Jack, and petting Jack's horse, he said, "I feel sorry for the horses! They can't go any farther today. What a heat wave, *what* a heat wave! The asphalt is like hot tar."

"You know what, Jack? Let's let the horses take a rest, and we'll go drink a cup of coffee. Moe and Nicky will stay with the horses."

Moe and Nicky, the two boys who worked as helpers by running up flights of stairs to deliver the fruits and vegetables, each stood guard like a wooden soldier by the horse of his boss.

Jack looked at the two grimy, sweaty boys and handed each of them a nickel, saying, "Buy yourselves an ice cream, and watch the horses."

Tony also gave each of them a nickel and added, "It's hot, it's hot. Buy yourselves a soda water, and watch the wagons too."

The two boys bought ice cream. They sat down on the edge of the sidewalk and ate the ice cream with wooden spoons. Suddenly Moe piped up, "You know, Nicky, we should have given the horses a drink. See how they're looking at us?"

Nicky stood up and, petting Garibaldi, replied, "You're right, but what can we do when there are no watering stations for horses to get a drink?" He gestured at the garage and said, "There are garages for thirsty cars; they have gasoline. Horses need water. There are a lot of gas stations for thirsty cars but not a single watering station for tired, parched horses. You can go fifty—what am I saying?—a hundred miles without finding a single watering station for horses."

"Jack says that a long time ago, before the automobile came along, it was different."

Moe and Nicky stood there, petting the horses and thinking about where they could get them a drink of water.

2.

Just then, they felt a stream of water on their legs.

Where was it coming from?

They quickly saw that several boys had unscrewed a hydrant on the street. The street was soon flooded, and it looked like a river. Moe cried enthusiastically, "Let's take water from the hydrant!"

But they had no bucket and couldn't do a thing. Soon a policeman came running up, screwed the hydrant back into place, and drove away the children.

Moe and Nicky looked at the horses, who were neighing and waggling their tails.

"There's nothing we can do," said Nicky, as he petted both horses.

Moe looked at the horses and exclaimed, "Nicky, let's buy a bucket of water in the garage for the dime that we have left over. We had ice cream, so we can go without soda water. We have to get the horses a drink!"

Nicky burst into laughter.

Seeing Nicky laugh left Moe embarrassed. He'd probably said something very foolish. "If you don't want to, we don't have to," he said.

The horses neighed again.

"Look, look, the horses are begging us to buy them a drink with that dime," Moe added.

Nicky handed over his nickel to Moe, and both of them went over to the garage.

3.

Moe shoved Nicky forward so he would go first into the garage, and Nicky shoved Moe forward to state their errand.

A man who was standing there polishing a car shouted, "Get out of here! What do you want? Home, go home!"

Moe and Nicky wouldn't budge. A garage worker came up and yelled, "Get outta here, I tell ya!"

The two boys still didn't budge. The garage owner approached the boys. Out of fear, Moe dropped the nickels from his hand. He bent over and began to stammer, "I—we—we, um," pointing at Nicky and himself, "we, um, we came to buy water . . . the horses . . . thirsty, we have a dime. . . ."

One of the garage workers guffawed and asked, "Oh, you want gasoline for the horses, and you have how much money?"

Moe showed his and Nicky's nickels and said entreatingly, "No, no—not gasoline—water, water."

The garage worker laughed even louder. But the louder he laughed, the more the two boys worked up their courage, until both of them said loudly and clearly, "You sell gasoline and water for thirsty automobiles, so sell us a bit of water for our thirsty horses . . . 'cause if you won't, they'll die."

The worker saw that the boys were not giving up; they were holding out their two nickels and asking for a bit of water for the horses, so he asked a question, "Where do you have your horses?"

The two boys led the worker over to the horses, who broke into loud neighing when they caught sight of Moe and Nicky.

The garage worker offered the horses water, and Moe and Nicky thanked him.

A car was parked near the garage. Inside sat a woman who overheard the boys asking for water for the tired horses and complaining that nobody thought about how there needed to be watering stations for horses who stay on duty and work hard all day.

4.

The next day, when Jack and Tony met up, one showed the other a news item in the paper that read as follows:

"The Society for the Prevention of Cruelty to Animals requests aid for horses. It wants to open two watering stations for horses this week: one on West Eleventh Street and one on Sheridan Square. The Society hopes to be able to provide water for the hundreds of packhorses on the streets of New York."

The news item ended this way: "Mrs. L., a member of the Society for the Prevention of Cruelty to Animals, thanks two boys, Moe and Nicky, for their devotion to living creatures and expresses the hope that Moe and Nicky will be rewarded for their benevolence."

Roosteroo

Ida Maze

IDA MAZE (MASSEY)

July 9, 1893–June 12, 1962

For biographical information on Maze, see "Where Stories Come From" in part 3. "Roosteroo" is concerned with questions of relational reciprocity.

— ℬ —

Roosteroo,
Your comb so red
I've got seeds for you
And crumbs of bread.

Give me a feather;
Why not give me two?
Wake me in the morning
With your cock-a-doodle-doo.

PART VIII

JEWISH FAMILIES, HERE AND THERE

From Labzik: Stories of a Clever Pup

Khaver Paver

KHAVER PAVER (GERSHON EINBINDER)
February 8, 1901–December 7, 1964

Eventually known by the pen name Khaver Paver, Gershon Einbinder was born in Bershad, Podolia, to a prosperous family of logging merchants. He studied in *kheyder* and attended yeshiva. Fleeing pogrom violence in the wake of the Russian Revolution, he moved to Romania in 1919 before emigrating to the United States in 1923 or 1924 (accounts vary). As a teacher in Romania, he began to write stories for his students. Once in New York, he taught in the secular Yiddish schools run by the communist-aligned International Workers Order (IWO) and contributed regularly to leftist newspapers and children's periodicals. He started out writing for children in the 1920s and '30s and eventually came to write fiction for adults as well.

In 1935, he published a book of linked stories about the mongrel pup Labzik and the leftist Jewish family that adopts him. Published and distributed by the IWO, the book's proletarian sympathies are vividly clear. Dwelling in the heart of the bustling working-class community of Brownsville, Brooklyn, Berl the sewing-machine operator, his wife Molly, their son Mulik, and their daughter Rifke offer a sympathetic portrait of Depression-era secularist Jews who confront life's adversities and adventures as a family. Like a situation comedy or radio play, each chapter of the Labzik tales features its own conflict, rising action, and resolution involving the heroism of the family's canine companion.

After publishing his Labzik stories, Einbinder moved to Los Angeles, where he wrote for the Yiddish film industry as well as continuing to pen fiction, plays, and memoir. His screenplay credits include *Der puremshpiler* (The jester) and *The Light Ahead: Fishke the Lame.* The "Chaver Paver Book Committee" saw to it that his work from this period was published.

— ℬ —

The Hard-Luck Pup

A woman from Brownsville laid her puppy in a basket so he couldn't see where they were going. But Labzik, the puppy, was *delighted* to be in a basket. So he lay there belly up, kicked his little paws, and beamed with joy.

The woman climbed up to the elevated at Sutter Avenue Station, tossed her nickel into the turnstile, and ran up to the tracks above. A train was already waiting: it would carry them lickety-split over all the rooftops and then underground, and then again over the rooftops, and once more underground.

As the train clacked along, the woman spoke to the puppy in the basket.

"Labzik, don't be mad at me for what I'm doing. It's because of the Depression."

"Woof, woof!" replied Labzik, as he tried to lick the tip of her nose.

The woman didn't allow the lick on her nose, but she went on, "And don't think, Labzik, that I don't like you. I love you, but there's nothing to give you to eat, and that's actually why we had to send away our little Emma to her aunt's house in Boston."

"Woof, woof!" answered Labzik, as he tried to catch her fingers playfully in his teeth.

The train ran above the rooftops and underground, and soon enough, they reached Jackson Avenue Station in the Bronx. The train stopped there for a full minute. The woman from Brownsville got up and turned Labzik out of the basket and onto the station platform, while she remained on the train. The doors closed, and the puppy ran alongside the moving train and shouted with all his might, "Woof, woof, don't leave me, don't leave me!"

But it had already happened. The train sped away with the woman from Brownsville, and the puppy was left alone in a strange part of the city with a note around his neck.

At first, Labzik thought it was all just a game and that someone would come back and get him soon. So he lay down in a corner and waited.

לאבזיק

פון כאַווער פּאַווער

(מייסעלעך
וועגן קלוגן
הינטעלע
לאַבזיק)

צייכענונגען פון
לואי בונין

He waited and waited as the day wore on and eventually turned into night. In a low growl, he began to cry, "Wherrre, wherrre, wherrre?"

Trains full of workers kept rushing into the station. The doors opened, and the passengers ran out quickly and bounded down the stairs. No one even glanced at Labzik.

He began to cry louder, "Whe-ere, Whe-errre?"

Another train rushed in, the doors opened all at once, the workers ran out and bounded down the steps.

Labzik picked himself up and began to stride back and forth across the platform with flattened ears, whimpering, "Wh-e-eere?"

Meanwhile, it began to rain. It got cold. Trains rushed in, people got out, but absolutely no one noticed the puppy with the note around his neck.

Labzik thought things looked very bad for him, that he might even die, and he began to feel very sorry for himself and to whimper like a small child, "Ay, ay, ay."

Let's leave Labzik crying on the platform for a while so we can tell about Berl the sewing-machine operator.

Berl had big, black eyes that were always merry. He had a capable wife named Molly, a little boy named Mulik, and a little girl named Rifkele. He'd been sitting in a window seat on the train, looking out.

"Ugh," he said, "it's raining. But gosh darn the rain, as long as there's a good supper!"

The Lexington Avenue express train stopped at Jackson Avenue, and out ran Berl the Operator with his merry eyes. But before he could head for home, he noticed the puppy with the note around its neck, trembling with cold and whimpering like a child, "Ee, ee, ee."

He bent down, and the puppy licked Berl's fingers. Berl liked that. He skimmed the note, which said, "There is a Depression on. My husband has no work, and we have nothing to feed this pup. Good people who still have work, please take him in. He's called 'Labzik.'"

Berl thought it over, wondering, "Should I take him home or not? Of course we'd have to feed him, and I have so little work. But gosh darn the scarce work! I *will* take him home."

Berl wrapped him up in the newsprint pages of the *Morning Freedom*,* and Labzik didn't object. He knew that he had found a real mensch.

I don't even have to tell you about the great joy of Rifkele and Mulik when their father brought the "hard-luck pup" into the house. They gave him warm milk, bathed him, toweled him off, and put him to bed in a cradle. Rifkele rocked it and sang softly, "Oh, Labzik, oh, sleep hard luck puppy, sleep. The Pioneers† will drive away the Depression. Oh, sleep, sleep."

Labzik obeyed and was soon fast asleep.

Labzik and the Strike

Part 1

One night at dusk, Berl the Operator came home, but he didn't say, "Good evening to you, my wife Molly, good evening to you my daughter Rifke, good evening to you my son Mulik, and good evening to you my doggie Labzik."

---

* A leftist daily newspaper begun in New York during the 1920s.
† A communist youth group.

No, he didn't say any such thing; he sat down at the table instead and worried. Molly sat down too, and so did Mulik, Rifke, and Labzik, and they all worried about what could be worrying Berl.

Suddenly Berl banged his hand on the table and blurted out, "Gosh darn it! What are you all worrying about? Why aren't you serving me dinner? I'm hungry."

"Nope," replied Molly, "I won't serve you your dinner."

"Why not?" asked Berl.

"The reason . . . ," began Molly, "well, because you haven't wished good evening to me—or the children or the doggie."

"I didn't say 'good evening'?" Berl asked, astonished. "Imagine that! Good evening to you, my wife Molly, a good evening to you, my son Mulik, a good evening to you, my daughter Rifke, and to you too, doggie Labzik. So, now would you serve my supper already?"

"No, I still *won't* serve your supper." She was still mad.

"Why not?" said Berl. "I've said a proper 'good evening' now."

"Yes, you said it," said Molly. "But we still want to know what you're worrying about."

"Ha! Molly, you think I'm worrying," said Berl. "Well, yes I am: about the strike."

"Strike?!" cried Molly, with a loud clap.

"Strike!" cried Mulik, his eyes widening.

"Strike!" cried Rifkele, slapping herself on the cheek.

"Woof, woof," barked Labzik. Of course he knew nothing about what was going on, but with everyone else talking, he had to say something too.

"Yes, a strike," replied Berl. "A strike against the boss. The boss wants us to work until nine o'clock at night, and we don't want to. We say that if we keep such long hours, we'll get sick from the hard work."

"Well, if that's how it is," said Molly, "let's finish up dinner quickly and go to bed early. I'd like to go with you tomorrow morning to the shop and help you strike."

"I'll also help you strike," called out Mulik.

"Me too," said Rifkele.

"Woof, woof," Labzik put in.

Berl looked over at Labzik and said, "Yes, that's all right, but what will we do with Labzik? He'll want to come too."

"Don't worry," answered the mama. "We'll tie him to the bed with some twine."

And so that she wouldn't forget, she took the twine out of a drawer and lay it on the table.

When Labzik saw the twine, he began to tremble. He knew from previous experience that a piece of twine always meant something bad for him. He walked up to the twine and began to bark at it. This made everyone in the house laugh.

Everyone went to bed, including Labzik. His dream was a long story, in which Moyshl the Boy Scout (whom Labzik already disliked) was chasing him with a piece of twine, and he was trying and trying and trying

to outrun the boy. He ran for an hour, two hours, with Moyshl always hot on his tail. He caught a Lexington Avenue Express and kept riding it the whole night. But suddenly, Labzik felt something choking him, and he began to pull against it. He woke up and saw that it was daylight. The length of twine was already around his neck, he was tied to the bedpost, and everyone was leaving the house. He tugged against the twine. He began to cry. But now the door was closed, and he could hear everyone going down the stairs. He felt very sorry for himself, that he should have to be tied to the bed, and he burst into tears like a little child, moaning, "Eeeeeee."

The street was still empty as Berl, Molly, Mulik, and Rifke made their way in the darkness to Jackson Avenue Station. They climbed the stairs, threw in their nickels, and stepped onto the empty platform.

Before dawn, there weren't many trains running at all. They strolled up and down the long platform, talking about the strike and looking into the distance from time to time to see whether an express was coming.

Eventually, they felt a vibration from afar. They began to hear the click-clack of the wheels, and they made out the train with its two large eyes. One eye was red, the other green. All of a sudden, the doors opened, and they boarded. They looked around, aha—he was there! Who was there? Why, obviously, it was none other than Labzik.

Yes, he was there. And a tiny bit of torn twine hung from his neck. Apparently he had chewed through it with his sharp little teeth. And now he was standing in the subway car with tears still in his eyes, but he was intensely happy. The train went very fast, and Labzik jumped from Rifke to Mulik, from Mulik to Berl, from Berl to Molly. He licked everyone's fingers and was so overjoyed that he didn't know what to do with himself.

As for the rest of what happened with the strike, it will be revealed in part 2 of this story.

Part 2

So Labzik was riding the subway too. Rifkele took him in her hands, sat him on the straw seat, and talked with him. She said to him, "Labzik, you're a bad boy."

Labzik answered her with a wag of his tail.

Then she asked him, "Labzik, do you even know what a strike is?"

He gave his ears a shake. That meant that yes, he understood what a strike was. But of course Rifkele knew that he was a big liar and he didn't understand, so she explained it to him. "A strike," she said, "is when the workers won't work anymore until the boss is good to them. Get it?"

At that, Labzik shut one eye and left the other open.

Talking that way, they arrived downtown at Thirty-Fourth Street. When they got outside, it was no longer dark. The sun shone golden on the houses. Many people hurried along the streets to work.

When the whole family arrived at the shop where Berl worked, they found lots of other workers milling about with large signs. The signs said, "We don't want to work until nine o'clock at night. We want to come home early and play with our children!"

The workers greeted each other all around and said, "Good morning to you, Berl the Operator. You've come to picket with your wife and children?"

"A good morning to you, comrades," Berl replied cheerfully. "Not only have I brought my family but also my doggie, Labzik. He also wants to picket the shop."

"Ha, ha!" laughed the workers. "A dog is going to picket the shop? Really, now!"

Labzik didn't know they were laughing at him. He was busy looking all around the street to see what he could do to help. He had just noticed a policeman, a mean-looking one with a club, standing across the street. Labzik recognized that very policeman (the one who had grabbed him and Mulik and Rifke once) from near the Jackson Avenue Station, and the dog threw himself onto him furiously. The workers barely managed to tear him off.

They chanted, "On the line, on the line," and picketed the shop. Molly, Mulik, Rifkele, and finally Labzik all marched in line. Berl didn't join the line; he said something quietly in his wife Molly's ear, so that nobody else would hear, and he entered the building through an open door. Nobody saw him except for Labzik. Did you think *he* wouldn't see? And instantly, he shot through the same door as Berl.

Berl began to climb the stairs. And Labzik went after him. Berl climbed from the second floor to the third to the fourth. And Labzik kept following him. Berl went from the fourth floor to the fifth, from the fifth to the sixth, with Labzik right behind him. Berl climbed from the sixth floor to the seventh, from the seventh to the eighth, and so on until the eighteenth floor, and the doggie was always right there behind him.

On the eighteenth floor, Berl paused and caught his breath. He quietly opened a door, and Labzik followed.

This was the shop where Berl worked. Eight men who didn't want to go down and join the strike were still sitting there at the sewing machines. When Berl went in, they all lifted their heads, and Berl spoke to them, saying, "Come down, let's strike, because if we *all* strike, the shop will be left empty; and when it's empty, the boss will see that things won't work his way, and then he'll treat us better."

But why was one of the eight men signaling something to him with his hands? What could he mean? What he meant was that Berl had better look out, because something bad was about to happen to him. But Berl didn't catch his drift, and he didn't look out, so he didn't see the boss, along with two gangsters, running toward him from behind. Labzik jumped up on them with his sharp little teeth, but he caught a hard kick in the head and fainted.

Labzik didn't know how long he lay there unconscious. When he finally picked himself up, he had a terrible pain in his head. He lay on the stairs and had no idea how he'd gotten there. Slowly it all came back to him, and then he jumped up with a start, because *where was Berl*? Where *was* he?

Labzik sniffed the stairs. He sniffed and ran up, up, up, from the eighteenth floor to the nineteenth, from the nineteenth to the twentieth, and so on for all thirty floors, until he came out on the roof, which was full of bright sunlight. Labzik would have liked to stop and notice how beautiful New York looked from such a high rooftop, but he had to keep his priorities in mind. Where was Berl? He sniffed the roof, sniffed and sniffed until he bumped into some kind of small enclosure with a locked door. He scratched the door with his claws and barked. He knew already that Berl lay there, because he could hear sighs from inside. But what would scratching the door accomplish, when it was so tightly locked? Labzik thought about it, turned himself right around, and raced down all thirty flights of stairs.

Mulik noticed Labzik running up to him. Labzik jumped up and tugged at his pants with great urgency and kept pulling him toward the entrance. The doggie also tugged at Molly's dress and at Rifkele. Molly sensed right away that something wasn't right. So she called all the other strikers over to join her in following Labzik.

In the end, they all climbed up after the doggie, and he brought them to the locked door. They broke down the door and found Berl lying there tied up. They untied Berl right away, and this made Labzik so happy. But Berl was even happier that they had unbound him. All the strikers went back to the shop, and there were so many of them that they were no longer afraid of the boss. The other eight workers went down with them and joined the strike. They all walked out together, marched back and forth along the street, and sang, "On the line, on the line, come and picket on the picket line."

The doggie with the white ears went first, of course, like a great hero, and he thought everyone was looking at him when they said, "What a clever Labzik he is! Truly priceless."

Labzik and Glikl

Khaver Paver

KHAVER PAVER (GERSHON EINBINDER)
February 8, 1901–December 7, 1964

For biographical information on Khaver Paver, see the preceding story, "*From Labzik: Stories of a Clever Pup.*" In 1947, Einbinder followed *Labzik* with the tales of his son Vovik, the family pet, fittingly, of a now-grown Mulik.

— ℬ —

I haven't yet told you the story of how Labzik got married and became a dad.

And I've also never told you about how Mulik got married and became a dad.

It happened like this:

One fine day after Passover, a big, heavy truck stopped right across from Labzik's house.

So right away, Berl the Operator, his wife Molly, his little daughter Rifke, his son Mulik, and of course also Labzik stuck their heads out the window to see what was going on.

First, they unloaded a big, blue sofa from the truck. After that, a heavy white icebox. And then, a wide, black piano. And finally, a lot of other household goods.

"Apparently they're moving into the apartment across the way," said Berl the Operator.

"They should just be nice people, the ones moving in across the way" said Mama Molly with a sigh.

"Gosh darnit!" said Berl the Operator. "Why shouldn't they be nice people? All people are nice."

"Yes," agreed Mama Molly. "Everybody's nice—except for those who aren't."

"For example?" Berl the Operator was getting mad at being contradicted.

"For example?" answered Mama Molly. "Kalmen with the long nose who used to live in the very same apartment across the way and who scalded our Labzik with hot water."

As soon as Labzik heard the name "Kalmen," he barked two or three times. He could still remember how the hot water had felt.

"You can't draw conclusions from just one person," replied Berl, getting madder.

Mama Molly knew of other people too who weren't so nice, but she decided to keep quiet. It wasn't worth fighting over.

Meanwhile, a second truck pulled up with more housewares: beds, chairs, tables, bundles of sheets, blankets, and pillows. A little dog with long yellow fur over its eyes and a curly white tail jumped right down.

"Oh what a pretty little doggie!" Rifke cried.

"Gosh darnit! It really is a pretty little dog," said Papa Berl.

"But look, look how its eyes are covered by long fur," added Mama Molly. "How can it see where it's going?"

"It can certainly see," answered Papa Berl, annoyed.

Berl was still mad from earlier, when Molly had argued with him about people being nice.

And Labzik? Labzik said nothing but let out a deep sigh.

What that sigh meant, nobody knew.

Perhaps his heart had already told him that he was in for it.

Meanwhile, as everyone was marveling at the little dog with the curly tail, a young girl with red hair jumped down from the truck too. Yes, she had red hair and laughing brown eyes.

"What a pretty girl!" exclaimed Mulik.

"Well, there you are!" grumbled Mama Molly, who was unhappy for some reason. "Okay, so maybe she has red hair—what's the big deal? That's nothing we haven't seen before."

"She is very, very pretty. I should be so lucky," said Berl with a cheerful wink.

"Just look at him," fumed the mama. "Now he's an expert."

"Gosh darnit, where's Labzik?" Mulik asked suddenly.

(Mulik liked to say "Gosh darnit" a lot, just like his father.)

Labzik was no longer at the window. He was already outside, down by the truck, barking sternly at the strange dog.

The strange dog began to bark back at him. This annoyed Labzik, and he began to growl at her angrily.

Labzik got even madder, and he bent his neck, stuck out his muzzle, bared his sharp teeth, and said, "Grrr, grrr, grrr."

The strange dog also bent her neck, stuck out her muzzle, bared her sharp teeth, and said, "Grrr, grrr, grrr."

"Glikl, Glikl, come here," the pretty girl with the red hair began to call. "Come here right this minute!"

"Ha, ha!" laughed Rifke loudly. "That a *dog* should be called Glikl? Glikl-Shmikl!"

"Gosh darnit!" said Papa Berl angrily. "What is there to laugh at? So, is *Labzik* a nicer name?"

"Mulik," pleaded Mama Molly, "run down fast and bring Labzik inside. Otherwise, they'll fight like, well, dogs."

So Mulik ran down, called Labzik, and chased him back inside. He bowed very politely to the pretty girl. He said, "Excuse me," and went back in.

And the story doesn't end there. In fact, it's just beginning. . . .

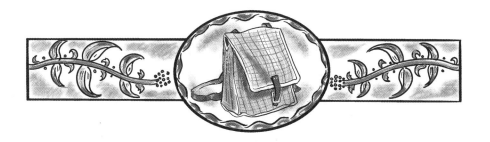

Evie Gets Lost

B. Oyerbakh

BERISH OYERBAKH (DOV AUERBACH)
1888–Summer 1941

Born in Plotsk, a small town in Poland, Oyerbakh studied in religious schools before attending university in Warsaw. He began his writing career in Hebrew but switched to Yiddish after moving to the rapidly industrializing city of Lodz in 1909. He contributed to several daily newspapers as well as to the literary journals based there. In 1922, he moved back to Warsaw, where he published stories for children in both Yiddish and Hebrew. Oyerbakh died of hunger in the Warsaw Ghetto in the summer of 1941; the exact date of his death is unknown.

"Evie Gets Lost" is a realistic story about a modern, prewar Warsaw of large apartment houses and daily newspapers. The story centers on the tensions and care in a relationship between older and younger siblings.

— ✼ —

Evie was a pretty little girl of five and a half with a round, clear face, big, shining eyes, and curly black hair. She had already known the alphabet for a long time. Back when her mother had bought her a little booklet with pictures of boys and girls, with doggies and an oven and a window, she had used it—that beautiful, new booklet—to teach herself how to read: bat, cat, dog, egg, fan, and many other short words of a single syllable in both Yiddish and Hebrew.

Evie was a happy little girl and a live wire; all day long, she would make mischief and jump around the house, from room to room. Sometimes her mother went out, and Evie would stay alone in her room for a while, climb onto a chair, and crawl up onto the window ledge to watch the children playing out in the courtyard.

Her parents loved her very much, and they delighted at how light she was on her feet, but at the same time, they also felt fearful, afraid for her, because she was so wild and always crept onto the window, lest—God forbid!—anything bad should ever happen.

Evie had a brother named Isaac. He was already a lad of eight years old who went to school. Every morning right at eight o'clock, after he had scrubbed his hands, face, head, and ears with soap and water and eaten breakfast, he would shoulder his book bag with his books and notebooks, button up his overcoat, take along the roll that his mother had given him for second breakfast, and head off to school.

Isaac loved his little sister Evie, and Evie loved her brother Isaac. Every afternoon they both played with their toys at their little white table with its two white chairs, which stood in a corner, near the big horse that their father had bought for them.

Sometimes they also quarreled as they played, but usually Evie was more to blame than her brother Isaac. That's because everything that Isaac had, anything she so much as spotted in his possession, she wanted him to give her right away. If she saw that Isaac had a pencil, she would go running right to their mother, crying, "Why does he get a whole pencil and I just have a small piece of one?" Then she would want Isaac to give up his pencil to her.

That's what she did whenever she saw that Isaac had received something that she hadn't. But Isaac was already older of course, so he understood that his sister was still a little girl—and he always gave in to her so that she wouldn't cry.

There was just one matter, though, where Isaac wouldn't give in to his little sister at all: Evie never stopped asking him to take her along with him to school and show her the teacher and students, the class, the desks, the classroom, and the pretty pictures of birds, lions, bears, and everything else that Isaac had told her about school—but Isaac wouldn't take her along for anything in the world. Nor had their mother given permission for her to go with him. Because she was still quite small—their mother said—she wasn't allowed to go with her brother, who was still just a little boy himself.

Once, Isaac was sitting at the big table doing his homework, and Evie was sitting at the little table in the corner and playing by herself with her toys.

Eventually she didn't want to play alone anymore at the little table, so she went up to Isaac and asked him to go play with her. But Isaac wouldn't play with her just then, because he still had homework to finish.

Evie went back to her little table and sat back down on her little chair feeling forlorn. Cradling her chin in her palms, she tilted her head sideways and trained her big, beautiful eyes sorrowfully on her brother, who was sitting at the table doing his homework.

As soon as Isaac finished his homework, Evie jumped up, ran over to him, and begged, "Isaac, Izzy dear, take me along tomorrow to school. I'll give you both of the red apples that Mama gave me today." So Isaac finally agreed and promised to take her along to school the next day, and he accepted Evie's red apples.

Evie was positively jubilant that she would be going along to school the next day, and all afternoon until evening, both of them, Evie and Isaac, played happily.

The next day, Isaac left early for school, just like every other day, and Evie was still asleep. When she finally got up an hour later and saw that Isaac was already gone, that he had left and gone to school by himself, she was annoyed at herself for oversleeping and angry at Isaac for not waking her.

But she didn't know that Isaac was already having second thoughts and no longer wanted to take her along at all because he was afraid of their mother.

When Isaac came home for lunch, Evie ran to meet him and reminded him of his promise the day before. But Isaac answered her with, "I don't want to take you along anymore because you're still too little. . . ."

This made Evie despondent, and she felt like crying and telling their mother on Isaac for taking both of her red apples the day before, but she felt embarrassed in front of Mother, so she stayed quiet, avoided crying, and didn't say anything at all.

That afternoon, though, when Isaac had once again taken his book bag and gone off to school, Evie could no longer restrain herself, and quietly, so that nobody would see, she ran after him.

When Isaac looked around and saw Evie running after him, he started to run faster so that she wouldn't be able to catch up; but Evie didn't turn back. She kept running after him.

Meanwhile, Isaac ran away until he disappeared and Evie could no longer see him. Evie was left standing there on the sidewalk, so she started looking around in every direction to see where she was. She looked and looked, this way and that, but she could no longer see the house where her parents lived; she was lost and couldn't find the way back to Mother.

She was very frightened and started to run farther, but suddenly she pulled up short and began to sob.

Many, many people, men and women, adults and children, passed her on the street, and all of them stopped and asked, "Why are you crying, little girl? Why are you crying? What's your name? What are your Mama and Papa's names?"

Though Evie hadn't stopped sobbing yet, she remembered and told the people that her name was Evie Lilienblum, but she didn't know the name of the street where they lived—and she couldn't stop crying. . . .

The people took pity on her, stroked her head, and tried to calm her. "Don't cry, don't cry, little girl. We'll get you home soon to your Mama."

But Evie was scared of all the strangers and couldn't stop crying.

It was already turning to dusk, and a young lady took pity on her, held her by the hand, and walked with her from house to house, asking, "Perhaps you recognize this lost child? Perhaps you know who she is, where this lost little girl is from?"

But nobody recognized Evie. Then an old woman came along, who had just crossed the street, and out of pity, she took Evie along with her and offered to keep the girl with her until they could write in to the newspapers and in that way let her parents know where she was so that they could come and pick her up.

Meanwhile back at Evie's house, there was a great lament. Her mother, who hadn't noticed when Evie went out of the house, realized only a couple of minutes later that she wasn't there and was immediately terrified.

All afternoon, Evie's father and mother had been looking around for her throughout the house, in the courtyard, and on the streets. It was dark already, and Evie still wasn't there. It was a terrible night for the unfortunate mother!

Father, who was himself very upset, tried to comfort Mother. But she wouldn't allow herself to be consoled, crying pitifully, "Who knows what could have happened to my child in the street? Who knows? . . . Oh, my God, my God. . . ." She sat there crying like that until well after midnight.

Isaac was absolutely devastated. He was afraid to admit to his mother that he was to blame for the entire calamity that had happened to Evie, and he couldn't hold himself back from crying. Evie's playthings stood there in the corner so forlorn and abandoned that he imagined they were looking at him reproachfully, with fury and rage. Isaac was afraid to look over in their direction.

Mother sat on a chair crying, so Isaac went up to her and snuggled his head against her knee, and hot tears ran down from his eyes and fell onto his mother's dress.

While Isaac and his mother were sitting there sadly, bathed in tears, Father dashed out to the newspapers' offices and let them know that his little daughter Evie had gotten lost that day. He wanted them to print a request that she be brought home to such-and-such street and such-and-such house number and such-and-such apartment number.

Early the next morning, two notices appeared in the newspapers, one right after the other. One read as follows:

"A girl of almost six with black, curly hair, named Evie Lilienblum, wearing a short, red-velvet jacket with red socks and yellow shoes, is located on such-and-such a street, in the care of so-and-so, at such-and-such address."

And the second read as follows:

"A girl of five and a half, with black, curly hair, wearing a short, red-velvet jacket with red socks and yellow shoes, by the name of Evie Lilienblum, got lost yesterday from such-and-such street, such-and-such number. Whoever knows of her whereabouts is asked to notify her parents. . . ."

Evie's father ran down very early in the morning to buy the papers. As soon as he read the first notice, he rejoiced and quickly ran to tell Mother and Isaac the good news, that Evie had already been found, and then he dashed over to pick up Evie and to thank those good people heartily for their kindness in taking his lost child into their home.

When Father got there, Evie was still asleep in bed. She looked tired, and her cheeks were streaked with dried tears.

For a short time, her father stood there beside the bed and gazed with compassion at the lost little girl, and only after a little while did he wake her; and then he could no longer restrain himself from taking her into his arms and kissing her little lips.

Waking with a start, Evie shrieked and fell into her father's arms, kissed him, and called out through tears, "Papa! Poppy-Papa!"

Evie's father got her dressed, thanked the good people, and took her home.

Oh, what joy soon overtook the household! Evie hurled herself onto her mother, and Isaac burst into tears and told the whole story of what had happened the previous day, imploring, "Mommy, Mommy, I won't do it again. It's my fault, I let her out into the street when she wanted to run to school with me. . . ." And Isaac cried for a long time, until Mother kissed him, and he and Evie covered each other with kisses too.

On his mother's orders, Isaac went up to Father, kissed his hand, and begged him to forgive his sin of leaving his sister on the street.

And from that day on, Evie and Isaac loved each other even more; and they played together every afternoon at the little table, and Evie told him so many stories about all that had happened to her on that awful day, how everyone stood around her on the street asking her questions, how the kind old lady had taken her home with her, and how she had cried for such a long time at the strangers' house.

Isaac listened to the whole thing and cried tears of pity for his little sister. She had gone through so much. He kissed her and promised her that from that day on, he would never again leave her behind and would always take care of her.

The Sick Chicken

Sarah L. Liebert

SARAH L. LIEBERT (SORE-LEYE LIBERT)
ca. 1891–January 28, 1955

For biographical information on Liebert, see "Moe and Nicky" in part 7. "The Sick Chicken," along with "Mirele's Birthday" (which follows), may reflect Liebert's experience helping Jewish farmers living outside New York City to organize Yiddish schools for their children.

— ℬ —

Mr. Fox, a farmer not far from Boston, had a little girl. She had curly, blond hair, large blue eyes, and white teeth, and she was called Mirele. She loved the geese, turkeys, and chickens on her father's farm.

Every morning, Mirele put on a long, wide apron—one of her mother's. She would put dry, yellow seeds into the apron's pockets and go with her father to the geese, turkeys, and chickens. As soon as Mr. Fox and Mirele got out to the barnyard, they heard the racket of the fowl.

"You hear that? And that?" said Mr. Fox to Mirele. "They're saying 'good morning' to us."

This made Mirele very happy, and she called out, "Good morning, dear geese! Good morning, dear turkeys! And good morning, dear hens and roosters!"

Mr. Fox unlatched the door to the coop where the geese lived. The door opened, and they all came running out. Mirele pushed her way through the flock of geese that were pecking at her clothes. One goose, with a long, white neck and a red beak, pecked at Mirele's hand, kissed her, and hissed hoarsely, "S-s-s-s-s-s, fassssster! We want breakfast!"

But the little girl with the long, wide apron wasn't in a hurry. Slowly she went over to the big tin bowl, filled it up with dry, yellow seeds, and said, "There you go. Eat and don't make a racket."

The geese stretched out their long necks and cried out, "S-s-s-s-s."

Mirele thought their "s-s-s-s-s" meant, "Thank you, little girl."

Mr. Fox filled the bowl up to the brim with corn, poured fresh water into the iron trough, and took Mirele's hand, saying, "Come on, my girl, to the turkeys."

Mr. Fox opened the door of the turkeys' coop, and all of them came running over. They puffed themselves up, spread out their large wings with the blue-green feathers, and cried out, "Gobble, gobble, gobble!"

"Good morning, good morning," Mirele answered. "I know what you want. You want corn and more corn. Here you go. Eat up and don't gobble anymore."

The turkeys puffed themselves up mightily. The comb of the largest turkey was red as fire. He stuck out his neck just as far as he could and cried, "G-o-b-b-l-e!" All the other turkeys chimed in, "Gobble! Gobble! Gobble!"

With the turkeys' food and drink taken care of, Mr. Fox took his little girl over to the chickens. As soon as they got to the chicken coop, they heard the clucking of the hens and the shrill song, "Cheep, cheep, cheep," of the little chicks. There were two bowls in the chicken coop, a large one for the big hens and a small one for the little chicks.

Mr. Fox walked over to the big bowl, and all the large hens followed him. Mirele went over to the small bowl, and all the little chicks followed her. All the big hens were white. All the little chicks were yellow. Mirele knew that the little chicks also wanted to have white feathers when they grew up.

As the chicks ate, Mirele stood there looking on. Suddenly, she cried out, "Daddy, Daddy!"

Mr. Fox came over, very frightened, and asked, "What is it, my girl?"

Mirele pointed at a small, yellow chick that stood on one foot and said, crying, "Look, look, Daddy, this chick has only one leg."

Mr. Fox waved his big, red hand, so that all the chicks ran away from the bowl. But one chick didn't run; it hopped away from the bowl on one foot. Mr. Fox took that chick into his hands. He looked it over and said, "This chick has a swollen foot. You know what, Mirele? This chick was bitten by a fly. Take it into the house, and you be the chick's doctor and nurse. If you can get the chick healthy, you'll receive it as a gift for your birthday next month."

Mirele took the chick from her father's hands, gave it a kiss, and said, "I'll get it healthy, oh yes, I will! I'm going to take my chick right into the house and become its doctor and nurse."

Mirele's Birthday

Sarah L. Liebert

SARAH L. LIEBERT (SORE-LEYE LIBERT)
ca. 1891–January 28, 1955

For biographical information on Liebert, see "Moe and Nicky" in part 7. "Mirele's Birthday" continues the story of Mirele's farming family outside of Boston, representing the integration of American customs like birthday parties into a modern Jewish home. Mirele places a great deal of importance on including her friend Johnny Smith in the festivities even though he does not speak Yiddish, the language in which most of the story takes place.

— ℬ —

1.

"Mirele, Mirele, get up. It's your birthday!"

Mirele opened her eyes to see her mother, already dressed in her coat, standing there trying to wake her.

"Where are you going, Mama?" asked a drowsy Mirele after a little while.

"Don't you know today's your birthday? I'm going shopping. Papa has invited all the farmers to your birthday party."

Mirele slowly dragged one foot out from under the comforter and then the second, until she was sitting at the edge of her bed, lost in thought. Suddenly she asked, "How old am I, Mama? Seven or eight?"

"What? You don't know how old you are?" asked Mama, a bit surprised. "Today, my girl, you're turning eight. You're not a baby anymore."

Mirele hugged her mother, saying, "Here are eight kisses for my eight years."

"Here's an idea, why don't you get dressed, and make it quick? If not, I'll give you eight *potches*.* Oh, and one more for the year to come."

With that, Mama tried to catch hold of Mirele, but the girl was faster than her mother. Before Mama could make a move, Mirele was hidden under the comforter, shrieking, "Ha ha! Where are my *potches*?"

Mama patted the comforter, but Mirele slid over quickly from one side of the bed to the other and finally slipped out from the other side of the bed onto the floor. She stretched out under the bed, grabbed her mother's legs, held them tight, and cried out, "Mama, where are my *potches*?"

Mrs. Fox bent down and tried to catch her mischievous little daughter. But Mirele was already on the far side of the bed, with only her head sticking out.

"Mama, catch me, catch me. Oh, this is such a fun game, and . . ."

Before Mirele could finish her sentence, she let out a sudden shriek, "Oy . . ."

She looked around and recognized the hands that were holding onto her feet. She knew who it was: her Papa. He gave the bed a shake and started to count, "One, two, three, four, five, six, seven, eight, nine."

Mr. Fox *potched* and counted, and Mirele laughed. Mr. Fox sat down on the bed and took his little girl onto his knee, saying, "And now, my little mischief girl, here are nine kisses, and go get dressed; wash up and then eat breakfast."

2.

After breakfast, Mirele ran out into the yard. She was going to visit her friends—the geese, the ducks, the turkeys, and the chickens—to tell them that today was her birthday. Mirele spent a long time in the hen house. She took the yellow chick and set it on her knees as if it were a child. She took its tiny head into both of her small hands, looked straight into the chick's eyes, and said, "Chickie, today you become mine, and you have to listen to me. You must become a big hen and lay lots of eggs and hatch them, little chick."

As Mirele spoke, the chick blinked.

"Good, you promise. Your eyes say so."

An automobile could be heard pulling up. Mirele swiftly left the chickens and ran up to the parked car. Aunt Bella and Uncle Sam got out, along with their three children. They were all carrying packages.

* Playful slaps.

Mirele knew that they were birthday presents, and she tried to start open-ing them. But Mr. Fox had already gotten there too. He snatched away the packages, saying, "Packages get opened in the house, not in the yard."

Inside, Aunt Bella went to work. She decorated the dining room with col-ored paper. More automobiles arrived. Mirele ran out each time.

She would take a look into each car to see whether a package lay inside, and then running cheerfully over to the kids playing in the yard, she'd clap her hands and say quietly, "Here it is. They've brought me something."

It was noisy inside the house. Every minute, there was another "hello" from an arriving guest. In the middle of the house stood a table covered with a white cloth. Each bit of space on the tabletop was occupied. Here was a plate of pears and apples, there, a plate of oranges, and over there, a plate of cookies. Around the table's edge lay red paper baskets full of nuts, raisins, almonds, and colorful candies the size of peas. The baskets beck-oned quietly to the children, "Come, take us. We're sitting here waiting for you."

Mrs. Fox came into the dining room, looked around, and took Mirele by the hand, saying, "Go on, my girl, put on your new dress."

It didn't take long for Mirele to come out dressed up all in white. But her shoes weren't tied, her hair wasn't combed, and in one hand, she held a long, blue ribbon. The guests burst out laughing, and Uncle Sam said, "Oh, Mirele still can't tie her shoes."

Aunt Bella called Mirele over and tied her shoes. She combed her hair. She made a big bow out of the blue ribbon and said, "Now you can go receive your guests. But don't forget to say 'thank you' for each present."

Mirele nodded and disappeared.

Finally they sat down at the table. Once the children were seated, there was an uproar and a ruckus. "Mirele, come sit at the head of the table!"

But Mirele wasn't there. "Mirele! Mirele!" they called louder—but no answer.

Mr. Fox walked around the farmyard, looking in all the stalls and enclo-sures. There was no trace of Mirele. He came back into the house and said, "Mirele is a mischievous girl. When she wants to, she can disappear all of a sudden. For her, it's like a game."

So they looked in the cupboards and closets, under the tables, behind the doors, and in every corner of the house. But Mirele wasn't there; she had vanished into thin air. Everyone was frightened, thinking about the same thing, but they were too scared to say it out loud. Mr. Fox threw himself down on a chair and blurted out, "Call the police! Maybe my child has been kidnapped."

A whisper went up throughout the house: "Kidnapped? Could she have been kidnapped?"

Mr. Fox took the phone in hand to make the call. No sooner did he start to say, "Hello, hello? I want the police," than a cry of joy rang out through the room: "Mirele!"

Mirele stood by the door holding hands with a little boy of about four. She looked around.

Then she ran up to her father and grumbled, "Papa, you invited all the other children, but you forgot to call my friend Johnny Smith. I had to go and get him myself. *Now* we can start the celebration."

Mirele took Johnny by the hand and led him to the head of the table. She pulled over a chair, sat Johnny down on it, and said, "Papa, I promised Mrs. Smith that I would bring Johnny home right after the party."

Aunt Bella was the first to recover. She walked up to the table and gave the command, "Children, begin!"

At once, all the children burst into resounding cries of "Happy birthday to you, Mirele."

Aunt Bella slid the round chocolate cake with the candles over to the birthday girl and told her to blow them out. Mirele blew, and everyone in the house shouted, "One, two, three, four!"

Once the candles were blown out, everyone started to eat the good-ies. Things grew cheerful. They clapped and sang songs. Johnny sat there looking around. He didn't speak at all. So Mirele took his hand and said in a friendly tone, "Johnny doesn't know a single Yiddish song. But he does know English, so he's going to sing English songs." All the children clapped their hands and shouted, "Johnny, a song!"

Johnny stood up on his chair and began, "Jack and Jill, Jack and Jill." But instead of going any further, he started again, "Jack and Jill"—and then, all of a sudden, he fell quiet. Then he began to cry. Aunt Bella calmed him down. She told him to eat some of the goodies, and then he sang a song that made all the children laugh and cheered everyone up. The children shrieked and clapped hands and enjoyed themselves until late in the evening.

From An Unusual Girl from Brooklyn
David Rodin

DOVID RODIN (ELYE LEVIN)
b. July 31, 1893

For biographical information on Rodin, see "*From* The Three Braggarts" in part 4. Rodin's 1973 story collection *An Unusual Girl from Brooklyn* describes the exploits of an adventuresome girl with an intense love of the written word.

— ℬ —

That's Shprintse!

In Brooklyn, there once was a girl named Shprintse. But all the children called her "Shprintsuh-Wheah-Awe-Yuh." Since Shprintse was an unusual girl, not like all the others, things would happen to her that amazed people and made them laugh. And here's why:

Shprintse liked to read—a lot. Wherever she was standing or walking, she carried around an open book and read. When she was absorbed in a story, she would forget where she was and what kind of a world she lived in, because she imagined that everything she was reading about was actually happening to her. If she read that the little girl in the story was sitting, then Shprintse sat; if she read that the little girl in the story was standing, then Shprintse stood up; if she read that the little girl in the story was going over to the faucet and starting to wash the dishes, then Shprintse went over to the faucet, laid down her book beside it, and while continuing to read, started to wash the dishes. And if the little girl in the book had a plate fall out of her hand and shatter, then a plate also fell out of Shprintse's hand and shattered.

All the things that Shprintse did while she was reading made people laugh. But a lot of the time they were also amazed at what Shprintse managed to do: when she read that the little girl in the story was climbing the stairs, Shprintse would pick up her feet just as if she was walking up a flight of stairs; and when she read that the little girl in the book was climbing a ladder—and there was a ladder nearby—Shprintse started to climb it. While she was reading, she often secluded herself in such unusual places that nobody could understand how she'd gotten there. Even Shprintse herself didn't know.

Every day at dusk, Shprintse's parents went out looking for her. Little Tsirke, Shprintse's younger sister, who couldn't speak clearly yet, would also help look; she ran up and down the street, calling, "Splintsuh-Wheah-Awe-Yuh?"

And all the children from the block would run along with Tsirke, helping her look and calling, "Shprintsuh-Wheah-Awe-Yuh? Shprintsuh-Wheah-Awe-Yuh?"

That's how Shprintse's name came to be known on the street as "Shprintsuh-Wheah-Awe-Yuh."

Once they searched for her for half a day without finding her. They didn't know what to think. Everyone was asking, "What could have happened to Shprintse?" And nobody could answer. They all went around feeling worried and sad.

Before nightfall, when it was just beginning to get dark, Shprintse was spotted creeping down from the roof. They asked, "Shprintse, how did you get up there?"

She drew out her words as she answered (which is how she always spoke), "H o w s h o u l d *I* k n o w?"

And truly how *should* she have known? All she knew was that, reading her book, she had wanted to seclude herself in a place where her sister Tsirke would not be able to find her and disturb her; and she'd spotted a ladder standing there, so she'd climbed up it; on the roof, she spotted a chimney, so she leaned against it and started to read. Nobody saw her, nobody heard her, nobody disturbed her, and the story she was reading was so interesting that she forgot where she was entirely. If it hadn't gotten dark, she would still be sitting up there and reading.

Shprintse's Name Becomes Known

The street where Shprintse lived was a pretty one and as quiet as in the olden days. The houses there were large, one-story brownstones; leading to each door were five wide marble steps with ornamented brass railings on either side; next to each house was a flower garden; in front of the house, trees; and between the trees, old-fashioned gas street lamps. Every evening, the lamplighter would come to light the street lamps, and every morning, he would come to extinguish the lamps and polish them. The street was paved with stones. When the city had wanted to lay asphalt over the street and introduce electric lights instead of the old-fashioned gas lanterns, the neighbors banded together and wouldn't stand for it. After all, if the street were paved over and electric lighting installed, then cars would begin to drive down that road, and it would become as noisy and chaotic as all the city's other modern streets. So it remained old-fashioned and quiet, in the midst of the large, noisy, new streets of the modern city of Brooklyn.

On that very street, in order that her little sister Tsirke should not disturb her, Shprintse would often seclude herself on the steps of a distant house—sitting there and reading her book. But once Tsirke found where Shprintse had hidden herself with her book, she would always come and interrupt her reading. So Shprintse started to look for a new place where nobody would bother her.

Shprintse walked down the street, an open book in her hand, thinking that she could again crawl up to the roof, as she had done more than once before, and nobody would disturb her there. But no. Her little sister Tsirke had already figured out how to crawl up on the roof, so she would climb up and bother Shprintse.

Absorbed in her book, Shprintse read as she walked. Now she was reading about a girl, the lamplighter's daughter, who helped her father to wash and clean the streetlights, how she would scale the ladder that her father had set up by the lamppost. . . . It seemed to Shprintse that *she* was that girl, who was scaling the ladder now, lifting her feet up high and stepping cautiously as if she were climbing stairs. . . .

Meanwhile, the *actual* lamplighter had just finished cleaning a lamppost and climbed down the ladder, and now he bent over his bag in order to put back all the things he'd taken out. At that moment, along came Shprintse with the open book in her hand, and lo and behold, there was a ladder! So she clambered up, seated herself atop the lamppost, and started to read. The lamplighter neither saw nor heard what had taken place behind his back, so he stood up with his bag in hand, shouldered his ladder, and went on his way.

Before eating lunch, they looked around at home, and realized that Shprintse was missing. They searched all her usual hiding places without finding her, so her mother called little Tsirke and said, "Tsirele, my dear, run out to the street, find your sister, and tell her she should come right away and eat."

So Tsirke ran out to the street, looked on all the steps, and called, "Splintsuh-Wheah-Awe-Yuh? Tum (come) eat! Tum, Mama thez tho (says so)!"

Once the children from the block heard this, they ran after Tsirke and helped her belt out, "Splintsuh-Wheah-Awe-Yuh? Mama thez eat! Splintsuh-Wheah-Awe-Yuh? Mama thez eat!"

But Shprintse wasn't on the steps or on the street.

Tsirke raised her head and began to look on the rooftops. So all the children lifted their heads and started to look up high, until one child called out, "Look, just look where Shprintse's sitting!"

"Where? Where?" all the children began asking.

"Up there, on the lamppost!"

With shrieks of joy, all the children made for the lamppost, looked up at Shprintse, and chanted,

> Shprintsuh-Wheah-Awe-Yuh!
> We looked and we found huh!
> Where? Where? Where?
> On top of a lamppost!
> Where? Where? Where?
> On top of a roof!
> Where? Where? Where?
> She's gone again! Poof!

But Shprintse didn't pay them any mind, because at that very moment, she was reading in her book about some children singing a song just like that to the lamplighter's daughter, who was sitting on a ladder.

So Tsirke ran back to their mother and called, "Tum, Mama! Look where Splintsuh's sitting! She tan't geddown! Duh wamppost is high up! She tan't geddown!"

When Shprintse's mother got to the lamppost and saw where Shprintse was sitting, she grabbed her own head and cried, "*Gevald*, Shprintse, what will become of you? *What* will become of you? How did you ever get up there?"

Shprintse answered in her drawn-out singsong, "H o w   s h o u l d   *I*   k n o w ?"

Her mother replied, "What does 'How should I know' mean? You climbed up there somehow, so how do you not know?! Now how am I going to get you down from there? The lamppost is high up!"

Shprintse shrugged and repeated, "H o w   s h o u l d   *I*   k n o w ?"

Meanwhile, more mothers and passersby gathered around the lamppost, and they all said to call the firefighters, who would come with their long ladders and bring her down.

The firefighters were called not only when there was a fire but also when someone had crawled into a tight spot and couldn't get out or even when a cat had crept into a hole somewhere—it might be crying in a chimney because it couldn't get out; so somebody would call the firefighters, and they'd come with their long ladders and rescue it.

Not far from there, on the street corner, was a red fire-alarm column. The fire alarm (which stood on many street corners) looked like a red person standing on one thick foot, with a red, rectangular face, two large, red eyes, and a yellow handle in the middle of its face, which looked like a long yellow nose. When you pulled on the yellow "nose," it let the fire station know which street had a fire.

One of the mothers, who could see how much danger Shprintse was in, ran up to the fire alarm and gave its long nose a pull. Soon a bell rang in its square face; its red eyes lit up and started to wink and blink with little red lights—right and left, left and right; and immediately a clanging and whistling could be heard on the street, and a low red wagon appeared with the pump engine. The engine looked like a dark, big-bellied, kneeling man that was whistling and panting, and from its bronze head came a spray of sparks and a wisp of smoke. After the engine came a red wagon full of long hoses; and on either side of the wagon stood firefighters wearing high boots, black raincoats, and brass fire helmets on their heads. After them came a long, red ladder wagon—full of ladders—on which sat two drivers: one in front, one in back; because the wagon was so long, one had to steer just the front wheels, and the other, just the back wheels.

The firefighters rode up to the fire-alarm column and called out, "Which house is on fire?"

The woman who had called them was still standing by the fire alarm, and she answered, "There's no fire, but you have to get down a girl from a high lamppost over there, where that group of people is gathered."

The firefighters drove up to the lamppost where Shprintse was sitting.

When firefighters are called, a newspaper reporter rides along with them, in order to describe everything he sees and hears. The newspaperman requested that before they take Shprintse down from the lamppost, he be allowed to photograph her sitting up there and reading.

They let him. After that, the firefighters brought over a ladder and brought Shprintse down.

All the people in the street laughed and rejoiced. And all the children jumped for joy, danced, and sang,

> Shprintsuh-Wheah-Awe-Yuh!
> We looked and we found huh!
> Where? Where? Where?
> On top of a lamppost!
> Where? Where? Where?
> On top of a roof!
> Where? Where? Where?
> She's gone again! Poof!

The next morning, all the newspapers printed a picture of Shprintse sitting atop the lamppost and reading, while down below, next to the lamppost, stood little Tsirke. Beneath the picture, it said, "This is Shprintsuh-Wheah-Awe-Yuh and her little sister Tsirke (the one standing under the lamppost), who calls her 'Splintsuh.'" Next to the picture, the entire page described what an unusual girl Shprintse was and explained why she was called "Shprintsuh-Wheah-Awe-Yuh."

From that day on, Shprintse's name came to be known far and wide.

ACKNOWLEDGMENTS

Although this anthology includes few fairy tales, its own trajectory traced something of a fairy-tale plot—rife with enchantment, obstacles, and special helpers who enabled me to overcome them.

Revising the syllabus for my elementary Yiddish-language class about seven years ago, I wondered whether there had ever been any children's literature in the *mameloshn* and, if so, how I might incorporate it into my teaching. Some cursory searching led me to the Yiddish Book Center's Noah Cotsen Library, a digital collection of synopses and scanned originals of hundreds of collections and freestanding books of stories, poems, and plays. I quickly realized that I had tumbled into an out-of-the-way treasure cave glittering with a riot of colorful gems. First, I am grateful to those who had the foresight to commission this collection and the volunteer readers who summarized nearly one thousand books.

Most treasure caves are guarded by fire-breathing dragons, but this one was attended by friendly ushers who tried to wave visitors *into* its gentle maw. Earliest among those helpers were the staff and faculty of the Yiddish Book Center's Translation Fellowship, where I joined the first cohort in 2013 and dared to dream that I might scoop up some pockets full of Yiddish treasure and haul them into the surface-level world of English. Sebastian Schulman inaugurated the fellowship program, and now Madeleine Cohen runs it brilliantly, staffing it with working translators as generous as they are expert, including Barbara Harshav, Danny Hahn, Bill Johnston, and Aviya Kushner, in all of whose debt I remain. Myla Goldberg was a perspicacious mentor for this project at an early phase of its development. Members of the classes of 2013 and 2019 are fellows in every sense, and since Labzik cannot properly express the gratitude he owes them, I must try to do it for him.

Over the years, so many colleagues have aided me with thorny translation questions: Shane Baker, Elissa Bemporad, Zackary Sholem Berger, Dovid Braun, Matthew Brittingham, Leyzer Burko, Sandra Chiritescu, Madeleine Cohen, Maia Evrona, Dovid Fishman, David Forman, Itzik Gottesman, Faith Jones, Daniel Kennedy, Eitan Kensky, Jessica Kirzane, Mikhail Krutikov, Jordan Kutzik, Kenneth Moss, Rukhl Schaechter, Gitl Schaechter-Viswanath, Seb Schulman, Sasha Senderovich, Paula Teitelbaum, Ri J. Turner, Arun Viswanath, Meena-Lifshe Viswanath, and Saul Zaritt all have my gratitude. Marc Caplan undertook an extraordinarily close, careful review of large portions of the manuscript; his expert interventions have made the whole more accurate and idiomatic, though I am responsible for any errors or infelicities that remain. This book's introduction is immeasurably better for Justin Cammy's reading and thoughtful critique. Likewise, I am grateful for the improvements suggested by the anonymous reviewers.

Jennifer Young, then at the YIVO Institute, invited me to teach this material for the first time, and I discovered a world of thoughtful readers hungry for Yiddish children's literature. Linda Elovitz Marshall, in penning her lyrical homage to Moyshe Kulbak, *Good Night, Wind* (2019), showed me just how fertile a soil these translations can be for growing new cultural fruits. Speaking of Kulbak, I never would have found his singular tale "The Wind That Got Angry" without the assistance of Amanda (Miryem-Khaye) Seigel at the Dorot Jewish Division of the NYPL. Later, she outdid herself in assembling a rudimentary sketch of Malka Szechet's life from ships' manifests, Social Security documents, and sheer willpower. Her good offices led me to an enriching trilingual friendship with R' Maximo/Mordkhe Szechet.

Josh Lambert, in administering the TENT seminar on Jewish children's literature with the generous support of the PJ Library, created further opportunities to place these stories before several cohorts of writers and illustrators who are constantly honing their craft on behalf of children everywhere. I learned so much from conversations with Chris Barash, Meredith Lewis, Lesléa Newman, Erica Perl, Alan Silberberg, and Jane Yolen. I wish long, robust life to Anna Caplan's new *Honeycake Magazine*, whose inaugural issue included Benjamin Gutyanski's poem "A Snow Grandma."

The chief obstacle to selling this book was that there aren't very many like it, and nobody could quite imagine how to classify and publish it. Allison Adams at Emory's Center for Faculty Development and Excellence saw the project's potential early on, and I am grateful that she invited NYU Press's

Eric Zinner to our campus. Eric was the visionary who held the magic mirror or crystal ball displaying a future in which these stories were already treasured classics. He was also patient, preferring to see the book published well rather than fast. With grace and professionalism, Dolma Ombadykow assembled text and illustrations and attended to every detail of manuscript preparation. Producing a child-friendly, illustrated volume is not usually the ken of an academic press, but the designers and production team at NYU Press took on the task with relish, much to the benefit of the volume's youngest readers. The fairy godmother of this book, who wields her tablet and stylus as a magic wand, is its illustrator, Paula Cohen Martin. Seeing her artistic vision realized here is simply magical. Susan Schulman, who has encouraged my highest aspirations since I was in graduate school, sealed the deal with her usual expertise and good counsel.

Time to work on these translations was provided, in part, by the Memorial Foundation for Jewish Culture and Emory's Interdisciplinary Faculty Fellowship. The latter furnished the opportunity to collaborate with child psychologist Marshall Duke and anthropologist Melvin Konner—both of whom revealed new dimensions of the Yiddish stories that we took as our primary texts for cross-disciplinary analysis. During the summers, I have delighted in the chance to place my Yiddish treasure before the young adults studying the language intensively at the Yiddish Book Center's Steiner Summer Program; I thank Asya Vaisman Schulman and her excellent colleagues for those opportunities.

This volume has been published as handsomely as it has owing to support from the Schofield Subvention Fund of Harvard University's Department of Comparative Literature as well as extremely generous funding from Emory's Tam Institute for Jewish Studies. I offer special thanks to my fellow members of the executive committee, chair Eric Goldstein and director of undergraduate studies Catherine Dana and to several other Emory colleagues as well: Paul Buchholtz, Lisa Dillman, Hiram Maxim, Kate Rosenblatt, Ellie Schainker, Caroline Schaumann, Juliette Stepanian-Apkarian, and Ofra Yeglin. Peter Höyng, my thanks to you are echoed by Wilhelm Busch's ghost. The fellows at Emory's Fox Center for Humanistic Inquiry saw a great deal of nuance in these stories as I turned to writing about them critically. I extend particular thanks to Falguni Sheth and Yanna Yannakakis for combining sisterhood with accountability. The field of Yiddish children's literary studies is still emerging, but it has already found a number of good friends and interlocutors, including Deena Aranoff, Marina Balina, Mara Benjamin, Jeremy Dauber, Charlotte Fonrobert, Rachel Beth Gross, Rachel Harris, Irene Kacandes, Yuliya Komska, Susan Lynn Meyer, David Mazower, Leslie Morris, Eddy Portnoy, Lawrence Rosenwald, Neta Stahl, and Steven Zipperstein. An especially close kindred spirit in this inquiry, though I never had the pleasure of meeting her, was the late Naomi Prawer Kadar. Jack Zipes has worked harder than anyone to see children's literature accorded its scholarly due; I am beyond grateful to have his approbation for this volume.

The journalists who have taken an interest in this work, Britta Lokting, Marjorie Ingall, and Rokhl Kafrissen, have fueled my hopes that the book will be widely enjoyed, intelligently critiqued, and adroitly contextualized.

Many of us keep a couple of projects going at once so that we have a constructive outlet for procrastination. Mine was attending rabbinical school. I extend thanks to the faculty, students, and fellow alumnae of Yeshivat Maharat, who remind me of how these stories and poems form a part of the eternal Jewish word at its most expansive and immediate.

Wendy Amsellem and Annie Washburn will each find a piece of verbal afikomen hidden among these translations. Chavi Karkowsky, you are one of the special helpers.

Deborah Fernhoff has helped me to see—and shift—the plot arc of my own story; I cannot thank her enough.

Most scholars have a *dokter-fater* or *dokter-muter*; I have a *dokter-mame* and a *dokter-feter* in the persons of Ruth R. Wisse and David G. Roskies. They bring me life in the world-to-come of Yiddish.

My parents taught me by example to take seriously the mental lives of children and to value the literature we set before them. Aaron and Ariel Udel each live surrounded by books, and I hope that both of them will enjoy this one. By publication time, my three sons will just about span the ages at which these works are aimed. Y2KM, over the past several years, I have thought of you collectively as "the focus group." Nothing is more important to me than being your mother and your teacher. I hope you will live by the honorable virtues on display in these tales, including good humor, self-irony, and fraternal affection.

Finally, I have the pleasure of thanking my scholarly interlocutor, my citizen-prince, the hero of my life: Adam Zachary Newton. Though your fiery steed be a green compact SUV and your castle a suburban colonial, you possess the quintessence of true nobility: your search for the good and the just, the only quest that truly matters, is never-ending. You have sacrificed so much that our family might thrive; I only wish for you to receive the kind of generosity that you have shown to me. Long may we keep rescuing each other, again and again, in all the ways that two people can.

ILLUSTRATION CREDITS

Illustrations on pages 20, 68, 148, 182, 206, 238, 256, and 276 and banners on opening pages of literature selections by Paula Cohen.

Illustrations on the following pages appeared in the original editions:

41   Original illustration by Isa. *Untern taytlboym*, 63.

152   Original illustration by B. Malchi. *Vaksn mayne kinderlekh*, 156.

192   Original illustration by V. Litvinenko. *Far kinder*, 88.

197   Original illustration by Yitzchak Lichtenstein. *Di dray barimer*, 11.

201   Original illustration by Yitzchak Lichtenstein. *Di dray barimer*, 177.

213   Original illustration by Z. Maor. *Der vint vos iz gevorn in kas*, 11.

215   Uncredited illustration (likely Yoysef Tunkl or Wilhelm Busch). *Dos ferd un di malpes*, title page.

216   Uncredited illustration. *Dos ferd un di malpes*, 9.

217   Uncredited illustration. *Dos ferd un di malpes*, 10.

217   Uncredited illustration. *Dos ferd un di malpes*, 12.

245   Original illustration by H. Krukman. *Foygl kanarik*, 16.

254   Original illustration by H. Krukman. *Foygl kanarik*, 11.

255   Original illustration by H. Krukman. *Foygl kanarik*, 15.

263   Original illustration by Boris Fridkin. *Buts un di sanitarn*, n.p.

264   Original illustrations by Boris Fridkin. *Buts un di sanitarn*, n.p.

265   Original illustration by Boris Fridkin. *Buts un di sanitarn*, n.p.

266   Original illustration by Boris Fridkin. *Buts un di sanitarn*, n.p.

280   Original illustration by Louis Bunin. *Labzik,* title page.

284   Original illustration by Louis Bunin. *Labzik,* 77.

288   Original illustration by Louis Bunin. *Labzik,* 51.

289   Original illustration by Moses Soyer. *Vovik,* title page.

290   Original illustration by Moses Soyer. *Vovik,* 10.

299   Original illustration by Mashe Fisher. *Mirele un ire fraynt,* 6.

305   Original illustration by Mashe Fisher. *Mirele un ire fraynt,* 13.

ORIGINAL SOURCES

"A Sabbath in the Forest," by Yaakov Fichmann, was originally published by Farlag Kultur-lige, Warsaw, 1924.

"The Magic Lion," by Yankev Pat, was originally published by A. Gitlin, Warsaw, 1921.

"The Mute Princess," by Zina Rabinowitz, originally appeared in *Der liber yontef* [The precious holidays], published by Farlag Matones, New York, 1958.

"Children of the Field," by Levin Kipnis, originally appeared in *Untern taytlboym* [Under the date palm], published by Farlag Matones, New York, 1961.

"What Izzy Knows about Lag Ba'Omer," by Malka Szechet, was originally published as a free-standing book in Havana, with no date or press information.

"A Village Saint," by Sholem Asch, originally appeared in *Far yugnt: Dertseylungen un bilder* [For youth: Stories and pictures], published by Farlag Kultur-lige, Warsaw, 1929.

"Señor Ferrara's First Yom Kippur," by Zina Rabinowitz, originally appeared in *Der liber yontef* [The precious holidays], published by Farlag Matones, New York, 1958.

"Kids," by Mordkhe Spektor, was originally published by Farlag B. Kletskin Kinder, Vilna, 1914.

"Gur Aryeh," by Rokhl Shabad, was originally published by Farlag Yudish, Warsaw, n.d.

"Don Isaac Abravanel," by Isaac Metzker, was originally published by Farlag Kinder ring, New York, 1941.

"The Story of a Stick," by Zina Rabinowitz, was originally published by the Yiddish School in Mexico, 1958.

"Where Stories Come From," by Ida Maze, originally appeared in *Vaksn mayne kinderlekh: Muter un kinder-lider* [My children grow: Mother and children poems], published by the Canadian Yiddish Congress, Montreal, 1954.

"The Magnate of Jerusalem," by Sholem Asch, originally appeared in *Far yugnt: Dertseylungen un bilder* [For youth: Stories and pictures], published by Farlag Kultur-lige, Warsaw, 1929.

"The King and the Rabbi," by Solomon Bastomski, was originally published by Farlag Di naye yidishe folksshul, Vilna, 1922.

"The Baker and the Beggar," by Kadya Molodowsky, originally appeared in *Martsepanes* [Marzipans], published by Farlag CYCO, New York, 1970.

"A Boy and His Samovar," by Jacob Reisfeder, was originally published by Farlag Yunge hertselekh, Warsaw, 1920.

"Roses and Emeralds," by Judah Steinberg, originally appeared in *Fragen* [Questions], published by Max N. Maisel, Idisher farlag far literatur un visnshaft, New York, 1918.

"The Red Giant," by David Ignatov, originally appeared in *A Shtetl*, published by Farlag America, 1921.

"The Jews of Chelm and the Great Stone," by B. Alkvit, was originally published by *Kinder zhurnal*, October 1925.

"Lemekh Goes Ice Skating," by Leon Elbe, originally appeared in *Mayselekh* [Stories], published by Farlag Di naye yidishe folkshul, Vilna, 1928.

"A Snow Grandma," by Benjamin Gutyanski, originally appeared in *Far kinder* [For children], published by Melukhe Farlag, Kiev/Lvov (simultaneous), 1940.

"Zelig the Rhymester," by Kadya Molodowsky, originally appeared in *Martsepanes* [Marzipans], published by Farlag CYCO, New York, 1970.

The Three Braggarts, by David Rodin, was originally published by Farlag Matones, New York, 1920.

"A Deal's a Deal," by Solomon Simon, originally appeared in *Khokhomim, akshonim, naronim* [The wise, the stubborn, the foolish], published by Alter Rozental Fund, Buenos Aires, 1959.

"The Wind That Got Angry," by Moyshe Kulbak, was originally published by Der tsentraler shul-organizatsye, Vilna, 1921.

"The Horse and the Monkeys" was translated into Yiddish by Der Tunkeler and originally published by Farlag Brider Levine-Epstein and Partners, Warsaw, 1923.

"A Nanny Goat with Seven Kids," by Leyb Kvitko, was originally published by Tsenterfarlag, Kharkov, n.d. [1928].

"Stories from Genesis: How the Birds Learned Bible Stories," by Eliezer Shteynbarg, was originally published by Farlag Kultur, Czernowitz, 1923.

"The Birds Go on Strike," by Lit-Man, was originally published by Kinderfraynd, Warsaw, 1936.

"The Bat," by Meyer Ziml Tkatsh, originally appeared in *Dos taykhl katshet zikh afn baykhl* [The river comes up to my tummy], published by M. Ceshinsky, Chicago, 1933.

"The Alphabet Gets Angry," by Moyshe Shifris, originally appeared in *Foygl kanarik un andere mayses* [Canary bird and other stories], published by Moyshe Shifris Bukh-Komitet, New York, 1950.

"The Teacher," by Mashe Shtuker-Payuk, originally appeared in *Gut yontef* [Happy holidays], printed by Julio Kaufman, Buenos Aires, 1957.

"A Story of a Schoolboy and a Goat," by Kadya Molodowsky, originally appeared in *Martsepanes* [Marzipans], Farlag CYCO, New York, 1970.

"The Chickens Who Wanted to Learn Yiddish," by Moyshe Shifris, originally appeared in *Foygl kanarik un andere mayses* [Canary bird and other stories], published by Moyshe Shifris Bukh-Komitet, New York, 1950.

"Questions," by Judah Steinberg, was originally published by Max N. Maisel, Idisher farlag far literatur un visnshaft, New York, 1918.

"Boots and the Bath Squad," by Leyb Kvitko, was originally published by Kinderfarlag fun USSR, Odessa, 1935.

"The Girl in the Mailbox," by Lit-Man, originally appeared in *Mayselekh* [Stories], published by Kinderfarlag Nad, Warsaw, 1936.

"???," by Ida Maze, originally appeared in *Lider far kinder* [Poems for children], published by Farlag Kh. Bzshoza, Warsaw, 1936.

"Moe and Nicky," by Sarah L. Liebert, originally appeared in *Mirele un ire fraynt* [Mirele and her friends], published by I. W. Biderman, New York, 1952.

"Roosteroo," by Ida Maze, originally appeared in *Lider far kinder*, published by Farlag Kh. Bzshoza, Warsaw, 1936.

Labzik: Stories of a Clever Pup, by Khaver Paver, was originally published by International Workers Order Press, New York, 1935.

"Labzik and Glikl," by Khaver Paver, originally appeared in *Vovik: Stories of a Brownsville Doggie*, published by Khaver Paver Book Committee, Los Angeles, 1947.

"Evie Gets Lost," by B. Oyerbakh, was originally published by Farlag Mitspeh, Warsaw, n.d. [1920].

"The Sick Chicken," by Sarah L. Liebert, originally appeared in *Mirele un ire fraynt* [Mirele and her friends], published by I. W. Biderman, New York, 1952.

"Mirele's Birthday," by Sarah L. Liebert, originally appeared in *Mirele un ire fraynt* [Mirele and her friends], published by I. W. Biderman, New York, 1952.

An Unusual Girl from Brooklyn, by David Rodin, was originally published by Farlag Y. L. Peretz, Tel Aviv, 1973.

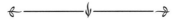

ABOUT THE EDITOR AND TRANSLATOR

Miriam Udel is Associate Professor of German Studies and Jewish Studies at Emory University, where her teaching focuses on Yiddish language, literature, and culture. She holds an AB in Near Eastern languages and civilizations from Harvard University, as well as a PhD in comparative literature from the same institution. She was ordained in 2019 as part of the first cohort of the Executive Ordination Track at Yeshivat Maharat, a program designed to bring qualified midcareer women into the Orthodox rabbinate. Udel's academic research interests include twentieth-century Yiddish literature and culture, Jewish children's literature, and American-Jewish literature. She is the author of *Never Better! The Modern Jewish Picaresque*, which received the 2016 National Jewish Book Award in Modern Jewish Thought and Experience.